THE BOOK HOUSE
NEW AND USED PAPERBACKS
692 PUCKETT DRIVE
MABLETON, GA 30126
770-944-3275

THE BOOK HOUSE
NEW AND USED PAPERBACKS

Shattered Dreams

by
Meshell

Bloomington, IN Milton Keynes, UK

AuthorHouse™
1663 Liberty Drive, Suite 200
Bloomington, IN 47403
www.authorhouse.com
Phone: 1-800-839-8640

AuthorHouse™ UK Ltd.
500 Avebury Boulevard
Central Milton Keynes, MK9 2BE
www.authorhouse.co.uk
Phone: 08001974150

This book is a work of fiction. Names, characters, places and incidents are products of the author's imagination or are used fictitiously. Any resemblance to actual events or locals or persons, living or dead, is entirely coincidental.

© 2006 Meshell. All rights reserved.

No part of this book may be reproduced, stored in a retrieval system, or transmitted by any means without the written permission of the author.

First published by AuthorHouse 6/23/2006

ISBN: 1-4259-3605-9 (sc)

Library of Congress Control Number: 2006904435

Printed in the United States of America
Bloomington, Indiana

This book is printed on acid-free paper.

Dedicated to my brother, Roger
who helped me see that I deserved so much
more than what I was settling for.
May he rest in peace.

Acknowledgements

This is a dream come true and I will be forever thankful. Lord, you have been the unmovable divine presence in my life that has made this possible. Thank you for the life experiences that aided in helping me write this book.

I am eternally grateful to my parents. Without your love, support, encouragement and discipline I would not be the woman I am today. Mama, it is because of your unwavering example that Janell and I learned to be strong women. Papa, your unfaltering love for your family continues to show us what a real man looks like. Thanks for being Mama's Jared.

To my son, Cameron, you are a daily inspiration and the light of my life. Thank you for the countless hours that you allowed me to sit at the computer and for offering to help by reading what I'd written. Your endless encouragement and pride in your mommies, "chapter book" warms my heart. Thank you for believing in me. Your patient and unchanging love is a blessing. Only God with His infinite wisdom could have known what you would add to my life.

Janell, you are always there when I need you. Thanks for having my back. No matter what happens in our lives I will always be grateful that God made us sisters and I will always love you.

Chloe', my blonde niece (smile), I look at you and see so much promise. I'm so proud of the young woman you are becoming. Remember, if you can dream it, you can be it. This book is proof of that.

TonYa, when I said, "I could have written this book," after I finished reading ……You throw my words back at me in the form of a challenge. To prove you wrong I wrote chapter one. After reading it you asked, "What happens next?" Those three little words set my creative juices on fire and I began this journey. From the beginning to the end you were everything from supporter to critic to editor to advisor; but the one thing that every reader should be the most grateful for is that you were my walking dictionary. Thank you, thank you, thank you. When you write your first Ton-tionary I promise to buy the first five copies.

To my original editors (you know who you are), words cannot express my gratitude. Thank you, thank you, thank you for helping me make this dream a reality. Whether you listened to my ideas or read the dreaded rough drafts my appreciation is overflowing. Thank you for your encouragement as well as your criticism. I love each of you for reassuring me and helping be believe I could do this. Without you guys I'd still be on page one.

To the women of the Vorsburgh clan, there is a little piece of each of you in this book. Thank you for allowing me to spend my entire young life listening to your stories. Without family we are nothing. I am grateful to be a part of yours.

To Tragedy, thank you for ministering to my soul. "Diamond In The Rough" is a work of art. You have used hip-hop to express God's love and forgiveness to our young people. What an inspiration! Continue to pursue your dream and God's abundant blessings are going to rain down on you.

To all of those women and men struggling through the remains of shattered dreams, know that our Father in Heaven loves us in spite of our imperfect nature.

Chapter 1

Keith climbed into his car after playing a pick up game of basketball with the fellas. The first thing he did was check his cell phone for messages. The automated voice sounded in his ear, "Three new messages are in your mailbox. Main menu. To hear your messages press one." Keith pressed one and placed the phone back to his ear. "First message today, 1:19 p.m." The automated voice continued. "Hey, it's Jaidyn. Tomorrow's my day off. I was trying to see what you had going on. Page me when you get a minute." The second message was from his mother and the last message, from Shelbi.

Shelbi McFadden was a trick he'd met a couple of years back. The first night he met her she'd walked right up to him and grabbed his dick. "Um nice," she'd said. She wasn't surprised when Keith did not flinch. In fact it was that exact arrogant, bad boy air that had caught her attention. She'd matched his attitude with her own overconfident one. "I've had my eye on you for quite awhile," she'd said still holding onto his prized possession. Keith's interest had grown just as fast as his muscle.

The next time he saw Shelbi they were at his boy, Markel's, housewarming party. She was with her husband. He was with a skeezer named Chevon that he'd eventually wish he'd never laid eyes on. As it turned out her husband and Markel were frat brothers. When her husband disappeared into the kitchen, Keith made his way over to her. "Are you still stalking me," he asked seductively as he moved into her personal space.

She'd smiled a sweet sexy smile and daringly said, "Why don't you meet me in the bathroom in five minutes."

Keith responded with, "Why don't we make it two." Two minutes and forty eight seconds later he had her bent over the sink laying the pipe to her ass and the rest is history.

Keith pulled into his assigned parking slot at his hideaway condo in Clear Lake for a late afternoon rendezvous just as Shelbi's message had instructed. When he unlocked the front door and stepped inside he heard muffled moans coming from inside the bedroom. The corners of his mouth stretched wide as he envisioned Shelbi and the purple glow in the dark vibrator they'd purchased already at work. "It sounds like you got started without me..." He was saying as he rounded the corner and found Shelbi and a young woman on the bed getting their groove on. Shelbi didn't hear him or notice him standing there but the young woman had. She smiled seductively at him, closed her eyes, and put on a small exotic moaning performance.

Keith couldn't believe Shelbi. She was eating the poonani like she was a pro, "Damn girl! What's up? You couldn't wait on me or what?"

Shelbi stopped and looked at him, "You took so damn long we got started without you."

"Is this the surprise you were talking about?"

"Yep. This is Alexia," Shelbi said rubbing the girl's nipples.

He'd be lying if he didn't admit it was a pleasant surprise. "Well don't stop on my account," he said still shocked that Shelbi went both ways. They'd done a lot of kinky shit together but he'd never thought she'd bend this far.

"It's nice to finally meet you. Shelbi has told me so much about you." Alexia moaned as Shelbi returned to the position he'd found her in.

"Sorry I can't say the same," he said seductively.

"Look, if you've got a problem with this you can turn yo ass around and..." Shelbi argumentatively said misreading Keith's hesitation.

"Chill out baby," Keith said stopping her before she flew completely off the handle. "I'm just wondering how long it's going to take y'all to break me off a piece?"

"Well, why are you still standing there? Take your shit off and join us," Shelbi said.

Keith took his time taking his clothes off. He wanted to enjoy the sight of the two of them as long as he could. Shelbi and Alexia were going at it like two tomcats. The sounds that were coming from the two of them had Keith's dick so hard he could split bricks. He massaged the "Dicktator" and got his first nut out the way while he enjoyed the show.

Alexia got up and came over to him. She took his hand away from his oozing muscle and placed her warm wet mouth on it. Now sure she had his undivided attention, she pulled him over to the bed where Shelbi anxiously awaited.

She motioned for him to lie on his back. Shelbi climbed on top of him, pulled his hands above his head, and hand cuffed him to the bed letting him know they were in charge. She kissed his neck, forehead and earlobes. He lifted his head to kiss her, but she avoided his lips. She kissed his cheeks, nose and finally his lips while Alexia continued working on the "Dicktator".

Shelbi then took two scarves and tied them around his ankles. She then tied the scarves to each side of the bed, leaving him in the spread eagle position. Alexia was now massaging the "Dicktator" and applying a large amount of Liquid Glide to his entire genital area.

She firmly gripped the bottom of the "Dicktator" and began slowly moving up and down his shaft, applying more pressure at the bottom then at the top. After she finished teasing him, Shelbi lay between his legs and licked everything from the top of his hills to the bottom of his valley. She was definitely hitting the spot and had every hair on his body stood at attention.

Alexia made a circle with two figures and held them firmly at the base of the "Dicktator". She used the other hand to give the "Dicktator" a deep tissue message. She was making a twisting motion with her hand that drove Keith crazy. She slowly increased the speed as Shelbi continued to massage his hills and valleys with her tongue.

When Keith seemed ready to go over the top the two women switched places. Keith didn't know how much longer he could hold the "Dicktators" urge to erupt at bay. Shelbi began tracing the "Dicktators" crown with her tongue, and Keith immediately knew he was in trouble. Shelbi always knew just the spot to hit that made the "Dicktator" want to expose its interior design.

With Shelbi working the "Dicktator" and Alexia working his hills and valley they brought his hot bubbling lava to the mouth of the volcano. Keith fought to keep it from spilling over. He began to choke under the pressure. The sensation in the "Dicktator" was building to a critical point, and the bubbling lava was filling his entire body.

Over and over they brought him to the edge of explosion without actually sending him over the top. This method only added to the intensity of the explosive contractions and made the "Dicktator" exude ash.

Shelbi finally saddled up and rode him like a cowboy on an open prairie. When he lost his condom inside her she climbed off, slipped her fingers into her opening and pulled it out. She climbed back on top of him bare back, riding him rough and hard like she was on a bucking horse.

"Shhhiiittt, who's pussy is this?" He managed to squeeze out.

Alexia massaged both of them before finally slipping her finger into Keith's anus and massaged his pressure point. *"Got Dammmnnn!"* He moaned.

Little by little the "Dicktator" chipped away at the dam that was holding Shelbi's river at bay. Once the "Dicktator" had knocked a hole in the wall and allowed the raging river to flow freely it was Alexia's turn. Alexia also had her way with him. She had a different riding style than Shelbi. She was a lot more timid. She rode backwards in the saddle, gripping his feet with her hands. She didn't want to bring her horse into the stable too quickly so she road at a slower pace, swaying easily in the saddle. With every trout, every rise and every fall she tightened her muscles, gripping the "Dicktators" head, making Keith's toes curl.

"Damn girl, work that pussy...Shiiiiiiitttttt!" Keith panted and quivered as Alexia drained the remaining life out of the "Dicktator."

Once their session had ended Shelbi quickly showered and excused herself. She needed to pick up dinner for her family and then pick up her son, who had stayed after school for a basketball game.

Keith tried to catch a quick nap while Alexia also got showered and dressed. Keith woke up three hours later ready for the next round only to be disappointed to find both women gone.

Chapter 2

After an afternoon of unbelievably good sex Keith lay next to Jaidyn stroking her head, deep in thought. He swore he'd never get this caught up in a woman but he realized that she was everything he'd ever wanted. She was the one and it was time he made sure that she stayed right where she was supposed to be, next to him.

He lay there with his nose in her hair, smelling her scent, reflecting on his past, and realizing that the ghosts in his closet were catching up with him way too fast. He had made many costly mistakes but had never viewed them as such until now. He had walked through life arrogantly thinking he would be a man that would never have to answer to anyone. Now it all seemed different and in the back of his mind he knew sooner or later he'd have to answer for this last skeleton he'd squeezed into the back corner of his closet. He'd thought about telling Jaidyn, unburdening himself but he knew that it could cost him everything. He had to secure his future with Jaidyn before that happened, but was this the right time he asked himself. If he waited any longer he knew he was risking his secret being exposed. Keith loved Jaidyn Nicolette Owens and had no intentions of ever losing her for any reason.

Jaidyn kissed Keith on the cheek, climbed out of bed and sheepishly went into the bathroom. Keith could see that all the long hours she was working was catching up to her. Once he heard the shower turn on he got out of bed, went into his closet and retrieved a small coffee can he'd stored in a shoebox. Suddenly he heard her turn off the water and he hurried back to bed. He emptied the can's contents into his hand, rolled the can under the bed and hid his surprise under the pillow. Then he waited for Jaidyn to come out of the bathroom.

Jaidyn stepped out of the bathroom dress in blue and yellow plaid boxer shorts and a yellow tank top. She had a refreshed, pleasant, faraway gaze on her face. He watched her, wondering what she was thinking as she walked past the foot of the bed. Her beauty struck him as if he were looking at her for the very first time. She possessed a rare form of beauty, beyond the grasp of most women. Her loveliness stemmed from back in the day, when make up wasn't needed to be strikingly beautiful.

Jaidyn had her hair pulled into a ponytail, allowing him to see the delicate details of her face. Her skin was the color of light brown sugar and as smooth as a baby's bottom. It looked as if she'd never had a blemish in her life. She had warm gray eyes, framed by long thick lashes. Her eyes seemed to draw him into her realm of essence.

Keith admired her long slender five-foot eight-inch, 140-pound frame. He was a breast man and made her perfect 36C's his playground. It was true, Aphrodite, the goddess of beauty, had taken her time with Jaidyn and made her every man's dream. Jaidyn was everything Keith desired in a woman; beautiful, intelligent, but most important she was a lady in public and a freak in the bedroom.

When Jaidyn climbed into bed, he took her into his arms and kissed her passionately. Keith's dick got hard instantly and he was ready to hit it, as usual. He reminded himself of the matter at hand and decided to ignore the "Dicktators" thirst for her attentive care. It was something he was not accustomed to doing. Keith sat up and took her left hand into his. He pulled a spool of white string from under his pillow and tied the end around her left third finger.

She burst into laughter, "What are you doing?'

His smile broadened, "Can you please just let me do this?"

"If you're planning on tying me up I think you're going to need a little more string."

"Jaidyn, please!"

"Ok, but you're going to need a rope if you're planning something kinky," she giggled. "Do you think your mother knows her son's a freak?"

"Do you think your mama knows you've turned me out?" They both erupted into laughter as the thought of their parents knowing what they did in their bedroom passed between them.

Keith's smile soon disappeared and was replaced by a loving gaze. "Seriously honey...I'm not being freaky...I've decided that I'm not letting the love of my life get away."

Jaidyn nervously hesitated unsure if he was serious or joking. "You're so silly!" she said deciding she'd rather not have that discussion.

"I'm serious. Do you have a problem with that?"

"That depends! Are you planning on tying me up and leaving me in this house forever?"

"Do you consider the rest of your life forever?" Jaidyn's face questioned his statement. He gently put his finger over her lips to silence the questions he knew would follow. He climbed out of bed and moved her to a sitting position on the edge of the bed. He dropped to his right knee. He pulled the string tight and placed a ring on the end that was in his hand. The ring smoothly slid down the string onto her finger.

In a smooth charming voice he said, "Jaidyn Nicolette Owens, I'm convinced you are exactly who God designed for me, and I have no intention on letting you get away. I can't imagine my life without you. Here with me is where you are suppose to be. I know this isn't a passing love affair because every time I look into your eyes the doors of heaven open. I finally understand what bone of my bone and flesh of my flesh means. Together you and I represent the totality of what God meant for a man and woman. I would be honored if you would be my wife." Tying the string around her finger had been something he'd seen in a movie but the words were his and he'd meant every single one of them.

Keith untied the string and waited for an answer. Jaidyn looked into his eyes as he looked into hers. As tears begin to roll down her face she looked down at the ring. It was beautiful. The one-carat princess cut diamond was ah inspiring. The rows of alternating round and baguette diamonds were in a platinum channel-bar setting. At that moment, words seemed to escape her. She looked up into his eyes and noticed he was near tears. How can I disappoint him she silently asked herself. Unable to believe the sweetness of this moment she wrapped her arms around him.

The "Dicktator" had been ignored long enough, and Keith surrendered to the physical force he was applying. He gently kissed her on the nape of her neck and pulled her closer. He wanted her to feel the "Dicktators" yearning. Jaidyn responded by placing her hands inside his boxers and slowly stroked him. She stroked his shaft with one hand while gently squeezing and stroking his head with the other. She knew all to well what drove him crazy. She had long ago learned that all the "Dicktators" nerve endings were in his head and slightly squeezing it made the "Dicktator" ooze with anticipation of what was to follow.

Keith removed her tank top and began kissing her breast. She continued stroking him and lavishing his earlobes with gentle nibbles and kisses. Keith's kisses turned into forceful bites as his hunger grew. He was having a hard time controlling the "Dicktator," who wanted to feel the pulsating warmth that awaited him between her legs.

She pushed him away and dropped to her knees. The "Dicktator" jumped with the anticipation of her warm, wet mouth deep-throating him. She looked up at him and took him into her mouth paying close attention to the "Dicktators" head. She teased his dick's opening with the tip of her tongue. Then she sucked it like it was a sour piece of candy. Keith's knees weakened. He found it hard to continue standing. He was momentarily lifted to another planet, another universe. Jaidyn was left alone with his muscle. It was in complete control of Keith's body. He fought for control, as goose bumps begin to creep up his legs to the small of his back. Jaidyn had damn near sucked the life out of him before he stopped her. "You're killin' me," he said pulling her to her feet.

Jaidyn momentarily let him fall from her mouth but continued to stroking him. She pushed him back onto the bed in an attempt to stay in control. Keith was a control freak. It wasn't often that he allowed her to be the domineering force in the bedroom.

Keith wasn't about to let her take control again. He needed to get his bearings before he lost it. He pulled her down on top of him kissing her intensely. He turned her over so that she lay on her back and kissed her inner-thighs. His goatee tickled her lower butt as he played with the little man in the boat. His tongue penetrated "The Palace" walls, and she melted. As she neared climax, he abruptly terminated all efforts and said, "Dr. Owens, I don't believe you ever answered my question!"

She wanted to slap the shit out of him but giggled instead, "I'm sorry Mr. Tyler I thought I had. Do you have any doubt what my answer is?"

"Nah, I just want to hear you say it," he said confidently as the head of his dick played with her clitoris.

"Keith Justice Tyler, I would be honored to be your wife."

Keith buried his head between her legs again and brought her to a climax. He then kissed her breast. He teased her with the head of his dick. She offered no resistance when she felt him slipping inside.

Keith couldn't believe he'd slipped inside her unprotected. She had always insisted that a layer of latex be between them. In the year they'd dated she'd never allowed him to sample the goods without a condom, but today her warm, wet pussy welcomed him. His dick extended another two inches.

As his quest for his first nut became more pressing, Keith began to bunny hop. Jaidyn hated when he banged the hell out of her. She preferred a slower, more pleasing groove. She wanted him to take his time and enjoy the climb to the top of the mountain. She flipped him over, straddled him, and guided him back inside. He put his hands on her hips and forcefully pulled her down onto him, allowing the "Dicktator" to go as deep as he could. Jaidyn moaned. Keith's toes curled. His eyes rolled in the back of his head with every rise and fall. His body finally stiffened and goose bumps covered him. Her hips made one last swaying motion, and he could no longer hold back. He exploded inside her.

"Shit baby," he said. He lay on his back trying to catch his breath and thinking if she hadn't always insisted on a condom it wouldn't have taken him so long to ask her to marry him. Now there was no doubt in his mind why she called it "The Palace." There was no doubt in his mind that he had hit the jackpot. Keith would be lying if he didn't say this was the best piece of ass he'd ever had. Most of the time his dick got hard just thinking about her. He still wasn't able to understand how she made him cum so quickly. For the first time in his life he admitted that he was pussy whooped, and he wasn't afraid to confess that he needed a woman for more than just a piece of ass. He wanted her, needed her, to keep doing what she was doing to him. To keep making him feel like he was feeling.

As usual Jaidyn wasn't satisfied but the "Dicktator" had given all he could and was falling asleep fast. She desperately tried to revive him, but it was too late. "Give me a minute to catch my breath." Keith said. Disappointed, she climbed off of him and lay in his arms. A few seconds later he was snoring.

Lying there she wondered what she'd done to deserve him. "Lord knows I've had more than my fair share of Mr. Wrongs," she said to herself. She'd waited her entire life for a man like him. He was breathtakingly sexy, charming and very successful. He was good for her, and she adored him. Eventually she'd love him the way a wife should love her husband. Sometimes fairytales really do come true, just not in the way we envision them.

Chapter 3

Jaidyn was anxious to get to church Sunday morning. She and Keith had spent the remainder of Saturday, after his proposal, in bed. So she had not told her family the news. Although her father had reservations about Keith the rest of her family seemed to like him.

It had been Jaidyn's family ritual to attend service together as long as she could remember. Her parents had always insisted on it. She could hear her father saying, "A family that prays together, stays together." So every Sunday she was expected to be at church along with her brother Lance, his wife Karen, her sister Joanna, her husband Remington and their four children. If anyone failed to show up they would receive a phone call from one of her parents wanting an explanation. The family always spent the remainder of the day at her parent's home eating dinner, watching football, basketball or movies. It was a tradition that Jaidyn had grown to love.

Keith hadn't attended church on a regular basis until he and Jaidyn started dating. She knew in the beginning he'd only gone to appease her but she thought that was changing. He seemed to enjoy service now.

Pulling into the church parking lot she contemplated whether to tell them as soon as she saw them or if it would be better to wait until service was over. Remembering Joanna and Remington's ordeal she decided it would be best if she and Keith told them together. The news would have to wait until service was over.

Keith was going to meet her at church but would be late. Jaidyn and his morning started off the same way their night ended. The escapade left Keith worn out. Afterward he'd fallen asleep and slept a little longer then he should have. She'd offered to wait on him but he wanted to drive his own car so he could get away right after dinner. He said he needed to get home to work on a campaign before his Monday morning's weekly staff meeting. She knew that work was only an excuse. He didn't like to spend Sunday afternoons with her family. She hoped once they were married that he'd grow to love the family time as much as she did.

Jaidyn admired her engagement ring one last time before taking it off and slipping it into her purse. As she entered the church she heard the choir singing "What A Mighty God We Serve." She scanned the pews for her family. She spotted them in their usual seats near the front. She put one finger up, walked up the middle isle and slipped into the seat beside Lance. Jaidyn leaned over and asked, "Where's Joanna?"

"I guess she's running a little late."

"Four kids will do that to you." They both laughed as Mrs. Owens turned around and gave them the eye. Some things never changed. They still talked, passed notes and ate candy in church and their mother still knew just what to do to get her disrespectful children to behave.

Lance wrote her a note on his program and handed it to her. She read it, "Where's Keith?" Jaidyn leaned over and whispered in his ear, "He's running a little late. He'll be here."

Just as the choir cued up for another song Joanna, Remington and the kids sat down behind them. Keith came in right after them and slid into the pew next to Jaidyn. He was looking debonair as usual. The cream colored Versace suit almost glowed against his dark chocolate skin. His wide shoulders, slender waist and six foot-two inch, two hundred twenty pound frame allowed him to look good in whatever he wore. She noticed the small diamond stud in his ear sparkling against the lights in the church. He kissed her on the forehead and flashed his irresistible Colgate smile. He was one of those brothas with a dynamic sexual presence that women, no matter the color, were drawn to. Being an ex-professional athlete he was used to the attention and took it all in stride.

He kept up with the latest fashions. Every time he stepped out of the house he resembled a dark chocolate runway model. His eyes were dark like coal. Cheek bones high, well pronounced. Lips full. Head bald. Goatee well manicured. He was sure of himself and confident in his abilities to please women. His pompous egotistical attitude worked to his advantage, making him even more appealing to women. There was very little that Keith Justice Tyler wanted that he didn't get.

Jaidyn turned her attention to the pastor. "Turn your Bible to Psalms 128," he was saying. "Today I want to talk about, 'How to Turn a House into a Home'."

"Every house you live in is not a home. You can have five bedrooms, air conditioning, a swimming pool, an alarm system, and a dog named Spot but I tell you sin will keep your house from being a home.

We live in a time that people believe in putting up facades. Even on Sunday we come to church with our church face on, like nothing is wrong. On our way home we're fighting or not speaking to each other. This is something that plagues us all.

My first point comes out of verse 1. "How blessed is someone who fears the LORD, Who walks in His ways." I want to talk to the single young sisters for a moment. Don't you ever believe as long as you live that you can change a man. If God does not win him with His love and he doesn't have a fear of God then you can't have a relationship with him. If you hook up with him you're going to experience hell on earth because you're God's child and he's the devil's child. Let's get it straight from the jump if he's the devil's child that makes the devil your father-in-law and he is always going to be in your house. Can I get an Amen..."

When the service was over Keith asked, "Where's your ring?"

"I put it in my purse. I didn't want anyone to see it yet. I wanted us to tell my family together." Keith smiled and reached for her hand.

As the Owens sat down to dinner, Keith said, "Mr. and Mrs. Owens, after dinner I'd like to talk to the two of you."

"Go ahead and tell us what's on your mind," Mr. Owens responded gruffly.

"Ok...yesterday I asked Jaidyn to be my wife and she's accepted." Everyone stopped eating. Jaidyn's mother got teary eyed and got up to hug them. After everyone saw the ring, hugged and congratulated them, they returned to their dinner. Mr. Owens had not moved or taken his eyes off of Keith. Once Keith sat down Jaidyn put her hand on his knee. He looked into her eyes and smiled. He reached for her hand and held it firmly. Returning to his conversation with Mr. Owens he said, "Sir, we'd like your blessing."

Russell Owens seemed to ponder the statement. "Would it matter if I didn't give it?"

"Russell!" Sarah Owens exclaimed in her thick southern voice.

"It's ok. I'd like to answer his question." Keith said turning his attention from Mrs. Owens to Mr. Owens. "No sir. I guess it wouldn't but it's important to Jaidyn that we have it." Keith said sliding his hand onto Jaidyn's knee.

There had been something about her father's demeanor with Keith that made Jaidyn uneasy. The unspoken vibe she'd gotten from him was becoming clearer by the second. "Daddy please." Jaidyn whined.

Keith was not who Russell would have picked for his daughter. As a matter of fact he couldn't stand the thought of the two of them together. He wasn't nothing' but a smooth talking, no good piece of shit as far as Russell Owens was concerned. He'd grown up with a hundred guys like Keith. He'd deliberately kept his distance from him hoping that Jaidyn would pick up on his disapproval. "Son, I'm old fashion and I'll do just about anything to protect my family. Next to Sarah, my children are the most precious thing on this earth to me…and…" Mr. Owens looked Keith straight in the eyes. "I'm not going to sugar coat it for you. You aren't exactly the type of man I had hoped she'd end up with."

Keith sat back in his chair, stunned by Mr. Owens words. Everyone in the dinning room was so quiet you could hear a rat piss on cotton. "But if you're who she wants to be with I guess I'll have to deal with that." Mr. Owens took a breath giving Keith a moment to absorb what he'd said.

Sarah could see her daughter's disappointment and her hurt feelings. When Jaidyn's eyes misted over her mother clasped her hands over hers, reassuring her. She knew it was important to Jaidyn that she had her father's approval.

Russell was being unusually tough and abrasive. The concern on his face reminded Sarah of the look he had the first time Jaidyn told him she had a boyfriend. There was no doubt that he still thought of Jaidyn as his baby.

"Look son! Jaidyn's our baby and we need you to promise us you'll take good care of her and never hurt her."

Keith felt like the wind had been knocked out of him. He knew how important this was to Jaidyn. He had a reassuring hand on her knee, which was bouncing a hundred miles a minute. "I'll do my best." He said earnestly.

"I hope so." Mr. Owens said returning to his meal.

A few minutes passed before anyone dared say anything. Finally, Remington broke the silence and tried to make light of the situation. "Hey Pop, I think you were a little softer on him then you were on me." The table broke into laughter as Remington reminisced on his conversation with Mr. Owens.

Russell Owens was a man of high statue, a man that demanded respect. When Remington asked Joanna to marry him she told her parents alone.

After hearing the news Mr. Owens asked Joanna to call Remington and have him come to the house so they could talk. When Remington arrived he recalled finding his father-in-law at the kitchen table cleaning his gun. Remington received a very different speech that night and had never forgotten it. He teased Joanna that he treated her so well because he feared her father's wrath.

Karen also shared her story. Hers was different than Remington's. Mr. Owens hadn't told her what he expected of her but rather what his expectations of Lance were as a husband and provider. He welcomed her into the family with open arms. He told her if Lance ever mistreated her that she was to let him know and he'd have a heart to heart with the boy. But Lance had never once disrespected or mistreated his wife. The Owens instilled the importance of the sanctity of marriage and family in all of their children.

After dinner the men retreated to the living room for an evening of football. Mr. Owens climbed into his brown vinyl lazy boy chair, also known as the "King's Throne." Lance and Remington sat on the couch and Keith excused himself saying he had to get home to get some work done before his Monday morning staff meeting.

The women remained at the table laughing and sharing stories of how Mr. Owens and Lance ran off every boy the girls brought home. They were always jealous of Lance. "No matter who the hood rat of the week was Daddy was nice to her," Jaidyn said.

"I can hear him saying, son..." Joanna said in a deep voice mimicking her father, "You play with fire you might get burned."

"You had it easy, you were the oldest. I had to put up with you and Lance. You weren't so bad because you came home from college and got married. Lance came home from college and made my life miserable. He acted like judge, jury, and executioner." They all laughed as they were reminded how protective Lance had once been. "Do y'all remember my first date? Lance threatened to beat Teddy up if the boy tried to hold my hand."

"That Lance was something else." Sarah Owens said chuckling.

"Hey!" Lance yelled from the living room. "The fools you were dating weren't worth your time. I did you a favor. The only one you ever dated that had any kind of potential was Jared and you kicked him to the curb. And Joanna I don't know what you're laughing at. Your high school sweetheart is a crack head right now. You're lucky my boy Remington decided to save you."

"I ain't trying to hear all that." Joanna said waving him off.

Being the youngest wasn't always easy. Joanna was ten years Jaidyn's senior and Lance eight. As a child they'd given her the nickname "Oops," because she'd come so many years after them that they'd told her she was an oops baby. Their mother would lovingly correct them, "I had three accidents not one, but all three were a gift from God."

They'd both watched her like a hawk and played the roll of judge, jury, and executioner her entire life. When she finished high school and left home for college at Baylor University, she'd suddenly found herself free from their watchful eyes and had gone buck wild. After being put on academic probation her first semester her parents threatened to make her come home and she settled down and concentrated on school.

Despite Joanna and Lance's meddling ways they were doting siblings and had spoiled her rotten. Over the years their relationships had changed. Joanna still wanted to take care of her, wanted to protect her. She still spoiled her with a home cooked meal at least once a week, with periodic shopping sprees, and with a $250.00 check on the first of every month. She justified it all with Jaidyn still being in school but Jaidyn knew it was just her way of making sure she didn't have to go without.

Somewhere along the way Jaidyn and Lance had become friends and confidants. Lance trusted Jaidyn's instincts and no longer felt like she needed protecting but he still spoiled her.

Chapter 4

Before leaving her parents on Sunday night Jaidyn had called Yasmine to invite her out to lunch the next day. She was anxious to share the news of her engagement but it would have to wait until her next day off. Yasmine Randall and Jaidyn had been inseparable best friends since they were seven years old. Yasmine's family had bought the house three doors down from Jaidyn's and the girls had become instant friends.

It had been Yasmine who had first introduced Jaidyn and Keith while at a jazz concert. Yasmine was a long time jazz fan and had two tickets to see Joe Sample in concert. Her husband Neal had gone on a business trip and was unable to attend. She called Jaidyn and invited her. Jaidyn had jumped at the chance to attend the concert with her.

During the concert they'd bumped into Keith and he'd made immediate advances towards Jaidyn. Yasmine, who was never short on words, came right out and told him to stay away from her. Nevertheless, he'd plunged forward and embarked on an intense exploration to add Jaidyn to his collection. Jaidyn had recently ended a relationship and did not return his attention. Driven by the challenge, Keith had been relentless in his pursuit and eventually changed her mind.

When Jaidyn told Yasmine that she'd agreed to go out with him her disapproval was evident. She warned Jaidyn of Keith's love 'em and leave 'em attitude. She'd said he thought he was Gods gift to women and his arrogant personality wouldn't allow him to treat women like they deserved to be treated. She said that no one was more important to Keith than himself. She claimed he'd written the book on how to be a playa'. She'd begged Jaidyn to be careful and to not fall in love with him but Jaidyn ignored her warnings and was now engaged to be married to him.

Yasmine was already seated at a table enjoying a glass of wine when Jaidyn arrived for lunch. "Hey girl." She said as Jaidyn sat down. Before Jaidyn could tell her about the engagement Yasmine started in on her, "Thanks for getting me out of the house, my mother-in-law is visiting and I needed to get away. That woman has been cooking and cleaning since she stepped in the door. Neal's all laid up like he's the king of Zambia and she's waiting on him hand and foot."

"Is he feeling any better?"

"Neal had a vasectomy, he didn't lose a limb. His ass is fine. It's been three days and he's acting like he's dying. When I gave birth to those kids I was up the next day washing clothes and cooking dinner. He even had the nerve to ask when he could get some. Now the tables are turned and I'm wondering the same thing," they both laughed.

"You know you're wrong. The man might be hurting."

"Jaidyn you're a doctor. You know better. The doctor told him he could go back to work the day after he had it. His ass is faking!"

"What brings your mother-in-law to town?"

"Her son called her after I told him I wasn't Hazel. She drove in that afternoon. You know that's her baaaby."

When the waitress approached the table to take their orders they were still giggling about Neal's unfortunate experience. Once she'd taken their orders Yasmine moved the conversation around to Jaidyn. "What was so important that you couldn't tell me over the phone?"

Jaidyn smiled. She'd deliberately placed her hands in her lap so Yasmine didn't get a glimpse of the ring. She was sure Yasmine would be just as excited as she was. Yasmine had always been her number one supporter.

Jaidyn launched into how wonderful her Saturday morning love session with Keith had been and eased her way around to how sweet Keith's proposal had been. Then she put her hand on the tabletop showing off the ring.

Yasmine was just as stunned by its beauty as Jaidyn had been. "I'll give it to the brotha, he's smooth but you can't be serious. I mean really," she said with her face contorting. "The rest of your life?"

Jaidyn pulled her hand away from her, "Can you please just be happy for me? You're my best friend and I want you to be excited for me."

"Look it ain't no secret that I can't stand you being with Keith and the thought of my best friend spending the rest of her life with him makes me sick." She said rolling her eyes.

"You two are friends and I don't understand why it's a problem for us to be together."

"Don't get it twisted, Keith and I have never been friends. I tolerate him."

"He's been wonderful to me. His past is his past. He hasn't once done any of the things to me that you claim he did in his past. Yasmine, *everybody* has a past. We've all made mistakes. He's not the same schoolboy you knew back in the day. I wish you'd stop all this and just be happy for us."

"You can save that BS for somebody else. The only thing that has changed about Keith Tyler is he's gotten better at the game. And I'm glad you're happy. I just wish you could be happy with someone else. Keith's a dawg."

"Fuck it Yasmine! I don't feel like having this conversation with you again." Jaidyn said rolling her eyes.

"Fine, but I only want what's best for you, and Keith ain't it. The brotha put the 'D' in dawg. Gurl leopards don't change their spots. They are woven into the fabric of who they are...Look, Keith's the type of brotha that's always had a lot of women and made each one of them feel like they were the only one. More then likely you're not..."

"Yasmine, that's enough. I'm sick and tried of hearing what a dawg my man is!"

"Then you need to take heed to what I'm saying and save yourself a whole lot of heartache." Yasmine stared at her with cold eyes while she waited on her to respond.

Jaidyn remained silent while the waitress delivered their lunch. "Is there anything else I can get you ladies," she asked. "No thank you," they both snapped. "Well my name is Amy, if you need anything let me know," she said before leaving the table.

"I know you have an attitude but can I say one more thing?" Yasmine asked determined to get her point across.

"It's best you don't! Now can we bless the table?" Yasmine rolled her eyes and bowed her head. After they blessed the table they sat in silence eating. Finally Jaidyn said, "I know it's killin' you so go ahead and get it over with, cause I don't want to hear this shit again."

"Are you sure Keith's the one? I mean I just don't see you spending the rest of your life with him."

Jaidyn was getting very agitated with her as she always did when it came to their conversations about Keith. "What part of 'I want to spend the rest of my life waking up to him' are you missing?"

Yasmine's face twisted and she spat Jaidyn's attitude back at her, "I guess I'm missing the part where you confess your undying love for him. You just seem to be..."

Jaidyn interrupted her, "I love him Yasmine and I appreciate your concern but will you please just be happy for me?"

"Humh...all I'm saying is you need to give this some serious thought. When my Granny used to tell us, Marry the one that loves you, not the one you love. The one you love will hurt you every time. The one that loves you will treat you like the queen you are and you'll learn to love him. She wasn't talking about a man like Keith. "

"Damn Yasmine!" Jaidyn practically yelled.

Yasmine realized she was pushing her luck and decided this was one of those times when her opinion was best kept to herself. "I only want what's best for you. Now that I've told you how I feel the rest is up to you. Even though I don't agree with your choice I wouldn't miss your wedding for the world. You're my girl and no man is going to come between us."

"I'm glad to hear that."

Sighing Yasmine asked, "When's the wedding?"

"Keith wants to get married right away."

"What's the rush?"

"No rush, it's just the best time. Although my call schedule isn't as rigid as it was when I was a resident, it's still hard. I've got a three day weekend coming up and if we don't do it then we'll have to wait until my fellowship is over and that's not for another six months. We won't be able to go on a honeymoon but we can go at another time."

"That just seems awful quick." Yasmine said disappointed that Jaidyn wasn't giving herself more time to consider what she was getting herself into.

"I know but you know how my schedule is and neither of us wants to wait a year."

"My friend the Surgical Oncologist, Keith does know how to pick them."

As they finished their lunch, Jared, Jaidyn's ex-boyfriend approached their table. Jaidyn was immediately taken aback. "Damn is it possible that his ass is finer than the last time I saw him," she asked herself. He was one of those brothas that had 'fuck me' written all over him. He was six feet-five inches of pure muscle, built like a Mack truck, and hung like a horse if memory served her right.

Yasmine caught a glimpse of Jaidyn openly admiring Jared, but then again it was hard not to. His dark gray silk sweater firmly gripped his wide sculptured chest, giving off just a hint of the six pack underneath. His biceps round and hard, well defined even with his arms resting at his sides. His deltoids formed perfect teardrops. The remarkable wings on his back gave flight to the imagination of what your hands could grip down below. His slender waist was attached to two perfectly muscular long legs that you saw the slightest hint of through the black silk trousers. His skin was the color of an Apache Indian. He had warm friendly hazel eyes, eyebrows thick, coal black wavy hair neatly trimmed. His voluptuous lips were thick, reminding her of LL Cool J. His goatee neatly manicured, trimmed to perfection. Women would die to have a man that looked that good on their arm. Curiously, he seemed oblivious to his good looks. It held no merit in his life.

"Hello ladies," he said with a warm genuine smile as Yasmine got up to hug him.

"Hey, how are you?" She asked excited to see him.

"I'm doing well. How's Neal and the kids?"

"They're all fine. I thought you were still in Japan. How long are you in town for?"

"Actually I just got here about an hour ago. I've been transferred back."

"That's great. Maybe we can get together for dinner soon." Now Yasmine knows she is going too far, Jaidyn thought.

"Let's do that." He said turning his attention to Jaidyn.

"Jai."

"How are you Jared?" She responded as she stood and nervously hugged him. They had never needed words to communicate and his close embrace told her more then she wanted to know.

"A hell of a lot better now!" He said molesting her with his eyes.

Jaidyn tried to ignore his eyes as they traveled down her. "You look great, Japan must have agreed with you," she said.

"It was a long year and a half. The hardest part was being away from the people I love." He paused making sure she understood what he was saying. In case she'd missed his point he made it clearer for her, "I've missed you. Can I take you to dinner?"

"...Thanks but my schedule is crazy right now."

"I won't take no for an answer. I'll call you?" He said noticing the engagement ring. He made a mental note to call Neal later to find out the deal.

Jaidyn could feel him staring a hole in her hand and placed it in her lap. She smiled politely as she dismissed him, "It was good to see you."

"Yasmine, tell Neal I'll give him a call. We need to get together and play some hoops."

"I'll do that and I'm serious about dinner. We need to catch up."

"Ok, that's a plan. See if you can get your girl here to join us."

"I'll do that," Yasmine said smiling.

"Jai do me a favor and make some time for an old friend. We need to talk." He said smoothly before walking away from the table.

Jaidyn peered at Yasmine with a knowing look. "What?" Yasmine asked.

"Heifer, you know what." Jaidyn said.

"Just because you two aren't together anymore doesn't mean that I have to dislike him. He and I were friends long before you decided to dump him. And besides he was good to you. Humh, that's who I thought you were going to marry." Jaidyn looked at Yasmine disapprovingly. "I wish you could have seen your face…from the way you two were acting y'all need to skip dinner and get a room." Yasmine said as she swirled around in her chair.

"There you go again." Jaidyn said unable to keep from laughing.

"What do you mean? There you go *again*?"

"Do you always have to be so messy?"

"Messy? You know just as well as I do, that man had you runnin' around here like a chicken with your head cut off." They both laughed.

"That he did." She muttered under her breath. The brotha had turned her out. She wasn't sure if it was his eleven-inch dick or that four-inch juicy tongue. Whatever it was, it had bordered on obsession and had once made her damn near lose her mind. Keith had satisfied her right before she'd left to meet with Yasmine but just thinking about Jared made her want to run home and fuck his brains out.

"Whatever huzzy!"

"Whatever tramp!" Yasmine said laughing.

Yasmine and Jaidyn walked to their cars still giggling. As Yasmine climbed into her Lincoln Navigator she yelled across the parking lot at Jaidyn, "Seriously Jaidyn, think about what I said."

"I always do," she called over her shoulder.

Chapter 5

    Getting into the car Jaidyn reflected on her relationship with Jared. She was still feeling a little discombobulated from seeing him. There was an inexplicable magical force that drew them together. Jared had always said that they were two halves to one soul. Whatever it was that drew them together was intoxicating and for three years he'd made her feel like they were the only two in existence.

    His attentiveness was still unmatched. He always made her feel like a queen upon her throne, making it easy for him to be her king. When making love he'd labored long and hard, leaving no stone untouched making sure she was satisfied before he erupted. Mentally and sexually he'd been the only man that took her to the gates of heaven on a chariot every time she was with him, massaging her body and mind. She wished Keith would learn this technique.

    He was the first man to free the little man in the boat. No one dared to do the things to her body that Jared had. In a sense she felt as though she lost her virginity to him. When a woman has her first orgasm she has a tendency to lose her mind. At the time Jared had her completely sprung. He had a strange power over her that she couldn't find the words to describe.

    The first time she was with him, she remembered he'd left the room, put on Johnny Gill's "My My My," and returned to the bedroom naked. She remember it had taken her by surprise since he'd left with all his clothes on and was only gone a couple of minutes. He'd returned to the room with a small tray of warm baby oil, a glass of champagne, strawberries and a bowl of whip cream. Jaidyn lay naked under the cover watching him as he prepared to take her to another level of ecstasy.

She quickly complied when asked to lie on her stomach. He rolled the sheet down to the small of her back and sprinkled the warm baby oil down the center of it. As he began to massage her she remembered how relaxed she became. He became her masseuse, taking his time, making sure he hit every spot; her neck, shoulders, spine, and butt. He pulled the bottom of the sheets up to the back of her knees. He massaged her inner-thighs, careful to only lightly touch the lips of her vagina. He pulled the sheet back to its original position, covering her naked body.

He rolled her onto her back, put baby oil into the palms of his hands and massaged the front of her body. Again, taking his time. Massaging from the temples of her face to the tips of her fingers.

The more he rubbed and kneaded her body the hornier she became. As she listened to Johnny sing, "my, my, my, my, my, my, myyyy you sho' look good tonight and you're so damn fiiiine," she wondered how much longer his elaborate seductive game was going to take. The urgency to have him inside her began to envelop every crevice of her body. Jared's ass was so fine with his clothes on she wanted to bite him, but now that he was straddling her naked and the muscle between his legs looked like it was at least nine-inches soft, she was doing everything she could to contain herself.

Jared kissed her softly, barely touching her lips as she came to a sitting position. He handed her the champagne glass of Moet. Taking a strawberry and dipping it into the bowl of whip cream he fed it to her. While she ate the strawberry he rolled the bottom of the sheet up to the tops of her thighs and massaged her legs and feet. Again, massaging far enough up to only lightly brush the lips of her vagina. Then he rolled the sheet back to its original position.

She hurried to finish the strawberry and the glass of champagne. She couldn't wait to see what was next. This was the type of shit she'd read about in books. He definitely had her undivided attention.

As she sat the wineglass on the nightstand he slid her down so that she lay on her back. Once on her back, he began kissing her passionately. She could feel him expanding. She was anxious to see what the brotha was packin' now that he was fully erect. When he lifted himself off of her she quickly glanced at his expansion. Jaidyn's eyes bulged as she openly gawked at the size of his dick. He not only extended a good two-inches but it was also thicker.

The first thing that came to mind when she saw it was an anaconda. The brotha was defiantly packing a full-grown anaconda. Unable to think clearly, she reached for it. She needed to get a quick feel, make sure her eyes weren't deceiving her. Before she could give him the proper hand test he pushed her down into the pillow and softly bit her nipples. His tongue slid down her rib cage leaving a path of tingles. Sliding her knees into a bent position he teased the area between her belly button and the top of her pubic hair.

Still dazed by what she had just seen, she wondered how long he would tease her. She tried to concentrate on his action and then, "*Oh my goodness, he's going to, aaaahhhh.*" She'd never forget the first time his tongue tickled her clitoris. It was the most amazing feeling. Her girlfriends had told her a hundred times how wonderful oral sex was but until that moment she had not experienced it for herself. They'd teased her, telling her she had no idea what she was missing and was still a virgin, so to speak.

As he gently pulled her lips apart licking, sucking and nibbling her clitoris. Jaidyn found it hard to control herself. The sudden gust of unimaginable pleasure surprised her. She involuntarily jumped, moved and maneuvered trying to get away from the pleasurable tingling sensation. Jared wrapped his arms around her hips and firmly held her as he continued his exploration. Then he did it! Slipping his tongue into her opening, inside "The Palace" walls, he drained all the juices from her body. Jaidyn held her breath, unsure if to cry or scream.

She didn't think she had the energy to take anymore until he skillfully slipped his eleven-inch snake of seduction inside her inch by inch. Pulling her into orgasmic overload. She moaned as he made slow circular motions with his hips. "Am I hurting you?" He'd asked. She hadn't answered him, her body continued to twitch as the tingling lingered on.

As soon as Jaidyn could gather some strength she asked him to turn over. He lifted himself and lay on his back. Now in control of her senses she made eye to eye contact with his rock hard erection. Still disbelieving its size, she climbed on top of him and guided him into that warm wet place once more. As "My My My" replayed they exploded together.

Jared held her close as they fell asleep.

Jaidyn had only slept for about an hour that night when her body woke her yearning for more. She listened to the soft sounds of him sleeping as long as she could before waking him.

Jared thought he was having an erotic dream when he woke to Jaidyn's tongue teasing the head of his dick. He made love to her several more times that night. Each time making her body convulse as she screamed with pleasure. The last time she surrendered to the overwhelming emotions and let herself go. When they were finished she lay in his arms overcome with emotion. No one had made her feel this way before. Making love to him only solidified the love she'd felt for him, leaving no doubt that he was the one.

Jaidyn would never forget that night. She'd cum more times then she could remember. It was that night that she'd learned where her g-spot was and the way Jared's dick leaned to the right allowed him to hit it over and over again.

When their relationship ended she threw out her Johnny Gill CD deciding it was only torture to hear Johnny sing their song. When she heard it on the radio it always brought back bittersweet memories. Jaidyn secretly hoped Keith would one day be able to take her to that level of ecstasy.

Chapter 6

Jaidyn was fifteen years old when her grandmother died from breast cancer. After experiencing her grandmother's tribulation she made a decision to become a Surgical Oncologist. Being a Surgical Oncologist meant she would be intensively trained in cancer surgery, which would allow her to treat people with a multitude of cancers; head, neck, thyroid, pancreatic, cervical, breast, melanoma, and other tumors of the skin. What better way of honoring her grandmother than to help people with this disease that intrusively plagued their bodies.

Jaidyn wanted to attend John Hopkins University School of Medicine for her residency since she'd decided to be a doctor. After working hard at Baylor and being accepted she was faced with the dilemma of leaving Jared. The five-hour trip from Houston to Waco every weekend had been difficult but now faced with moving to Boston seemed inconceivable. She couldn't bare the thought of tearing herself away from him. Therefore, The University of Texas Health Science Center in Houston would have to do. After all, it was a good school and M.D. Anderson Cancer Center was one of the best cancer facilities in the country.

Her residency schedule was so hectic she might well have been in Boston. The schedule required her to be on call forty-eight hours at a time, during which she was unable to leave the hospital. She and Jared made the doctors call quarters their home away from home during those times. After being on call for two days she would be off for twenty-four hours and then have to return to the hospital for another forty-eight hours of call. On her day off she tried to catch up on sleep, study and spend as much time with Jared as possible, making love to him every chance she got.

In early November of that year Jared's boss delivered a devastating blow. Jared would be transferred to Japan for an undisclosed period of time. The transfer would happen sometime in January and could last up to four years. Despite Jared's attempts to evade the transfer, the move was inevitable. He would have to go.

When she heard the news she become bitter. She had given up an opportunity to attend John Hopkins for him but he couldn't find a way out of the transfer for her. In late November Jared asked her to marry him but marriage would mean moving to Japan and giving up her dream of becoming a doctor. Jaidyn felt that she had already given up one dream and wasn't willing to give up another. Jared argued that she would only have to put it off for a few years but Jaidyn wouldn't hear of it.

Adding insult to injury, a week later Jaidyn found out she was pregnant. She had always insisted that Jared wear a condom but some time in September they'd gotten caught up in the moment and Jared hadn't worn a condom or pulled out in time. Paranoia invaded her good sense and convinced her that he knew before the first of November that he would be transferred and was trying to get her pregnant so that she would quit the residence program, marry him, and move to Japan.

In early December, after making love to him, she lay in his arms and told him that the relationship was not working out and she no longer wanted to see him. She'd said that a long distance relationship was out of the question and that they both needed their space. The following week, despite Lance's disapproval, he'd taken her to have an abortion.

The day after the abortion Jared called. "Hey, I'm going to swing by to see you?"

"Today isn't a good day. Can I talk to you tomorrow?"

"Are you still tripping? What's up with you?"

"I don't feel like this today, I'll call you tomorrow." Jaidyn said harshly.

"Shit Jaidyn, yo ass is really trippin'."

"Look, I'll talk to you tomorrow."

"I'm a few blocks away. I'll be there in a couple of seconds, open the door baby."

"Not today Jared."

"I need to get the remainder of my things. I'm pulling up in the parking lot now."

Jaidyn let him in. She needed to let him get his things so he wouldn't have any excuses to continue to harass her. Her anger began to disintegrate as soon as he walked in. Since the first day she'd laid eyes on him, he'd been her weakness. She remembered the entire room lit up with the smell of Calvin Klein's Eternity. Every time she'd seen him she wanted to fuck the shit out of him, that day was no different. He was the only man that ever affected her in this manner. In the three years they dated, her appetite for him never wavered.

He didn't say a word as he walked past her. He went into the dinning room and picked up a box that she'd packed for him. As he got ready to leave he undressed her with his eyes. Jared thought, what the hell and in one swift motion he put the box down, pulled her into his arms and kissed her. She felt herself melting and pushed him away. "I'd like you to leave," she said fighting to hold back tears.

"Don't act like this. Tell me what's wrong."

"Please just go." She didn't look like she was budging so he picked up the box and walked out. Tears rolled down her face as she slid down the wall. What the hell had she done, she questioned.

A knock on the door brought her out of her trance. She dried her face and opened the door. Jared walked past her without saying anything. She looked in the direction he was walking and noticed he had left his keys on the kitchen counter. Oh shit! His keys were sitting on top of the papers she had gotten from the abortion clinic.

"What is it now? You can't just be walking in here like you own shit." Jaidyn yelled trying to get his attention before he reached the keys.

It was too late. He was already picking up his keys and noticed the paper underneath them. He picked it up and began to read it. His brow became tense and the vein in the middle of his forehead began to protrude, "What the hell is this?"

"Some of my stuff for school. It's none of your business. Get your keys and get out!" She said snatching the papers from his hands.

Jared stepped in front of Jaidyn pinning her in the kitchen. She felt trapped like a dog in a kennel. There was no way out. His hazel eyes narrowed on her and his jaw muscle tightened, "Jaidyn, are you pregnant?"

"Don't be ridiculous." She said as she tried to move around him.

He backed her against the wall, "Did you have an abortion?"

"No!"

Jared untied Jaidyn's housecoat and noticed she had on her period panties. She had taught him that a woman should have two kinds of panties, period panties that they only wore during their monthly cycle and everyday panties. Jaidyn's period panties were big cotton bloomers. Her everyday panties were sexy bikinis or g-strings. He put his hand around her throat. "This ain't the week for your period. I keep up with that shit better than you." Before the words were out of his mouth he was already trying to figure out when was her last cycle.

She hesitated not sure what to say, "Will you please let me go?"

"Not until you tell me the truth."

"Jared please," she pleaded. Jared had the spirit of a lamb and she knew he'd never hurt her. She didn't want to hurt his feelings. If he knew the truth it would kill him.

"What have you done," he demanded.

"I had a abortion! Are you happy now?"

Jared became irritated, "what the fuck," he said shaking his head. "You killed our baby! How could you be so fucking selfish?"

"What?"

"You heard me!"

Jaidyn flew into him, giving her best impersonation of Laila Ali. He quickly put his arms up to protect himself. Her fists were striking him in the face, top of his head, arms and chest. The more he tried to dodge the hits the more punches she landed. He finally pushed her off of him. She hit the back wall of the kitchen with a thud. "Dammit Jaidyn," he complained. "I'm sorry, I didn't mean to push you so hard."

She picked up a glass out of the drain board and threw it at him. He ducked and it crashed against the refrigerator.

"What in the hell is wrong with you?"

She picked up another one. It hit him above his right eye. Blood instantly began trickling down his face. He reached up to touch the spot that was stinging. He pulled his hand back and noticed the blood, "Dammit Jai!"

"Get the fuck out!" She screamed as tears of hurt and anger ran down her face. "Get out of my got damn house Jared!"

He lunged at her grabbing her hands before she could throw something else, which only seemed to make her madder. "Calm yo ass down," he said as she tried to pull her hands free.

As he loosened his grip she flew into him again this time kicking him. Her foot struck its target on the third attempt. Jared doubled over grabbing his testicles. She took full advantage of his posture and jumped on him, biting, scratching and hitting.

"Girl, I promised you I'd never hit you but you're pissing me off!"

He bear hugged her, picked her up, took her into her bedroom and body slammed her on the bed.

"Fuck you Jared. Get the fuck off me." She said struggling to get free. "Let me go." She hissed, trying to catch her breath. He held her until he began to feel her relax.

Calming down she noticed how good the warmth of his body felt against her skin. How safe she'd felt in his arms. The feelings infuriated her all over again. She refused to be sucked back in by him.

Jared finally broke the silence, "If I let you go are you going to stay calm?" She didn't answer him. He slowly released her. Jaidyn got out of bed and went into the bathroom. Once the door was locked she sat down and cried.

When the tears finally stopped she could hear Jared moving around in her room. She knew no matter how long she stayed in there he would wait. He wanted an explanation and he wouldn't leave until he had one.

She wet a washcloth, cleaned her face and examined the bruises that were already appearing on her forearms and hands. There was a golf ball size goose egg that had already turned purple on her lower arm. Her knuckles had begun to swell and had turned a light shade of blue and purple. Four of her fingernails had been broken. The people at the hospital were going to wonder if she'd been in a war, she thought. She looked as if she'd lost the battle but the truth was he had never laid a hand on her.

She couldn't believe he said she was selfish. He'd never spoken to her so harshly before. He'd deserved the beat down she'd given him. He'd think twice before disrespecting another woman.

Deciding to tell him the whole truth. She said a prayer before she left the bathroom,

> *Father, please forgive me for what I've done and please help me forgive myself. Help me to make Jared understand. And give me the strength I need to say good bye to Jared.*
>
> *Amen*

Unlocking the bathroom door she found Jared sitting on the edge of the bed reading the abortion papers. Jaidyn took the papers from him and put them on her dresser. Jared put his elbows on his knees he hung his head.

Searching for the words she finally said, "I had an abortion yesterday. I didn't tell you because I knew you would try to talk me out of it." When he looked at her, his hazel eyes were slightly pink and the thought of him crying pierced her soul, making her regret her actions even more.

"What the hell were you thinking?" He asked softly allowing a tear to roll down his face.

"I wasn't." She painfully attempted. Jaidyn tried to appear strong but his tears destabilized her stance. She looked at him as tears freely flowed down her face.

"Don't give me that shit. Everything you do is carefully planned."

She couldn't hide from his merciless judgment. His raw emotions made her feel naked and exposed. "I was thinking I'm in medical school.

I'm trying to make something of my life and a baby would only complicate that. It's the last thing I need right now."

"This wasn't your decision to make alone! Did your selfish ass ever consider what I might have wanted?" Jared said hurt turning to anger.

"Yes, I considered how you'd feel. That's why I didn't tell you."

Jared stood up and came towards her. She hoped he was about to take her in his arms, tell her that everything would be all right and that he still loved her. She hoped that he was going to say he forgave her and he understood why she had to do it. "When are you going to stop doing what everybody else thinks is best for you and do what you want? I bet you don't even know what that is anymore. You're so busy trying to make your parents proud of you." He said through clinched teeth.

"Don't blame this on my parents. They don't know anything about it."

"Yeah, I know. You'd never let them know that their precious baby got pregnant!"

"This doesn't have anything to do with anybody but us." She said wiping away tears.

"You know how much I love you. I'd marry you tomorrow so don't give me that. This is about you. It's always about you. When your ass got pissed off at me last month and went out with the dude from the hospital that was about your selfish ass."

"Look, I don't want to hurt you."

"You didn't even tell me you were pregnant before you went and killed our child! What the hell do you mean, you don't want to hurt me? You've already done that…you could have at least talked to me first." Jared said as he hung his head.

"I'm sorry I didn't tell you but it doesn't change the facts. I love you but," her voice trailed off.

"But what? Being a doctor is more important then anything else! Even our fucking child?"

"Baby I'm just not where you are. I'm not ready to be a wife and mother. Being a doctor is very important to me and I can't do both. I can't finish med school with those type of responsibilities." The look of disgust and disappointment in his eyes penetrated her heart and left a gaping hole in it. She had never imagined things would come to this. "I'm sorry. I never meant to hurt you. But let's just face the truth, how can you be a father from the other side of the world? Your number one priority is your career. Not me or a child."

He shook his head, completely disgusted with her. How could she have done this? He thought he knew her so well. He stepped closer to her, gathered her into his arms and kissed her on the forehead, "That's bull shit and you know it. This wasn't about anyone but you. I won't take the blame for it," he said softly.

She'd never thought about it in those terms. She only did what she thought was best for her at the time. It wasn't until then that she'd realized how paranoid she'd been. She'd acted on the stressful emotions of not having things her way and hadn't thought logically or dealt with the reality of the situation. His comment had hit its desired target and stung. Nothing hurts more than the truth.

They didn't speak again until January when it was time for Jared to leave for Japan. His secretary, Naomi, gave Jaidyn his complete itinerary and she'd met him at the airport. He was surprised to see her. He was still angry with her, which made the goodbye even more difficult. She'd tried again to explain away the pain. Five months after he left he sent her flowers to apologize for his behavior. She hadn't heard from him again until today at lunch with Yasmine.

She'd loved Jared completely innocently, with the eyes of a child. She loved him before life's issues had taken their toll on her. It was a love so trusting and naive that it only comes along once in a lifetime. Everyone experiences it at least once in his or her lifetime. She deeply regretted how things had turned out. It broke her heart to think about all she'd put him through. She knew she didn't deserve him. A piece of her was still with him and losing him still haunted her.

Life's experiences have a way of robbing you of your innocence. Jaidyn's had changed the way in which she was able to love her future husband. Yasmine had been right, she'd never love him like she'd loved Jared but she'd love him the best she could.

Chapter 7

Jared shook his head and smiled when he thought about how good Jai was looking. Milk without a doubt was doing her body good. He couldn't believe that she was getting married. He thought about the ring and worked the possibilities of it through his mind. Maybe it isn't an engagement ring. Nah, that isn't possible. It's definitely an engagement ring. Nobody gives a ring that size as a token of friendship, he thought.

It wasn't until Jared was living in Japan that he realized how incomplete his life was without her. He had every intention on coming back and picking up where they left off. They needed to squash all that shit they had gone through and let the past be the past. Everybody makes mistakes. He never considered when he returned that she would be engaged. He'd expected her to wait on him because she'd felt the same way he did.

He'd been angry and hurt when he walked out of her apartment that cold December evening. He'd not tried to understand the reason she thought she had to abort their love child. When she showed up at the airport he was pleasantly surprised but he made the mistake of playing the hard-core roll. He'd wanted her to run after him. When she did he'd rejected her because he wanted to make her pay for what she'd done. Looking back on it, he'd been a damn fool.

He realized that he had defiantly been on an ego trip. He had let his pride and ego stand between him and the love of his life and he deeply regretted it. His ego had damn near stepped in and became his ruler. He'd been too stupid to realize that he was locked inside a prism of his own pride. His vises kept him from the one person that made him whole, complete. His pride wouldn't let him forgive her for aborting his child and his ego wouldn't let him pass on the promotion he was offered in Japan.

While in Japan he had taken time to take inventory of his life. Although he'd longed for a certain degree of success, everything he was achieving seemed useless and invalid without her. Coming to this conclusion forced him to take a long look at his roll in the demise of their relationship. In asking her to quit medical school and be his wife he'd accused her of being selfish, but the truth was he was the selfish one. He didn't have to take the promotion and move, but it would have enabled him to become the youngest partner in his firm. He hadn't told her the whole truth. He could have stayed right where he was and passed the promotion over. Once again his own demons, pride and ego, were his inward devils.

If loving Jaidyn was all that mattered he realized that he was going to have to take the advice of Iyanla Vanzant. He'd read in one of those books of hers that if he wanted to be happy, the days of his ego and pride ruling his life would have to be put behind him. Now that he'd done that there was no way he was going to let Jaidyn marry someone else.

"Damn," he said to himself, "I loved that girl more than life itself. I almost let my greatest treasure slip away." He remember something his mother use to say about the two of them and he repeated it out loud, "We're two halves of one soul…Not even another man could change that."

The love jones had set up camp in their lives. What they had was forever. God had clearly preordained it. Predestined it. Ordered it into existence before we even knew each other.

Jaidyn doesn't know it yet, but love, true love, never really dies. You can run from it but it's always there, down in your soul trying to tunnel its way out, he thought. From the response I got when I held her, there is no way she doesn't still care. I know every inch of her body better then she does and the responses of it. She melted in my arms. It felt like home, right where she's supposed to be. That doesn't happen when you don't love someone. Yeah, it's kismet, and it's time we stop running from it.

Since he'd seen her he had been unable to think of anything else and it was driving him crazy. He couldn't get her out of his system. He'd have to find a way to get her back. That damn ring would have to go. Who is this brotha? She was just going to have to turn him lose. Nothing against him but nah, it isn't going down like this. I'm not ready for it to be over. I've got to do something to keep the door open but, what, he wondered.

Jared had attempted to call Jaidyn at the last number he had but the number was no longer in service. He had stopped by her old apartment and she'd moved. He had allowed his mind to run wild. If she was living with this man he would lose his mind. He'd gone by the hospital several times but always came up empty handed. Knowing that she spent Sunday with her family he'd taken a leap of faith and gone to her parents' house on Sunday afternoon. Her mother told him that she had to work and hadn't been able to come. He'd had a long talk with Lance and Mr. Owens but every time he brought Jaidyn up Mr. Owens had quickly changed the topic. He had sent flowers to her at her parents address everyday for the last week and she still had not called him.

As a last resort Jared decided to call Yasmine. After leaving several messages and playing phone tag with Neal he decided to stop by after work. He'd sat in their living room catching up on all that he'd missed, hoping that one of them would mention Jaidyn but neither of them did. Frustrated he finally said, "Hey...how's your girl?"

"She's fine. You know Jaidyn, she's working way too hard. She started her fellowship a couple of months ago. After that she's going into private practice," Yasmine said.

"I see." He said. "Is her schedule still two on and one off?" Jared asked trying to get as much information as he could. The more he knew about her schedule the better his chances of catching up with her.

"No. The fellowship schedule is completely different. She's supervising the residents and reports directly to the doctors. She's on call twenty-four hours a day, seven days a week but there aren't any in house calls unless there's a problem. She's at home every night." Yasmine knew exactly what Jared was trying to get her to say but she wasn't playing his game.

Although Yasmine was answering his questions she wasn't coming right out with any extra information. Yasmine was too smart to fall into that trap and he knew it. He was going to have to come right out and ask her. "Yasmine why must we go about this the hard way?" He chuckled. "You know what I'm asking!"

A sly smile crossed her face, "No Jared, I don't." She said continuing the game of cat and mouse.

"What's up with the ring she was wearing?"

Yasmine hesitated then smacked her lips, "Why don't you ask her?"

A show of frustration flashed on Jared's face. "Cause I'm asking you. Is she engaged or what?"

"Yes."

Her answer cut him and he seemed to deflate a little. "Ssshhh, to who?"

"This brotha named Keith Tyler."

"Hhmmm...when are they getting married?"

"I think you need to talk to her about all that," she said seriously.

"I've tried to contact her but she's moved and her phone number has changed. I've gone to the hospital and her parents but she wasn't at either place. And I've been sending flowers to her parents house for the past week."

"Well it sounds like you've done just about all you can do. I'm sure she's getting the flowers."

He knew she'd given him all the information she was willing to give but he thought he'd try anyway, "Where's she living?"

"I'll let her know that you asked about her Jared."

"Yasmine I need your help. Call her, let me talk to her."

Yasmine shook her head. "I'll give her a message for you. If she wants to talk to you she'll call you."

"She's just going to have to turn this brotha loose. Nothing against him but it's not going down like that. I'm not ready for it to be over between us."

Yasmine was taken aback by his comment. "I know you didn't, what do you mean you're not ready. You ended it when you left and moved to the other side of the world. What was she supposed to do, wait on you?"

"Man," Jared said looking at her crazy, "We had something special."

"It couldn't have been too special, you left her. What exactly did you expect?"

"I expected her to wait." Jared said with an attitude.

"Wait for what? If I heard the story correctly you broke things off before you left."

Jared shot her a look of confusion, realizing Jaidyn had not told her the whole story. "That was a mistake. I got transferred, what was I supposed to do?"

"Jared be for real."

"What's that supposed to mean?"

"You're one of the most educated brotha's I know, you've got a Bachelors in Finance and Business Economics from Xavier University and a MBA in Financial Management from Stanford. People are beating down your door to give you a job."

"That's not true."

"You can tell that lie to someone else. You don't graduate at the top of your class and can not find a job. My company is one of those who would love to have you work for us. So save it."

Jared switched gears, "She's known this guy for all of two minutes. What is she thinking?"

Neal remained quiet but shook his head. Jared had crossed that imaginary line in the sand and Neal knew all to well that Yasmine was going to go off. Yasmine and Jaidyn were the best kind of friends. They could talk about each other. They could argue, fuss, and fight, but anybody else that had the nerve to open their mouth about one of them had a fight on their hands. He knew from experience that there was no winning an argument with Yasmine and now Jared was about to find that out too.

"She's moving on with her life. Do you realize how much you hurt her?" Yasmine got pissed off just thinking about it. "She walked around here for months like a damn zombie. She lost weight cause she wouldn't eat. She wouldn't fix herself up. She stayed at that hospital twenty-four hours a day seven days a week trying her best not to think about you. She stopped talking to everybody who cared about her. She did just what she should've done. She moved on."

Jared's heart sank. He had no idea she'd been so hurt. "I'm sorry."

"Humh!" Yasmine said shaking her head.

"You know I wasn't trying to hurt her."

"That's all fine and dandy but it doesn't change the facts. Y'all brotha's think y'all can just do anything to sistas and we're supposed to take it. Y'all think 'I'm sorry' solves everything. Women ain't taking that no more. Those days are over. Jaidyn is doing what she has to do to move forward with her life. Yo ass missed the boat. You should have jumped on it when you had a chance. You move you lose."

"Yasmine, I ain't trying to hear all that. I said I made a mistake and I'm asking you to help me correct it."

"Look, I don't have anything against you but if you looking for sympathy you've come to the wrong place. I'm not about to get between you and Jaidyn. I'll give her any message you'd like but that's it."

"Give her a call and let me talk to her. What can a simple phone call hurt?"

"Jared, I'm sorry," Yasmine said shaking her head.

"Neal man, talk to your wife."

"Maaannn, you're on your own. I'm not about to get in the middle of this."

"Fuck it then. Can yall just answer one question for me? When are they getting married?"

"Hm," Yasmine said as she got up and left the room.

"Yasmine," Jared called after her.

Neal sat smiling and shaking his head. "Man I see nothing's changed. Jaidyn still got yo ass pussy whooped. The power of the pussy is hell on a brotha. She's got both you fools runnin' round here losing yall's damn minds. Tell me this, what the hell did she do to you?"

"Man, it ain't like that. She's a hell of a woman and I fucked up."

They sat in silence for a few minutes watching the baseball game. Neal finally said, "Man they're getting married in three months. Jaidyn moved in with her parents until the wedding. I don't know nothing else. So don't ask and keep that shit to yourself. You didn't get it from me."

Chapter 8

Yasmine hadn't gotten a minute alone the night before so as soon as she got her family out of the house the next morning she sat down to call Jaidyn and tell her all about Jared.

"Hey girl." Yasmine said when Jaidyn finally came to the phone.

"What's wrong?"

"Why does something have to be wrong?"

"Because it's eight o'clock in the morning, you had the nurse page me and then you waited for me to come to the phone instead of leaving a message."

"Alright!" Yasmine said unable to hold onto it any longer. "You'll never guess who stopped by last night."

"Who?" Jaidyn asked unimpressed.

"Jared."

"What did he want?"

"You!" Yasmine said instigating.

"Gurl, whatever!"

"I'm not kidding! He said he's been trying to contact you but hasn't had any luck and that he's sent you flowers everyday last week but you still haven't called him. Says he made a mistake and wants you back. He said you're getting ready to marry Keith because you're on the rebound and that you don't really love him. He said you're still in love with him and," Yasmine remembered something Jaidyn used to say about Jared all the time and added it in for good measure, "Something about you being the other half of his soul. He intends on getting you back. Said he knows you better than anyone and that hug at lunch the other day wasn't just a hug. That he knew you creamed your panties right then and there." Yasmine said trying not to let Jaidyn hear the humor in her voice.

"Go to hell Yasmine," Jaidyn said laughing, "He didn't say that."

Yasmine broke into laughter, "What's wrong, the truth hurt? Alright, he didn't say that last part but he said everything else. What has little Ms. Jai gotten herself into?"

The thought of Jared made Jaidyn's heart sink. This was the last thing she needed. He'd sent her every variation of Calla Lilies she'd ever seen. Calla Lilies were his signature flowers. When they were dating she never received any other flower. The flowers had arrived everyday since she'd seen him at the restaurant with the same message written inside the card, "I need to see you. You're the other half of my soul. I made a mistake letting you go. Please call me at (713)545-0838." She'd hoped if she ignored him he'd go away but the flowers had arrived again this morning like clockwork. She pulled the card out of her pocket and read it again, "Marrying anyone besides me would be a mistake. Let me prove it to you over dinner. (713)545-0838. The other half of your soul, Jared."

Memories of them had saturated her mind. She felt like she was drowning in them when Yasmine asked, "So you going to see him or not?"

"I don't know. I don't think I'm strong enough for that...shit, what am I suppose to do?"

The uncertainty in Jaidyn's voice set off alarms in Yasmine's head. She light heartedly said, "I thought you were head over hills in love with Jared, I mean Keith."

"Ha ha ha, I'm glad you're having fun. Keith's my heart. Jared's the past, all that stuff with him is over." She said stronger then what she needed to.

"Are you saying that for my benefit or yours?" Yasmine said teasing.

"You know you're full of jokes today. Don't you have someone else to torture?"

"Come on now it's me. I know you better than you know yourself. After seeing you with Jared the other day there is no doubt in my mind where your heart is. So you can save that BS for someone else."

"I love Keith."

"Humh, then you need to ask yourself if it's possible to be in love with two men at the same time."

"What exactly are you saying?"

As usual Yasmine felt she had to drive her point home, "The same thing I've been saying, you're settling for Keith. I don't doubt that you care for him but you're still in love with Jared."

Yasmine's presumption aggravated Jaidyn. It was the last thing that she wanted to hear. She needed her help getting out of this predicament not her sarcasm or her wishful thinking. Things between her and Jared ended when she decided to have an abortion and he decided to move to Japan.

"Look girl, all kidding aside, Jared's a hell of a man. Whatever it is that draws you to him is genuine and shouldn't be ignored. I'd forgotten what you guys were like when you were together but looking back on it you were happier then I've ever seen you. There's no mistaking it, he's right when he says you're two halves to one soul. Anyone who sees you together can see it. He's the full meal deal and if I were you I wouldn't let him get away."

"I wish it was that easy."

"Do you remember when we dreamt about finding that old school love like our grandparents had?"

Jaidyn laughed, "Girl we were 14 years old. We didn't have a clue."

"That's true," Yasmine said laughing. "We didn't have a clue how much work it was to hold that kind of relationship together, but I got lucky. I found it in Neal and you can have it with Jared. You really need to think about what you're doing. You've got to make a choice Jai. Some things are simply kismet. You can delay them but you can't avoid them. You can still end this thing with Keith. It's not too late." Yasmine said seriously.

"Oh wise one, don't you have any better advice than that?" Jaidyn said sarcastically.

"Follow your heart Jai. You never go wrong when you do...Hey tell me something, besides getting transferred, what exactly happened between the two of you?"

"Nothing."

"Girl, as heartbroken as you were I had to miss something."

Although Yasmine was Jaidyn's best friend she'd never told her about the abortion. "You know everything. He got transferred, asked me to marry him, I said no and he moved to Japan. End of story. It was really just that simple."

"I've never understood why you would tell the man of your dreams no." Yasmine pushed, not believing Jaidyn's explanation.

"I was in med school."

"And?"

"And it was my first piority!"

Jaidyn's attitude was evident so Yasmine backed off a little. "It sounds like it was just a matter of geography. You were in one place and he was in another. That's not something to end a relationship over. When you love someone you learn to deal with that kind of stuff. Lots of people have long distance relationships. Shit Jai, he asked you to marry him. What else was he supposed to do?"

"A lot has happened since then."

"Hum. Well, do you still love him?"

"I don't know."

"You don't know or are you afraid to admit it?"

"I said I don't know!" Jaidyn snapped.

"I've never known you to be indecisive." Yasmine said gingerly.

"I'm not being indecisive. I'm marring Keith in a couple of months and that's the end of it!"

"Chill, you don't have to convince me."

"I've got to get back to work. I'll talk to you later."

"If you need to talk..." Yasmine started to say.

"I know."

"Girl, I love you."

"I love you too. Talk to you later."

Jaidyn's mind was racing when she hung up. Seeing Jared had stirred up feelings that her heart wouldn't allow her to throw away. She had been content with them lying dormant in a dark corner of her heart. She had explained it away to herself as the way every woman felt about their first love but then she'd seen him and she wasn't sure that she could continue to put what she felt in that category. She silently prayed as she walked back to the doctor's lounge.

> *Please Lord, give me a wise and discerning heart. I know You're trying to teach me something but please bring me through this lesson gently. Help me to be a wise, sensible, levelheaded woman so that I may recognize Your will for my life. Give me the courage to surrender to Thy holy will. In the name of my Lord and Savior Jesus Christ.*
>
> *Amen.*

The inner turmoil had her stomach in knots. On one hand Keith was a good man and he had been good to her. She didn't want to hurt him, but on the other hand was Jared. She never felt as complete as she did when she was with him. She'd be lying if she didn't say that he wasn't the love of her life, but things were different then. They both had changed and evolved into different people.

Jaidyn convinced herself that it was best if they let the past be the past. No matter how sweet his gestures were there was no use in taking a trip down memory lane and wondering what could have been. It was best if she let sleeping dogs' lye and ignored Jared's attempts to contact her. There was no turning back. Her wedding was right round the corner and she needed to concentrate on the preparations. She was about to marry Keith and attempt to have a storybook life.

Chapter 9

If someone would have told Neal that Jared crashed Jaidyn's wedding there is no way he would have believed them, but Neal was seeing him with his own eyes. He'd spotted Jared as he entered the church parking lot. Before he climbed out of his car Neal was on his way over to him. He couldn't believe this shit. He had to hear this story for himself.

"My man, what the hell are you doing here?" He asked shaking Jared's hand.

Jared knew he'd have to hear this shit for the next fifty years but he didn't care. His need to be with her was overpowering. "You know how it is man," Jared said.

"Nah dawg, I don't. Yo ass got some brass balls."

"Shit, what can I say? I've got to see her."

"I hear you..." Neal said still a little blown away by Jared's appearance. "Well if she ain't glad to see you, Yasmine will be. She hasn't been in the best mood. She's not happy about this marriage at all."

"I just can't let it go down like this. We need to clear up a few things before she does this. I wish I would have talked to Yasmine sooner but you know how things are."

"You should've did this shit last week when Yasmine told you."

"Yeah, I know." Jared's pride had taken over and he hadn't wanted to talk to Jaidyn before now. Yasmine had called him the week before and gave him all the information he needed to contact Jaidyn.

"Make sure none of her family sees you," Neal said.

"Don't sweat it..." Jared said. "Do you know where she is?"

"Yeah, they're in the back. Go around to the side door, it's open. It's the third door on the right," Neal instructed.

"And hey, you know I got yo back."

"Thanks man. For everything," Jared said shaking Neal's hand and giving him a manly hug.

As he entered the side entrance he was careful not to run into the groom or Jaidyn's family. After finding the room Jaidyn was in, Jared took a minute to collect himself before knocking on the door. When Joanna answered the door she was speechless. Jared could see Jaidyn standing in the middle of the room, looking like a beautiful princess. He eased his way around Joanna, the last thing he needed to do was lose his nerve before he got a chance to speak with Jaidyn.

Jaidyn was wearing an ivory strapless Vera Wang wedding gown. Yasmine was crowning the princess with her tiara. Her sandy brown hair framed her beautiful face. The dress was an A-line gown with a dropped waist. Her 36C breasts were nicely contained in its straight fitted top. The top of the dress was embellished with beads. The dropped waist showed off her slender hourglass shape and the five foot beaded train was spectacular. The platinum vintage style pear shaped center necklace and tear dropped diamond earrings mounted in platinum added an impressive elegant finish to her attire. Jared's eyes clouded. She should be his bride, he thought. She was simply breathtaking. He stood watching her, unable to move as a flood of regret rushed in on him.

"You look absolutely beautiful." He said struggling to get the words out.

Jaidyn immediately recognized his voice. She quickly turned to find him standing behind her. Her eyes locked onto his. She wasn't sure what to say. Oh shit not now, was all that came to mind. The weakness she felt for him put a death grip on her stomach muscles.

"Can I speak to you alone? It will only take a minute."

"Jared this isn't the time." Joanna said sympathetically.

Acknowledging Joanna's presence he said, "Joanna it's nice to see you." He gave her a soft hug and kiss on the cheek.

Yasmine's delight in seeing him was evident and she smiled widely. When Yasmine had called him she put him to the test before she'd voluntarily given him the information he needed to stop this wedding. Her final question was, "What is it about her that makes you love her?"

He'd responded sincerely saying, "It's not just one thing. It's everything about her. I love the way we laugh and joke together. The way she makes me feel when I'm with her. The peace she brings me. I love the way we bring balance to each other. I love her intelligent mind and the way she challenges me to be the best. She's my best friend." Yasmine could hear the love in his voice and her stance was weakened by it. It was that single statement that convinced her she was about to do the right thing.

"It's about time one of you came to your senses," Yasmine said.

He smiled agreeably, "Yasmine you look beautiful too."

"Thank you," she said grateful for his presence. Someone needed to talk some sense into Jaidyn. She was about to make the biggest mistake of her life.

Jared returned his attention to Jaidyn. His mesmerizing hazel eyes seem to hold her in a trance. "Ladies can we have the room for a couple of minutes," he requested.

"Joanna let's give these two a few minutes alone," Yasmine said before she could object. As she passed him she whispered into his ear, "I hope it's not too late to talk some sense into her. She won't listen to anything I have to say. Hopefully she'll listen to you."

"Jaidyn if you need me sweetie I'll be right outside," Joanna said from the doorway.

Jaidyn was still speechless. She was finding it difficult to move or think clearly. Her mind was racing. Why did he still have this effect on her?

Finally finding her voice she said, "I'm sorry, I didn't see your name on the guest list, were you invited?"

"Still the same old sharp tongued Jaidyn I see," Jared mused.

His mouth was moving but she didn't have a clue what he was saying. She was submerged in her own world, struggling to get her mind and body free from the way he smelled, the way he looked. Was it possible that his ass was finer today then he was four months ago? He was dressed in a dark navy Georgio Armani suit that was tailored to perfection. His Versace tie was navy pattern on a light blue background. He was sporting the David Yurman engraved cufflinks she had bought him and the smell of Armani Mania engulfed the room.

She was transfixed by the mere smell of him. How could he know that Armani Mania is my favorite? Isn't it a new fragrance? It couldn't have been out when we dated. Agitation overtook the corners of her mind as she struggled with the prospect of drowning in his efforts to pull the love she felt for him to the surface. The nerve of this bastard!

"Jared, lets cut the small talk. What the hell do you want?"

"I wanted to see you and when I spoke to Yasmine about the wedding..." his voice trailed off as Jaidyn interrupted him, "Yasmine? That's it, I've had enough of her meddling!"

"Wait a minute," Jared said grabbing her arm as she tried to storm past him to get to the door.

"Yasmine has nothing to do with me being here. She didn't know I was coming."

"What do you want?" She asked yanking her arm from him as his touch sent chills through her.

"I told you I wanted to see you, make sure you were ok."

"Give me a break, on my wedding day you decide to show up because you want to see me! What do you want?" She hissed, more aggravated with herself then with him.

He looked at her and smiled. She was beautiful when she was pissed. They had never fought much but when they did she always gave him a run for his money. She was strong willed. It was one of the things that attracted him to her.

"Passion," he said. She'd hated when he called her that. It had been his pet name for her. He'd said it fit her perfectly because she was all the things that passion was, love, warmth, desire and of course fire.

This wasn't going how Jared had hoped. He tried to start over. "Give me a minute. Just hear me out. I wanted to make sure you were happy. After I talked to you on the phone last week I just felt like I needed to see you."

"You know, you never did tell me how you got my cell number." She said curious but still wanting to argue with him.

He wasn't taking the bait and ignored her comment not wanting to divulge his source. He'd promised Yasmine he'd never tell Jaidyn that she'd given him all of her information. "Look, I came here because I needed to see you. I know you and I know how emotionally detached you can be over the phone but when I look in your eyes..." his eyes were fixed on hers. He seemed to look right into her. She turned away not wanting him to see the answer to his questions.

"Jared, this is my wedding day," she said impatiently.

"I know and I didn't come here to upset you."

"If you didn't come here to upset me, what did you think you were coming here to do? I thought I made myself clear when I spoke to you."

Before he could answer Keith walked in followed by Lance, Markel, Remington, Joanna, and Yasmine. "Is there a problem here," he asked.

Jaidyn was startled. Jared turned to look at him but had no intention on answering any questions from him. Without taking her eyes off of Jared, Jaidyn said, "No there's no problem."

"What the hell is wrong with you? Do you have a death wish? Get the fuck out of here and leave my wife alone before I kick yo muthafuckin' ass!" Keith said getting into Jared's personal space.

"Your wife?" Jared said mockingly.

"Keith please," Jaidyn exclaimed trying to stop the pissing match before it ensued any further. "Have you forgotten we're in a church?"

"What the fuck are you doing here," Keith asked again.

"Just calm down! For your information I invited him." Jaidyn said to everyone's surprise, including Jared and Yasmine who knew she was lying.

"You invited him?" Keith asked in a tone that told her he knew she was lying.

"Is there a problem with that?"

"What, yall friends and shit? How long this shit been going on?"

"Keith it's not like that."

"What the fuck is it like," Keith yelled.

Yasmine was enjoying every minute of this. She'd known Jaidyn all her life and didn't know she had it in her to spin a lie that fast. It was always Yasmine that got them out of tight spots. Then again it was always Yasmine that got them into tight spots in the first place. If Jaidyn were pushed into a corner eventually she'd fold and tell the truth, but apparently she'd been holding out or taking lessons.

"It's exactly what I just told you it was!"

"What the fuck are you saying?"

"I'm saying either you trust me or you don't. I'm going to have male friends. If you don't think you can handle that then maybe we need to stop this whole thing right now."

Keith was taken aback by her tone. "Alright, if that's the way you want it. If you think this shit's acceptable we gone go with that. But make damn sure you mark this shit down. I won't soon forget it." He stormed out of the room unable to believe this shit. She had just tried to turn the tables on him. Her ass had the nerve to get an attitude with him over another man. Alright, that shit's cool he thought, but it works both ways.

"Will you guys please give us a few minutes," Jaidyn asked the remainder of the rescue team.

"Are you going to be alright?" Lance asked.

"Yeah."

"You sure?"

"What do you guys think he's going to do to me? If he hasn't done it by now then he ain't gone do it!"

"Jaidyn, calm down. Take all the time you need." Yasmine said as she shuffled everyone out the room. She knew better then to mess with her when she was like this. Once pissed off she lost all ability to reason and her sweet demeanor turned into a snake with poisonous venom.

Once everyone was gone Jared laughed, "Damn girl! Is it like that?" He'd always found the sharp tongue of a black woman sexy. It was often her best defense. Black women fought off some of their worst enemies with their mouth.

"Look I don't need this drama. What do you want?"

"I'm not here to cause drama. I'm here because I needed to see you." He said with a serious undertone in his voice.

"Jared...."

"Listen to me," he said cutting her off. He closed the gap between them and grabbed her hand. He needed her to look into his eyes, he needed to make sure she understood, "I never found the words to come to you and say the things I should have. I guess I'm paying for that now but I'd give anything to have another chance."

The softness of his words melted her heart. "We've never needed words. I've always known how you felt." Jaidyn mumbled.

"I should've...."

"We can't go back, Jared." She said tenderly.

"I know that. We can move forward. You don't have to settle for this guy."

"Jared..."

"Jaidyn I've loved you since the first day I laid eyes on you. It's no secret that I screwed up and let my pride keep us apart. But my love and affection for you hasn't changed. Being away from you has made me see just how much you mean to me. You're the other half of my soul and I'm lost without you. Loving you is all that matters. Baby, it's not too late for us to walk out of here."

Jaidyn could feel part of her soul evaporating. How had she gotten to this place in her life? No longer able to fight back the tears, they begin cascading down her face. It wasn't until now that she fully understood how much she loved him. It was beyond comprehension. She had once been completely entangled in his web, helplessly captured. The memories they'd shared would forever be etched in her soul but she couldn't hurt Keith, not now, not like this. She owed him so much.

Struggling to breathe she said, "You've always been in my heart, you're a part of who I am. And a part of me is always going to love you, but…" No longer able to hold himself back he kissed her. She'd never been able to resist him and nothing had changed. She closed her eyes and allowed their tongues to do a sensual dance. Their kiss was soft but forceful. It was deep and meaningful allowing both of them to have a near drowning experience.

"He'd better cherish you. There will never be another like you." He said running the back of his fingers over her cheeks, wiping away some of the tears.

"You know that I love you. I always have," she said.

"I know, you're just not brave enough to walk away from this. But I'll be brave for both of us…If you just say the word, we'll walk right out of here."

"I'm sorry…" she said in a whisper.

He put his finger over her mouth to silence her. He couldn't bear to hear what would follow. "I'm always going to be here for you. I'll always treasure you, Passion." He said cupping her face in his hand and kissing her one last time.

Without another word he turned and walked out the door, past Jaidyn's rescue team and into the cool brisk day.

Yasmine and Joanna rushed back into the room to find Jaidyn crying inconsolably. Yasmine hugged her while Joanna handed her tissue. "You don't have to do this Jaidyn." Joanna said.

Jaidyn's head bobbed, "Yes I do."

"This is ridiculous! You don't cry over one man and marry another one. The way you feel about him isn't going to change. It's going to eat you up inside and make you miserable." Yasmine advised.

Chapter 10

Keith and Jaidyn settled into a nice routine. It had been six months since their wedding and marital bliss hadn't stopped. Jaidyn had pulled herself together and married the man she planned on spending the rest of her life with. She was Keith's wife and nothing was ever going to come between their union.

Jaidyn's beauty and flippant attitude was what had captured Keith's attention. It had been years since he'd had a woman flat out refuse his advances. She'd made the chase difficult yet amusing. He'd wanted to break her down, make her fall in love and then use her until he decided to move on, but somehow during his pursuit he'd fallen in love. He hadn't been ready to get married but he couldn't resist her and now she was Mrs. Keith Tyler.

His mother had always told him it would happen that way. She'd said, "Some girl's going to come along and turn your world upside down and all those scally's in those streets won't mean anything to you." She'd been partially right. Jaidyn had come along and turned his world inside out but he'd remained faithful to the teachings of his father. Richard Tyler had taught his son early in life in order to have a happy marriage every man should keep a little somin' somin' on the side. As far back as he could remember he'd accompanied his father to his lady friend's houses. He would sit on the couch watching cartoons while his father and his friend would be in the back of the house handling their business.

Richard told his son many times, "No one woman can fill all a man's needs. As long as you go home at night and make sure the bills are paid, a woman shouldn't have anything to say about a man's private business."

Keith's life style as a professional athlete only added to this mentality. The women he dealt with didn't seem to care how many other women he had as long as he kept a few dollars in their pocket.

He'd had a thing about hood rats as long as he could remember. He'd never been able to pin point exactly why. Maybe it was the way they squeezed all that ass and tits into their clothes, or maybe it was the way they all seemed to fuck the shit out of him. Whatever the reason he had to have one on his team, but they couldn't be his main woman.

Zaria, his latest hoochie, had been filling that place in his life for almost three years. She was a bobcat in bed, a freak to the core, but she didn't know how to be a lady and every hood-rat had her place. He'd be her jockey as long as she'd allowed him to ride her every chance he got. He had planned on ending things after he and Jaidyn were married, but after that stunt Jaidyn pulled with ole' boy at the wedding he felt justified in continuing to have her as part of his collection.

Keith was surprised when his secretary buzzed him saying that Zaria was waiting to see him. Zaria noticed the irritation on Keith's face as soon as she stepped into the office. She knew that it was against the rules to show her face at his office but she thought that he might make an exception in this case. Before he opened his mouth she showed him the brown paper lunch bag she brought with her. "Hey baby. I thought I'd bring you lunch."

Zaria knows better than to bring her ass to my office he thought. She'd called him several times but he hadn't returned her calls. This better be good. She wanted to know when she'd see him. He knew what that meant. It was the first of the month and the rent was due. He'd been messing around with her so long he knew her game better than she did. Her ass would get him over there, sex him down and then spring it on him. He'd paid her rent for the last year and had told her two months ago that she was going to have to get a job and start paying it herself. She must be desperate he thought. There's no way I'm paying for pussy today. She's going to have to get one of her baby's daddies to pay her damn rent. Tramps never change he thought. If her ass ain't careful she's going to find herself sitting on the bench and he'll have a new starting line up. If I hadn't made so many wise investments then her ass would have been out of luck way before now.

"What did you bring," he asked dryly.

She emptied the bag contents onto his desk. Keith burst into laughter as he looked at the array of condoms. There were ribbed tipped, rough riders, seven studded, pleasure plus, texture plus, lubricated, glow in the dark, lambskin and dental dam condoms. There were also yellow, red, and orange colored ones with reservoir tips. They were an assortment of flavors; strawberry, chocolate, vanilla, banana and mint condoms. There were condoms on lollypop sticks. Condoms in candy wrappers. You name it. She had it. The one thing that seemed out of place was a package of Hall's strawberry cough drops.

"Can I show you how to use them?" She asked seductively. She walked around the desk, climbed onto his lap and kissed him.

Picking up the mentho-lyptus cough drops he asked, "What are these for?"

"Added stimulation."

"You trying to teach me something new?"

"I sure hope so," she said as she untied his tie and unbuttoned his shirt. The "Dicktator" had a jump-start on them and was standing to attention. Zaria responded with her own salivating ooze. She unbuttoned his pants and he pulled her clothes off as fast as he could. Their hunger for each other was growing urgent.

In one swift move he stood up, lifted her off his lap allowing his pants to drop to his ankles, wiped his desk clean, and placed her on the top of it. He entered her with such force it made her tremble. Devouring her breast he thrust in and out. In and out. Moans and groans consumed the room. Easing out of her, he brought her to a standing position and turned her around. As he kissed and licked her shoulders and back, he gently enter the forbidden zone. She bent forward onto the desk, giving him full access. Making circular motions with his hips the strength in his knees begin to deteriorate. He slowed his strokes and placed his hands around her waist in search of the warm wetness between her legs. While firmly continuing his slow methodical strokes he found the little man in the boat and teased him. Deeper and deeper the "Dicktator" prowled, on an endeavor to reach the very depths of her soul.

She shivered over and over again. Wanting to increase the pleasure of her orgasm he slid out of the forbidden zone and re-entered the warm moist space between her legs. She could no longer hold it. No longer control it. "Harder, harder." She blew out in a frenzy. With an earthquake size tremble he brought her to a climax and her essence spilled onto Keith's desk.

Knowing he had satisfied her the "Dicktator" withdrew in an attempt to escape the magical atmosphere of her trembling walls but it was too late. Goose bumps had begun marching up Keith's spine. Keith forced his way back inside her and pumped once, twice and then again. The "Dicktators" jumped as his veins began to bulge and overflowed. Keith's legs had taken a beating and been weakened. He was no longer able to support his weight.

He lay back on his desk, trying to clear his mind, regain control and gather his strength for round two but Zaria wasn't wasting any time. She was on top of him reinserting the "Dicktator". As she began to perform her mouth-watering magic on him he sent telepathic messages to the "Dicktator" ordering him to slow his roll, it wasn't quite time for number two yet.

"Ooh Shhhhiiiitttt!" Keith moaned. *"You love this dick don't you?"*

"Mum hum."

"Dammmnnnnn…fuck me girl!"

Just as the "Dicktator" began to respond to Keith's commands Zaria cut off all communications. She had slipped a cough drop into her mouth then devoured him causing the ultimate chaos. The cough drop produced a mint phenomenon and Keith Tyler's descendants embarked on a frantic search for an exit. His body involuntarily reacted, he deliriously gripped the back of her head and made love to her mouth. She slipped her finger into his rectum massaging his pleasure point and Keith's offspring evasively entered her mouth. Zaria consumed his army and stayed on task, allowing the "Dicktators" veins to be emptied.

Lying on his desk trying to catch his breath he wondered why he would ever consider giving her up. What Jaidyn didn't know wouldn't hurt her.

Jaidyn pulled into the parking garage of Keith's downtown office building and noticed his car in its normal slot. She parked beside it, grabbed her purse and started towards the lobby. She walked through the lobby having an ideal conversation with the building security guard that had accompanied her from the parking garage. She knew that he had a crush on her and she was flattered. She couldn't help but to smile and bat her eyes in the flirtatious way women did when they knew a man was smitten with them. The security guard was bold. He saw what he wanted and went after it. He could care less that she was someone else's.

When Jaidyn arrived in Keith's office she asked his secretary if he had any appointments on his schedule.

"He's free for the next two hours but he's with someone right now," she said.

"Do you know if he'll be finished soon?" Jaidyn asked before taking a seat in one of the office chairs.

"I'm sorry I don't." The secretary said trying not to offer her boss's wife any more information than she asked. "This is exactly what his lying ass gets," she thought. I want to see how he's going to get out of this one.

"I'll just wait a few minutes." Twenty minutes later Keith and Zaria emerged from his office.

Keith was completely taken off guard to find Jaidyn waiting but being the playa he was he recovered quickly. "Hey!" He said as if he was excited to see her. "I thought you had hospital rounds this morning."

Jaidyn made eye contact with the young woman. Zaria looked at her and smiled, showing off her gold tooth. Zaria found it amusing and exciting at the same time that Keith's wife had been sitting just on the other side of the door while she was fucking his brains out. It made her pot of gold tingle and she wanted to take him back into the office and do him one more time. She smiled and said to herself, "Gurl, he ain't got nothin' left for yo ass. I just finished fucking his brains out."

Jaidyn found Zaria odd. She seemed out of place in this office. She was dressed more like a hoochie than a client, she thought. Keith kissed Jaidyn on the cheek hoping to divert her attention, "So what brings you here?"

"I thought maybe we could go to lunch."

"Mummm, as much as I'd love to I can't. I have too much going on here."

"Let's go in your office so we can talk."

Remembering the condoms still covering his desk and the smell of sex in the air Keith said, "I've got to run down to my boss's office for a quick meeting."

"Oh," Jaidyn said surprised. "Well I guess I'll see you at home later."

"I'm sorry baby," Keith said smiling at her.

Chapter 11

Jaidyn arrived at Copeland's for dinner with her husband fifteen minutes early. She decided to get a table, order a glass of wine, and enjoy the atmosphere while she waited for him. The place was packed so she anticipated having to wait to be seated. As she stood at the hostesses' station waiting on a table she surveyed the restaurant and noticed Keith was already there. He was standing at the bar engrossed in a conversation with a cute young woman.

Jaidyn deserted the hostesses stand and moved through the crowd towards them. As she got closer to them the young woman became more familiar but she couldn't place her. Keith seemed irritated. She got close enough to hear Keith say, "I'm getting tired of yo shit," and someone grabbed her by the arm. "Hey Jaidyn," Markel said pulling her into an embrace.

"Markel. What's going on? I haven't seen you since the wedding." She said hugging him tight.

"My boy has been trying to keep you all to himself," he said smiling. Jaidyn smiled back at him. "You're looking beautiful as usual."

"And you're charming as usual." She responded. "Are you meeting someone here?"

"I spoke to Keith earlier and he invited me to have dinner with you guys. I hope that's alright."

"Oh, absolutely." She said trying to look in the direction she'd seen Keith.

"Keith tells me that you're getting ready to open your own office." Pulling her attention back to him.

"Well, I'm joining a practice with several other colleagues."

"Are they finishing school with you?"

"No. They've been practicing for a few years. We are moving to a larger office space that will accommodate our needs a little better."

"Oh, okay."

"One of the doctors I'll be in practice with is single and around your age."

"Oh, no." He said shaking his head and smiling. "No blind dates, but thanks any way."

"Don't say no until you've met her. Why don't you come to the offices' open house and you'll meet her without any pressure."

Markel laughed. "I'll think about it."

Keith had spotted them and ended his conversation. He'd casually walked through the bar before approaching them, hoping it would appear as if he hadn't seen them. "Hey dawg what's up?" Keith asked as if he was surprised to see them standing there. He shook Markel's hand and kissed Jaidyn, "Hey sweetheart. When did you guys get here?"

"We both just walked in. We've been here just long enough for your wife to try to set me up."

"With who?"

"Regina." Jaidyn answered.

Keith shot Markel a look of approval. "She's alright man."

After the three of them sat down to dinner the guys talked non-stop about draft picks for the upcoming basketball season. The conversation eventually switched from basketball to football. Jaidyn sat quietly listening to them. She hadn't been able to get her mind off of the woman that Keith was talking to. She looked so familiar. She knew she had seen her somewhere before but she couldn't place her. Although she had only heard a small portion of what Keith had said it was enough to send her woman's intuition into overdrive. Curiously, when he came over to her and Markel he seemed fine.

While the guys talked she tried to put the image and words out of her mind, but her woman's intuition kept pulling it back to the surface. Markel excused himself to the bathroom and gave Jaidyn the window of opportunity she'd been waiting on. "Who was the girl you were talking to at the bar?"

"Who?"

"The girl you were arguing with?"

"What girl?" Keith asked as if he didn't have a clue who she was talking about.

Jaidyn's radar was all over the place, something wasn't quite right about his denial. "Keith, the young woman with the strapless black dress and the Stiletto hills."

"Oh, baby that was nothing."

"It looked like yall were arguing from where I was standing and I thought I heard you say 'you were getting tired of her shit'."

Keith smiled as if Jaidyn's assumptions were preposterous. "You're kidding right? You can't be jealous of some skeezer getting up in my face." He said turning the conversation around.

"Keith, I just said it looked like you were arguing. I didn't say I was jealous."

"Look Baby," he said gently cupping her hand in his. "These skeezer's recognize me from the league and they try to holla. You know that."

Jaidyn shrugged the thoughts off and thought how insane she must sound to him. This type of thing had happened to them many times. She couldn't believe that she was feeling insecure.

Before dinner was over Keith announced that he'd have to attend a seminar in Lake Tahoe the following Thursday and wouldn't be back until Tuesday. Markel knew he was lying. He had told him earlier that Zaria had been nagging him for not spending enough time with her since he'd gotten married so he was taking her on a mini-vacation. He picked that weekend because he knew Jaidyn was on call.

Markel had once admired Keith's smooth way with the women, but things had changed. Markel and Keith had grown into very different men. Markel had grown up with two different stepfathers that both ran around on his mother. He promised himself that he'd never put anyone through that. When he got married the days of not being able to remember the girls name that had sucked his dick dry the night before would be over. He had warned Keith that Jaidyn was not one of his usual dumb women and if he didn't curve some of his habits his wife was going to become suspicious of his extra circular activities.

After dinner Keith and Markel walked Jaidyn to her car. Keith kissed her good-bye and told her he would meet her at home. She said her good-byes and drove off.

"Man, thank you for running interference with Jaidyn. I didn't see her come in," Keith said.

"You need to get yo shit together. When I saw her she was on her way over to you guys. You need tell Jaidyn the truth before Chevon does. You've let this shit go on way too long. When she showed up at the wedding you should have handled your business then, instead of trying to ignore her. You're lucky ole' boy showed up and got everyone's attention. And why in the hell would you meet Jaidyn at Chevon's hang out?"

"Man, I tried to get her to go some place else but she insisted on coming here. I don't know what I'm going to do about Chevon. I thought I had this shit under control. That ho is driving me crazy. This morning when I left the house her ass was sitting outside waiting on me. She followed me all the way to work. She said I've left her no other choice but to put those white folks in my life."

"Playa it's time to handle up. You've got to deal with Chevon for the rest of your life. She doesn't deserve to be treated like this and neither does Jaidyn."

"Handle up! Shit that's what I'm doing. I make sure I take care of mine!"

"Well, maybe you should consider taking her to court and getting something in writing."

"You must be out yo mind. I'm not getting those people in my business. I rather deal with Chevon's bull shit."

"Man you need to talk to Jaidyn before Chevon does."

"Shhhhiiii! That's the last thing she wanta do! She keep fuckin' with me the only thing she's goin' get is an ass whoopin'."

Chapter 12

Jaidyn and Keith hadn't spent any time together in the last two weeks. She was in the last weeks of her fellowship and her schedule had become crazy. Between her hospital patients and trying to set up her new office she hadn't had any time to spend with him. She'd left home before he'd ever gotten out of bed and came home after he had dinner. Last night she was home for about an hour, just getting ready to sit down to dinner when she was paged and had to return to the hospital for an emergency surgery. Her patient had not done well so she spent the remainder of the night at the hospital instead of returning home. Although Keith never complained when things like this happened she always felt bad. After making her morning rounds she gathered her things and went home for the day.

Jaidyn was pleasantly surprise when she pulled into the garage and found Keith's car in it's spot. She climbed out of her car walked into the house and found Keith lying on the couch, watching TV, in his silk pajama pants. She knew she would find the shirt at the foot of the bed waiting on her. He always wore the pants and left the shirt for her.

"Hey baby. Did you decide to stay home today?" She asked him with excitement in her voice.

"Yeah, something like that." Keith said dryly.

"Maybe we can catch a movie. I heard that new movie with Taye Diggs and Sanaa Lathan is wonderful."

"Sounds like a plan. Do you have to go back to the hospital?"

"Later tonight I need to check on my patient but the day belongs to you, if you'd like."

"I'd love to spend the day with my beautiful wife." He said pulling her down on top of him and kissing her. They both enjoyed the tender affection. She had been missing him just as much as he was missing her.

Jaidyn suggested that he join her for a shower and Keith jumped at the chance. Since they'd been like two ships passing in the night. They hadn't had dinner together in two weeks and lately their lovemaking had been rushed. Although he knew she was tired and sleep deprived she never refused him when he needed her, but there was always an urgency to their lovemaking. She knew him well and knew how to get him to a climax quickly but he wasn't going to let her off that easy today. Whether it was a quickie or an all nighter, anytime he lay with her it was ecstasy.

Jaidyn and Keith started their lovemaking in the shower and moved into the bedroom. Jaidyn was pleasantly surprised by Keith's stamina. It had been a long time since he had completely worn her out, "Are you going to keep me in this bed all day or are we going to the movie?"

"I kind of like the position you're in right now. How about we stay home and order something to eat?" Keith said as he got up to get the delivery taxi menu out of the kitchen. After he'd ordered lunch they settled back into each other's arms.

"What made you stay home today?"

"I quit my job." He said in a matter of fact tone. "I thought I told you that."

Jaidyn was glad she was lying in Keith's arms and he couldn't see the concerned look on her face. This story had better be good she thought. "No." Jaidyn said shaking her head. "You failed to mention it."

"Well, I quit my job."

"What?" Jaidyn asked astonished. Keith looked at her as if to say you heard what I said. Jaidyn tried to keep her voice pleasant. "When?"

"A week and a half ago."

"Why?" She knew the tone of her voice was shitty and immediately regretted the slip up.

"Damn what is this twenty questions?"

Jaidyn took a deep breath, "I'm sorry honey. I didn't mean to sound so anxious."

Keith took a minute before he started talking again. "At the Monday morning staff meeting the new company management informed us of the new changes that they would be implementing. I didn't feel that I could comply with their wishes, so I quit. I'm tired of working for someone else. I'm going to start my own marketing company. It's something I've wanted to do as long as I can remember."

"Baby I think that's an absolutely fabulous idea but do you think it was wise to just quit? What about your two weeks notice?"

"What about it?"

Jaidyn sat up in the bed and looked at him as if she was expecting for him to say something else. "So you quit this past Monday?"

"No, the Monday before."

"That was two and a half weeks ago. Why haven't you told me?" Jaidyn asked, no longer concerned with hiding her attitude.

Keith matched her attitude with his own, "Because I didn't realize I had to report to you."

Jaidyn calmed her voice. "You don't have to report to me but this type of decision doesn't just affect you. We're married and should consult each other when we are making life-changing decisions."

"This has nothing to do with our marriage. This is about my dreams."

"Any decision made about pursuing our dreams has to do with this marriage! And you need to consult with me."

"I don't remember that being in our wedding vows. Are you making up your own rules for marriage as we go along?"

"Keith you're being ridiculous. Nothing you do anymore is about just you. It's all about us!"

"Maybe you ought to share the Jaidyn Tyler Handbook on Marriage with me so I'll know the rules. You should have shared that shit with me before I married you." He yelled as he got up and put his pants on so that he could answer the door. Keith was pissed that she had the audacity to be upset about him quitting his job. "As matter of fact you don't seem to be bothered that I'm supporting you while you are pursuing your dream." He said as he left the room.

"You knew that I was pursuing my dream when we got married! So I don't want to hear that shit." Jaidyn yelled after him. She was pissed that he was trying to turn things around. What in the hell was he thinking? You don't just quit a six figure a year job to pursue a dream without some type of planning. You pursue the dream on the side and keep the job until the dream can support you.

While Keith was at the door paying the deliveryman Jaidyn made an escape to the shower. She needed a few minutes to calm down, gather her thoughts and get her attitude in check. She knew she needed to support her husband but he couldn't have been thinking clearly. You don't just quit your job when you have a family. When she got out of the shower Keith was already eating. She joined him at the table.

"Look Keith, I'm…" Jaidyn started but was interrupted when Keith's cell phone began to ring. Keith looked at the caller ID then answered his phone with a grumpy, "Hello."

"Hey you," Shelbi said.

"Hey."

"Doesn't sound like you're having a good day." She observed. There was silence from Keith's end of the phone. "Can you talk?"

"Let me hit you back man. I was just sitting down to lunch with Jaidyn." Keith said his voice more lighthearted this time.

"Oh, is she there?"

"Yeah, I can meet you at the gym."

"The gym," Shelbi snickered, "That's not exactly the kind of work out I was hoping for." Keith kept his face straight although his mind was jumping with excitement. "Can you meet me around…umm…how about an hour?" Shelbi asked.

"Sounds like a plan."

"I just love to talk to you when she's sitting right there. Something about it turns me on." Shelbi said before hanging up.

Keith smiled and hung up. He looked back at Jaidyn, "What were you saying?"

"I was apologizing to you." Jaidyn paused trying to remember what she was about to say. "I understand your dream. I really do and I support you but I'd be lying if I didn't say this makes me nervous. I wish you would have talked to me before you made this kind of decision."

"Look, this conversation is over."

She couldn't believe he was attempting to end the conversation. She felt compelled to get her point across. If he were able to make these types of decisions without her, he would do this forever. This could set the tone for their marriage and she was never going be a do as I say woman. Jaidyn charged forward, only this time with a softer tone. "All I was trying to say is this type of decision affects our household. I have to get my name out there and build a new patient base in this practice before I start making any real money and I don't know how long that's going to take. It would have behooved both of us if you would have waited another eight to ten months before you made this type of move."

"Behooved us? Don't you mean you? I don't know what the hell you're doing with your money but you haven't paid a bill in this house since we got married. Don't you think it's about time you step up to the plate!"

Jaidyn was shocked, "I was wondering when this shit was going to come up. The only reason I haven't contributed is because you've continuously insisted that you're the man of this house and that it is your responsibility to take care of the bills. Every time I open a bill you get pissed off. You got that damn P.O. Box so now I don't even see the bills but, now it's my fault I don't contribute?"

"Look, I'm not going to argue with you about this. The pennies you're making will be fine until I get this business off the ground and besides I have some savings and my retirement."

They sat in silence for a few minutes before Jaidyn started in again, "What have you done to get this business off the ground?"

"Nothing yet…You need to understand something, I'm starting this business with or without your support. I don't give a damn what you think or want."

Please don't tell me that he's got the nerve to have an attitude with me. He has to be losing his mind. He quit his job and has the nerve to be mad at me. He has definitely lost his mind.

They ate the reminder of their lunch in silence. As Jaidyn was clearing the table Keith's cell phone rang. That cell is the first thing that has to go she thought. When you don't have a job you can't have the benefits of one.

Keith went to answer his phone. When he returned he was dressed. He walked into the kitchen picked up his keys and walked out the door. Jaidyn followed him to the garage and asked him, "Where are you going?" He looked at her, got in his car, and backed out of the garage.

Ok she thought, two can play that game. You don't want to talk, we don't have to. I can show you better than I can tell you. On top of being frustrated with him she was tired and her mood had turned sour so she gladly accepted his absence. She went to her room and lay down.

After her nap she went to the hospital to check on her patient. When Jaidyn returned from the hospital Keith still wasn't home. It was almost time for dinner so she tried calling him on his cell phone. When he didn't answer she left a message asking if she should cook something or was he going to pick something up on his way home.

At nine o'clock she tried calling him again but still didn't get an answer. She couldn't remember the last time she'd called Keith and he didn't answer his phone. That phone was his Siamese twin, he didn't go to the bathroom without it. So she knew him not answering meant he was still pissed off.

Chapter 13

At three a.m. Jaidyn heard the garage door go up. She had been unable to sleep and had tossed and turned most of the night. Keith had not called or come home since the argument earlier that day. He was pushing the 'I'm pissed' thing way too far, she thought. When he came in slamming doors and turning on lights she reconsidered her position on arguing with him. It was what he expected, what he wanted, but he wasn't going to get it. She was tired, had to be up in three hours, and didn't want to entertain this drama tonight. It would have to wait until tomorrow.

When the alarm clock began buzzing at 6 a.m. the first thing she noticed was that Keith had not gotten into bed. Jaidyn climbed out of bed and went into the living room to see were he was. She found him on the couch asleep. The smell of alcohol seemed to be bellowing out of his pours. She retrieved a blanket from the hall closet and covered him up.

She went back in their room and got into the shower. What had seemed so horrible yesterday had been cured by a few hours of sleep. She had never been able to stay mad very long and being married hadn't changed that. Arguing over spilled milk seemed useless today. There was nothing she could do about him quitting his job. All she could do was to support him and help him in whatever way she could. She'd call him later to apologize and give him her support.

Over the next three days Jaidyn tried endlessly to talk to Keith. She called him when she was at work but he refused to answer his cellular or the home phone. When she'd arrived home from work he'd conveniently not be there and he was making it a habit to not come home until after she was in bed. When she got up to go to work she'd find him asleep on the couch or in the guestroom. Things were getting a little ridiculous she thought.

Deciding to put an end to the stalemate she left the hospital a little early to get home before he left. When she drove into the garage there was a brand new two door Mercedes-Benz parked in Keith's spot. It was a brilliant black, hard top two-seater convertible. Her heart stopped beating as alarm ran through her veins. Somehow she instinctively knew her fear of the car being his was right on target. Before she got out of the car she went over best and worse case scenarios in her mind. She took several deep breaths trying to pull herself together. She tried to come up with something to say that wouldn't cause an argument. A therapist would tell her to tell him how she felt in the same loving words that she would want to hear so she pondered on the right words. Forget this shit she thought. All she wanted to do right now was kick his ass. She took a minute to pray before she got out of the car.

> *Lord, please don't let this man have bought a new car. Let it be someone else's. Help me to control my temper and control my tone when I speak to him. Lace it with love and patience. I'm frustrated and need Your guidance Father. Help me to understand what possessed him to spend this kind of money when he doesn't have a job. And Lord keep me from putting my hands around his damn throat and choking him to death.*
>
> *Amen.*

She got out of her beaten up old Honda, went over to the Mercedes, and kneeled to look at the license plate. The buyers' name on the paper license tag said, 'Keith J. Tyler'. She peered in the window of the car and was unable to believe her eyes. She needed to take a closer look so she opened the door of the car and climbed inside. The black leather seat felt heavenly. The layout of the navigation system and the walnut colored wood trimmed in leather helped create an awe-inspiring interior. She was in complete disbelief and words escaped her. She got out of the Mercedes and went around to the opposite side of the car to get a look at the sticker price, $96,990 was neatly typed on the bottom line. She gasped, feeling like the wind had just been knocked out of her. The alarm that was sprinting through her veins had found a resting-place, inside her head. She intuitively put her palm to her forehead as if she could stop the alarm from pounding against her temples. She felt like a small artillery explosion had just taken place inside of it. She leaned against the garage wall pulling her purse open and searched from some aspirin. When she found the bottle she opened it and popped three pills in her mouth and swallowed them without the help of water.

This could not be true. Somebody please wake me up from this nightmare. This muthafucka has lost his damn mind. *What part of no J-O-B is he missing?* We're going to end up in the poor house trying to pay for this thing. Forget the thin ice his ass has been treading on, he'd fallen through it and sank to the bottom she thought. "Lawd, what have I gotten myself into?" She asked out loud.

When Jaidyn walked into the house Keith was getting his things together to leave.

"Hey, you got a few minutes? We need to talk?" She said trying to keep her voice steady and calm.

"No."

"No? You got someplace to be? The last time I checked yo ass didn't have a job!"

"What part of no did you not understand? The N or the O?"

This was the type of shit that made women beat the hell out of men. His ass was asking for it. "I didn't understand the N or the O!"

"Jaidyn your ass is buggin' and I don't have time for this shit."

Keith picked up his keys to leave and Jaidyn stepped in his path, "We need to talk about this shit right now."

"You better get out my way."

"You want me to move? Move me! This shit has gone far enough." She said stepping in front of the garage door. She wasn't going to let him leave without having this discussion. Shit, fuck a discussion it was all out war. Her present disposition wouldn't allow her to sit down and have a calm discussion with this damn fool. Her $25,000 a year salary and his NFL retirement could barely pay their bills let alone a $100,000 car note. She was afraid to find out how much the payments on the damn thing were.

"I can't believe you have the nerve to have an attitude. What the fuck is the problem now?"

"That $100,000 car sitting in the damn garage is the problem. You don't have a job or a way to pay for it, that's the fucking problem. And don't give me that shit about me having the nerve to be pissed off. I have every right to feel the way I do. My damn husband is acting like an irresponsible teenager."

"What the fuck are you talking about? Have you missed any meals?"

"That's not the point. How in the hell do you expect for us to pay for that car and the rest of our bills? We can't live in a car."

"What I do with my money ain't none of your got damn business. If I want to buy a car or anything else as long as it's not affecting you then I don't want to hear yo shit. I'm getting sick of your shit Jaidyn." He said walking around her to get to the garage.

"Where in the hell are you going?" Jaidyn said stepping in front of the garage door so he wouldn't leave.

"Step the fuck off Jaidyn. I ain't playing with you."

Before either of them knew what happened she slapped him. The slap surprised them both. She hadn't expected to go there with him. She had never acted like this with him nor had he with her. He pushed her against the wall and pulled his hand back, her eyes registered surprise and he caught himself before he hit her. She flinched, bracing herself for the hit that she thought would follow.

He grimaced at the thought of hitting her and pushed her to the side. "Jaidyn I told you to step the fuck off!" He said as he opened the door to leave. He'd lost his temper before and had hit a woman but the thought of him ever laying a hand on Jaidyn made his stomach churn.

Jaidyn watched him back out of the garage then she did what most women do when they are in a crisis, she went inside and called her mother. Jaidyn sounded rattled on the phone so her mother drove over. After arriving at her daughter's home the first thing she heard was, "Mama he's insensitive and irresponsible." Mrs. Owens countered with, "No baby, he's a man. You've got to understand, men are different than we are."

Jaidyn thought if she told her mother every detail of the past three days that she would be just as pissed off with Keith as she was, but her mother said exactly what Jaidyn should have expected, "You young people don't know nothin' about stickin' out hard times. Baby, this is just one of those things that couples go through. You need to give your husband all the support you can. This isn't any easier on him than it is on you. You've got to let a man be a man. You can't tell him what to do and if you do you've got to be clever enough to make him believe it was his idea in the first place. If you're sharp you can make him do just about anything and get him to believe it was his idea the entire time."

"Mama he quit his job. What kind of man quits their job?"

"Honey, you've got to support him no matter what. There are times when you've got to stand beside him and there are times, like this, that you've got to stand behind him and hold him up."

"I can't do that."

"That's ridiculous, of course you can."

"You don't understand. He's not like Daddy."

"Jai, your father is the man he is because he's got a good woman standing behind him to hold him up when he needs me to. There were a lot of days that I wanted to give up. He wasn't always the man he is now. I always tried to approach our problems with the idea that tomorrow was a brand new day filled with brand new blessings. If we could just make it through the day we start over on a new day tomorrow." Jaidyn bobbed her head although she wasn't buying what her mother was saying. "Now you call that man and apologize. When he gets home have him some dinner cooked and be in one of those nice negligees. Show him how sorry you are."

"I'm not apologizing to him!"

"Well you've got to do what you think is best. Just think about what I said."

In retrospect Jaidyn knew she shouldn't have called her mother. She was old fashioned and didn't understand. She thought arguing was useless and you need to do what your husband thought was best for your family. She should have called Yasmine or her girlfriend Anna. They would have told her just how handle his ass.

Chapter 14

Keith was only a block away from home when he decided to call Markel. He asked him to meet him at VII, a sports bar, to watch the game. He needed to drink a few beers and unwind. Jaidyn had pissed him off. She was going to have to straighten her attitude out. He was the man of his damn house and she better learn to recognize that.

When he walked into VII Markel was already there. He was sitting with a few of the fella's they frequently hung out with. They spent the remainder of the evening drinking and shooting the shit. Around 11 p.m. most of the guys begin heading home to their families but Keith decided to have one last drink and convinced Markel to stick around with him.

"Man, don't you think you've had enough? You've been drinking those Heineken's like they're water."

"Just one more beer man." Keith said walking over to the bar. As he stood waiting on the bartender to get him a beer he noticed Jared sitting at the other end of the bar. When he and Jared made eye contact he yelled out, "What the hell you looking at?" Jared ignored him, which pissed Keith off so he walked over to him and repeated his question, "What the hell you looking at fool?" Jared glanced over his shoulder at him then returned his attention to his drink. This brotha has got to be losing his mind, coming over here getting up in my face. He better step the fuck off before I send his ass home in a pine box. He must not know who he's messing with. I ain't one of these weak muthafucka's he can punk.

Keith tapped him on his shoulder, "You hear me talking to you?"

"Look Man, don't get salty. I don't have no beef with you."

When Markel finally looked around and saw the two of them standing toe to toe he quickly made his way towards them. What the hell is Keith doing he wondered. I don't feel like this shit tonight, he said to himself.

Keith was drunk and had lost his good sense. The alcohol wasn't going to let Jared off that easy. "Fool, I'll knock you're ass smooth out!"

This fool really has lost his damn mind. I've been trying to be cool because this muthafucka is drunk but he's going to make me kick his ass. He's taking my kindness for weakness. "I'll be the last muthafucka you knock out. You keep walking yo ass up in my face and yo boys goin' be yo pallbearers. I'll make Jaidyn a widow tonight."

Markel caught the tail end of what Jared was saying. He stepped between them, facing Jared. "Hey man, my boys drunk. Yall need to settle your differences some other time. This ain't the time or the place." Jared stared at him. His jaw muscle tightening. Markel turned to Keith, "Hey playa lets get out of here."

Keith ignored Markel and addressed Jared, "Bitch it's best you keep my wife's name out yo mouth." He said pointing his finger at him.

"Yo wife is the only reason I haven't gotten on yo ass. Now you need to take yo partner's advice and take your ass home before I give you that ass whoopin' yo partner knew you were fixin' to get before he came over here."

In the blink of an eye all hell broke lose. Keith came across Markel's shoulder with a right hook, hitting Jared in the jaw. Jared quickly responded with a roundhouse left. Then his arms pumped with a controlled urgency of a master boxer. Markel got sandwiched between them. Jared pushed him out of the way he quickly came down on Keith with his left elbow. Upon impact Jared could hear the crack of Keith's nose braking, then he saw the blood began to gush from his nose.

When the phone rang at 3:32 a.m. Jaidyn was startled out of her sleep. She answered the phone in a panicked voice. The voice on the other end said, "You have a collect call from Harris County Jail. Push eight to accept, push four to decline, or simply hang up."

"What," Jaidyn asked sitting up. After a couple of seconds of silence the mechanical voice repeated itself as if it understood her question. They've got the wrong number she thought before she hung up the phone. By the time she closed her eyes and got comfortable the phone rang again. "Hello!" She irritatedly yelled into the phone. The mechanical voice repeated itself, "You have a collect call from Harris County..." Jaidyn reached for the lamp on the side of the bed. Once the light was on and she could see Keith had not come to bed, panic begin to run through her. She looked at the clock again, 3:42 a.m. "Yes, yes!" She said into the phone and then pushed eight. When Markel's voice came through the phone Jaidyn was relieved. Keith must be on the couch, she thought. She got out of bed and headed for the living room.

"Jaidyn, this is Markel."

"Markel, what's going on?"

"Hey ah, Keith and I had an altercation in VII's. We're ok but we're in jail." Jaidyn stopped dead in her tracks. "Can you come bail us out? We're in the Harris County Jail."

"An altercation?"

"Yeah, can you come get us?"

"Where's Keith?"

"He's here, he's alright. Can you come get us?" Markel had gone over what he was going to say to her before he'd picked up the phone to call her. He didn't want to veer off the subject because he didn't want to answer any questions. He thought Keith should explain his stupidity to his own wife.

When Jaidyn walked into the Harris County Police Station she ran head on into Jared and Julian. "Jared, what are you doing here?" He looked at her as if she was utterly worthless, beneath his consideration. If looks could kill she would have died on the spot.

Julian looked at her up and down and sucked his teeth, "You act like you're surprised. You're my girl but you need to put yo man in check before..."

"What are you talking about?" She asked cutting him off, "What happened?" She directed the question more to Jared than to Julian.

"Man, leave her alone. Lets get the hell out of here." Jared said.

"Jared what happened?" Jared pushed the glass door open and walked out with Julian in tow.

What in the hell is he talking about, she wondered. As soon as she got to the bonding window she asked, "What are the charges on Keith Tyler and Markel Martin?" The woman behind the bulletproof window asked for their SPN number. Jaidyn gave him the numbers that Markel had given her and repeated the question.

The middle-aged woman behind the window peered at her over the top of her reading glasses. She seemed to be annoyed by the urgency in Jaidyn's voice. She slowly typed the numbers that Jaidyn had given her into the computer, "They were both charged with assault. Do yo want to post bond?"

"Assault?"

"Yes ma'am," she said. "Do you want to post bond?" The woman asked, still peering over the top of the reading glasses.

After Jaidyn paid both their bonds the woman told her to have a seat, it would be a few minutes before they came out. Jaidyn sat down and went over all the scenarios she could imagine.

Obviously the altercation had to be with Jared and Julian but what happened? Had Jared approached her husband? What in the hell had Jared done to him? The longer it took for them to let her husband go the more pissed off she became. Jared had taken this shit too far.

She knew Jared was a thug at heart. Although he claimed to be reformed there was still a hardness to him. Behind that beautiful face was a roughneck brotha. He hid it well but it was always right under the surface. He'd grown up in Brooklyn and his parents had tried to perform an exorcism by sending him and his twin brother Julian to Xavier University. They had hoped removing them from their environment would help to remove the thug mentally from them, but New Orleans was full of thugs and they fit right in. It wasn't until Jared began to attend Stanford for his MBA that he decided to leave that life behind. The Ivy League education helped him refine the roughneck in him but it didn't remove it completely.

Jaidyn grimaced at the possibility of Julian being involved. Julian wasn't Jared. If he was involved she knew that things had gone badly for Keith and Markel. Just like Jared he had a sweet, loving demeanor, but if you crossed him he could be deadly. Julian was a street pharmacist turned computer graphic designer; however, he was a straight up hoodlum. No amount of education could change him. His nine-millimeter was part of his everyday wardrobe. With all his dealings it was surprising he wasn't in the state penitentiary.

She recalled when Jared got pissed off he had been known to have a flash back or two. Although he'd never flashed on her she had been a witness to that side of him. The first time she saw it they were in a club. When he went to get them a drink a brotha approached her and asked her to dance. She refused, the guy went off, called her a wanna be ho and Jared acted a damn fool. Jaidyn sat there with her mouth open, unable to believe that this sweet, loving, educated man acted like that. It surprised her that he had it in him.

After seeing it that first time she began to pick up on small things, the attitude, his conversation when he was talking to the fellas, his habits, and his impatience with clear people outside his work environment. Even his dress outside of work was tinted with a little hip-hop flavor. It had been that bad boy attitude that had made him sexier to her.

By the time Keith and Markel came out Jaidyn was ready to ring Jared's neck. When she saw Keith's face she had to fight back tears. He had two dark circles under his eyes, his lip was cut, his nose swollen which made his entire face look swollen. He resembled the elephant man. Jared and Julian must have taken him off guard she thought.

"Baby are you alright," she asked touching his arm gently.

"Let's go, I just want to get out of here." He said with an attitude.

Markel was holding his side and was obviously in pain. "Markel, are you alright?"

"Yeah, can you take me back to VII to get my car?"

She stopped walking and attempted to examine Markel's side, "Does this hurt?"

"Aaaaarrrrrhhhhh," Markel yelped.

"You guys may need to see a doctor. Let me take you over to the hospital."

"I'm fine." Markel said.

"You're not fine. You could have a broken rib."

"I'm cool. Can you please just take me to my car?"

"Okay. But promise me that you'll see your family doctor tomorrow."

"Okay."

Although Keith's face was swollen he seemed to have the attitude from hell so she didn't press the issue with him. She would take a look at him when she got home. Their car ride was quiet. Jaidyn had a million questions but she knew it was best if she spoke to Keith alone. When they arrived back at VII, Keith and Markel returned to their cars. Again she encouraged Markel to see a doctor first thing in the morning and he thanked her for her concern and for bailing him out. He kissed her on the cheek before he got into his car. She waited on Keith to get into his car so that she could follow him home. They'd had enough drama for the night and didn't need anymore.

Once inside the safety of his own home Keith sat on the couch and turned the TV on. Jaidyn went into their bedroom, got him some PJ bottoms out of the draw and went into the bathroom to draw bath water in their Jacuzzi size bathtub. After she turned on the jets she sprinkled Epson Salt in the water to help with any soreness he may have.

"Baby, I drew a bath for you." She said returning to the living room.

"Thank you." He said struggling to get up off the couch.

Keith went into the bathroom and climbed into the tub. Jaidyn let him relax for a few minutes before she went back in to discuss the night's sequence of events. When she returned to the bathroom Keith was laying back on the tub pillow with his eyes closed. She took a seat on the toilet and watched him for a few seconds.

She got up, picked up the sponge, lathered it and began rubbing his chest. He pulled her close to him and kissed her. "I love you." She smirked and continued bathing him. "I'm sorry we argued earlier. But you're driving me crazy. I'm the man of this house and I'm going to handle everything. You need to trust me!"

He still seemed to have an attitude but curiosity was killing her so despite her apprehension she plunged forward with her inquiry into the night's events. "What happened tonight?"

Keith sat up abruptly, "That pretty muthafucka you fuckin' with jumped me! That's what happened."

"Who jumped you?" She couldn't believe he was accusing her of messing around.

"Oh you having difficulty hearing tonight? You know who I'm talking about unless you fuckin with more then one brotha!"

She knew exactly who he was talking about but she repeated the question anyway, "Who are you talking about?"

"Ok...now you going to play boo-boo the fool! Jared, ain't that yo homeboy's name?"

"Who?"

"You heard me the first time. Ain't that that nigga's name? You da one fuckin' him. Shit, you ought to know." She couldn't believe he was making these crazy accusations.

"Jared jumped you?" She asked the question more out of astonishment than the need for him to repeat it. Although she herself had first thought the exact same thing she didn't realize how ridiculous that assumption was until Keith said it.

"Did I stutter or som'n? He walked up in my face talking shit. His ass got your name coming out his muthafuckin' mouth? What the hell are you doing with him?"

His ass has gone too far she thought. He is beginning to piss me off. I've had enough of hearing this bull. This is a game I'm already tried of playing. If he wanted to argue he was going to have to do it by himself. Because Jared got on his ass doesn't mean that we are sleeping together or that he has to take the shit out on me. "Jared's my friend and I'm not fixin' to keep on explaining that to you. We don't have to be sleeping together to be friends."

"Don't kid yourself. He isn't interested in being yo damn friend. A piece of ass is exactly what he's after. At least that's what he said."

"I just can't believe Jared would say something like that."

"Now you goin' defend the nigga? I'm yo fuckin' husband and you goin' pick that high yella muthafucka over me. I done went to war with that muthafucka and you goin' stand here and tell me some shit like that! Get the fuck out my face. I'm through talking to you."

Jaidyn left the bathroom without saying another word. It was useless to try to talk to him when he was like this. She was going to have to talk to Jared and see what really happened. She wondered what exactly Jared had said to him. The way he and Markel looked Jared and Julian had jumped them but he'd never mentioned Julian. What the hell happened, she wondered.

Chapter 15

Living with Keith was becoming unbearable. Jaidyn felt like she was dying internally. This is not what marriage is supposed to be like. She reflected on all the fights they had over the past few months. Keith had become jealous and had begun to continually accuse her of messing around. She was having a hard time faking the part of a good wife. She wasn't sure who he'd turned into but he wasn't the man she'd married. He'd been sweet, loving, and kind until they were married. He'd changed and the man she thought she loved no longer existed.

Since he'd quit his job and started his own business they'd been passing each other like ships in the dead of night. She intentionally stayed at the office or hospital as long as possible. When she was home he retreated to the study which was now doubling as his office. The fights were more frequent than ever and were beginning to break her down, making her question why she'd chosen to marry him. The conversations between them were no longer pleasant and natural, but rather forced and difficult. She felt like she was lying next to a stranger at night. Even making love to him had gotten to be mechanical. Something she did out of obligation not desire. She was getting tired of kissing his ass to try to get along with him. She always thought it was the woman who was supposed to inflict the silent treatment and act like the man didn't exist, but in their case her husband was the king of that tactic.

Lying next to Keith, waiting on the first light of the day, she decided that yesterday was the last day they would waste on bickering. It was Friday and her friend Anna was coming from San Francisco for a visit in a few days so they needed to put this crap between them to rest. Today was a brand new day and things between them needed to change. They had been neglecting one another in every way and she knew she was going to have to step up and handle her business. As the dark began to welcome the morning light she climbed out of bed and went into the kitchen. She couldn't remember the last time they'd had breakfast together. So why not start there. Breakfast in bed would surely end the stalemate between them, it would be a nice icebreaker.

She'd prepared eggs, bacon, toast and freshly squeezed orange juice, she picked up the paper off the driveway and slid it into the side pocket of the tray. She returned to the bedroom with a feast made for her king. Before she entered the room she took a deep breath and forced herself to smile.

"Good morning." She said turning on the light with her elbow and walking over to the bed.

Keith rolled over and sat up, "What's this?"

"I wanted to cook my husband breakfast," she said smiling.

"Oh, thanks," he murmured taking the tray from her.

Jaidyn was momentarily taken aback by his dryness, but plunged forward with her attempt to smooth things over. "Baby I was hoping we could put these ridiculous disagreements we've been having behind us. I hate arguing with you and I miss us."

"Is that right?"

"I'm sorry honey. I really am." Her apology seemed to fall on deaf ears. She attempted to show him how genuine she was with a smile and a gentle rub of his leg. She sat on the end of the bed hoping he would say something, but he ate in silence. When he was finished eating he lifted the tray off his lap, put it on the bed and went into the bathroom. Jaidyn sat on the bed as long as she could. When she heard the shower turn on she got up and returned the tray to the kitchen.

When he came out of the bathroom she was back in the same place he'd left her. He sat next to her and she rubbed his back while he put on his socks. "Can you please talk to me? Things have gotten so out of hand. It feels like we've done nothing but argue since we've gotten married. I miss you. I want things back the way they used to be. I miss the way we used to make love." She said pleading with him.

"Jaidyn, it's early and I need to get some work done. I have a meeting in a couple hours on a major account. This will have to wait until later." As he got up Jaidyn grabbed his hand, he looked down at her and gave her a weak smile. It looked like it pained him to do so, she thought.

She uncurled her legs, stood up and kissed him softly. "I love you," she said.

He gave her another half smile and headed for the study. "Can I ask you something?" She asked stopping him. Keith turned around and waited for her to go on. "What's it going to take for us to get back to where we were?"

"I don't know."

"Humh…why'd you ask me to marry you?"

"Because I was in love with you." Keith answered as if that was the dumpiest question he'd ever heard.

"Honey, people in love work out their differences."

Keith seemed to think about what she'd said. "I'm not sure if I'm still in love with you or if I just love you. When I figure it out I'll let you know."

Jaidyn tried not to act too dumbfounded but she was. He'll let her know! Does he have any idea what marrying him had cost her? She remained quiet until her voice was calm, "It doesn't sound like you want to be married."

Again Keith considered what she said thoughtfully. "I want to be married, I'm just not sure I want to be married to you."

On her way to the office, her cell phone rang. She was surprised to see her home number on the caller ID. "Dr. Tyler," she said in a dry tone.

"Hey…ah…. thanks for breakfast. Have a good day." Keith said. Without giving her time to respond he hung up. Jaidyn looked at the phone before she flipped it closed wondering if he realized what he'd said to her twenty minutes before.

> *Can You believe this? Of course you can…I'm at a loss here. Can You please help me out. Open his eyes so that he can clearly see the consequences of his behavior. Ah…I just… can't believe him! Give me strength Lord.*

Chapter 16

Jaidyn drove towards the hospital and reflected on everything that had transpired between her and Keith. Her mood was sour as it was much of the time these days. Stephanie Mills, The Comfort of a Man, softly played on the radio and began to pull her out of her mood. Meli'sa Morgan followed Stephanie and Jaidyn turned the radio up a bit. She couldn't help but sing along, "Here we are in this big old empty room staring each other down. You want me just as much as I want you, let's stop fooling around. Take me baby kiss me all over…" Then the DJ sent the Isley Brothers through the airways making her forget the stress that had been weighing her down. "Drifting on a memory, ain't no place I'd rather be then with you. Loving you. I might as well sign my name on…" Jaidyn sang louder than the radio.

She was lost in the music and missed her exit. She continued on the freeway in the direction of downtown. Twenty-minutes later as she sang, "I must have rehearsed my lines a thousand times. But when I get up the nerve, to tell you the words never seem to come out right. If only you knew how much I…" louder then Miss Patti, she pulled into the parking garage of the building that housed Jared's office.

She got out of the car, went into the building, found the elevator, pushed the button for the sixty-fourth floor, and moved to the back of the elevator as people piled on trying to get to work on time. She wondered what in the hell she was doing? What had she been thinking? Her car must have been on autopilot. The higher the elevator climbed the faster panic invaded her chest. Her throat went dry, her lungs tightened, and her stomach did flip-flops. She wanted to bolt as soon as the elevator doors opened, but the elevator was packed and she was in the very back corner. She was getting claustrophobic and there was no escape. "What am I doing?" She asked herself. Struggling to keep her composure she decided to ride the elevator until it emptied out and then return to the parking garage. There will be no harm done as long as I don't get off this elevator, she thought.

When the elevator stopped on the sixty-second floor Naomi, Jared's secretary, stepped on. "Jaidyn!" She said with an air of surprise and excitement as she maneuvered towards her.

"Naomi. It's so nice to see you," Jaidyn said reaching to give her a hug. Jaidyn missed Naomi. She genuinely liked her. She was a lovely sixty-ish black woman, who was not only Jared's secretary, but she was one of his mothers' oldest friends. Naomi had also become somewhat of a surrogate mother to him and Julian. In the absence of their mother she'd doted over them as if they were her own children. Naomi's approval of Jared and Jaidyn's relationship was evident from the very beginning.

Jaidyn's residential schedule worked against a meaningful relationship but Naomi had done everything in her power to make sure Jared's schedule was conducive with Jaidyn's. Jaidyn provided her with her call schedule and she tried to make sure that on her off days Jared could spend the day working from home. Although it didn't always work out, her efforts were greatly appreciated by both of them.

"I'm surprised to see you. Do you have an appointment with Jared?" Naomi asked absent-mindedly. "I mean...I don't remember seeing you on his schedule."

It wasn't a big surprise that Naomi hadn't expected to see her. Jaidyn was surprised to be there herself so she tried to ignore her first question. She tried to change the subject by asking, "Are you still working for Jared?"

"Of course. I don't think he'd have it any other way."

"I thought you were reassigned when he was transferred to Japan."

"I was, but when he returned he insisted that I be returned to his office," she boasted proudly. "Says he hated being in Japan all those months without me. You know he called me once a week just to see how I was getting a long. He tried to get me and James to join him there, but we couldn't leave our kids and grandchildren."

"I didn't know that. He's always raved about how indispensable you are."

Getting back to her original question she said, "By the way, did you say you had an appointment?"

Now she knows I didn't have an appointment, Jaidyn thought. Jaidyn knew she knew Jared's schedule by heart. Jaidyn knew she was caught but she wasn't sure what she was caught doing. The only thing on the top fifteen floors of this building was the company Jared worked for and she couldn't come up with an excuse for being in this area of the building. "No. I was in the building visiting a friend down at the credit union and thought I would drop in and say hello." She regretted the lie as soon as it exited her mouth. It was only 8 a.m. and the credit union on the first floor wasn't open yet.

"Oh, I see," Naomi said looking at her suspiciously.

"Well, I mean, ah...if Jared isn't busy I was going to poke my head in and say hello. If he is I'll just talk to him some other time." Jaidyn said as Naomi stepped off the elevator. Naomi put her hand on the elevator door to hold it open for Jaidyn who hadn't moved from her the spot she was standing in. Jaidyn hoped that she would say that he was in a meeting and she could ride the elevator back to the first floor without having to get off.

"Oh, don't be silly. He's never too busy to see you and I believe his schedule is clear so you can visit as long as you like," Naomi said.

On their way to Jared's office Naomi asked Jaidyn, "Dr. Owens, can I ask you a question?"

"Sure!" Jaidyn braced herself for what would follow. Naomi was famous for her up-front nature and she was sure that Naomi knew everything that had transpired between her and Jared. Whatever she wanted to know couldn't be good.

"How many times have you been to this building to see Jared?"

Damn, Jaidyn knew exactly what she was asking but hadn't expected for her to come right out with it. She attempted to play the dumb roll, "I'm not sure what you mean."

"How many times...have you...ridden that elevator, but been too scared to get off since Jared has been back here?"

Jaidyn stood there in complete disbelief. She was definitely caught. She was unsure what to say. She was afraid to admit that this was her first time actually getting out of her car and getting on the elevator but she'd sat in the parking garage too many times to count.

"I see," Naomi said understanding Jaidyn's silence. "Take some advice from an old woman, we can derail our destiny. If you don't get it right in this life time you'll have to do it all over again in the next life." Naomi said in a concerned tone. "When you find a love like the two of you have you can't run from it. It's always inside of you and it shows in everything you do. Sometimes it hurts like hell but if you're going to have a chance at happiness you've got to accept it. Running from it is only going to make you unhappy and drive everyone around you crazy."

"Yes ma'am," was all she could say. Naomi's wise heartfelt words pierced her heart as they hit their desired target.

Naomi walked into Jared's office followed by Jaidyn. "Look who I bumped into this morning. We were in the coffee shop together and I convinced her," Naomi was stopped mid sentence when she saw the lovely young woman that Jared was lipped locked with. It was obvious by Naomi's reaction that she had no idea that Jared was with someone. Everyone, with the exception of the young woman, was stunned. Naomi being the oldest of the group kept her wits about her, she cleared her throat and apologized for interrupting. Then she backed out of his office, almost backing over Jaidyn.

Jaidyn's feet wouldn't move. Her heart had dropped into her stomach and cut off the blood supply to her feet, paralyzing them. Naomi gave her a little push moving her out of the doorway. Once the door to Jared's office was closed Jaidyn begin frantically searching her purse for her car keys.

"Jaidyn...sweetie, I'm sorry I had no idea he had someone in there with him." Naomi said sympathetically.

Jaidyn gave her the best smile she could muster. "Now look who's being silly. You don't have to apologize. I need to get going anyway."

Jaidyn didn't know what she was expecting but what they'd walked in on wasn't it. Seeing him with another woman made her jealous.

Before Naomi could think of any soothing words to say Jared and his young friend walked out of his office. She wished both ladies a good day as she walked by. Naomi was not surprised that Jared looked just as bothered by what they had walked in on as Jaidyn did.

"MMMRRRSSS. Tyler is there something I can help you with?"

His condescending tone immediately pissed her off and his formal approach was equally irritating. It felt wrong for him to greet her formally like it was all business. "No, Jared! I don't think so." Although she kept her voice calm her irritation was clearly detectable.

"Well, obviously you came here for some reason. What might that be?" Almost before the words exited his mouth he wanted to take them back. He couldn't stop himself from being a condescending smart-ass. The compromising position she had found him and Faith, his new girlfriend, in had put him on edge and made him feel guilty and defensive.

"Not that it is any of your business but I bumped into Naomi and wanted to visit with her for a few minutes." Turning her attention to Naomi she said, "It was nice to see you again. Thanks for the advice. I promise to give it some thought." She turned and headed back down the hall towards the elevators. She made a mental note to send a card to thank Naomi for being so nice.

When Jared turned around to look at Naomi she gave him a disapproving look and sat down at her desk. "What's that for?" He questioned her.

"What is what for SIR?" If he had any previous doubts they were removed when she called him sir. She only did that when she was annoyed with him.

"Naomi, what do you want from me? She's married!"

Naomi put her elbows on her desk, leaned forward and maintained that motherly disapproving gaze. She didn't answer his question but she breathed in heavily and let it out with a sigh reinforcing her annoyance with him.

"Stop looking at me like that." Jared said then went down the hall after Jaidyn.

Jaidyn stood at the elevator frantically pushing the down button. She was hurt more than she could have imagined. Seeing Jared with someone else cut her deeply. Somehow, no matter how irrational it may have been, she thought he'd wait on her. She took for granted that he'd always be there, waiting for her when she was ready. "How could I have been so stupid," she asked herself.

> *Father you know my heart. I don't understand this hold he has on me. Open my eyes so that I can see things clearly. Show me how to let go if that is Your will. I thought I was past him but I know I'm not. I thought I could handle this, but I can't. I need your help. Order my footsteps. My path is Yours to guide not my own. I surrender to Your will Father.*

"Hey Jai," Jared said interrupting her talk with God, "As long as you're here why don't you come into my office and have a cup of coffee with me."

"Oh, now I'm Jai. What happened to MMMRRRSSS. Tyler?" She asked sarcastically. "No thank you. I don't have time to play games with you."

"I'm sorry Jaidyn. I didn't mean to patronize you. Please don't make me cause a scene."

"I really don't care what you do."

He smiled, he knew her better than she knew herself. He knew the one thing she couldn't stand was to have a public disagreement. So he got loud with her, "Mrs. Tyler we are not finished with our meeting. It would benefit both of us if you would return to my office!" Jared said loudly.

She couldn't believe his ass had the nerve to be trying to front her in his office. Her eyes darted around as she tried to see if anyone was listening. She attempted to match his volume, "Trust me Mr. Mitchell you don't want to finish our business. I'm sure the results won't be nice."

Jared took her by the arm and led her back to his office. She gave him some resistance but finally complied. When they walked past Naomi's desk she tried to look busy as if she didn't notice them come in.

Once the door to Jared's office was closed he let her arm go. Wanting to keep the distance between them Jared took a seat behind his desk. Jaidyn sat in the Windsor chair in front of his desk wondering what the hell she was doing there. Although his demeanor was strictly business there was something warm about him. It's his eyes, his exotic beautiful eyes looked right into her, she thought.

"So, what's up Jai. I know you weren't just in the area. You've come here with a purpose. So…" Jared's words echoed in his ears. He just couldn't stop being an ass.

His condescending attitude only pissed her off. Her emotional state was volatile and she only needed the slightest thing to set her off. She didn't have to put up with this bullshit she thought to herself as she rose to leave. She touched the doorknob and abruptly turned back, "You know what, I did come here with an agenda," she blurted out angrily. "I wanted to tell you to stay the hell away from my husband." She had no idea where that came from. The fight had been months ago and she hadn't thought twice about talking to him about Keith but it was the only thing she could think to argue with him about. She felt like a fool after she said it but there was no turning back now.

"Stay away from your husband? You can't be serious! Don't you think you need to be telling him to stay away from me." Jared said almost laughing.

"Jared I don't appreciate you lying to Keith and telling him that we were messing around."

"Is that what he told you? Hum…he disrespected me. You know how it works, when someone is disrespectful they have to be taught a lesson. Sometimes that lesson is a hard one." He said in a sarcastic street tone.

"I'm not interested in your street justice bull shit. I don't appreciate you and Julian jumping him. It was childish. Your problem is with me not Keith. If you want to be pissed off at someone you don't need to look any further than yourself. If your ass wouldn't have been so selfish and self-centered then we wouldn't be where we are. Keith is being the man you wouldn't be!"

Naomi wasn't eavesdropping but it was hard not to hear Jaidyn shouting. She got up and closed the main door to her and Jared's offices so no one would hear the two of them. The last thing they needed was for someone to interrupt them she thought. It was time these two kids worked this mess out before Jaidyn went and got herself pregnant and an innocent child was caught in the middle.

She's got a point Naomi thought he doesn't have anyone to blame but himself. He should have never left her and went to Japan to begin with. Naomi was glad that Jaidyn was finally telling him what she herself had thought. Lord knows that poor boy was a complete mess after he went to that child's wedding. She'd tried to comfort him but there's no running from a broken heart. As the old saying goes, your trash is another man's treasure.

As Jared sat listening to her go off he couldn't get past how damn sexy she was. He must have been dumb, deaf, and blind to let her sexy ass go. He'd never find anyone closer to all his dreams. "Is that what *your husband* told you?" Before Jaidyn could answer Jared went on, "That's bull shit. Keith got his ass whooped because he got up in my face talking shit. I tried my best to let him make it but he wouldn't let the shit go. His boy even tried to get him to step off but he wasn't having it. His ass punched me first. That's why he got his ass whooped. It's unfortunate that his boy got caught in the middle of us. As for Julian, he wasn't there so that's another lie. I gave him the beat down he was asking for by my damn self. As far as talking about you, don't flatter yourself, your name never came out my mouth."

Jared wasn't surprised that Keith had lied to her. As a matter of fact he had suspected it, it's what he himself would have done. No man in his right mind would tell his woman that her ex whooped his ass after he got in his face.

Jaidyn sat down in a chair and quietly tried to digest everything Jared had just told her. She wasn't surprised but Jared's recollection of the fiasco took her a little off guard. The real problem was that her senses had been jolted more by what she was feeling for Jared. His mere presence was driving her out of her mind. She hadn't realized how much she'd missed him. If she told anybody they'd swear she was sprung and missing the sex but it wasn't about sex. She missed their endless conversations. Laughing with him. His friendship, at one time he'd been her very best friend. She missed complaining about him leaving the kitchen in a complete mess when he'd cooked. She missed never having to stop for gas because he'd filled her gas tank a couple of times a week. She missed the attitude he got when she borrowed his shirts and didn't return them. She missed him, everything about him. What they once had was gone and now it was hard for them to sit in the same room and have a simple conversation.

Jared misinterpreting her silence, drove his point home, "If you don't believe me ask the brotha that was with him." She didn't need to ask Markel she believed every word that came out of his mouth. She just wasn't sure how to respond to it. It all made sense. This had to be the reason that Markel had stopped coming around and why Keith got pissed off every time she said she spoke to Markel. Why he said that he wanted her to stay away from Markel.

As they sat in silence he wondered what she was thinking. He wondered if she remembered how they used to hold each other in bed and watch movies. He missed those days. She never made it through a movie. She would always fall asleep in his arms and he'd hold her until the movie was over. He wondered if she remembered how they just needed to be with each other. Did she remember how they fell so helplessly in love. Did she remember all the future plans they made together. It made his heart sink to think of her making future plans with another man. Did she remember the endless hours they played Geusters and cards with Yasmine and Neal? All the laughter they shared while beating them. An air of jealousy hit him when he thought of her and Keith hanging out with their friends. Did she remember how things used to be when they were together? How happy they were? He still spent endless hours thinking about her. There was a lingering reminisce of her sprinkled every where he went.

Her mind drifted to all that had transpired between them to bring them to this point. She'd been trying her best to let go but she couldn't. The memories kept rushing in on her. They were beating the hell out of her. She was torn and had been trying her best to think of him as just another old boy friend but she missed the friend she found in him. There was a point in time when she woke at night with something on her mind she'd wake him no matter what time it was and they'd talk about whatever was keeping her awake. He helped her clear her mind. He was her therapy when she felt like she was losing it. When he was in Japan she missed him but not as much as she did now. She needed his friendship now that things seemed crazy. Now she was wondering what she had gotten herself into.

She wondered why flash backs of the two of them continued to invade her every waking moment. She'd been trying to understand why she was feeling this way. She'd been denying what she knew was true but sitting in his office with him and seeing him with another woman made it clear. She was part of a masquerade, pretending to be a loving wife. She had everyone around her hoodwinked but she couldn't fool her heart. Her heart knew the truth and now so did her head.

Her silence had disarmed him and he wanted to close the distance between them. He eased out of his chair and took a seat in front of her on the end of his desk. He interrupted her thoughts when he leaned over and tenderly cupped her hands in his, "Passion, that fight was months ago. You want to tell me what you're really doing here? Is everything alright?"

She avoided eye contact in case he could still read her thoughts. "What's her name?" Jaidyn asked trying to change the subject.

"Who?"

"Your new girlfriend." She said, regretting the question before it was out of her mouth. What she really wanted to know was if he touched her or held her like he used to hold her. She wanted to know if he loved her the same. If their loving making was as passionate as theirs had been.

Jared stared at her blankly. She always changed the subject when she didn't want to answer his questions. "Her name is Faith…Can you please answer my question."

"Do you love her?" She knew she was asking for it but she couldn't help herself. She had to know if Faith had taken her place in his heart. She wished she could be happy for him but…it hurt.

Jared ignored her question and as softly searched her face for an answer to his question. "You know I would never do anything to hurt you. I want you to be happy, even if that means you being with another man."

His touch was soft and sweet, his voice low, almost a whisper when it happened. The magnetic force that pulled her to him took over and discombobulated her senses. She drifted in the moment and before she could stop herself her lips were touching his. His lips were still soft and warm. She wanted to climb inside his mouth and be absorbed by his soul. She was completely engrossed in the kiss when he pulled away, *"WOW"* was all he managed to say. He sat on the end on his desk peering at her.

Shit, I shouldn't have done that she thought. What in the hell was I thinking? She couldn't believe she'd just made a complete fool of herself. She searched his face for some sign of what he was thinking, feeling, something, but all it displayed was shock. Jaidyn began fumbling through her purse looking for her keys again. She had to get out of there and get some fresh air to clear her head.

This damn girl is married, he thought. What the hell is going on? He was trying to keep his composure but how could he when she was coming at him like this. *Shit, shit, fuck.* He wasn't trying to break up her happy home. He wasn't that type of man. Then again it couldn't be too happy if she was in his office kissing him. Homeboy must not be handling his business because Jai ain't the type of woman that messes around. Something was definitely up. She couldn't be happy because she wouldn't step out on her man. She's a damn good woman.

When Jaidyn stood up to leave he took her hand in his. He continued to study the floor for some type of answer. He rubbed his thumb across the back of her hand and light heartedly said, "*Damn girl.* You really know how to mess up a brotha's day."

"Sorry. I was completely out of..." Jared kissed her before she could finish her sentence. The kiss was different then the last one. It was deep and meaningful. Strong but not forceful. Dynamic yet sensual. The little man in the boat jumped wildly. A tingling sensation began creeping up Jaidyn's back and she stepped into him. Without breaking their lip lock Jared stood up and pulled her into his arms. He wanted her to feel what she was doing to him so he lightly pushed his erection into her.

The kiss had awakened a small amount of sensation in her body but merely brushing against the anaconda's rock hard surface had awakened every sensation conceivable. The wetness between her legs pulsated and it scared her. She swayed away from him, "I'm sorry."

"For what?"

She thought he could read her mind if he looked into her eyes so she diverted them. Her heart was so full she couldn't explain to herself or him what she was feeling but her need to be close to him was overpowering.

"What is it baby...what's on your mind?" He pulled her trembling hand to him and french-kissed it, then he slowly sucked each one of her fingers. She wouldn't look at him so he put his finger under her chin and lifted her head. He gently ran the back of his fingers under her eyes to clear away the tears that were escaping. "I miss you." He said pulling her back into his arms.

"I miss you too." Echoed inside her head. Being in his arms felt too damn good. She pulled away and dropped her head, "I can't do this. I came here to see if we can be friends."

"Friends? Oh, I'm not interested in being your friend." He said sliding her hand down his chest to the crotch of his pants so she could feel his hardness. Her hand lingered there and she took a deep breath. Jared slid his hand under her dress and pulled her panties to the side. His fingers found the wetness of her raindrop and he played in its puddle of water.

"*Fuck!*" Jaidyn screamed to herself as she allowed him to slip his fingers in and out of her. "*Pleasssee!*" She said trying to pull away from him.

"It doesn't feel like you're interested in being my friend either." He said seductively as he nibbled on her ear.

"No Jared. I can't." She said struggling to pull away. He held her tighter making her efforts useless. She took a deep breath and held it as his fingers caressed the little man in the boat.

"Baby you're so damn wet." He moaned into her ear. "Friends don't get that way when they're together." His magical fingers knew her pleasure points well. The hurricane he had created had the little man in the boat about to lose his mind and jump overboard. When Jaidyn finally freed herself from his grip she was only seconds away from a climax. She took several steps away from him trying to regain some type of control before it evaporated completely.

"Listen to me...." She said. Jared leaned back and tried to keep himself from ripping her clothes off. "The only thing we can be is friends. I'm..."

Jared knew what she was about to say and it irritated the hell out of him. He interrupted her, "You're married...to the wrong damn man!" She hated it when he completed her sentences. "Okay Jai, let me get this straight, you're in love with me. You miss me as much as I miss you and you want to be friends?"

"I don't want to lose your friendship is all I'm saying."

"Well, first off we can't be friends because I'm not interested in being your damn friend. Secondly, I'm still in love with you just as much as you're in love with me...don't you get it? We...WE are still in love with each other. Fuck that friendship bull shit."

"Jared you were just in here with another woman."

"And what exactly does that mean? You go home to another man every night."

"Don't turn this around. We're talking about you. What was that all about?"

"What do you want me to say? I'm not married or committed and the woman I love is married to another man...Passion, you're killin' me softly baby. How can you be jealous of me being with another woman when you're with another man?"

Silence momentarily flooded the room. Killing him, she thought to herself. Being without him was torturing her. It's the closest thing to hell on earth that she could think of. Her anxiety about Jared and another woman was ridiculous and she knew it but she was still in love with him. That reality was never clearer. She was mad at herself because of it.

He knew by the look on her face that something wasn't right with her. He hadn't seen her look so stressed out in a long time. He softened his tone and lowered his voice, "When you're near me I want to touch you and not like a friend. I can't be your friend. I need more from you than friendship. Shit baby, my dick's so hard right now it's throbbing. All I want to do right now is lay you down. To hell with that married shit. You hear what I'm saying? You can't come at me like this and expect me to behave and be your damn friend."

"I'm sorry. I shouldn't have...."

"Let me ask you something, can you honestly tell me that you aren't still in love with me just as much as I am with you?" He asked. "Can you tell me when you're lying in bed at night, next to him, you don't think about me?"

"Jared."

"Nah Jai," he said interrupting her, "You and I both know the truth and your husband knows it too. He came at me like he did because of it. This friendship thing is about you wanting to have your cake and eat it to. Well I'm not having it. You're either going to be with him or with me. You can't have us both...nothing's changed between us. I'm still the man that loves you unconditionally. The one who knows you better than you know yourself. And you're still the woman who sees what no one else sees. The one who completes my sentences. The one I want to walk with the rest of my life. You're the woman that inspires me and makes me feel like I can do anything. The woman I want to be the mother of my children. What we found in each other, I never thought possible. You and I are two halves of one soul. Being married to someone else isn't going to change that. I want to spend the rest of my life waking up to you. If that's not possible, so be it. I want you to be my very best friend until I take my last breath, but if I'm not with you then being your friend just isn't something I'm willing to settle for."

What she felt for him scared the hell out of her. She was doing exactly what she promised herself she wouldn't do; but every time she saw his face, every time she smelled his cologne, every time she was near him she couldn't help herself. Her heart beat with fear. She wanted to scream "I made a mistake, I never stopped loving you," but her voice box collapsed trapping the words inside it and she choked back tears.

As Jaidyn turned from him to leave he said, "I'm in love with you. You can't expect for me to be able to be your friend…" Jaidyn reached for the door handle and Jared added, "Don't expect for me to be here waiting on you when you figure out that you've made a mistake. It's time for me to move on with my life."

Chapter 17

Keith's meeting had gone better than he'd expected. He would be flying to New York next week to close a multi-million dollar deal with an up and coming black owned entertainment company. "Adding a deal of this magnitude to the other projects I'm already working on will require an office space, and I'm going to have to hire several employees," he thought to himself.

Keith smiled as a million thoughts ran through his mind. "It's time to celebrate," he said out loud as he drove towards home. He picked up his cell phone to check his messages. The first one was from Jaidyn. "I guess I missed you. I was hoping to catch you before your meeting to wish you luck. Oh well. *GOOD LUCK!* Let me know how things go." The second message was from Zaria. "I need a hot beef injection. If you ain't careful somebody else is gonna be over here handling your business." The third message, "Hey this is Shelbi. I was hoping to see you today. Give me a call in my office when you get a chance." The fourth message was Jaidyn again, "Heyyyy, I forgot to remind you that my office's open house party is tonight, and Mama Nat called. She want's you to swing by the house so she can ride with you. If you can't pick her up call Markel. I spoke to him earlier and he said he'd be happy to pick her up for you."

Keith dialed Jaidyn's office number. "You've reached Houston Surgical Oncology Associates. If you need to make an appointment please press one. If you need to speak to a nurse please press two. If you need to speak to an operator please press zero," the computerized voice said. Keith pressed zero and waited. "Good afternoon Houston Surgical Oncology Associates. This is Darcy may I help you?"

"Hey there Darcy. How are you today?"

An immediate smile flashed across her face. "Hello Mr. Tyler. Can you hold? I'll get Dr. Tyler for you."

"Wait a minute Darcy! How's your day going?"

"Pretty good. Things are crazy around here with all the party stuff going on."

"I see. Are you going to be at the party?"

"Yes. Are you coming?"

"Yea. I'll be there."

"Good, you know I had the strangest dream about you last night. Hopefully I'll get a minute to tell you about it." Darcy said in a flirting tone.

"I look forward to it." Keith said a little aroused.

"Hold on a minute I'll get Dr. Tyler for you."

A minute later Jaidyn was on the line. "Hey honey. How'd your meeting go."

"Fine. What's this about Markel picking up my mother?" Keith asked in a strained voice.

"When I spoke to him earlier he said if your meeting ran over that he'd pick her up for you."

"I don't need him to pick up my mama. If I can't pick her up she can drive herself." Keith said annoyed.

"Keith," Jaidyn said as if he were being ridiculous. "When I spoke to your mother she said she didn't want to drive into town by herself. Markel was just trying to be helpful."

"And what in the hell are you doing talking to Markel?" Keith said irate at her defensiveness of him.

Here we go with this shit again, Jaidyn thought. "I called Markel to remind him of the open house. Remember I told him I'd like to introduce him to Regina."

Keith remembered the conversation but he was still infuriated. "You ain't Ms. Matchmaker. Let that nigga find his own woman."

There was no point in arguing over this with Keith. He would only end up being pissed off with her but as soon as he saw Markel she knew he would act like nothing had happened. His insecurity issues were beginning to get on her nerves. She couldn't talk to another man without it being a problem. If she saw one of her male patients in the mall and stopped to say hello Keith would interrogate her. If a brotha looked her way more than once he wanted to know if she knew him.

Deciding not to get entangled in an argument with him she lied and said, "I've got a patient waiting. So I've got to go. The party is from five to nine. Are you going to be able to make it?"

There was a long silence from the other end before Keith said, "Yea. I'll be there."

"I'll see you at five. I love you," she said before hanging up. "Ummm hmmm," she heard him saying. She knew when she hung up the phone she'd talked to him about 5 minutes too long. Now she'd have to hear his shit when she got home.

Keith hung up with Jaidyn and dialed Shelbi's number. Her secretary said one of her kids was ill and she had to pick him up from school. They didn't expect her back in the office until tomorrow. Damn, he said to himself before dialing Zaria's number. Twenty minutes later he was sitting on Zaria's sofa getting his dick sucked.

Chapter 18

Jaidyn moved through the crowded lobby of her new office casually talking to her colleagues and friends. Although a smile was plastered across her face, internally anger and disappointment filled her. She kept watching the door and checking her watch. It was almost 8 o'clock and she was hoping that Keith would show up any minute.

The overall turn out of the opening was better than Jaidyn or her colleagues had expected. Mama Nat and Mr. Joe, her gentleman friend, along with her parents and Markel had all come to support her. Yasmine and Neal had also shown up but only stayed for about an hour. They had to get home to relieve Yasmine's mother from her baby sitting duties.

Mama Nat, Mr. Joe and Jaidyn's parents had been laughing and talking like old friends for quite a while when Mama Nat caught Jaidyn's eye. Jaidyn had noticed her continuing to stare but did not want to look in her direction. She didn't want to answer any questions but now their eyes had locked and Mama Nat mouthed the words, "Where's Keith?" Jaidyn hunched her shoulders as if to say, "I don't know." Mama Nat gave her a disapproving look and she returned it with her own facial disappointment.

Jaidyn continued to wear a smile just as she had all evening. When the door opened her eyes darted in its direction, it wasn't him. She looked down at her watch just as she had a hundred times since the party started. "Where is he," she wondered. Dr. Jacobs, a colleague, interrupted her thoughts when he came over to say good-bye. "Thank you for coming. I look forward to working with you in the future," she said graciously.

The door opened again and Keith stepped in looking like a piece of chocolate candy. He wasn't handsome but his ass was so damn sexy it didn't matter. Jaidyn looked at her watch a final time, 8:17 p.m. Before Keith could make his way over to Jaidyn his mother cornered him. From a distance they looked like they were having a friendly conversation but Jaidyn knew Natalie Tyler was reading him his rights.

Jaidyn scanned the room once more and noticed her father and Mr. Joe looking at Keith critically. "Why does he have to pull bull shit like this when they are around," she asked herself.

"My wife understands I've got to make a living too." Jaidyn heard Keith saying to his mother as she approached them. Mama Nat didn't attempt to hide her frustration with Keith's tardiness. Keith ignored his mother's harsh words and death stare and wrapped his arm around Jaidyn. Natalie shook her head in disgust before walking back to Mr. Joe and the Owens. Keith kissed Jaidyn on the forehead and said, "Babe it's a great turn out." Jaidyn kept the smile on her face but pushed away from him. "Don't tell me you're trippin' too."

"We started at five, it's 8:30. This is important to me. Couldn't you think about anybody besides yourself for once?"

"I'm not fixin' to listen to this shit." Keith said harshly as he spotted Darcy, Jaidyn's receptionist, by the mini-bar.

"Then why don't you leave," she said, her smile widening as she caught her parents looking in their direction.

"Whatever," he said blowing her off and walked towards the makeshift mini-bar they had set up.

Darcy caught his attention with her flirtatious smile, big blue eyes, and cute little body. Her long auburn hair didn't hurt either. "So tell me about this dream." He said as he walked up beside her. She turned in his direction and he flashed his beautiful, sexy Colgate smile.

"Are you sure you can handle it?" Darcy flirted back.

"Try me," he said looking at her seductively.

"It involved me, you, and my vibrator."

Keith laughed, surprised at her bluntness. "Hmmm," he said urging her on. For the remainder of the evening every time he was near her she whispered dirty little innuendoes in his ear. He laughed each of them off until she said, "I've never been with a black man before. How about you, me and a piece of Saran Wrap go back to my place?" Keith had never been one of those men who would fuck anything. He was picky about the pussy he chose to dive into. Everything that looked good and smells good isn't always good. White women had never been his flavor but there was something about this one that made his dick hard. "I can suck a golf ball through a garden hose." He heard her saying as he thought of a way to get out of going home with Jaidyn. Right then and there he thought about taking her in one of the exam rooms and tappin' that ass, but it was too risky.

Jaidyn's funky little attitude gave Keith the prefect opportunity to cop his own attitude. Before the party ended he'd convinced her that she'd pissed him off so badly that he didn't want to be around her. The truth was he'd made plans to meet Darcy around the corner and follow her back to her place.

Once Keith and Darcy were safely inside her apartment she showed him exactly what she'd dreamt. He watched her intently. Her hips slightly moved as the vibrator she was using tickled her pleasure point. She had placed her head in Keith's lap. Her eyes were closed so she couldn't see his face but she could feel his dick poking her in the back of her head and it turned her on even more. She slightly opened her mouth letting out tiny little moans of pleasure. Keith's dick got so hard she thought it was going to split her head open.

Keith rubbed her breast, her face, and her stomach before slipping his fingers into her mouth. Allowing her to show him exactly what she planned to do with his love stick. Before the end of the night she'd bent her body in positions that most women could only dream of. She'd suck his dick until his body was covered in little pimples and he'd begged her to stop. She'd proven to be a worthy adversary by pushing Keith to the limit and had blown his mind in the process.

After cumming for the fourth time that night Keith looked at the clock, 4 a.m. He jumped up and ran into the bathroom. He didn't have time for a shower so a wipe up would have to do. He hurried to get dressed, kissed Darcy a final time and raced to the parking lot. When he got to his car he frantically searched for his keys. *Shhiit*, he thought, this is the last thing I need. He went back to Darcy's apartment and banged on her front door. Fuck, I'm in deep shit, he mumbled to himself.

"I knew it was just a matter of time before you came running back for more." Darcy giggled.

"I forgot my keys," he said anxiously.

"They're on the dresser," Darcy said disappointedly. Keith walked passed her without a second glance and picked up his keys. "Call me," she said as he past her on his way out of her front door.

Back in his car he looked at the clock, 4:20 a.m. He still had a fourty-five minute drive home. Keith knew that he was going to have to listen to Jaidyn's shit. "Fuck," he yelled hitting his steering wheel with his hand. "Fuck, fuck, fuck! What in the hell am I going to tell her this time," he wondered.

Chapter 19

The party had been a success and before Jaidyn's head hit the pillow she was asleep. At 1:30 a.m. the neighbors barking dog woke her and she got up and went to the bathroom. When she returned to bed she looked at the clock and noticed how late it was. Keith still wasn't in bed. She went into the living room to look for him. He wasn't there. She went into the kitchen, his plate was still on the stove. As she walked into the study, alarm momentarily rushed in on her but it only took her about ten seconds before anger hit.

She was too pissed to go back to bed so she turned on the TV and tried to watch a rerun of the Cosby Show. After 2 a.m. had come and gone she decided to get in her car and check all his normal spots, maybe something had happened to him. After not finding him she returned home.

At 4:45 a.m. she sat in the darkness of the living room waiting on him. She had blown up his cell phone, calling every ten minutes but only got his answering service.

> *I saw all the signs but I choose to believe all Keith's lies. My eyes have been opened. He is selfish and self-centered and I guess living with him is my punishment for not allowing You to choose my path. I accept that this is my burden. But Lord, can You do me a favor? While I'm enduring this burden please keep me from killing this man.*

She couldn't take the waiting so she called Yasmine. When Neal answered Jaidyn apologized for calling so early and asked to speak to Yasmine.

"Jai, what's wrong? Did something happen?" Yasmine said with a panic stricken voice.

"I'm sorry Yasmine, everything's fine, if you call not seeing my damn husband since nine o'clock yesterday fine. Where in the hell could he be?"

"Wait a minute, back up." Yasmine said sleepily, "Where are you?"

"At home."

"Do you need me to come over?"

"No." Jaidyn said embarrassed that she had called Yasmine to begin with.

"Have you tried calling his cell phone?"

"Yes, I've even gone to all his normal hangouts and he is no where to be found."

"Have you called Markel?"

"No, but I went by there. He wasn't there either."

"You drove to Markel's this time of night?" Yasmine said looking at the clock.

"Girl I am so pissed off I am seeing stars. When his ass steps in that door he better have a damn good lie or I swear I'm going to kick his ass."

"Will you listen to me for once, he ain't no good and I told you that. You need to turn that fool loose. If you let him get away with this, he's going to continue to do you like this. You've got to put a stop to this before it gets out of hand. Keith isn't the kind of brotha you can let get away with stuff like this. He'll take your kindness for weakness and become a repeat offender."

"Yasmine, I don't need to hear that shit from you right now. Damn can I ever call you and you just be supportive?"

"Uh, don't be getting pissed off at me. I didn't stay out all night. You know you always have my support, but don't expect to not get the truth. It sounds like you're getting lied to enough."

"I've got to talk to you later, Keith is coming in the door." Jaidyn said slamming the phone down.

Keith did his best to be as quiet as possible. He had not parked his car in the garage in fear that the noise from the garage door opening would wake her. It was 5:12 a.m. and the last thing he wanted to do right now was go head to head with her. After he unlocked the front door he eased it open. He took his shoes off so they wouldn't make any noise on the marble entryway. When he entered the house it was so quiet you could hear a rat piss on cotton. Everything was dark. Good, he thought, she's asleep. He was half way across the living room when Jaidyn turned the light on. She was sitting on the couch next to the lamp watching him.

"Shit baby, you scared me half to death!" He said.

"Where in the hell have you been?"

Keith got an instant attitude. He knew how this was about to go down. "Here you go. I'm not trying to hear yo shit." Keith said putting his stuff down and walking into the kitchen.

His words stunned her. She followed him, "My shit? Have you lost your damn mind? It's five o'clock in the fuckin' morning!"

"And?"

"And, as the old folks say ain't nothing open after two o'clock but legs and restaurants. And I know yo ass ain't been in no restaurant because if you had you wouldn't be in that damn refrigerator."

Keith slammed the refrigerator door. "Look, I ain't trying to go there with you. I've been at Markel's. I went there after my meeting to watch the game and fell asleep on the couch."

Jaidyn was in his face before he knew it. She took her finger and pushed it into his forehead, "You're a damn lie. I went to Markel's and all the rest of your hangouts and yo ass wasn't anywhere to be found. You had me worried as hell. The least you could have done was called and said you weren't dead. You've got to come up with a better lie than that."

"The last time I had a curfew I lived with my mama."

"And if you ain't careful that's exactly were you're going to be --- back with yo mama!"

"I'm a grown ass man and I don't have to answer to nobody. So you don't need to ask me where in the hell I've been. I was where I was at."

"What the hell does that mean?" She asked wanting to go upside his head.

"I was where I wanted to be. You need to get the hell out of my face before I tell you something you don't want to hear."

"What? Another one of your lie's, that's the only thing I don't want to here. You know what...*FUCK YOU Keith!* Where ever the hell you were, you need to take yo black ass back there. You out chasing women and shit while I'm at home worried to death. I'm not going to have it. If that's what you want all you need to do is say the word."

Keith laughed. "Chasing women. Is that what you think? I don't have to chase no damn body. The ho's out there," he said pointing to the door, "Throwing pussy at me."

Jaidyn's temper was at a boiling point. It took everything she had to keep from going up side his head. "You muthafucka, I don't have to put up with this shit. You can't have the best of both worlds. You can't hang onto me and have those tramps in the streets too. You've got to make a choice. I won't be a good little woman while yo ass do whatever the fuck you want to do. I'll walk away from all this before I let that shit happen. You goin' have to bring yo ass in at a decent hour, period, or you're going to find yo ass out there with them ho's."

"Have to bring my ass in...have you lost yo mind? All I have to do is stay black and pay taxes."

"I am so sick and tired of being sick and tired of putting up with yo shit." Frustration showed on Jaidyn's face.

"I suggest you build a bridge and get over it." He said laughing.

"You bring yo got damn ass in here one more time at five o'clock in the morning ..."

"Get the fuck out my face Jaidyn." Keith warned as he walked into the bedroom and started taking off his clothes. "I don't know why I'm entertaining this bull shit with you. I pay bills in this muthafucka! If you don't like it you can get the fuck out!"

Jaidyn wasn't sure what to say to him, all she wanted to do was beat the shit out of him but she was trying to control herself. She stood and watched him start to undress. This muthafucka has lost his damn mind, she thought. There was no way she was going to put up with him treating her like this.

All Keith wanted to do was get in the shower and go to bed. He wasn't trying to hear that bull shit from her. This conversation was over. He knew he was wrong and felt bad for treating her so harshly but what else was he to do. He should have just kept his mouth shut and listened to her rant and rave. Arguing with her hadn't accomplished anything. He had said things he hadn't meant and knew when the sun came up he was going to have to kiss her ass or buy her something expensive to make up for it.

He was sitting on the bed pulling his socks off when he noticed that he had put his boxers on inside out. "Fuck, Jaidyn didn't miss shit," he thought. He hoped she was so pissed off that she wasn't paying attention. With one sock on and one sock off he got up and started walking to the bathroom. He wanted to get away from her before she noticed.

As Keith walked to the bathroom she couldn't believe what she was seeing. His underwear and T-shirt were turned inside out. He was a perfectionist when it came to the way he dressed. Every inch of him was flawless before he left the house. She fought back truth that was now running rapidly through her mind. She'd been trying to deny what she already knew was true since her woman's intuition had kicked in before she went to bed. But there it was, truth. Standing there taunting her, daring her to try to ignore it. The old saying was true, "There isn't anything open after 2 a.m. but legs and restaurants." Her fucking husband had been between some ho's legs. She struggled to blink away tears.

"This muthafucka has to pay for this shit," she mumbled to herself. Before she could stop herself she flew into him like wonder woman. His back was to her and he hadn't expected this. He stumbled forward and hit his head on the armoire. "Fuck," he yelped. Jaidyn didn't let up. She was relentless. The continuous explosive blows were coming too fast for him to duck and weave. She was whooping his ass like she was fighting a bitch on the street.

Keith tried to push her off of him but was unsuccessful. In order to get her to stop he was going to have to fight her like a dude. He didn't want to hurt her so he continued to try to avoid and sidestep the blows she was throwing at him.

By the time Jaidyn stopped hitting him angry tears ran down her face.

"Shit, do you feel better now?" He yelled. His question infuriated her all over again and she ran at him. By the time she was finished with him she didn't want to look at him. She picked up his clothes and threw them at him. "Get out."

"What?"

"Did I stutter?"

"This is my got damn house. How the hell you goin' put me out?" He said with some amusement in his voice.

"The house you pay the bills at --- you fixin' to get yo shit and go. Whatever rock you climbed from up under, take yo black ass back to it."

Keith dismissed her by walking into the bathroom. Jaidyn stormed out of the room like a woman on a mission. When she came back Keith was in the shower. She swung the shower door open, "I'm not playing with you. You gonna get yo shit and get the fuck out."

"Bitch you need to step the fuck off before I whoop yo ass." Keith threatened her.

Jaidyn wasn't phased by his antics. "You gon' walk out of here on your own or they're going to take you out on a stretcher." She said showing him the box cutter she had retrieved from the garage.

Keith smiled. "Come on now," he said reaching for her.

Jaidyn pulled away from his attempt to touch her. "I wish you would. I'll cut yo ass from ass hole to elbow. Don't play with me." She said pulling the box cuter back in a swinging motion.

"This crazy muthafucka has lost her damn mind," Keith thought. He got out the shower and got dressed. Jaidyn calmly sat in the living room waiting on him to leave. When he came into the living room there was a deafening silence. "Baby, this shit has gotten out of hand. We need to talk. Let me explain."

Jaidyn put her hand up, "I don't want to hear it."

"Alright baby, I know I fucked up. I'm sorry. We need to talk and straighten all this out." Jaidyn walked over to the door and opened it. There was an eerie calmness to her and Keith knew she meant business. He picked up his keys and walked over to her. When he leaned over to kiss her on the cheek she moved back. "I don't know where your mouth has been." She said avoiding his attempt at emotional drama.

"Ok, that's how it's goin' be --- Cool."

A minute later she heard the screeching of his tires as he backed out of the driveway.

Lord, I know You know where You're taking me and I've got my hand in Yours but please Father convert him, change him, convict him or move him out of my life.

Chapter 20

"Hey dawg. Sup? You got company?"

"Nah man, I'm by myself. Sup with you stranger? I haven't heard from you in a minute."

"Wanted to see if you were up for a work out or maybe a game of racquetball.

"Sounds like a plan. I haven't whooped yo ass in racquetball in a while." Markel said.

"There you go talking that smack. You want to put your money where your mouth is?"

"I've got two Benjamin's on the best two out of three."

"Alright. I'll come by and scoop you up."

"Cool."

Five minutes later Keith was pulling into Markel's driveway. On their drive to the gym Markel asked how things were going with Jaidyn. Keith told him how ridiculous Jaidyn had behaved after he'd came in late.

After Keith finished Markel asked, "Man why did you get married?"

"What kind of question is that? I love my wife."

"If that's the case what the fuck are you doing out here chasing these tramps?"

"Man, I ain't chasing these women. They're throwing the pussy at a brotha."

"You fowl man, you're one dirty muthafucker, you know that? You keep this up and you're going to lose Jaidyn."

"Jaidyn's never going to leave me man. She's wants me to think she's crazy, but as long as I'm taking care of home she doesn't have anything to complain about. Look, Jaidyn isn't like other women. She doesn't want to be lied to so she doesn't ask questions because she doesn't really want to know the truth. She doesn't expect me to be faithful for the next forty years. If she did it would be an unreal expectation. Long as I am not throwing the shit in her face it's cool. I fucked up and I know that. I should've had my ass in the house long before five o'clock. Shit it was a mistake and it won't happen again."

"You can't let these freaks mess up what you have at home. These days quantity will get you killed but quality will keep you happy and healthy. Shit dawg, the older I get the more I'm into quality. I'm not into quantity any more. You better learn that shit quick or you're going to fuck around and lose the best thing that's ever happened to you. While you're bull shittin,' there's a lot of brothas out here that would love to have a woman like Jaidyn, including me. All a brotha has to do is put a little salt in your game. I'm telling you man, you need to leave that playa shit alone. Cherish what you have."

Keith made a mental note to watch Markel when he was around his wife, he was a little too interested in her. "Man, don't hate the playa, hate the game. These tricks out here don't mean anything to me. Jaidyn is always going to be first. She can get anything she wants out of me. She's my heart. I make love to Jaidyn. I fuck these tricks. I fuck those ho's so hard, I try to knock the bottom out of their shit. It's not like that with Jaidyn. My business has taken off so the sky is the limit when it comes to her."

"With a woman like Jaidyn it isn't about the material things. She can get those things for herself. You've got to give her what she can't buy. Man you've got it all and you can't see it. Ain't nothing out here but a bunch of tramps. The grass isn't greener on the other side, the shit is brown."

This conversation had gone on long enough, "What the hell is up with you? You act like you want to fuck my wife."

"Come on now man. I've got a lot of respect for her. She's a hell of a woman and yo black ass is lucky to have her. I would hate to see you fuck things up with her. She cool people."

"Well, you don't have to worry about that! We said until death do us part and that's the way its going to be."

"Alright Pimp Daddy, I hear you." Markel said deciding to drop the subject. He knew it was useless to try to make Keith see the error of his ways. They'd been friends long enough for him to know that Keith wouldn't realize how good he had it until it was too late.

Keith spent the remainder of the day with Markel. A little after 7 p.m. Keith went home to face the music. When he pulled into the driveway he pushed the button on his garage door opener but it wasn't working. "The battery must be dead," he thought. He parked his car in the driveway and went to the front door. When he unlocked the door he found that his key no longer fit. How the hell she gon' change the locks on my damn house. Keith forcefully pounded the door with his fist. Keith yelled for her to open the door. *"Why you trippin? Open this door!"*

Jaidyn sat at the kitchen table and listened to him bang on the door. She wasn't ready to deal with him yet. She was thinking about all the lies he would tell when the phone rang and brought her out of her trance. She got up, went to the phone hanging on the kitchen wall and looked at the caller ID. Keith's cell phone number flashed across the screen. Without answering it she returned to the kitchen table where she was reviewing upcoming surgery candidate charts.

Annoyed by Keith's fifteenth call she answered the phone, "What Keith?"

"Baby, come on now. Don't you think your taking this a little too far?"

"Keith, I need some time. I'm tired of all the BS. I told you that this morning."

"I know baby. That will never happen again. I don't know what I was thinking. I should have told you the truth from the beginning. I drove to my mothers after I left your office. I waited on her to get home so that I could tell her about the contract I'd gotten. After you acted so shitty I went and had a few drinks. When Mama got home I was passed out on the couch. She knew I'd been drinking so she let me sleep it off. When I realized what time it was I jumped up and came home. I didn't call because I knew you would be in bed."

"Sounds like another lie to me."

"Baby you can call my mother and ask her. I talked to her today and asked her why didn't she call you to tell you I was there. She said she thought you knew. She didn't realize that I hadn't told you. I'm a little surprised she hasn't already called you. She was upset when I told her what happened. She let me have it. She was worried about you being upset so I thought she would have called you by now."

"Keith look, I'll talk to you tomorrow. I need to go." Jaidyn said in an unbelieving voice.

"Baby wait. I left something at the front door for you."

"Good night Keith," Jaidyn said and hung up. She went to the window in the front of the house to see if he was still in the driveway. He was gone so she went to the front door. When she opened the door he had two bears kissing each other along with three dozen long stem white roses. She brought the stuff inside and opened the card attached to the flowers,

"Being away from you is tearing me up. Forgive me for the things I said. You stepped right out of my dreams and are all the woman I'll ever need. I adore you. I need you. But most of all I love you."

Before she could close the door the phone rang. She sat the flowers down on the entry way table and she went to answer the phone, "Hello."

"Hello Baaaby. How are you?" Jaidyn hadn't expected to hear Natalie Josephine Tyler's heavy Cajun accent on the other end of the phone when she answered.

"Oh Mama Nat! I didn't expect to hear from you."

"Well, I hope this is a pleasant surprise."

"It's always a pleasure talking to you." They both laughed. "How are you? And how are things going with Mr. Joe? I'm sorry I didn't get a chance to talk to you last night." Jaidyn said trying to sound as up beat as possible but in reality she was annoyed and depressed. She didn't want to involve her mother-in-law in her and Keith's problems.

Jaidyn loved her mother-in-law, she was hard not to like. Her and Jaidyn hit it off the first time they met. She had a quiet almost reclusive demeanor that was often misinterpreted as stuck up and stand offish, but she was a very sweet and loving person. Jaidyn was not only Natalie's daughter-in-law but confidant as well. She confided in Jaidyn how she was forced to be an introverted person. She'd told about her violent marriage to Keith's father, which helped to give Jaidyn an insight into her personality. Keith's father had been verbally and physically abusive. She'd stayed in the marriage out of fear rather than love. After twenty-five years of marriage he'd left her for a younger woman and for the first time in Natalie's life she'd been able to have a life outside her home. The long-term abuse had taken its toll on her. It had made her somewhat fearful of sharing too much with people.

Mr. Joe, Natalie's beau, was a wonderful man who loved her dearly. He'd asked her to marry him several times but Jaidyn knew that Natalie would probably never marry again. When Mama Nat shared her story with Jaidyn it had somehow bonded the two women and made them more than just in-laws.

"We had a good time last night."

"I'm glad. So, Mr. Joe told me he asked you to marry him."

"Will you stop with that marriage stuff. I've told you and Joe that's for young folks. I like things just the way they are. After all he just lives across the street. We can see each other anytime we like and when we get sick of each other we don't have far to go to get home. How are you baaaby? When are yall going to give me some grandchillin?"

Jaidyn laughed, "I'll make you a deal. I'll stop asking you about marriage when you stop asking me about grandchildren."

"Ok baaaby," Natalie Tyler said laughing "Where is that son of mine?"

"He's not here Mama Nat. I'll be sure to tell him you called when I talk to him."

"Baaaby, I really called to talk to you. I don't want to get in the middle of yall's private business, but Keith called me and asked me to give you a call."

"Mama Nat that's not necessary."

"Baaaby, men can be just plan old inconsiderate at times. I don't want to get into y'alls business but you have to decide what's best for you. Can't nobody tell you what you should and shouldn't do."

When Natalie Tyler hung up with Jaidyn she felt horrible. Although she hadn't lied to Jaidyn she felt like she'd deceived her by not correcting the lie she knew Keith had told. "Nobody deserves to be lied to," she thought. She made a vow to never deceive or lie to Jaidyn for Keith again. Deception was just as bad as lying, they go hand in hand. It was time that Keith learned what she'd always told him, "What's done in the dark will come to light sooner or later."

She picked up the phone to call him. "Hey Ma, did you talk to Jaidyn?"

"Yes but let me tell you something. Right is right and wrong is wrong. I won't uphold you when you're wrong. If Jaidyn asked me any questions I'm going to tell her the truth. So it's best that you don't get me involved in yall's personal business."

Jaidyn stood in her kitchen running what Mama Nat had said back through her mind. It was what she hadn't said that had caught Jaidyn's attention.

> *Lord I love you and I need you. Come into this house and into our hearts and bless us. Help me to make since of the things Keith does. In Jesus Name,*
>
> *Amen*

Jaidyn was still holding the patient's chart in her hand that she was about to review before Mama Nat called. She returned it to the table and went into her bedroom to get the cordless phone so that she could call Keith. As she picked up the phone her mind shifted back to the chart she'd been about to review. She went back in the kitchen to look at it again. Although she hadn't reviewed it something had caught her attention and she wanted to dispel the anxiety that was running rapid through her veins. When she got to the table and picked it up again she was taken aback, *"Uuuhhh God... Hobgood, Naomi, date of birth May 22, 1940. Shit!"*

She took a seat at the table, opened the chart and began reading it as fast as she could. Breast cancer! Doctor Davide Abounasr referred her for a radial mastectomy. She had already undergone several chemotherapy treatments.

Jaidyn went to her purse to get her Palm Pilot. She hoped that the receptionist had down loaded the patient appointment schedule to it so that she could see when her appointment was. The new receptionist had proven once again to be a lifesaver. Naomi's appointment was the last appointment on Monday.

Chapter 21

Jared hands explored Jaidyn's sexy smooth body as his tongue traveled south. "The Palace" welcomed the wetness of his tongue as he slipped it inside the opening the anaconda had escaped moments before. Plunging into its golden walls he could feel her pulsating pleasure. He softly kissed her lips then gently sucked her clitoris all the time working his fingers in and out. She twitched and jumped letting out a high pitched sigh as she dripped with approval. He tasted her sweetness one last time before her essence overflowed.

Jaidyn pushed him back onto the couch and mounted him. She sat astride like she was on a custom built Harley Davidson. While she used him as a masturbation toy he watched her beautiful face, chin up, eyes closed, pure unadulterated pleasure was written all over it. As the anaconda probed as deep as it could go she road the Harley with the expertise of a skilled rider. With every rise and fall, every twist and turn she swayed, matching the movement of the bike. Knowing just what to do to make her scream the Harley accelerated and she moaned passionately. Jared clung to the pillow beneath his head as their love juices burst into each other.

The intense tingling jarred him from his dream. He sat up on the side of the bed with the sheet draped across his hard dripping muscle. He looked at his bare feet as if he were expecting them to tell him why this continued to happen.

Faith, the woman he'd been sharing his bed with for the last few months soothingly rubbed his back. "What's wrong? Did you have a bad dream?" She asked sheepishly. "Man if you only knew," he thought, it was more like a fantasy gone wrong. Unable to will his tumescence muscle down he turned to Faith closed his eyes and pretended she was the woman in his dreams.

Chapter 22

Jaidyn missed sleeping next to Keith and regretted not calling him and telling him to come home. She wondered where he'd spent the night. She picked up the phone to call him. His cell phone answering service came on immediately. She decided not to leave a message and returned the phone to the cradle beside the bed. She'd wait until later to call him back. She got out of bed, went to the garage and re-plugged the garage door opener into the outlet. She had unplugged it after he left Saturday morning knowing he would try to use the garage to get back in the house.

After a sleepless night Jaidyn got out of bed early wanting to get an early start. Jaidyn took a shower, changed and rushed to get to the hospital. She needed to make rounds early so that she could pick up Anna from the airport and make it to church before 11:00 a.m. service.

Anna Monroe and Jaidyn had been friends since they were eleven years old. Jaidyn met Anna when she was visiting her father's family during a summer trip to Barbados. The two had become instant friends. They'd maintained their friendship through an endless array of letters and during numerous summer vacations to Barbados.

Anna was now living in San Francisco, working as a Fashion Merchandiser. She was also pursuing her dream of becoming an artist on the side. She was meeting with the Museum of Fine Arts to discuss a potential exhibit of her work. She also had a meeting with The Shrine of the Black Madonna to sign a contract for an exhibit she had scheduled in the next few months.

Jaidyn was thankful it was Sunday. More then ever she needed to go to church and have her spirit renewed. She took a minute to pray as she walked down the hospital corridor:

> *Father God, here I am again standing in need of Your refreshment, Your wisdom, and Your divine guidance. Lord, hold Naomi in your loving hands, and heal her body. Give Naomi the hope, strength, and courage she will need to endure the things she's about to undergo. Replace the fear she will inevitably have with faith and trust in You. I ask for Your abundant blessing on her and her family in their time of need. Lord, allow Your loving kindness, grace, mercy, and favor to rain down onto this entire family.*
>
> *Thank you for giving me the gift and knowledge of healing. I am Your instrument please use me, consecrate the abilities You have given me for the healing of this woman. Allow my efforts to not be in vain.*
>
> *Now Father God please bless my marriage. After our fight my first impulse was to call Jared. Although I didn't, I wanted to. Please remove this temptation from my heart. Help me to understand why it continues to happen. Keith and I need your guidance. His attitude and tantrums are chipping away at my tolerance little by little. Please send peace and love into this marriage. In the name of my Lord and Savior Jesus Christ.*
>
> *Amen.*

The smell of cooking bacon woke Keith. He rolled over and looked at the clock. If he was going to meet Jaidyn at church he was going to have to get a move on. He didn't have a suit with him so he was going to have to go by the house to change.

After he got dressed he walked into the living room. Zaria was in the kitchen cooking breakfast and those four bad ass kids of hers were parked in front of the TV watching cartoons.

"Good morning," Zaria said.

"Hey."

"Give me a couple of more minutes and breakfast will be ready."

"I'm not hungry," Keith said as he sat down at the bar and put on his shoes.

"But I cooked just for you. The kids ate cereal."

"Thanks but I'm not hungry."

"Where are you going?"

"Home."

"Uh, well can you leave me some money to pay the rent?"

"Hell no! I told your ass I wasn't paying yo damn rent anymore. I meant that."

"Well what am I suppose to do?"

"I really don't give a damn. Get one of yo kid's daddy to pay it or try getting yo lazy ass a job!" Keith said as he picked up his keys and walked towards the door.

"Fuck you Keith."

"You did that last night," he said as he slammed the door.

Jaidyn couldn't remember the last time Keith went to church with her but she wasn't surprised when Keith slipped into the pew beside her and Anna. When he attempted to hold her hand she pulled it away from him. His mere presence pissed her off all over again. It occurred to her that his mother hadn't said that Keith was with her. She had only tried to be of comfort to Jaidyn. She didn't need his mother to confirm what she already knew, Keith wasn't with his mother. It was just another lie.

When church service was over Lance pulled Jaidyn to the side while the rest of the family talked to other members of the congregation. He asked if Anna, Keith, and her would be joining them for dinner at their parents. Jaidyn told him that they would be. Lance asked Jaidyn about the tension he had been noticing between her and Keith. Jaidyn got an instant attitude and asked him to stay out of her business.

After her talk with Lance she wondered if anyone else had noticed the tension between her and Keith. She didn't have to wonder for long because Anna was the next to inquire about her intense disposition. Before she could tell Anna about her and Keith's fight, he approached them kissed Anna on the cheek and said hello. He put his arm around Jaidyn and pulled her closer to him. He kissed her on her forehead as Anna divulged her plans for later that evening.

When Keith and Jaidyn were safely out of everyone's hearing radius he asked, "How did you sleep?"

"Fine," Jaidyn said with a hint of an attitude.

"I love you baby."

"Hum."

Keith ignored her obvious attitude, "How long is Anna going to be with us?"

"Just a few days."

They spent the remainder of their day at her parents home enjoying the company of her family. Keith told everyone about his new contract and his plans to open a new office and hire some employees. Jaidyn enjoyed their conversation. She was never able to stay mad long and she found herself happy to see him smiling. She couldn't remember the last time she'd seen him so happy.

She was excited for him but no one was happier to hear the news than Mr. Owens. They all got a lecture on how money problems can create problems in a marriage and how young people need to learn that the success of marriages are determined by the couples ability to stand together against adversity and weather any storm. Jaidyn got the distinct impression that her father thought that her and Keith's problems stemmed from money. Although his lecture was directed at all of them she felt like it was clearly for her and Keith. It was then that she realized that although she hadn't discussed their marital issues with anyone lately, they were evident to everyone.

After another wonderful Sunday afternoon with her family Jaidyn headed home and Anna headed to meet some friends at an art gallery opening. Jaidyn pulled into her driveway, raised the garage door and was completely flabbergasted by what she found there. A silver BMW SUV with a big red bow was parked in her spot. After getting out of her car and walking into the garage she pulled a card off the windshield and it read; 'For my wife. Thank you for putting up with me. I never thought it was possible to love you more today then I did yesterday but I do.' "Oh my goodness I can't believe this. It's beautiful. No wonder Keith left my parents early," she thought.

When she walked in the house it was like walking into a fairytale. There was an aisle of white and red rose petals from the garage door to the bedroom. When she opened the bedroom door the room was illuminated by a plethora of warm inviting Aromatic candles. A beautiful array of roses in every color covered the bed.

Keith stood in the bathroom doorway watching her. He enjoyed making her happy. She really was the love of his life, "I was out of line last night. I'm sorry for the way I spoke to you." Jaidyn had expected flowers to be on the doorstep this morning or at the hospital. She'd expected some small expensive gift. That was normally what she got after they'd had a blow up. Everyone thought her husband was an ideal husband and told her how lucky she was. The truth was she only got this type of treatment when they'd had some type of altercation. A new car, she hadn't expected this. Her mind was screaming at her, "This only solidifies what you already know. He was with someone." She tried to push the thought to the back of her mind.

"Do you like your present?"

"I love it honey." She said rushing into his arms to kiss him.

Keith took her by the hand and led her into the bathroom. The bathtub was also illuminated by candlelight. She was enthralled in the moment and didn't know what to say. Keith had always been a romantic, but she hadn't seen this side of him in a long time and it had taken her by surprise. The new SUV was breathtaking and all the trouble he had gone through to set this up was heart warming. "How did you do all this?"

"I can't give away my secrets."

"Thank you." She said as Keith undressed her. When she climbed into the bathtub she waited on him to get undressed but he didn't. He disappeared into the bedroom and put on a CD. When he returned he was carrying one glass of wine. He handed it to her and took a seat on the floor next to the bathtub.

"Aren't you going to join me?"

"No. I just want to enjoy watching you."

"Please join me." She said waving him over to her. After he'd undressed he climbed into the bathtub behind her. She settled back onto his chest and enjoyed the music.

"Where did you get this CD?"

"I made it for you."

"Wow. Thank you. It's incredible." She said listening to it intently. He had put all her favorite love songs onto one CD. It had everything from Marvin Gaye to India Arie to Heather Headley. A romantic evening was just what she needed and it was no surprise that she quickly forgot about everything that they'd been going through and just enjoyed being in her husband's arms.

Keith sat behind her tenderly rubbing her shoulders and arms. The more gentle touches he embellished her with and the closer he held her to him the more she wanted him. She enjoyed his attention. It was very seldom that she got the star treatment from him. He always said that he was concerned with satisfying her but she knew better. He was always ready to pound away at her but once he was satisfied he'd climb off of her and fell asleep faster than she could blink an eye. She knew if she didn't get hers in the fifteen minutes it took him to get his she was shit out of luck.

He ran his fingers through her hair. When he cupped her breast she turned around and kissed him. She wanted to make love to him right then and there but he refused telling her that they'd have the whole night for that. He said he wanted to admire her and to enjoy holding her.

She stood in front of the bathroom mirror drying off she noticed that Keith had written 'I love you' in soap on the mirror. All of this was just too much to take. She was so excited she said to hell with her negligee. She wanted to get into bed with her husband as quickly as possible. He had already mesmerized her and her body was screaming for him.

When she climbed into bed Keith took her into his arms and made love to her tenderly, like it was their first time together. He took his time, moving along her body slowly and carefully. He made sure that he meet every expectation and need that she had. Their lovemaking was sweet and meaningful. It had been a long time since they made love all night long and he'd held her afterwards.

When the sun began peaking through the blinds she snuggled a little closer to him. Not wanting their romantic escapade to end, but she had a day of shopping planned with Anna, so she was going to have to pull herself out of bed soon.

Jaidyn, Keith and, Anna were just sitting down to breakfast when the phone rang. Keith got up and went to answer it while the two ladies continued to laugh about the men Anna had met the night before. "When I asked him what his name was he said Torture. I said I'm sorry I didn't hear you. He said it again, Torture. I looked at him puzzled, like I know your mother didn't name you Torture." Both ladies laughed. "Girl get this. He said, it's Torture because you're torturing me with your sexy ass."

Jaidyn was laughing so hard tears were falling from her eyes. "That brotha put the T in tired. I know you didn't give him your number!"

"Girl please! I told him he was torturing the hell out of me with his tired ass pick up lines. But that didn't seem to discourage him. I don't know what you guys are feeding these brothas in Houston."

"A brotha like that gives the rest of us a bad name." Keith said coming back to the table and handing the phone to Jaidyn. "It's for you."

Keith leaned over close to Anna's ear as if not to disturb Jaidyn's phone call. "A sexy ass woman like you needs a man to come at her from the side. If he has to use an opening line it should be something like...can I have a picture of you so I can show Santa exactly what I want for Christmas." The way he was talking to Anna made her uncomfortable.

"Hello." Jaidyn said into the receiver. When she heard the voice on the other end she instantly went into business mode. "Yes, this is Dr. Tyler." She paused as she listened to the person on the other end of the phone. "I'm not on call today. Have you tried calling Dr. Santos." Jaidyn was silent as she listened to the person on the other end of the phone again. "I see...I'll be there as quickly as I can." Jaidyn was incensed when she hung up. The look of disappointment on her face told Anna exactly what she was about to say. "I've got to go to the hospital to check on a patient. I'm sorry but it should only be about an hour."

Keith snickered. "Welcome to my life Anna. Now you see what I put up with. Everything takes a back seat to Dr. Tyler's patients." He said with a sarcastic undertone.

"You want a woman that makes the big bucks you've got to put up with this type of thing." Anna said in Jaidyn's defense. Turning her attention to Jaidyn, "It's no problem girl, go do your doctor thing and I'll hang out here."

"Anna and I will be just fine. If you take too long we'll find something to do." Keith said looking at Anna with lust filled eyes.

Before Jaidyn was out the house Keith was making moves on Anna. He'd said a few things to her before but she'd ignored him or laughed them off. She'd been unsure if he was serious or if she was misjudging his flirty ways. "So Anna, Jaidyn tells me you're not only beautiful and sexy but you're also very talented...can you show me some of the artistic talents you possess."

Anna looked at him as if she was puzzled when he picked up her hand off her lap and ran his fingers through hers. She jerked her hand away from him and said, "I don't want to misunderstand what you're saying but I know you aren't trying to..." before she could get the sentence out Keith had pulled her into his arms and had his tongue down her throat. She tried her best to bite his lip off as she pushed away from him. She stepped back and tried to slap the taste out of his mouth. "You sorry sack of shit. I don't know what kind of impression you got but Jaidyn is my fucking friend... You son of a bitch."

"I see you like it rough." Keith said laughing a seductive laugh. "Damn girl you're sexy as hell when you're mad." He said trying to pull her back into him.

"How could you? Jaidyn's my fucking friend. You a dawg ass nigga!" Anna said horrified.

Keith laughed, "You know what dog spells backwards...com'on you know you want it."

Anna hit him again. Only this time she closed her fist and drove it into his private area. Keith leaned forward moaning in agony. Anna was standing over him yelling when he hit her. He hit her so hard it knocked her off her feet. "Bitch you have lost you're muthafuckin' mind!"

When Jaidyn got home Anna was gone but she'd left her a note,

Meshell

Jaidyn,

They've had an emergency at the office. They need me back ASAP.

I called the Museum as well as the Shrine and will meet with both of them before my 2 p.m. flight. I'm sorry, I know we had plans.

Tell Yasmine I look forward to meeting her on my next trip. I'll call you in a few days.

Anna

Chapter 23

Jared had been in Japan on a business trip and had been unable to be with Naomi and her family during her surgery. When his meetings ended he got on the first plane back to the States. When he arrived at Bush Intercontinental Airport he retrieved his bags and headed straight for the hospital. He'd spoken to Naomi's husband several times. He'd told him that things had gone better than they expected. Although Naomi still had a long hard road ahead of her and would have to undergo chemotherapy, James report that Dr. Tyler thought she'd gotten all the cancer. Jared knew that Jaidyn was the right person to recommend to Naomi. He knew that she would take extra special care of her but he was still anxious to see Naomi for himself.

When Jared walked into Naomi's hospital room the last person he excepted to see at 5 a.m. was Jaidyn but there she was sleeping in the chair next to Naomi's bed. He picked up a blanket off an adjacent chair and draped it across her. He gently pulled a lock of hair that was dangling across her face to the side. She looked like a sleeping angel that had lost her way from heaven.

"What are you doing here so early?" Naomi whispered. "And when did you get back in town?"

"I thought you were sleeping." Jared whispered back then leaned over and kissed her on the forehead. "How are you feeling?"

"Not too bad. What day is it?" She asked with a confused furrow in her brow.

"Saturday morning."

"Saturday? I didn't think you were due back until Tuesday."

"I finished things up early so that I could get back here and make sure you were doing everything the doctors told you." He said in a hushed voice.

"Jaidyn is taking good care of me."

"She looks like she is giving you around the clock service." Jared said looking in Jaidyn's direction.

"That child has slept in that chair for the last two nights. I didn't have a good night last night and they called her at home. She came up around midnight and spent the remainder of the night here with me. She came in tonight at about 2 a.m."

"Another bad night?" He asked with concern in his voice.

"No. I'm a little uncomfortable but I'm fine. I don't know why she came in tonight. Said she wanted to check in on me. When I took my pain medicine she was right here holding my hand. When I opened my eyes again you were standing here." A pained look crossed Naomi's face and Jared motioned for her to rest. He pulled up a chair beside her bed and held her hand as she drifted back off to sleep. Forty-five minutes later a nurse came in to take her vital signs and give her more pain medication.

As he sat quietly watching them both sleep it was hard for him not to reminisce on his time with Jaidyn. The memories they shared would live forever in his heart. He'd felt like he was in the arms of an angel when he was with her. He'd been dating, trying to replace her but she was simply irreplaceable. He knew sooner or later he'd settle for someone but Jaidyn would always be a part of him and he'd never feel complete without her by his side. He had gotten all kind of advice from his mother and Naomi and they had both been right. He finally understood what his mother meant when she said that the worst way to miss someone was to be sitting right next to them and know that you can't have them. He was experiencing that at that very moment. Still waters really do run deep.

On his way to the hospital he'd listened to a CD by Gospel rapper, Tragedy. She'd said that time heals all wounds and she was right. Time had put distance between him and the pain but the love he had for Jaidyn hadn't changed. He suspected it never would. He'd love her to the end of time. It was anchored deep down in his soul. He tried to fight it but when she was around him his resistance was low. Her hauntingly beautiful face wouldn't let him breathe. She haunted him in his dreams and preoccupied his every waking thought. It was worse than any drug. He'd give up all he owned just to be with her. He couldn't get her out of his system. He was strung out. An addict that fiend for just one hit of her. He remembered a time that their thirst for each other had been addictive. Like all addictions their habit was so strong that if ignored it woke them in the middle of the night. He had to laugh at himself because he knew he was a straight up base head for her love.

Jaidyn woke to find Jared sitting across the room. He was looking down at the floor lost in thought. She watched him and wondered what he was thinking. He was one beautiful specimen she said to herself. He was one of those beautiful people who commanded your attention when you saw them.

She smirked as a memory from the past tiptoed softly across her mind. There were so many things in her daily life that struck a cord and took her back to happier times with him. When she wasn't busy or when she was alone and everything was quiet and still they'd gently push their way into her thoughts and linger there. She'd stop wrestling with attempts to push the memories out of her mind and had learned to cherish them.

Jared let out a little mischievous laugh. "What's so funny?" Jaidyn asked.

He looked up surprised, "Ah...nothing. Just laughing at myself." He said unable to contain his smile. Feeling like he'd just been caught with his hands in the cookie jar he quickly tried to change the subject. "I thought you were still sleeping," he whispered.

She surprised herself and said, "No. I've been sitting here admiring you." Her comment made him a little uncomfortable. She got up, put her shoes on, folded the blanket, and placed it in the chair. "I thought you were in Japan. How long have you been back?"

"I arrived about two hours ago."

"How was your trip?" She whispered.

"Productive. Thanks for asking." As he sat there hoping that she would say something that would give him an excuse to take her into his arms and lavish her with kisses, but it was a foolish thought. This wasn't a prefect world and he knew that.

Jaidyn could feel her temperature rising just as it did every time she was near his fine ass. "I better get out of here. I need to see a few patients." She said as she walked towards the door.

Jared got up and followed her into the hallway. "Hey Jai, spending the night here is going above and beyond the call of duty. Naomi's really special to me and aaaahhhh...I just wanted to thank you."

"You're welcome. She's a very special lady," she said turning to leave.

"Hey can you aaaahhhh...give me an update of her condition?" Shit! What am I doing? I'm acting like a damn schoolboy. Get it together Jared, he said to himself.

Jaidyn's intelligent eyes looked right into his. "Her prognosis is good. The surgery was a success. We did have to have do a radical mastectomy but the good news is that the lymph nodes were benign. She will still have to undergo chemotherapy. She's a fighter but she'll need lots of help and prayer to deal with everything she is going through. M.D. Anderson has a support group for breast cancer survivors. I think it would be wise for her to attend a meeting as soon as she's feeling up to it. Although chemotherapy affects everyone differently, it is extremely difficult on the patient as well as the family and they'll need as much support as they can get."

Jaidyn's words became jumbled as Jared watched her sexy lips moving. "Does this girl have any idea what she's doing to me?" He asked the powers that be. Dammnn, I fucked up! When he tuned back in she was saying, "I don't see her going back to work anytime soon."

"Wow. Thank you Dr. Tyler."

Jaidyn smiled warmly realizing he was mocking her. She'd been speaking to him in the manner in which doctors did when they didn't have social interaction with the patient or their family. She giggled and changed her tone, "You're welcome. Why don't you get some rest. You look exhausted and Naomi doesn't need to be worried about you right now."

"Will do…And hey thanks again." He knew Jaidyn was right, if Naomi thought he was tired she would worry so he was going to head home to get some rest. Naomi was like a second mother to him and her family had become he and Julian's family since they'd been in Houston. He had every intention on standing beside her during this ordeal.

Jared walked back into Naomi's room to get his keys and found Naomi lying in bed awake. "Hey you're awake! I'm going to head home and let you get some rest. I'll be back later. I'll call before I come to see if you need anything."

"…Was that Jaidyn you were talking to in the hall?" She asked, her voice heavy with sleep.

"Yeah. She said you're doing fine but you need to rest so she's chasing me out of here." He said kissing her on the forehead, "So rest, I'll come by to see you later." Before he could get the words out of his mouth the drugs had called her back into a quiet slumber.

When Jared came out of Naomi's room he spotted Jaidyn sitting at the nurse's station writing in a chart. He walked over to the counter and leaned over and said, "Dr. Tyler can I speak to you for just a minute?"

"Sure! Just let me sign this chart." After signing the chart she walked around to the front of the nurse's station, sure he had more questions about Naomi.

Seeing her had awakened something in Jared. It was a desire he'd prayed that the Lord would take from him but there it was still burning a hole in his chest. He wanted to talk to her, touch her, just be around her.

"Be straight with me. Is she going to be ok?" Was all he could think of to ask.

Beneath his polite surface Jaidyn thought she sensed nervousness. Her eyes filled with compassion, "We're going to do everything in our power to help her."

Why does she have to look at me like that, he questioned. Why in the hell am I so weak for this woman? "What exactly does that mean?"

Jaidyn looked at him benevolently, "Why don't we have a seat in the lodge and I'll explain everything to you."

To Jared's surprise his heart was thumping so loudly it was ringing in his ears. That hadn't happened around a woman since he was in high school. "Can we talk about it over breakfast? My treat!" There it's out. That's what he really wanted, to be with her outside of this hospital.

Silence.

Jaidyn starred at him blankly surprised he even wanted to talk to her but more than that, surprised he'd consider sharing a meal with her. After their last encounter she had been left with the impression that he wanted nothing to do with her.

"I mean, I haven't eaten since yesterday and I'm starving." Man, you're batting zero, he said to himself.

She studied him thoughtfully. She had to be misreading him, she thought. Is he nervous? "Well, I need to check on another patient but if you can wait that sounds wonderful. How about the hospital cafeteria in about twenty minutes?"

"Uh..." he said still stumbling, "I'd like some real food if that's ok with you. I've been in Japan for two weeks and powdered eggs aren't what I had in mind."

Jaidyn laughed, he was definitely nervous. "Where did you have in mind?"

She still had that laugh that could melt ice, he thought, and still sensual beyond belief. "I'll let you pick," he said.

She didn't want to read more into his invitation or his uneasiness than there was. It was best if she left her assumptions about his anxiety to his concern for Naomi. He'd always been a quiet worrier. He was one of those people who liked to get all the information he could then figure out how to fix the problem. So it came as no surprise to her that he wanted to know as much as he could. "If you want more information about Naomi I will be glad to sit down with you after I've seen my next patient. You don't have to buy me breakfast."

"...This isn't about Naomi. I just want to buy an old friend breakfast... that's if she'll let me."

There was silence as she considered what he'd said and smiled. "An old-friend umm…," she mused trying to conceal a smile.

"I'll pick you up in front of the hospital in twenty minutes?"

"Ok," Jaidyn said, completely bewildered. He'd told her there was no way they could be friends, what had changed, she wondered.

"Oh and Jaidyn…," he said smiling. He stepped closer to her and fought the urge to kiss her inviting lips, "Thanks." He gave her a lingering kiss on her forehead and she shivered. Damn, his ass is fine as hell.

Keith was hoping to surprise Jaidyn by bringing her a bite to eat for breakfast. She'd worked crazy hours the past few days and he was feeling sorry for her. She'd gone to bed around 8:00 p.m. and had been getting up sometime during the night to attend to a sick patient. When he spotted her car he pulled into the space next to it. He had asked her numerous times to not park in the parking garage but as usual she hadn't listened to him. He'd told her how dangerous these things were for women but Jaidyn was stubborn and had a mind of her own. Before he climbed out of his car he made a mental note to speak to her about it again.

Jaidyn took a little longer than Jared expected. When she finally arrived in the lobby he was waiting patiently. "Sorry I took so long."

"No problem. My car is just right outside."

"Good, I'm starved."

"How's Mama's Kitchen sound?" He asked.

"That sounds wonderful. I haven't been there in…forever."

"I'm surprised you used to love that place."

I only loved it because I was with you, she thought.

Jared opened the door of his Hummer and helped her inside. Jaidyn smiled as she got in. Jared's ghetto'ed out car reminded her how different he was than he appeared to be. When in the business world he was professional, highly intelligent, ambitious, well groomed and very well spoken. He was the young, gifted black man that every company wanted working for them.

When you took him outside of the business environment he was a straight up homeboy. His entire demeanor was different. His speech changed, the clothes he wore were different, even the car he drove was different. His work car was a wide body Mercedes but his weekend car was a Hummer, it was his baby. The black on black SUV Hummer had twenty-four inch chrome rims, the inside had a DVD player, three TV screens, and a hell of a sound system.

Jaidyn used to refer to him as a modern day Dr. Jekyll and Mr. Hyde. His response was always the same, "I'll play the game but won't let the game play me." He played the game very well. Depending on which world you knew him from it was hard to imagine him in the other world.

He was one of those six-figured brotha's who hadn't forgotten where he'd come from or who helped him get there. He was deeply embedded in his roots. He believed in trying to help empower other black people. He'd been honored for his example to black youth as well as his ongoing contributions to the community. He'd been a mentor for 100 Black Men of America as long as she'd known him. He joined the organization when he was in high school. He was completely devoted to their mission. She could hear him saying, "I stood on a lot of shoulders and had a lot of people prop me up to get where I am. I have to give back." He was not only a strong, beautiful man he was also intelligent and his down to earth personality was an added prize.

Jared was also involved in a mentoring program through his church. The teenager he mentored was named Tye. He'd made it his mission to not only be Tye's mentor but to also be the father that Tye never had. She greatly respected and admired his dedication to his community.

The first thing Jared noticed when he climbed into the truck was her scent. He missed the sweet smell of the fragrance she wore. He missed her soft skin next to his, he missed holding her small slender hand. He missed the floral smell of her hair and how it tickled his nose when they spooned.

As Keith approached the front entrance of the hospital he spotted Jaidyn exiting the hospital laughing with someone. As he got closer he was able to make out who the man was. He couldn't believe what he was seeing. Jaidyn was getting in the car with Jared. What the hell, he thought. He'd felt sorry for her and it turns out her ass had been lying about a sick patient!

He watched them drive away. "Son of a bitch," he yelled. He turned around and went back to the parking garage. When he finally got to his car and got out of the garage they were no where in sight. He circled the entire area looking for them but they'd vanished.

"How's Tye," she asked once he got in the car.

"He's great. He's struggling a little bit with Chemistry right now but over all he's good...has Yasmine told you that he's sweet on Noelle?" Noelle was Yasmine's oldest daughter.

"No she hasn't."

"Every chance he gets he's trying to get me to take him over there. Noelle's playing hard to get but he's wearing her down."

Jaidyn laughed, "Make sure he respects my goddaughter." The ease of their conversation reminded her that their karma had always seemed to be intertwined.

"You don't have to worry about that. He's a good kid. He always asks about you, maybe I'll bring him by to see you some time."

Jared thought about the first time he met Jaidyn. It had been her beauty that had first attracted him to her but once he'd spoken with her he realized she was witty and down to earth. She was also one of those people who had every social grace she needed to adapt to any situation. Their conversation had depth. They sat and talked for hours like they'd known each other their entire lives, making them feel like old friends.

He'd never been one of those brotha's that had a hard time finding a woman or one that had to run game for a piece of ass, some hoochie was always in his face. But a good woman was hard to find. From the first time they'd had a conversation she had been that one that just fit. There was no pressure, no stress, and no drama. Their Christian and spiritual values were intertwined and their dedication to family and marriage were identical. She was the one and he'd known that since their first conversation.

Jaidyn had ordered her usual eggs, grits, toast, pan sausage, and large orange juice with ice. He watched her while she ate. She was so damn beautiful. He'd be lying if he didn't say that he loved everything about her sexy ass. From her deep dimpled smile and funny little laugh to the way her gray eyes softened when she looked at him.

He smiled. "What?" Jaidyn asked smiling back at him. Jared wasn't looking at her like a friend. He was looking at her the way a man looked at a woman.

"Nothing," he said diverting his eyes away from her. She studied him as she waited on him to respond. "I'd forgotten that you mixed your eggs and grits together before you ate them." He admitted.

"Why don't you try some?" She said offering him a spoon full. He allowed her to feed him and was surprised that it tastes so good. Jared looked at her seductively and she quickly pulled the spoon from his mouth. Ooohhh, his ass is too damn fine, she said to herself.

"Mmmmm! That is good. I wonder why I've never tried it before." He said looking deeply into her eyes and realizing what he loved most about her was the way he felt when he was with her. It just felt right. She knew him better than anyone. She was his best friend and he missed the hell out of her.

Chapter 24

Keith was sitting in front of the TV watching ESPN when Jaidyn walked into the house. She leaned over and kissed him, "Hey baby. How was your night?" Keith didn't answer but she didn't notice. She went into the bedroom to get a shower. She'd told Yasmine and the kids that she'd meet them at the Gallaria to go ice-skating.

When she finished her shower and got dressed she felt fresh and rejuvenated as she walked into the kitchen. Keith had sat the bag of breakfast tacos he'd gotten for her on the cabinet. She peered in the bag and returned to the living room, "Are these for me?" Although he didn't answer she thanked him and told him how sweet it was. She kneeled behind the couch, put her arms around his neck and kissed him on the cheek.

He moved her hands and sat forward. "What's up baby? Is there something wrong?" An image of *them together* ran through him and scared the hell out of him.

"What?" Jaidyn asked.

He turned on her like a raging bull with smoke coming out of his nostrils, "I saw you with his ass!"

Panic ran through her veins like ice cold water but she never stumbled or wavered, "What are you talking about? Saw me with who." Here we go with this bull shit again, she thought. She didn't feel like this today. She didn't have a clue what he was talking about but his accusations were driving her crazy. He'd been accusing her of fooling around so long she couldn't remember when it started or what had set it off. He wouldn't let up long enough to get over it. Every man that looked her way he wanted to know if she knew them. If she did he wanted to know if she'd slept with him. His jealousy had gotten on her last nerve. He couldn't possibly have known how childish he sounded

"You know what I saw. Don't play crazy."

She decided not to let Keith bait her in. "This isn't getting us anywhere. If you've got something to say you need to say it."

"I ain't no damn fool. I saw you leaving the hospital with him this morning."

She knew she was caught but if she tried to explain how innocent her breakfast with Jared was things would go from bad to worse. If he wanted an explanation he was going to have to spell it out for her and right now she just might deny it. Maybe she should take the approach men took, if you didn't talk to me or touch me it wasn't me. Regardless of what she said she knew a fight was inevitable and he was going to act like a damn fool.

"I don't have a clue what you're talking about." She said in a dismissive attitude. "I'm going to meet Yasmine and the kids. Do you want to come along?"

When he didn't answer she took that to mean no which surprised her because she didn't go anywhere without him trying to tag along. She kissed him on the cheek and picked up her keys. She wasn't supposed to meet Yasmine for another hour but she wanted to get out of there before Keith had the chance to blow up. She didn't feel like haggling over this subject with him. Her and Jared's breakfast had been extremely pleasant and he wasn't about to make her feel guilty. They'd sat for a little over two hours laughing and talking about life. There was nothing pressing or devious about their breakfast. Their past relationship or how they now felt about each other never came up. They simply sat like two old friends and caught up on what life was serving them at that very moment. Keith's insecurities were just that, his insecurities, and he'd have to live with them. She wasn't about to let him make something out of nothing. If she indulged in his temperamental Virgo tantrum it would only make things worse so the best thing to do was ignore him.

Chapter 25

By the time Yasmine and the kids arrived at the ice skating rink Jaidyn had decided she needed to tell Yasmine her secret. She couldn't keep this to herself. She needed to hear the words out loud and see someone else's reaction to her confession. There was no way she could tell anyone but Yasmine. She knew if she didn't see her today she would probably lose her nerve. Getting together had become more about her own desire to unburden herself than it was about seeing her oldest girlfriend. For years Yasmine had doubled as her friend and her therapist. Today she needed the therapist because she wasn't quite able to figure out why she felt so bubbly yet so guilty.

Yasmine and the kids were late as usual but Jaidyn took the time to think about her encounter with Jared. She was deep in thought when Yasmine and the kids finally showed up.

"Noelle I'm sick..."

"And tired!" Noelle said finishing her mother's sentence.

Jaidyn snickered under her breath but Yasmine didn't find anything funny and hit Noelle in the back of her head. "Alright...I can show you better than I can tell you." Noelle rolled her eyes when Yasmine turned her back.

The kids gave their Auntie Jai a hug then went to get their skates. Once they were on the ice Yasmine started talking. Jaidyn listened to how Noelle was at the age that she thought she knew everything and it was beginning to drive Yasmine crazy. The truth was that Noelle was exactly like her mother and Yasmine was having a hard time dealing with her grown up attitude coming back at her from her own child.

"I swear that child is giving me gray hair. No matter what I say she's always got something else to say. I've resorted to popping her in her mouth but that's not working. Through all the tears she still has to get her point across. I don't know where she gets it from."

"You don't," Jaidyn asked smiling.

"We were never disrespectful to our parents. When they said something that was it. There wasn't any discussion. We either did it or we got knocked out. These kids got it too easy."

"Give the poor girl a break, her hormones are going crazy right now."

"I've got her damn hormones. There's only room for one queen in my house and I'm it."

"If I remember correctly you were the same way the only difference is that you were smart enough to mumble from across the room or under your breath on the way out of the room." Jaidyn said giggling.

"That's bull and you know it. I was never disrespectful."

"Girl please! I remember your mother throwing that blue lamp at you because she couldn't get to you fast enough."

Yasmine started laughing, "That only happened once."

"That's because she broke the lamp."

"Mumh…I still have flashbacks about that ass whoopin!" They both broke into laughter. "You're little goodie two shoe ass don't know nothing about those type of whoopins."

"My Mama and Daddy didn't get a chance to whoop me, Joanna and Lance beat my butt enough for everybody. Lance's behind was borderline abusive."

"Ouh, girl do you remember that time we were running through the clothes racks in Weiners and Lance took the belt off the rack and beat our ass?" Yasmine asked.

"Girl Lance still acts like that. Joanna's kids know Uncle Lance doesn't play."

"That Lance was something else…You look great today. Things at home must be getting better."

Jaidyn shrugged, "Not really." They both looked over at the kids. Noelle had stopped skating to talk to a boy that looked about her age, Nicholas was trying to do tricks, and Nicolette had found a new group of friends that she was playing with. Jaidyn looked at her godchildren and wondered where the time had gone. They were growing up way too fast. Noelle had matured into a beautiful fourteen-year old young lady. Nicholas and Nicolette were almost six. Nicholas was a sweet quiet child but then again he didn't have much of a choice, Nicolette, Jaidyn's namesake, had always talked enough for the both of them. All three of them had their fathers paper bag brown complexion. Noelle was the only one so far that had her mother's African Queen beauty and shapely figure.

Seeing the kids brought back memories. She and Yasmine had planned out their entire lives. They were supposed to graduate together and go to the same college. They were going to have a double wedding and they were going to marry men that were best friends. They'd planned to have children at the same time so that they'd be like sisters and brothers but things hadn't worked out as they'd planned. Yasmine had opted to graduate from high school a year early and go away to college instead of attending the University of Houston like they'd planned. While Jaidyn decided to make Baylor University her school of choice. When Yasmine was in her second year at Xavier University she married Neal. Eight months latter she was pregnant with Noelle. When she finished school they both found jobs in Houston and returned to the city. Although Jaidyn adored Neal, Yasmine hated Keith and Neal wasn't all that friendly towards him either. Regardless of the choices they had made their friendship had stood the tests of time and remained strong.

Right now Jaidyn desperately needed that friendship. She contemplated how to approach her concerns with Yasmine. If anyone would understand, it would be her. One thing she never found when she went to Yasmine was condemnation, no matter what she'd done.

Yasmine looked at Jaidyn. Her eyes seemed to be sparkling, "So what's up with you?"

Her morning encounter had left her in good spirits. She replayed the scene from breakfast in her head. Played it once, played it again and said, "I had breakfast with Jared this morning."

"You did what?"

Jaidyn gave her a cowardly smile and averted her eyes, "It was nice."

"Nice?"

"Yeah. It was...I don't know...just nice." That was an outright lie. Breakfast with Jared was better than nice, it was...incredible, she thought. Instantaneously Jaidyn knew why she felt so guilty. It wasn't breakfast with an old friend. It was the revelation of what she'd been hiding and denying. What she'd been living with all balled up inside of her, Jared was her happily ever after. He was her meant to be. Tears burned the back of her eyes and she blinked quickly.

Yasmine's face contorted, "What?" She asked concerned. Jaidyn shook her head and continued to wildly blink the tears away. Yasmine sat quietly waiting for her to explain. She knew Jaidyn needed her to listen more than she needed her to talk.

Jaidyn finally spoke, "Do you remember what you asked me before I got married?"

"What?" Yasmine asked wrinkling her brow.

Still slightly discombobulated by the revelation she said, "You asked if it was possible to be in love with two men at the same time."

Jaidyn definitely had her attention now. "Yeah. I remember."

"I think I finally have an answer."

"Alright?"

"I don't think you can, but I think it's possible to love two men at the same time."

"What?"

"I've finally come to terms with how I feel about him."

Yasmine was dumbfounded. What in the hell was this girl talking about? She stopped watching the kids and gave Jaidyn her full attention. She didn't want to miss anything she had to say. She'd thought that Jaidyn had dealt with these demons but sounds like she was wrong. When it came to Jared, Yasmine had the hardest time figuring Jaidyn out. Maybe it was because Jaidyn had the hardest time figuring herself out.

"What does that mean?"

Jaidyn looked at Yasmine then back at the kids. "I guess it means I know the difference in loving someone and being in love with someone."

Yasmine wasn't sure where she was going with this. She was going to have to break it down to her like she was a child because she wasn't making sense. "What exactly does that have to do with Jared?"

Jaidyn considered the question carefully before she answered. She knew if she let the words escape her mouth there was no going back. There was no denying it, "I'm still in love with him."

"What?" Yasmine asked puzzled. Jaidyn turned and looked at her and Yasmine repeated her question as if she hadn't understood what Jaidyn had said, "What?"

Jaidyn looked her straight in the eyes and repeated herself, "I'm in love with Jared." She looked back at the kids and allowed her words to soak in.

Yasmine was still looking at her as if she had been speaking a foreign language. She took in a deep breath as if she was inhaling Jaidyn's confession then said, "Let me get this straight…You think you're in *love* with Jared Mitchell?" Yasmine drew out the words as if she was speaking to someone from another country. This wasn't earthshattering news to Yasmine she had suspected it but she was still dumbfounded by the confession. As if she was still processing it Yasmine said, *"In love with Jared!"*

"Lord knows I care deeply for Keith but I got into this marriage without resolving my feelings for Jared. Deep down I knew I shouldn't have agreed to marry Keith but I guess I was afraid to be alone."

Yasmine took her by the arm and directed her to a bench. She was completely astonished. What in the hell was this girl thinking. Didn't I tell her this shit before she married that fool, she thought.

"I'm in love with Jared and have been as long as I've known him. Being married to Keith hasn't changed that. I see Jared and I melt. It's incomprehensible to me. I'm trying to do what's right but when I see him or spend time with him I want to walk away from this charade I call a marriage. I don't know what I'm doing anymore but I know I'm tried of running from what I feel."

"Back up a minute, what makes you think you're in love with him?"

"Everything. I thought I was passed it but I guess I was scared."

"Girl, you've got to break this shit down to me like I was a child. When Jared showed up at the church why didn't you walk out of that church with him? What were you afraid of?"

"I guess I was afraid of having no control over how I felt. There is nothing comparable to how I feel about him. He gives me something no one else ever has. It's nothing he does. It's just him. He's amazing. I love everything about him. The way he makes me feel, the way he thinks, his laugh, his smile. I love the way he gets inside my head but most of all I love his willingness to put up with my shit. He's unbelievable…and I love the way he makes love to me…" She confessed with conviction.

"What?" Yasmine broke in. "Y'all having sex?"

"I wish!" Jaidyn said with a conniving smile. Yasmine had brought a memory to the surface that had been hovering underneath her subconscious. Jaidyn allowed the memory as well as a dream she'd had to run rapid through her mind for a minute. She looked back at Yasmine when she was finished fantasizing. Yasmine was looking at her with that I know you ain't considering it look.

"I think about what I walked away from all the time. I was just scared. Keith was safe and stable. Jared was unpredictable or should I say we were unpredictable when we were together."

"Dick will do that to you!" Yasmine said sarcastically.

"Mmmmm…Especially that one." Jaidyn muttered.

"So…what's changed? Why the new epiphany?"

"I've changed I guess." A show of uncertainty flickered across her face. "I couldn't forgive myself for what I had done and I couldn't understand how he could forgive me or want to be with me."

A puzzled look crossed Yasmine's face, "Forgive you for what?"

Shame shadowed Jaidyn's eyes. "I had an abortion." She confessed.

"*Ooooooohhhhh Jai!*" Yasmine paused for a moment taking in a deep breath. "Why didn't you tell me." She said with her voice was full of compassion for her friend.

That was a good question. Yasmine had been the keeper of her secrets almost her entire life but this was one of those secrets that Jaidyn thought she'd never tell anyone. It was a humiliating situation she'd hope to take to her grave. "I don't know." Jaidyn said looking down at her hands for a long moment then back at Yasmine. "When he found out he was really hurt. He didn't want to have anything to do with me."

"You didn't discuss it with him before you did it?"

Her eye's misted over, *"No,"* she said with her voice cracking. Yasmine placed her hand on her back as she continued. "You were right when you said he's everything I ever wanted. No one has ever had this affect on me." Jaidyn paused gathering her thoughts, "He makes me float. You know what I mean?"

Yasmine listened intently. She always had all the answers but this had knocked her for a loop. She had never heard Jaidyn speak so passionately about anything except being a doctor.

Yasmine's mind was going full throttle. I can't believe this. That's why they broke up… They've got to be seeing each other more than she's saying. I wonder how long this has been going on? Jared's ass has had his damn feet under my dinner table at least twice a week, why hasn't he mentioned it? …Maybe he told Neal. I'm going to kick Neal's ass if he knew and didn't tell me…wait a minute…why did it take Jaidyn so long to figure this shit out?

Jaidyn let out a genuine laugh. "What?" Yasmine asked.

"Isn't it ironic how the advice you've been giving people your entire life turns out to be the worst advise in the world when you apply it to your own situation? Do you know how many times I've said, 'don't nothing help you get over one man like another man.' Now I realize it only camouflages the how you really feel."

"Why did it take you so long to figure this out and why did you marry Keith to begin with? Didn't I tell you…" Yasmine stopped herself and let out a heavy sigh.

Jaidyn considered both questions before she answered. She flashed a weary smile at Yasmine, "Marrying Keith was momentary insanity I guess. I never considered the price I'd pay for saying I do."

Yasmine exhaled heavily, "Tell me what happened at breakfast?"

"Nothing really. We talked for about two hours but nothing happened. We didn't discuss anything important."

"Am I missing something? How long has this been going on?"

"You're not missing anything. I've told you everything."

"What does Jared think about this revelation?"

"I haven't told him but I'm sure he knows. He's always read me so well." She said smirking. "He knows what I'm thinking before I do."

Yasmine shook her head. "Do you have any idea how you sound?"

"Yeah, like I'm in love with him."

Yasmine shook her head in disbelief. They sat quietly for a few minutes while Yasmine replayed everything that Jaidyn had just told her.

"So what are your plans?" Yasmine inquired.

"I don't have any. I guess I've made my bed and I have to lie in it. There's really nothing I can do, I'm married."

"Have you thought about leaving Keith?" Before Jaidyn could answer Yasmine was throwing another question at her. "What the fuck are you going to do?"

Barely audible she said, "I don't know."

"Have you considered what they both bring to the table?"

"Yeah. They each bring something different."

"I've heard what Jared brings but what does Keith bring?"

"...Heartache."

"Shit Jai. That's deep. What are you going to do?"

"I don't know." She said shaking her head. "All I know is I've got to get control of my feelings before they take control of me and I end up having an affair."

"An affair? You're already doing that! You can have two different kinds of affairs, sexual or emotional. It would be better if you were having a sexual affair. They're easier to handle. They're strictly physical. The kind of affair you're having is an emotional one. For women that's the worse kind. First it's emotional and sooner or later it ends up sexual. Then you end up not wanting your husband to touch you."

Jaidyn looked at Yasmine in surprise. She hated it when she read her mind. How did she know that the sight of Keith made her sick? And when he touched her she wanted to vomit. "Come on, you can't be serious. I had breakfast with him once," Jaidyn said, faking disbelief.

"Let me ask you something…be honest…do you love Keith?' Jaidyn's silence answered the question for her. "It doesn't matter what you're doing with Jared. The point is you're emotionally unavailable to Keith."

Jaidyn smiled, "Alright Dr. Randall!"

Yasmine laughed along with her, "This session will be $150.00 and I don't take checks."

"Put it on my bill," Jaidyn said still laughing.

"You ever asked yourself what people do when their reality falls short of their destiny?"

Yasmine thought about her question and then about Jared. Since he and Neal had become good friends, he was always at the house. Although he was dating Faith he never hid how he felt about Jaidyn. "Jai, you need to talk to Jared. I bet he feels the same way you do," Yasmine encouraged. "The two of you can figure this whole thing out."

Jaidyn flashed her a weary smile hoping she was right but the thought made her feel selfish and greedy.

"It's not too late for you to end your marriage. You guys don't have kids yet and you don't really have anything to fight over."

"I feel so horrible for Keith. None of this is fair to him. It isn't like I married him completely unaware of what I was doing."

Chapter 26

Jaidyn arrived home to find that Keith seemed to have snapped out of his mood. When she climbed into bed she was surprised that he nestled up next to her and asked her about her afternoon with Yasmine. She quickly went into his arms welcoming his warmth.

While she was talking he got out of bed, lit a candle and put on a CD. Although she was tired she was all too happy to oblige in his pursuit. While he was putting on the CD she snuck up behind him, put her arms around him and ran her tongue softly down his back. When he turned she dropped to her knees, quickly freed the "Dicktator" from his boxers and took him into her mouth while he was still limp. She covered as much of it as she possibly could and he quickly grew inside of her mouth. She kissed, licked and sucked the "Dicktator" until he could no longer stand the pressure.

Keith hadn't expected her to be so enthusiastic about giving it up, but as usual she rose to the occasion and had damn near robbed the "Dicktator" of all it's treasure. Keith knew better than to let her take control right off the bat. She knew just what to do to bring him to his knees. He had never been able to stand up to the pressure she applied. He'd crumbled every time and tonight was no different. He'd be the first to admit that his wife had his ass whooped. No matter how many other woman he had sex with this was the best piece of ass he'd ever had.

Jaidyn freed the "Dicktator" and pulled Keith towards the bed. Keith shook his head and pushed her against the wall. With her back against the wall he spread her legs and began performing cunnilingus on her. She had come to dread this part of their escapades. He was rougher than she liked. His nibbles were actual bites. His tongue an invasive probe. It wasn't unpleasant just insensitive and raw. As he bit and licked the wet spot between her legs he caressed her breast. Once he tasted the juices of her orgasm he stood up and picked her up. With her back still against the wall, she wrapped her legs around his waist and allowed him to enter her. With every rise and fall "The Palace" put a death grip on the "Dicktators" head. Taking control again she slowed her falls and refused to give the "Dicktator" open access to "The Palace." She allowed his head to peer into the gates but wouldn't allow him completely inside the walls. When she finally gave the "Dicktator" full access Keith moaned with pleasure as the "Dicktator" exploded, spilling his jewels onto "The Palace's" floor.

Keith was far from being done with her. He carried her to the bed and put her down. He rolled her onto her stomach and pulled her butt into the air. Although she never complained he knew that the rear-entry position was the one she disliked the most. He was gentle when he entered her but once "The Palace" was warmly lubricated again he manhandled her. The force of the "Dicktator" was hard, rough, almost brutal. Jaidyn struggled to get away from him but he wouldn't let up. She begged him to stop but he only got rougher. He fucked her so hard his balls made a clapping sound as they hit her.

Keith reached around her and played with the little man in the boat. Jaidyn pushed his hand away and he forcefully pushed his fingers into her mouth, making her taste her own essence. Her ass would know better than to try to fuck over him again he thought. "Who is the got damn man now? I know that fool couldn't put it down like this!" He said. If his wife was going to act like a ho than he was going to treat her like one, he thought. Sometimes you have to remind these ho's who the king of the jungle is and straight up jungle fucked the shit out of them.

Chapter 27

Jaidyn passed an unfamiliar car with a female driver sitting in it as she pulled into her driveway. "She must be waiting on someone," Jaidyn said to herself. Before Jaidyn could unbuckle her seat belt and get out of her car the woman was standing on the driveway waiting on her. There was something vaguely familiar about the young woman but Jaidyn couldn't place her right off.

"Hi." Jaidyn said extra friendly, hoping the girl would give her a clue as to where she knew her from. "Is there something I can help you with?"

"Hi Dr. Tyler. I'm Chevon Ramsey. Is it ok if I come in and talk to you for a few minutes? It's about Keith." Chevon wanted to get right to the point. There was no reason to drag this out. She had been over it in her mind a thousand times.

"You look very familiar. Have we met?" Jaidyn asked feeling uncomfortable.

"My father's one of your patients." Chevon replied easing Jaidyn's nervous.

"I see." Jaidyn said smiling at her. Jaidyn unlocked the front door and stepped inside. A look of confusion crossed her face, "I thought you said this was about Keith."

"It is."

"Okay.," Jaidyn said questioningly. "Come on in. Why don't you have seat on the sofa." Jaidyn directed as she sat her briefcase in the study. "Can I get you something to drink?" Jaidyn called from the study.

"No thank you," Chevon called back.

Jaidyn came into the room smiling warmly. That won't last long, Chevon thought. By the time she finished her story a heaviness gripped Jaidyn. Although Chevon apologized over and over Jaidyn felt like a fool. She'd always known in her heart that she wasn't the only woman in Keith's life but she'd never suspected he had a child. She'd ignored all the warning signs and they'd been right in her face. She took a minute to digest everything that she'd just been told.

Chevon knew exactly how Jaidyn must have been feeling. She herself had felt it when she found out what she thought was real was all a lie. The first time she saw Keith and Jaidyn together she wanted to curl up into a little ball and die. Keith had looked straight at her, grabbed Jaidyn's hand and walked past her like he didn't know her. At that moment something inside her twisted, turned, and broke. She couldn't believe it was happening. She'd told him the week before that she was pregnant and they'd started making plans. She'd thought about going off on his ass but she played it off because she was with her girlfriends and they were waiting to see her act a fool. She remembered wondering how could he do this to her and his unborn child.

The day after she saw them Keith called her to tell her that he'd asked Jaidyn to marry him and she'd said yes. After that she'd found out all she could about Jaidyn and tried to contact her several times to tell her about the baby, but Keith had always stopped her. After they were married she'd gone as far as to sit outside their house hoping to get up enough nerve to go knock on the door. She'd seen them again at Copeland's and was going to talk to her but Keith interfered. The last time their paths crossed Jaidyn was her fathers' doctor and that was when she decided she had to tell her the truth.

Chevon's familiar face finally registered in Jaidyn's mind. She remembered seeing her arguing with Keith at Copeland's. Her intuition had told her there was more to their argument than Keith had said but she'd brushed the feelings aside. She'd also seen her sitting outside the house several times but hadn't paid much attention to her. This bitch has been stalking me, she thought. I thought that she was waiting on a neighbor and all along she was looking for me. Jaidyn's blood began to boil. How dare she come to me with this bull shit.

> *Lawd, please keep me from putting my hands around this bitch's throat.*

Jaidyn's feelings were hurt but when she opened her mouth all that came out was anger. "*You need to get out my house with this bull shit,*" Jaidyn said, pointing to the door.

Chevon stared at Jaidyn as if she didn't understand the words that were coming out of her mouth. "I'm sorry," Chevon said softly.

"*Sorry! You dun lost yo muthafuckin' mind,*" Jaidyn yelled. "This is all Keith's fault."

"*You know what? You need to get the fuck away from me before I...*" Jaidyn stopped mid sentence as recognition twisted through her mind with the force and destruction of a tornado.

Chevon had done what she'd come there to do but her feet would not move. She had not expected Jaidyn to respond like this. She'd met her several times and couldn't have imagined her being anything but kind.

"Ramsey...Otis Ramsey...that's your father?" Chevon's head bobbed, realizing that Jaidyn was putting two and two together.

"*Oh my God!*" Jaidyn said as if the wind had just been knocked out of her. "Otis Ramsey, was in my office last week. *Ooooohhhhh my God!*" She said again trying to gather her thoughts and pull herself together. "K.J." Jaidyn said the child's name as if she were asking a question.

Chevon's head bobbed again, "Keith Jr."

Jaidyn sat down on the couch trying her best to gather what small amount of dignity she had left. Otis Ramsey was one of her favorite patients. His grandson K.J. and his wife, Betty, accompanied him to every visit. A tear tickled down Jaidyn's cheek.

"I'm sorry." Chevon said as she studied the floor. "I told Keith I was pregnant the week before he asked you to marry him. Until then I thought I was the only one. That's when he told me about you. He said he was going to ask you to marry him and begged me to have an abortion. When I wouldn't he said he didn't want anything to do with the baby or me. I swear I didn't know anything about you until then." She tried to explain.

"Why are you just now telling me this?" Jaidyn asked trying her best to keep the tears that were flooding the back of her eyes from falling.

"I don't want him if that's what you're wondering." Chevon said as tears started rolling down her face. Chevon paused as if there was something else she wanted to say but didn't know if she should. "Last week at my daddy's visit, my parents said K.J. was whining because he was hungry and you gave him a bag of chips out of your lunchbox."

All of a sudden Jaidyn had an epiphany and finished her sentence for her. "K.J. saw a picture inside my box!" Jaidyn made a sound as if all the air had been knocked out of her. Another tear fell, "He pointed to it and said, 'da da'." This time Jaidyn couldn't stop the tears from flowing.

Chevon finished the story for her. "My parents said you told him that that was your husband. But when you showed the picture to them they knew. My mama wanted to tell you right then about Keith's scandalous ass but my daddy stopped her." Jaidyn had smiled at the child and thought he was mistaken.

Chevon's heart ached for her. "Since you've been my father's doctor, I've gotten to see another side of you. You weren't the evil person Keith made you out to be." Jaidyn looked at her as if to say what did he say. Chevon understood her questioning eyes and said, "He said he didn't want K.J. around you. He said that you were mean to children because you didn't like them. He said he didn't trust you"

Chevon could see the hurt in Jaidyn's eyes and now she was sorry that she'd ever come there. Her confession had been much more informative than she'd intended. She'd given Jaidyn a blow-by-blow account of her entire relationship with Keith and she didn't know why. There was something about Jaidyn that made her comfortable, something that made her want to confide in her. It was as if Jaidyn had used a can opener to open her up and everything inside her came pouring out.

She had first noticed Jaidyn's ability to pull the words right out of someone when she was treating her father. Jaidyn had come into his hospital room like she was an old friend rather than his doctor. Before she discussed his health they talked easily about the Green Bay football game. Then she'd moved to grandchildren. She'd used the two things he loved the most, Green Bay football and his grandchildren, to get him to relax. She'd simply eased her way into the sensitive subject of colon cancer. It was hard for everyone in the room not to immediately like her. She had treated him with the respect and dignity of a friend rather than the harsh, abrasive bedside manner of so many doctors. She was very impressive.

Now she had done the exact same thing to Chevon. It wasn't anything she had said, Chevon thought. Although she was very upset she had still been a thoughtful listener and seemed to have carefully considered every word Chevon had said. That alone had made Chevon tell her more than she had intended.

All kinds of bells and whistles where going off in Jaidyn's head. She'd hugged and kissed little K.J. before he'd left the office last Tuesday but she'd never suspected. "Let me get this straight. Your parents had no idea I was Keith's wife?"

Chevon shook her head, "But they knew he was married."

"How old is he?"

"Thirteen months."

Jaidyn's eyes narrowed on her, "You've known who I was all this time."

Chevon knew it was a rhetorical question but she felt compelled to say something. "I'm sorry. You don't deserve what he's doing to you."

Jaidyn looked stunned as she caught Chevon's words, "What he's doing to me?...Is there more?"

"With a man like Keith there is always more."

Jaidyn's mind was in overload and she wasn't sure she wanted to hear anymore but she charged forward. "What else is there?"

"You'll have to ask Keith. I came here to tell you about our son."

Jaidyn had perfected the ability to stay calm, levelheaded and rational during times of high stress. As a doctor it was something she had learned but she was losing the ability to apply it to this situation. She momentarily lost her cool and yelled, "What else is going on?" Realizing her tone she fought to regain her composer. She tried to incorporate the techniques she used when dealing with grief stricken patients. "I'm sorry. Can you please just tell me the rest."

Tears continued to roll down Chevon's cheeks, "Keith has been sleeping with Zaria. She's one of my so-called friends."

Now things were becoming clearer. This wasn't about K.J. or what he was doing to her. This was about Chevon getting back at Keith for fucking with her friend. Who the hell does this tramp think she is coming in my house with this shit, Jaidyn thought.

The uncomfortable quietness was getting to Chevon. "I'm sorry I swear I never wanted to hurt you. I didn't know anything about you until it was too late."

Jaidyn wanted her out of her house as soon as possible. The sight of her was making Jaidyn nauseated. Her stomach was in knots and she could feel a migraine coming on but she still had a million questions. "How old are you?" Jaidyn asked in a nasty tone.

"Twenty-two."

"Does Keith help you?"

"Yes. He pays for day care, buys all K.J.'s clothes, and pays our rent. He says he doesn't want his child growing up in the projects."

That tit-bit of information was more than Jaidyn could handle. "That's it," Jaidyn said holding up her hand, "Don't..." Jaidyn started to say as Keith walked through the front door.

"Hey," Keith said as he put his keys down on the table. Jaidyn's face was white as a sheet and she looked at him like she wanted to go upside his head.

"What's going on here?" He asked with an attitude.

Jaidyn's gray eyes locked on him like a heat-seeking missile. *"I know you didn't!"* She said sounding more pissed than hurt. He couldn't believe he'd walked into the middle of this bull shit. Where in the hell had Chevon parked her car he wondered, cause it wasn't in the driveway. If it had been there was no way he would have walked his ass into the middle of this shit.

Meshell

He couldn't believe this shit was going down like this. This bitch needs a good old fashion ass whoopin' he said to himself.

"Didn't what?" He asked indigent.

Jaidyn's head snapped back in his direction. I don't believe this mofo. She looked at him as if she didn't understand his question. Keith got the message, "Look I'm not fixing to deal with this bull shit."

"Keith you can cut the act. I told her everything," Chevon said.

Keith immediately went into defensive mode. "Look I am not going to deal with the chaos. You want to believe this tramp." He said looking Chevon up and down. "That's on you!" He said picking his keys up and heading back out the front door.

Jaidyn closed the front door, locked it and slid down the back of it. She was finally alone and able to have a bonafide breakdown all by herself. The tears were quick and disorienting. They'd seemed to be firmly rooted somewhere deep inside her and she couldn't find a way to turn them off. Her head was pounding so badly it was making her want to throw up. She got up and ran towards the toilet. She barley made it before everything she'd eaten that day came up. Vomiting almost seemed to help her head stop pounding.

She went to the medicine cabinet, pulled out a bottle of Motrin, twisted the top off and dropped two pills into her hand. Deciding two wouldn't kill the pain she drop another one into the palm of her hand. Popping the pills into her mouth she turned on the sink faucet and put her mouth under it, washing the pills down.

With her head still pounding she went back in her room and lay across her bed. She felt dishonored, disrespected, shamed. She felt like a fool. She'd been a good wife to this man, why would he do this to her. It was as if the more he hurt her the more she tried to love him. She shook her head in disbelief of her own stupidity.

She got up and began pacing the room. Her mind racing as she started trying to rationalize the entire situation. Number one, Chevon has a child that she says is Keith's, but that isn't a proven fact. The bitch could be lying. "First thing we need to do is get a blood test," she thought. Number two, if this child wasn't his why is he paying her bills? Maybe that's another one of her lies. Number three, I deserve what I'm getting. After all I am married to one man and in love with another. Maybe this was Satan's little revenge, his pay back. Number four, shit there is no number four. No matter how much I try to rationalize this shit the fact is, his ass is lying and has been all this time. "He's a sorry sack of shit!" She screamed through tear drenched eyes.

Looking back I guess I've always known Keith was a two-timing, self-centered son of a bitch. Lawd knows I would be justified in leaving him after all the heartache he's sent me through. He's hurt me more then once and I won't take anymore of his BS. "*Shit!*" She yelled.

Chapter 28

Two hours later Keith was unlocking the front door. Jaidyn watched him as he closed the door and dropped his keys on the table.

Father give me strength…on second thought don't because I just might wrap my hands around his lying throat and choke his ass to death.

"How could you? Do you have no shame? That girl is still a child. You're thirty-seven fucking years old. What were you thinking?" Was the first thing she said to him.

He wasn't ready to have this conversation with her. He needed more time to figure out what he should do. They were so far from where he wanted them to be. He knew he was going to wreck their future if he kept running from his past. There had to be a way out of this. He needed time to think. He couldn't believe this trick had walked into his house and dropped this shit on his wife like this. "Baby that tramp is just pissed off because I don't want her ass."

"Keith, I'm not ready to have this conversation with you. I can't honestly tell you that I will be anytime soon. Knowing you've been cheating on me all these months is hard enough, but to think that you have another family is more then I can deal with right now."

"She came over here to cause trouble. She came onto me and I told her I was married. She's trying' to get back at me. Her ass has been straight up stalking me…."

"Are you saying this is all a lie? This baby isn't yours? You haven't been taking care of her and that child since he's been in this world?"

Jaidyn looked straight into his eyes. She wanted him to look her in the face and lie to her. But his eyes shifted away from her as he lied, "Of course it's not mine. I never slept with that tramp." He had lied to her so many times she knew the signs.

"So if we get a DNA test there is no way this child is going to be yours?"

"Didn't I just say that I never slept with that tramp. I can't believe this shit." He said forcefully.

Jaidyn studied the floor as he continued. She finally held up her hand, "Stop," she said. "The sound of your damn voice pisses me off."

"Are you going to let this skeezer walk in our house and run game on you like this?"

"I want you out of this damn house, now!"

"I'm not going anywhere until we straighten this out!" He yelled.

"I don't think there's anything to get straight. You're a lying, cheating, self-centered ass hole. Why don't you try being a man and tell the truth instead of lying all the damn time."

"Baby I'm not going to lie to you. You don't understand how much I love you."

"Don't give me that shit. You don't know what love is! I'm not fixing to get myself upset over this nonsense."

"Honey I'm sorry."

If he says another fucking word to me I swear I'm going to jump on him. "If I hear 'I'm sorry' one more time I'm going to lose it. How hard is it for you to tell the truth? How hard is it to give me an ounce of honesty? I'm tired of you playing these games. I'm trying to love you but you…" realizing what she'd just said Jaidyn hesitated.

Keith heard her too. His eyes darkened and narrowed on her as he looked at her. "Trying to love me? You're my fuckin' wife! What the fuck do you mean trying to love me?"

"You know what I meant. Don't turn this around," she said getting her purse and keys.

"No. I know what the fuck you meant, I know what you said…where are you going?"

"As far away from you as possible," she said.

Keith grabbed Jaidyn by the arm. "I'm not through talking to you yet."

Jaidyn looked down at his hand on her arm then back up at him. She tried to pull her arm way and he tightened his grip. Jaidyn swung her purse and hit him across the head. In a matter of seconds she'd gone so crazy on him that she scared the hell out of herself. "You ever put your muthafuckin' hands on me again I'll kill you." Jaidyn said picking up her purse and keys.

After Jaidyn had driven away she could hear her mother saying, "Baby, accept your defeats with the grace of a woman not the grief of a child." "How do I do that Mama," she asked aloud?

She was tired of the struggles of this marriage. She was too drained to cry and too weak to fight for it. She'd refused to admit it to herself or anyone else but below the surface, under the smile she tried to wear daily, depression was beginning to fester and was doing silent damage. She was trying to snap out of it but she was beginning to realize as long as she was in this situation it was going to be next to impossible.

Chapter 29

The smell of food surrounded Jaidyn as soon as she stepped inside Yasmine's front door. She looked down at her watch and realized it was dinnertime. The kid's schedules combined with Yasmine and Neal's work schedules didn't allow Yasmine's family to sit down to dinner together every night; however, Yasmine insisted that they sit down to dinner as a family at least three times a week and of course tonight was one of those nights.

"I didn't mean to disrupt your dinner." Jaidyn told Neal as he led her into the dining room.

"Now you know you're always welcome. We're just getting ready to sit down. Why don't you join us?"

"No thanks, I've already eaten," she said trying to sound upbeat but a show of exhaustion was on her face.

When she entered the dinning room Yasmine was just sitting down. She invited her to eat with them but Jaidyn declined, giving her the same excuse she had given Neal. She'd been starving before her encounter with Chevon but had since lost her appetite. Jaidyn sat down in the adjacent family room. She attempted to act as if nothing was wrong as she engaged in idle conversation with the kids and Neal. The kids absolutely adored their Auntie Jai and never felt like they got to see enough of her.

As the kids bombarded her with the latest things happening in their lives Yasmine remained quiet, occasionally eyeing Jaidyn and urging the kids to finish their dinner. The more Jaidyn talked to the kids the more convinced Yasmine became that something was wrong. She took special note of Jaidyn's attempts to act upbeat. Jaidyn couldn't hide heartache behind a smile with her. When you had been friends as long as they had you instinctively knew when the other was upset.

The longer Yasmine sat listening and watching her, the more pissed off she got. It had to be Keith. She lost her appetite and excused herself from the table. She asked Neal to finish up with the kids and asked Jaidyn to join her in the study. Yasmine closed the door behind them and asked, "Do you want to talk about it?"

Jaidyn had known as soon as she stepped into the dinning room and looked at Yasmine that she'd made a mistake coming there. Yasmine always read her like a book and today was no different. She knew Yasmine knew something was up because her attitude had changed from pleasant to perplexed. On one hand she wasn't ready to tell anyone about all Keith's lies but on the other hand she was anxious to get this off her chest. She wanted to come clean not only with Yasmine but with herself. She wanted to face this with her eyes open. She did not want to hide behind another lie. She had to accept what she knew was the truth, Keith was a lying, cheating dog. She knew if she told Yasmine that she'd have to hear the dreaded 'I told you so.' Yasmine believed in tough love and Jaidyn knew she wouldn't sugar coat any advice she gave. So she tried taking the high road, "There's nothing to talk about. I just dropped by to check in on you guys."

Different day, the same old shit, Yasmine thought to herself. "Who do I look like, Sally Sponge Head," Yasmine asked rolling her eyes. "Haven't you had enough of his shit...what has he done this time ...Let's get this over with because we both know as soon as he calls your cell phone you're going to run home to him."

"Don't start," Jaidyn said a little stronger than she'd intended.

"Hu*mmm! Don't get an attitude with me. I ain't the one fuckin' over you,*" Yasmine peered at her for a long time. Jaidyn's eyes were puffy, she could tell she had been crying. Keith had broken her down, literately drained the life out of her. She used to fix herself up, but for the past few months she looked tired and miserable all the time. Her hair was always pulled up in that damn ponytail and the little bit of make up she used to wear, she'd stopped wearing all together.

The tension in the room was thick, "Let's just drop it." Jaidyn said.

Yasmine softened her tone trying not to add to Jaidyn's issues, "Alright, have it your way. Just tell me when we like him, when we hate him, and when we need to kill him and dig a hole."

Jaidyn laughed, "I'll do that." The room began to close in on Jaidyn. She needed some air before she told Yasmine everything.

Before Jaidyn could get out of the room Yasmine hugged her and tears came gushing out. Everything that had been happening came pouring out of her. Jaidyn wanted to drown in her own misery. Yasmine sat quietly holding her hand, rubbing her back, listening as she cried and told her about how Chevon had shown up at the house. How Keith had continued to lie and tried to deny everything. She told her about Zaria. She told her how she had been checking his cell phone messages while he was in the shower and someone named Shelbi had been leaving messages saying she was horny as hell and needed to see him. She told her how Lance had seen him at lunch with Alexia, one of his friend's younger sister. And how when she asked him about it he claimed she was a potential client. She told her how she was always finding phone numbers in his pockets and how they'd be out together and he'd give women his business card. She told her how he'd been behaving lately. How rough he had treated her during sex after he saw her with Jared. She told her how she and her mother were having lunch at the Cheesecake Factory and saw Markel. He was having lunch alone so they invited him to eat with them. When she told Keith he told her to keep her ass away from Markel. She told her how he'd trip every time she got home five minutes late.

Jaidyn was a complete wreck. Yasmine wanted to wrap her arms around her best friend and make all this go away. "What do you want to do?" Yasmine asked sympathetically.

"I don't know. What am I supposed to do?" Jaidyn asked still wiping her nose.

Jaidyn's weak pathetic attitude pissed Yasmine off. "Don't be a damn fool. Leave his ass! You know what he's doing so if you're not going to do anything about it you need to stop sneaking around looking for trouble. All you're doing is hurting yourself."

"But..."

"There are no buts. You don't need him. You deserve better! But you've got to make up your mind that you don't want to be treated like this."

There was an uncomfortable silence before Jaidyn said, "I wish you could go kick his ass for me."

"I can arrange it," Yasmine said smiling at her. "You need to get yourself together, stop this crying and handle your business. When you've done all that you can you can't let Keith get the best of you. He's only going to treat you like he knows he can. If he can't treat you like you want to be treated you need to leave his sorry ass."

"I know."

Yasmine could tell that Jaidyn was mentally and physically drained. She retrieved a blanket from the closet and suggested Jaidyn try to rest for a couple of hours.

Meshell

Before Jaidyn closed her eyes she said, *"I've got my hand in Your hand. You know where you're taking me. Be light and strength to me Father."*

Chapter 30

"Hey son," Mama Nat said. "What are you doing out so late?"

"Hey Ma." Keith said kissing her on the forehead.

"I was just about to have some sweet potato pie and a glass of milk. You want some?"

"Sure," while Ms. Tyler was getting the pie Keith took a seat at the kitchen table. "Jai and I had a fight. She left the house in a rage. I think she's going to leave me this time."

"Stop talking that nonsense son. After she cools off she'll be fine. Jaidyn loves you."

Between bites of his mother's sweet potato pie Keith told her how Chevon had wronged him. "When Chevon told me she was pregnant I panicked. I asked her to have an abortion but she refused. I knew if Jaidyn found out she would leave me. I wasn't ready to get married but it seemed like the only answer at the time. I did what I thought was right by Chevon and paid all her doctor's bills. I thought when the baby was born I'd pay child support and that would be it. But when she went into labor she called me and asked me to come to the hospital. I waited until the next day to go see her. When I walked in the room she was just about to give birth. When K. J. was born I was standing right there. The first time I looked down into his little face I knew he was mine. Chevon doesn't have to ask for anything. I make sure she has the things she needs for K.J. and I try to see him a couple times a week. I ain't sorry like most brotha's. I take care of my kid. That tramp can't get anything else from me after this. She's going to have to take me to court."

"So what your telling me is I've got a grandson. You've known about him since before he was born and you never told Jaidyn or me."

"Yes Ma'am."

Ms. Tyler sat looking at Keith and shaking her head. She'd suddenly lost her appetite. She got up, put her pie in the trash and began washing the dishes.

"I never wanted to hurt Jaidyn. It never occurred to me that she would find out. This is tearing me up. I can't stand fighting with her." Ms. Tyler didn't respond to him. The longer she stood at the sink the madder she got. An angry silence hung in the air.

"Mama say something."

"What do you want me to say?"

"I don't know...something."

Ms. Tyler turned off the faucet and dried her hands on a towel. She threw the towel onto the counter top then turned to face Keith, "You triflin' and sorry just like yo damn daddy. All I've heard you say since you walked in that door was me me me. Have you thought about what you've done to that girl or that child? Jaidyn don't deserve anything like this and that baby and his mama sho' don't deserve it. I've told you over and over what's done in the dark will come to the light." She picked up her cigarettes off the table and lit one.

Keith already felt horrible for hurting Jaidyn and his mother's disappointment and tongue-lashing wasn't making it any better. "I'm sorry."

"You sorry...for what? You sorry that you got caught or you sorry it ever happened?" Keith knew it was a rhetorical question so he remained quiet. "Your sorrys don't mean a damn thang."

"I made a mistake. What am I supposed to do?"

"You know I did the best I could with you. I tried to make sure that you grew into a good man. I didn't want you to turn out like the rest of these fools around here. You saw what your father put me through. What would possess you to turn around and do the same thing?" Keith knew better than to open his mouth, it would only make things worse. When his mother went off like this he reverted back to childhood state.

"You damn men let yalls little heads do the thinking for yalls big heads. You around here laying up with all these tramps. That poor girl waiting on your triflin' ass to come home while you out making babies. I thought I raised you better than that."

"Mama it ain't like that. I'm..."

"Boy don't you back talk me!" Keith sat quietly waiting on his mother to finish. "If you came here looking for me to tell you that you made the right choices or sympathy for what you're going through then you've come to the wrong place. You've brought all this on yourself."

Jaidyn keeps giving you chance after chance and you're still finding ways to mess things up. Despite the stuff you're putting her through she's still with you. Why she continues to put up with you is beyond me. But let me tell you something, you're not invincible. I don't know what you lookin' for in those streets but there ain't nothing out there. You better cherish what you have at home. There is no guarantee that Jaidyn's always going to be there. Every good woman has her breaking point." Mama Nat took a long drag off her cigarette. She squinted as the smoke floated past her eyes. "Mark my words. You'll have to live with the things you do and say to Jaidyn for the rest of your life. Although you don't see it right now, life's a wheel baby. What goes around comes around! Are you going to be able to handle it when it comes back to you? You a damn fool if you think you are."

By the time she sat down at the table Keith felt battered and bruised. No one knew how to verbally beat him better than his mama. She'd never had to whoop him. The verbal lashing he got from her was more than sufficient. It always left him feeling worse than any beating could have.

Ms. Tyler pulled another Kool cigarette out of the pack, rested it between her lips, got up from the table, turned the stove burner on, leaned over the fire, and lit the cigarette. There was an uncomfortable silence while she took a long drag. Keith was staring a hole in the kitchen floor. She leaned against the counter top and folded her arms across her chest. "When am I going to get to meet my grandson?"

"Whenever you're ready. Wait until you see him, he's beautiful. He looks just like me but he's light skinned like his mother."

Chapter 31

Jaidyn woke to a quiet house. She quietly gathered her things and headed for the door. She was surprised to find Nicolette sitting in front of the TV in the living room. "Hey you, what are you doing up so early," Jaidyn asked in a hushed voice.

"Watchin' cartoons…where are you going?"

"Home," Jaidyn said still whispering.

Nicolette frowned, "But we haven't had breakfast yet."

Jaidyn kissed her on the head, "How about we do breakfast some other time?"

"Just us?"

"Sure. Just you and I."

"Can we go to Mama's Kitchen," she asked excitedly.

"Absolutely," Jaidyn said smiling.

Nicolette jumped into Jaidyn's arms, "I love you Auntie Jai."

"I love you too," Jaidyn said hugging her. The innocent pure love Nicolette had for her touched her heart.

When Jaidyn got into her car she thought about Nicolette. She wondered at what age the innocence of children is first compromised. When do we forget how to love each other purely, without reservation, without lies and deceitfulness?

Lord, when there's no place left to go I always end up here with You. Once again I'm standing in the need of Your guidance, Your truth, Your discernment and Your comfort. Lord most of all I need Your love and understanding. I'm tired Lord, completely worn out. I'm turning all this insanity over to You. You know what's best for me and You are in control of my life. I will stand on Your word and allow You to direct my path.

Rain down Your peace upon my household. Help me to forgive Keith. Help me to see the man I married and not the demon he's become. Holy Spirit minister to his spirit. Teach him to surrender to Your will.

Lord, Your loving kindness continues to get me through each day. Thank you for showering me with Your unmerited favor Father. In the name of your darling son, Jesus Christ I pray.

Amen

When Jaidyn arrived home Keith was sleeping on the sofa. She stood over him watching him. "What in the hell did I ever see in this fool," she wondered.

He was startled to find Jaidyn standing over him. The look in her eyes scared him. "Are you alright?" He asked. Jaidyn walked away from him like he didn't exist. Once she was in her room she closed the door behind her. It was only 7 a.m. but to deal with this shit he was going to have to get hisself a drink, to ease his mind. Jaidyn had gone so crazy on him the night before he was sure he'd pushed her too far this time.

He couldn't stop wondering where in the hell she'd been all night. Maybe she'd been with that nigga, he thought. Naw, he said reconsidering, she wouldn't do that to me. Then again you can't ever tell what these hoe's will do.

He poked his head in the door, *"Where in the hell have you been all damn night?"*

"You know what," her head snapped around and she looked at him evilly. *"I don't feel like that bull shit!"* She walked into the bathroom and she slammed the door behind her.

Keith got the message. Keith sat on the bed and waited on her to finish her shower. By the time Jaidyn emerged from the bathroom he had rethought his approach. "Baby we need to talk."

"About what? You want to tell me more lies?"

"I never meant to lie to you," he said as he sat down next to her on the bed. "I'm a fool. I was just taking the easy way out. I didn't want to lose you. I'm going to make things right. This doesn't change anything."

"It changes everything."

"It doesn't change how much I love you."

"Sometimes love just isn't enough Keith." When she looked at him all she saw was deceit. How could she have been so blind?

"We can work through this. I'm willing to do whatever it takes. Whatever you want."

"The only thing I want is for this whole thing to go away, for it to never have happened. You knew this before you married me and you should've told me. I didn't sign up for this."

"I know but I couldn't tell you. I couldn't hurt you like that. I had hoped that the baby wouldn't turn out to be mine. I wouldn't hurt you on purpose you know that. We can work this out."

"How many times do we keep trying? It's just not working. Things can't be turned around."

"What are you saying?"

"I don't know what I'm saying. All I know is I can't keep living like this. You've made me so many promises and nothing ever changes. I need some time. I need to get away from you so I can figure things out for myself. I can't do that as long as I'm here with you."

"You're my wife and I'm not going to let you walk out on everything we have." Keith's tone was harsh. He attempted to soften it, "Don't leave, I'll move into the guest bedroom. Give me a chance. Give us a chance. Tell me what to do to make things right. Please forgive me. I can't stop loving you. I need you."

She wondered if he would change in time. If he'd ever realize her worth, "Keith you hurt me."

"I know. It'll never happen again. I promise."

"It's not that easy, our problems aren't just Chevon..." Keith gave her a confused look. He thought they had a great marriage. He waited on her to explain. "We used to talk. We used to spend time together. You used to go to church with me on Sundays. Now the only time you go is when I'm mad at you...You used to hold me at night but all that changed after we were married."

"Those aren't problems. We're married now. We don't need to date anymore. And we do talk. As for church...I don't have to go to church to be saved."

Chapter 32

Father, it's as if something inside me has broken, simply fallen apart. After being mistreated and neglected for months I think I've finally cracked under the pressure...I can't seem to get things back on track. I don't know how much longer I can do this. I never thought I would have to go through something like this. It's been two months since Chevon showed up on our doorstep and I've felt like the rug's been pulled from under me every since.Like I've come unglued.

I know I insisted that Keith start getting K.J. on the weekends and bringing him to the house but seeing them together makes me...I don't know...resentful...ANGRY! I mean...I guess...I'm jealous...but I don't know why. I don't get it Lord, you know the last thing I want is a child...I'm amazed at how good Keith is with K.J. and how much K.J. absolutely adores his Father. On one hand I think it's great that Keith is trying to be a good father and I encourage that. But on the other hand I'm resentful and angry. I know my anger isn't fair to either of them. But when I see them together I can't help it. I can't control the anger. Help me Lord...I mean...K.J. is too cute. He's got a smile that lights up a room. I can't help but smile when he looks at me but the second Keith enters into the equation I get instant attitude...

Markel stopped by yesterday. It was K.J.'s weekend to be with us. It was the first time anyone besides Mama

> *Nat and my family had seen us interact as a family. It was so humiliating. When Markel looked at me all I saw was sympathy. Why did this have to happen? This entire situation is so degrading. I don't know. I just...don't know.*
>
> *This is so much more than just K.J. and Chevon. I care for Keith but when he touches me I want to throw up. When I make love to him it feels like a violation. This has been happening for months and nothing's changing. I don't know...I feel so empty...I'm not sure things will ever change.*

The phone began to ring and Jaidyn reached to pick it up, "Hello."

"What's up girl?" Anna asked in an upbeat warm voice.

"Not too much. What's going on?" Jaidyn asked dryly.

"You alright? It sounds like I woke you up."

Jaidyn cleared her throat, "No, I was...ah...just laying here." Although it was Sunday evening Jaidyn and Anna's normal time to talk on the phone Jaidyn didn't feel like talking today.

"It doesn't sound like this is a good time. Why don't I give you a call next Sunday." Anna suggested.

"I'm sorry Anna. I'm just...we'll talk next week."

"Girl don't worry about it," Anna insisted.

"Thanks Anna."

"Hey, you and I really need to have a heart to heart talk."

"You sound serious. What's up?"

"It's not important right now. There's just something I should have told to you a long time ago and I didn't...we'll talk next time."

"Are you sure."

"Yeah," Anna said trying to sound like it was no big deal but knowing it was going to be one more thing to add to Jaidyn's list of problems. Anna knew Jaidyn was going through a lot but she just couldn't hold on to this anymore. It was time that she told her everything that had happen between her and Keith. She should have told her what Keith did to her. It had never seemed like the right time but lately it was really weighing heavy on her. Today just didn't seem like the right time to dump that cramp on her.

Chapter 33

Jaidyn was having a bout with the blues and had been having sleepless nights. She and insomnia were becoming good friends. As she lay listening to the rain cascading down her window she dreaded having to get out of bed when the sun came up. It was only 3 a.m. and it was already one of those days that she couldn't wait until it was over.

She'd been feeling overwhelmed lately. Her husband was driving her out of her mind. On top of the relentless headache for the past two weeks she'd been feeling like she had the flu. She was having an emotional melt down and had been fighting hard to function as if nothing was wrong. She knew she could contribute all her symptoms to stress. She grimaced as she realized that she was having a bout with depression or maybe it was just plain old heartache.

Silence was Keith's newest way of torturing her. They'd been living in complete and total silence for weeks. When she tried to talk to him he would ignore her or only answer her question. There were absolutely no conversations.

Although they still shared a bed the thought of Keith touching her again was repulsive. When he did touch her it made her skin crawl. She'd forgotten what made her love him in the first place. There really was a thin line between love and hate and he had finally pushed her across that line.

It had been two months since Chevon's secret had shattered their lives and they'd grown farther and farther apart. Keith hadn't changed. He was still the same man she married but the things she used to be able to tolerate and ignore were no longer acceptable. She couldn't count how many times he'd gotten out of bed at 11:30 and said he was going to the car wash because he couldn't sleep; or how many late night trips he'd made to the post office. She could no longer count how many times he'd been on the phone and the conversation would end abruptly when she walked in the room.

The endless amount of flowers or sweet gestures she received after one of his late nights was maddening. The elaborate steps he went through to convince her that he was sorry for whatever the current offense was all a game. He was always scheming and when he got caught, he had an innate ability to make you think it was all in your mind. She use to think he was someone he wasn't but now the blind folds were off and she didn't like what she saw. She wasn't only disappointed in who he had turned out to be but also in herself for putting up with him.

She didn't know what kept her holding onto this marriage. Every time she packed her bags and decided to leave he'd begged her to stay claiming he needed her. He'd promise to change. He'd promise things would be different if she stayed, and they would be for a couple of days but within a week they'd be back at square one. He'd go right back to hanging out with the guys Thursday, Friday, and Saturday nights and staying out all times of the night. Sunday was still her day but when Monday rolled around it was Monday night football with the fellas.

She had spoken to her mother about the situation. Her mother told her, "People make mistakes." Which only furthered confused her. She thought she should allow time for the confusion to dissipate before she made any impulsive decisions. She thought by staying and working things out that something would change but they hadn't. She thought that maybe he would learn to appreciate and respect her but that was turning out to be a pipe dream as well. She hadn't left because she didn't want to make the mistake of coming back.

The longer she stayed the more bitter she became. Keith was poison to every woman he touched and she wondered how much longer she could live with the venom that he poured over every crevice of her life.

Jaidyn climbed out of bed careful not to wake him. She picked up a pair of jeans and T-shirt off the chair and retreated into the hall bathroom to get dressed. She wanted to take a drive to clear her mind.

She'd been in her car five minutes listening to the smooth sounds of Magic 102's 'Quiet Storm' when Luther came on the radio and Jared trickled into her thoughts. She picked up her cell phone and dialed his home number.

Chapter 34

Jared was jarred out of a deep sleep when the phone rang at 4 a.m. It was Jaidyn, she asked if she could come over. He looked over at the clock, 4 a.m., "Is something wrong Passion?"

There was silence from the other end of the phone and then he heard a small, "No," escape her lips. But he knew differently. He could hear it in her voice and for her to call him at 4 a.m. something had to be wrong. He was trying to be indifferent to the things she was going through but it was killing him softly.

Jaidyn checked in on Naomi a couple times a week. Jared had made it his business to stop by Naomi's house on those days. If anyone asked, Naomi would swear it was a coincidence, but being the busy body she was, she faithfully called Jared to inform him what time and day Jaidyn would be visiting her. They had even shared a meal at Naomi's on more then a few occasions but Jaidyn seemed oblivious to the fact that Naomi had made dinner just for the two of them. Jaidyn always tried to appear upbeat and happy but he'd seen straight through her charade. Naomi had also seen it. She'd pointed out that Jaidyn wore unhappiness as part of her wardrobe.

When Jaidyn walked into his downtown loft the pounding rain had her dripping wet. She resembled a lost angel that needed rescuing. Her body seemed to glisten when she stepped into the foyer light. Her sopping wet T-shirt clung to her making her hard nipples transparent. Her hair was dripping wet and her shoes made a soggy squeaking sound as she walked across his doorstep.

"What happened to your umbrella?"

"I don't know," she said shaking her head. "I think I may have left it at the hospital."

"Let me get you a towel," Jared said disappearing around the corner. He came back with a towel, a pair of socks and some sweats. "Here, put these on."

"Thank you," she said as she retreated to the bathroom to change. Jared watched her walk towards the bathroom and admired her tight little butt. His dick twitched and he ran his hand across it to reposition it as it tightened.

Jaidyn came out of the bathroom wearing the clothes he'd given her and with her hair pulled up into a ponytail. She looked around his loft, nothing had changed. He bought it while they were together and she'd helped him with the decorating.

The loft was maculated yet warm and inviting. His living room had two expensive looking dark leather sofas positioned around a beautiful mahogany table. Behind one of the sofas was a sofa table with an array of family photo's. One side of the spacious living room was a wall of ceiling to floor tinted windows with an amazing view of downtown Houston. She noticed that her picture no longer sat with the other family photo's he had sprinkled throughout the loft.

He watched her as she looked around and made herself at home on his sofa. Trying to be lighthearted Jared said, "Ooww, she's a brick...house. The clothes she wears, her sexy ways can bring a strong man to his knees."

"I don't think those are the exact words to that song," she said laughing. A tinge of nervousness hit her as it suddenly occurred to her that she was in his apartment, in the middle of the night, alone with his fine ass.

Jared forced his hands into the pockets of his jeans and fought the urge to touch her just as he did every time she was near him, "So...sup girl?"

"Not much. I wanted to stop by and see what was going on with you. I'm sorry it's so early. I didn't mean to wake you. I thought maybe you were still an early bird."

"I am! I still go to the gym at 6 a.m. but I don't normally get out of bed until around five."

"I'm sorry."

"Don't sweat it," he put his hand on top of hers and interlaced their fingers, "...You want to tell me what's wrong?"

Why does he have to touch me every time I'm around him? Doesn't he realize my stuff starts tingling when he does that? "Nothing, really," she said in a barely audible angelic voice. "I just stopped by."

"Oh yeah, is that why your face is dragging on my floor? I've got skid marks all the way down my hallway," he said jokingly.

Jaidyn laughed, "My face isn't dragging."

"Whatever!" He got up and retrieved a small hanging mirror off the wall and held it in front of her. "Do you see what I see?"

She burst into laughter. "What? Pure beauty?" They both laughed. "You're still silly. That's why I came over here. I needed to laugh."

"At 4 a.m.? I was hoping this was a bootie call," he said half teasingly. This time she gave him a weak forced smile as she entertained the thought. "You want to talk about it?"

"Not particularly," Jaidyn responded.

"How about some coffee? French vanilla still your favorite?"

Jaidyn shook her head, "Yeah, that sounds wonderful."

While Jared was in the kitchen Jaidyn lay her head on a pillow that Jared had left on the arm of his sofa. Her thoughts traveled back to Keith and how he'd been treating her. Anger and bitterness had replaced sadness as the angry tears begin spilling from the corners of her eyes and she thought of evil things she could do to him.

Jared stood in the kitchen watching her wipe her face. As the coffee brewed he came around to the living room, lifted the pillow she had her head on and took a seat under it, laying her head in his lap. He rubbed his hands through her hair and along the side of her face, "Passion we don't have to talk if you don't want to but by now you know you can trust me."

Jaidyn's emotional dependence on Jared had not changed. Being in his presence still seemed to pull her raw emotions to the surface and made her feel free to express them. She hated being that way with him. It didn't allow her to hold how she felt back. She buried her head deeper in the pillow and had herself a good cry.

The harder she cried the more he felt like his heart was being torpedoed. The urge to pull her into his arms was tugging on his insides. He hated to see her in this much agony. He took the thought process out of it and did what was natural. He pulled his T-shirt off, lifted her head off his lap, he put his leg behind her and lay down pulling her onto his bare chest. He used his T-shirt as a tissue to clean her face. To his surprise she did not resist. She squirmed around until she got comfortable.

Laying in Jared's arms felt like heaven...like home...where she was supposed to be. His chest held her nicely and when he put his arms around her it was as if he engulfed her. She wanted to melt into him. She wanted him to simply absorb her, like a sponge absorbing water. She couldn't seem to get close enough to him. Jaidyn sat up and removed her top then snuggled against his bare skin. She needed his warmth. This was once a routine when they were dating. If she was upset about something she lay in his arms naked being comforted by his warmth. It was her therapy, a temporary refuge. When she was in his arms she was always able to find that place inside herself where there was perfect peace. She wasn't living in a fairytale and she knew this current soothing method wouldn't last, but for the moment it took her away from all her worries and her tears quickly subsided.

She felt his dick growing and she smiled to herself. It was nice to know that she still had the same affect on him that he had on her.

She was asleep within minutes of her head hitting his chest. She slept soundly, like she hadn't slept in months. Jared held her tightly for almost two hours. He'd never paid much attention to how quietly she slept. The steady rhythm of her breathing mixed with her heart beating next to his felt like a dream. The pleasure of having her in his arms made him desire her more than ever.

They lay skin to skin. Heart to heart. They danced the same rhythmic dance making it hard for him to distinguish hers from his. He finally rolled her onto the couch, retrieved a blanket from the closet and covered her. He pushed her hair out of her face and admired her beauty. Looking down at her he thought about what she must be going through. She looked weak and fragile, like a vulnerable angel that needed rescuing. If Keith knew her at all he had to know that she was unhappy. If he loves her he'll fight to change things between them before it's too late, Jared thought. He stole a kiss from the sleeping beauty before he went into his study.

When Jaidyn's pager went off it startled her out of a deep sleep. She was momentarily disoriented as she looked around Jared's partially lit loft. "Oh my God, what time is it?" Jared heard her stirring, got up from his desk, and went into the living room. He turned on the light just as she was looking at the number on her pager. She squinted against the light, "It's my parents. I left my cell in the car, can I use your phone?"

"Sure thang," Jared said picking up the cordless phone off the sofa table and handed it to her. When she finished her conversation she hung up and looked at him. He'd become her guardian angel. There had been so many days that she'd gone to Naomi's with hopes of finding him there. He seemed to have become her quiet gentle savior, always standing guard over her from afar. Her day would be unraveling, she'd go to Naomi's and there he'd be waiting with a smile. She'd be in her office and problems would be tumbling around her and he'd call just to say hello. She wondered if he knew what a comfort he'd been to her.

"Everything alright?"

"Yeah," she said yawning, "I missed church service this morning. They were just checking to see if I was going to be able to make it for dinner."

"You guys still doing dinner at your folks every Sunday?" Jared asked. Jaidyn shook her head. "Well you better get up and get over there."

"Not today," Jaidyn had a meltdown in church the week before and didn't want to face her family. The pastor had spoken about the sins associated with divorce. She had sat in church countless times and listened to pastors tell their congregations divorce was a sin. Sunday's message hadn't been any different but when she'd heard the sermon instead of it being uplifting and encouraging it had penetrated her heart and made her feel condemned to a life of hell. Whether it was on earth with Keith or in the eternal place of damnation the effect at the time was equally devastating.

She'd called the assistant pastor during the week and sat down with him. He reassured her that, "We've all sinned and fallen short of the glory of God." He went on to explain that, "Sin is simply missing the moral mark of God. Because we have been justified by the blood of Jesus we have been freed from the penalty of sin. God does not condemn you to a life of hell, He forgives you. His grace and mercy saves us from ourselves." Although their conversation made her feel better, she was still carrying around the guilt of being in a loveless marriage and the possibility of divorce on the horizon.

Jaidyn looked at the clock, "Hunh, I'm sorry. I didn't realize it was so late. It looks like I've made you miss service too," Jaidyn said regrettably. Jared had a strong spiritual foundation and hardly ever missed church service.

"We just added a Saturday evening service so I went last night."

"Mumh." Jaidyn said relieved that she hadn't kept him from his plans. "Why did you let me sleep so long?"

"Neal came by and we went to the gym. You were still sleeping when I got back. The only time I've known you to sleep like that is when you were working nights. So you must have needed the sleep."

"Huh," she said putting the palms of her hands on her forehead. That's all I need is to have to hear this from Yasmine, she thought.

He seemed to sense what she was thinking naturally, "He didn't see you. I met him downstairs."

Jared looked at her sympathetically. Her eyes were puffy from a combination of sleep and crying. He sat next to her and she ducked under his arm, resting her head on his chest. They continued the conversation with ease, "Why did you let me come here?"

That was the million-dollar question that he'd been wondering his damn self. It was as if she'd cast a spell on him and it prevented him from telling her no. No other woman could dare dream of getting away with the things she did. Faith, his current girlfriend, had voiced her concerns many times about Jaidyn's ability to disrupt their lives. "I don't know. On the phone you seemed like you could use a friend."

As she gazed at him she seemed to be pulled into a trance by those big hazel eyes of his. There was no mistaking that she loved him beyond her own understanding. She'd tried to escape it by marrying Keith and for a while she did, but she still yearned for him. He was her deepest desire. Most people thought of desire in a sexual manner but her desire for him was so much more than just sexual. This longing, yearning she had for him was centered on what she'd never found in another man. He was the life support that kept the blood pumping through her veins, the caretaker of her heart. She could never have dreamt of finding a love like she had in him and that is what made her crave him even more. He was the other half of her soul, he completed her. Being away from him had been the most painful thing she'd experienced.

"Thanks Jared."

"For what?"

Her voice broke, "…Being a friend." She gave him a weary smile.

He kissed her on the top of her head and pulled her closer to him. If she only knew that he was in heaven having her there with him. He'd rather have a piece of her than none of her at all he thought. It was unbearable to imagine her with another man but the alternative of not imaging her in his life at all was earthshattering.

She knew letting him hold her like this was dangerous but she needed the comfort. She wanted to forget all the things that she'd been going through lately. His erection was poking her and making her juices flow.

She wanted to tell him all about Keith's betrayal. She wanted to tell him about the war that had been going on in her soul. How she finally realized the things she'd been denying and simply living through.

When he began to rub her arm it was too much to bear. She looked up at him and he kissed her. Jaidyn closed her eyes and floated in the moment. The taste of him made her quiver. *SSSShhhhhhit,*" she screamed in her mind as the earth began to move. It got too good to her and she pulled away, "Jared, I'm sorry I've got to go." She struggled to get to her feet and find her shirt.

"Wait a minute Passion. Don't leave," Jared said arming her wrist.

"I'm sorry. I shouldn't be here. My life is in shambles and I don't want to pull you into that insanity." She said as she put his sweatshirt back on. As she reached for her keys he placed his hand on top of hers trapping it in place. She knew she couldn't resist if he pursued this any further so she kept her back to him.

He pulled her hair to the side and lightly kissed her on the nape of her neck. He made a trail of kisses up her neck to her ear lobe and lightly nibbled on it. She damn near lost her balance. "Why do you keep running?"

"Mmmm…please…" She struggled to get the words out, "…I'm…married."

"Yeah, to the wrong guy." He hit the nail on the head with that one. There was no denying it. She was married to the wrong man. When she turned around he kissed her deeply. He lifted her shirt and made a nibbling path down to her breast. Then he pulled her back into his arms and devoured her lips. The anaconda was rock hard against her and she creamed her panties right there. As if a thunderstorm had rolled in, clothes began to plummet to the floor like lighting bolts. A flood of regrets inundated every crevice of her mind. Like drizzle on a warm summer's day tears began falling from her eyes and Jared licked each and every one of them. "I know," he whispered. "You don't have to cry."

Jared kissed her breast and traced her nipples with the tip of his tongue. Experiencing a bittersweet warm tingling sensation, a battle between Jaidyn's mind, body and heart raged inside of her. *"Shit, shit! What am I doing,"* she questioned? *"Aahhh, that feels so good…God, I love this man."* Rang inside her head.

"I can't do this," she screamed inside her mind before letting the words part her lips.

"What are you afraid of," he asked?

Getting caught up is the first thing that came to mind. Never going home was the second. When she looked into those hazel eyes of his she wanted to confess all her deepest darkest secrets. She pushed him off of her. Wanting to put some distance between them. She looked around the room for her clothes. The room looked like a tornado had hit it. Clothes lay in complete disarray around the floor.

Jared watched her as she hurried to get dressed, *"Answer me!"*

Tears glistened in her eyes, "I can't hurt you again. I won't pull you into this. It's not fair to you. I realize that I'm married to the wrong man. You are the love of my life and I'm tired of running from what I feel for you."

"Did she just say what I think she said?" He asked himself.

"Loving you is one of those bittersweet experiences in life that I would never change."

His expression was a mix of surprise and happiness, "Wait Passion…what did you just say?"

"…I don't want to hurt you anymore than I already have."

"No baby, what did you say?"

She looked at him puzzled, "I don't know, what did I say?" At that instant the unveiling of the truth she had just told him hit her like a ton of bricks. She hadn't meant for it to come pouring out but it had and it was too late to take it back.

Before she could answer him Faith's voice sounded from behind them, "Am I interrupting something?"

Jaidyn turned around and found her standing in the doorway. Everyone stood frozen, unsure who should speak next. Jaidyn recognized that this was the prefect time to make her get away. "No. This is prefect timing. I was just leaving," Jaidyn said as she picked up her keys and started towards the door.

"Wait a minute Jaidyn," Faith said stopping her. Jaidyn's blood ran cold. She wasn't ready to play out this potentially disastrous situation. "You forgot your purse," Faith said handing her purse to her.

"Thanks," she said relieved that was all she wanted. Jared still had not spoken. It wasn't clear if he was caught off guard when Faith interrupted them or if he was thinking about her confession. Whichever it was Jaidyn was grateful to be out of there.

"Looks like I interrupted something." Faith said throwing her keys down on the table. "Why don't you go after her?"

"What?" His face contorted. "I'm not going to have this conversation with you," Jared said abruptly.

Chapter 35

Keith spotted Jaidyn maneuvering through the parked cars towards the garage elevator. "Shit!" He said scrambling to get Alexia's head out of his lap.

"Wait a minute daddy. I'm almost finished." She said as she deep throated the "Dicktator" one last time. Keith pushed her off of him. "What's wrong with you? I thought you were enjoying this," she said.

"My fuckin' wife just walked right in front of us."

"Mummm. That makes things a little more exciting," Alexia moaned. Keith struggled to get his pants zipped and buttoned. Alexis pulled against his efforts, "Where are you going," Alexia asked in frustration.

Keith reached in his pocket and threw a hundred-dollar bill at her. "I'll holla at you later," he said getting out of the car still buckling his belt.

As she pulled her clothes back on she asked, "You want me to wait on you?" Keith slammed the car door and ran towards the stairs before she was able to get the sentence out of her mouth.

Jaidyn thought surprising Keith at his office for an early lunch might break the ice. They'd had a fight that they were both still pissed off about but lunch had proven to be another one of her feeble attempts to rectify a no win situation.

After the lunch from hell she hadn't wanted to go home. She called Keith at his office and told him that she was going to have to go back to work and would be late. She'd gone to the movies then walked aimlessly through the mall window-shopping. She'd considered calling Yasmine and asking her to join her but she really just needed the time alone.

When she got home Keith was in a bad mood. To avoid dealing with him Jaidyn had gone into their bedroom and taken a shower. Keith was on a rampage. He had found a Victoria's Secret bag in her car. She still didn't know why he was in her car to begin with and at this point it wasn't important.

Keith had come into the bedroom while she was getting ready for bed and said, "I thought you had to work late. This receipt says that you bought this today."

Jaidyn looked at the Victoria's Secret bag he was holding. She hadn't had any intention on buying anything at the mall but an older gentleman had flirted with her and made her feel desirable and attractive. Keith hadn't made her feel that way in Lord knows how long. After the gentleman had said some very nice things to her she'd went into Victoria's Secret and bought the purple colored negligée. "I stopped by the mall on my way home," Jaidyn said with a flippant attitude.

"To see who?"

"Why does it always have to be that I was with somebody?"

"You must have been with somebody to bring home some shit like this."

"You need to fix your tone and stop talking to me crazy!" Jaidyn said as she sat on the bed.

Keith held up the negligée she'd purchased, "Who the hell did you buy this for?"

"I'm not going through this with you." Jaidyn said trying her best to keep her voice as calm as possible.

"Who the fuck you going to wear this for? I know it ain't for me. I can't remember the last time your ass wore something like that. All I ever see you in is some damn sweats with your hair up in a fucking ponytail, looking like a dude around here. Shit yo ass sleep with two feet in one sock. What the hell you need something like that for?"

Jaidyn snatched the purple negligée out of his hand. "I'm going to tell you like you tell me, 'build a bridge and get over it."

Keith charged out of the bedroom and went into the garage. When he came back he had a laundry basket and a can of gasoline. He went into the closet, got all of Jaidyn's negligees and put them in the basket. He came back into their bedroom, sat the basket in the middle of the floor and poured gasoline on them. Before Jaidyn could react he lit a match and set the basket on fire.

"Now whoever the muthafucka is you seeing can buy yo ass some more!" Keith shouted at her. Jaidyn flew across the bed so fast it took Keith by surprise. She was fighting him like a man on the street. He was going to have to knock her out if he wanted her to stop.

At that moment the line between the past and the present was blurred. Everything he' done to her ran through her mind and she wanted to make him pay for it. When he finally hit her in self-defense it infuriated her even more. She grabbed her mouth and glared at him. When the shock had worn off she picked up the TV remote control, threw it at him and flew into him again. "You mother fucker every body told me you were a bitch before I married your ass!" She threw the clock radio. "If you had any kind of dick you wouldn't have to worry about who the hell I was fucking!" The lamp followed the radio. "You sorry sack of shit, I sleep with two feet in one sock because the thought of you touching me makes my skin crawl." Throughout the entire episode hot angry tears rolled down her face. By the time the night was over they were both battered and bruised.

A week had passed since that fight and she had yet to regret anything she'd said or done. The entire ordeal had been an awakening. She'd taken this past week to go back inside herself and reclaim who she was. In doing so she had made up her mind that it was time to get rid of all the lies, betrayal and confusion in her life. With everyday that passed the lies were becoming more and more visible. She couldn't find forgiveness in her heart for the things Keith continued to do to her.

She decided that the cause of her depressive attitude was this marriage. She knew it was time to embrace and acknowledge its failure. They'd grown too far apart to bridge the distance between them. Somewhere down the road they'd become something that she didn't recognize. In the back of her mind she'd always known no matter what Keith promised nothing was going to change. She was either going to have to accept who he was and live with it or walk away from this marriage.

There was no way she could live the rest of her life with all the lying and cheating. The only thing left to do was to write off the losses of the marriage and move forward. She had finally given herself permission to release all the meaningless crap in her life, starting with him. Since she'd married Keith turmoil had been circling her like a vulture stalking its prey. Somehow she had become entangled in Keith's issues and forgotten who she was and what she really wanted out of life.

It had once been a story book romance. She was once hypnotized by his charm. She recalled when he proposed to her. She'd felt like Cinderella and he was her Prince Charming that had given her the glass slipper, but that was all the past. It was time to stop hiding and denying the truth. It was time that she conceded to what had been staring her in the face for months. It was time to throw in the towel and concede to defeat. No matter how much they fought to salvage what was left of their marriage, it was clear it was over.

Meshell

Lord have mercy and forgive me. You are the source of my existence. Without You I can do nothing. Come into my life and my heart, live in me and through me. Help me to forgive Keith for the pain he's caused during this marriage and help him to forgive me for the things I've done. I know that am not without blame for its demise. I will not pretend that I was blind when I choose to marry this man. Somewhere deep in my subconscious I knew who Keith was and I made a conscious decision, but living this lie is pure hell. If leaving him means I can stop this downward spiral then I've got to do it.

Your word promises healing and peace Lord. In the name of Jesus I ask that You bless us both with those gifts. And Father, thank you for loving me enough to forgive me for my sins.

Chapter 36

Jaidyn had her receptionist clear her schedule for the day and after she made rounds at the hospital she met Joanna and Yasmine. They had both insisted on going with her to find a new place to live.

"Hey, you guys ready to go?" Jaidyn asked cheery. They both looked at her like she had lost her mind. Over the past few months Joanna had gotten to know a side of her sister that she hadn't known before. Most people in her situation would be falling apart but she seemed to have an eerie calmness about her. When most people lost control she seemed to hold tighter to it. Joanna wondered how long it would be before the emotional roller coaster she was on came crashing down on her. "What," Jaidyn asked.

"Nothing," Yasmine said dismissing Jaidyn's question. "Who's driving?"

"I will," Jaidyn said.

Once they were in the car Joanna asked, "Jai are you alright?"

"I'm fine. Will you two stop worrying about me. I've made up my mind, I want to be free from this and I know it's not going to be easy. It's time that I move on with my life. I'm killing myself trying to maintain this illusion. It's time that I let it go and this is the first step."

"You're doing the right thing. It's never easy but sometimes for your own peace of mind you've got to walk away," Joanna said.

"This isn't all Keith's fault Joanna." Jaidyn said defensively. It was time that she stopped blaming the destruction of this marriage completely on Keith. The truth was that she had been just as deceptive as he had been. "Our problems aren't just about Chevon and K. J. It's much deeper than that."

"I know that. If Keith knew you at all he would know that too. It's not hard to see that your problems started way before Chevon showed up."

Jaidyn pulled over to the side of the rode and Yasmine knew that she was about to go on a rampage. She wondered if Jaidyn finally realized that she was no longer willing to put up with Keith's BS because she finally realized she could not make what she felt for Jared go away.

"I never loved Keith like I should have. I've been in love with Jared since before I said, "I do." No matter what I do I can't make it go away. I've tried to love Keith but my heart just won't do what my mind is telling it."

"Girl please..."

"Let me finish. I love everything about him, the way he speaks, the way he thinks, the way he looks at me, the way he touches me, most of all the way he supports me. I haven't wanted to tell anyone. I didn't want to admit it to myself. If I continue to live this lie I'm only going to hurt Keith more than I already have."

"Everybody but you seems to know that. I wondered how long it would be before you figured it out." Joanna nonchalantly responded. Jaidyn's face showed complete disbelief. The only person she seemed to have fooled was herself.

Jaidyn fell in love with a quaint cozy little house in the Rice Village area. After she'd taken care of the necessary paper work. They spent the remainder of the day shopping for furniture. By the time they returned to Joanna's they had bought enough furniture to fill the entire house. She still needed linens, kitchen utensils and tons of other small things but overall it was an extremely productive day.

Chapter 37

Jaidyn was relieved when she arrived home to find Keith gone. She wanted some time to pack a few things before he came home. She went back to her car to retrieve a few empty boxes she'd collected. As she started to pack the first box she heard the garage door go up. Jaidyn wasn't sure how he would react if he found her packing so she went into the living room and waited on him to come in. She hoped to defuse a potentially bad situation by telling him up-front of her plans to move.

"Hey baby," he said.

"Hey. You're late, where have you been?"

"Traffic."

She hadn't meant to sound so sarcastic but she couldn't help it, "Hmmm, that's an original. What a surprise."

"Here you go again. Don't yo ass get tired of fussing?"

"Don't yo ass get tired of lying?" She said as she went back in the bedroom. She wasn't going to fight with him and get drawn back into his insanity one more time. She couldn't take anymore of this nonsense and wouldn't be his fool for one more day. I've been through way too much with this fool for him to keep disrespecting me, she said to herself.

She hadn't planned on moving out tonight because her new place wouldn't be ready for another two days and the furniture wouldn't be delivered for another three. But he had just pissed her off for the last time and she'd rather stay with her parents or in a hotel then put up with him one more night.

When Keith came into the bedroom his heart sank. She had never gone as far as to pack her things before. "What are you doing?" Jaidyn pissed him off when she walked past him as if he wasn't there. As she came out of the bathroom with an arm full of her things he grabbed her by the arm, "I asked you a question."

She gave him a look that would melt the North Pole. Jaidyn pulled her arm away from him. "I'm not putting up with your shit anymore. I'm leaving!" She hadn't meant for it to come pouring out like that but there was no use in crying over spilled milk. She might as well cut straight to the chase.

"You what?"

"You heard me."

"You got to do what you got to do." Keith knew as soon as the words exited his mouth that he didn't mean it but what was he supposed to say? He left her packing, went into the kitchen, and got himself a beer. Then returned to the bedroom doorway and watched her. "So, who is he?"

"This isn't about a man. This is about how you treat me. You've hurt me for the last time. I can't even cry anymore. I forgive you but I'll never forget all the shit you've done. We've tried but it's not working out. It's time to move on."

"Can we talk about this?"

"No. I'm through talking. You've lied to me for the last time."

"Fuck it then. I'm not going to beg your ass. Get yo shit and get the hell out my house and make sure you leave my key."

"Your house? I thought this was our house!" Jaidyn said infuriated.

"This is my muthafuckin' house! You walked in here with the clothes on your back and you leaving here with the clothes on your back," he said as he retreated back to the living room.

Jaidyn picked up a box and headed towards the door. She took one last look around the bedroom to make sure she didn't forget anything that she would need in the next couple of days. "I'll come over in a few days to get the remainder of my things. I'll return your key then." She said as she walked past him feeling a strange mix of anxiety and relief.

> *Heavenly Father, Thank you for giving me the courage to walk away from this. Thank you for pulling me out of this mess. Thank you for being with me and not leaving me all alone to face this alone. I can not believe how peaceful I feel about leaving my husband.*
>
> *Thank you for giving me a discerning heart. I will never understand some of the decisions I've made in this marriage. You were patient with me when I didn't listen*

and chose my own path rather then allowing You to take me where You wanted me to go, and I am eternally grateful.

Forgive me for ignoring the signs You were giving me. Father You have been my protector, my healer, and my guiding light. You are forever faithful and just towards me, and I am so grateful.

Amen

Chapter 38

Jaidyn and her parents sat down and had an old fashion powwow. Before their conversation ended Jaidyn and her mother were both in tears and her father had his healing arms wrapped around them. Neither of her parents could believe what Keith had been putting her through. It was her mother who'd asked the one question that she hadn't expected, "Is it possible that he knows how you feel about Jared?" The question stunned Jaidyn and the room fell silent.

The way her parents were looking at her let her know at some point this had been a topic of discussion. Feeling like a child that had been caught doing something wrong a wave of panic ran through her. "I…" She hesitated not sure how she wanted to answer. She could feel her father's disappointing eyes slipping over her. Despite their disappointment she knew that they'd be right there for her because that's just how they were. She had hoped to avoid this conversation as long as possible but deciding there was no point in lying to them she said, "I'm not sure. I thought I was hiding it pretty well."

"Honey you'd have to be blind not to see it." Mrs. Owens responded in a concerned mother tone. Jaidyn was stunned again and her eyes questioned her mother's statement. "I knew it after I saw you two together at that revival." Jaidyn remained silent as she thought back on the revival. Mama Nat had called and invited them to a revival at her church. After the three of them had been seated Jaidyn had surveyed the crowd. She was surprised to see Jared seated in a pew two rows in front of them. The remainder of the evening her eyes had continuously wondered in his direction. After service she'd excused herself to the bathroom. When she'd come out she'd found her mother talking to him. She'd approached them and said a friendly hello. The moment had been uncomfortable but she hadn't thought much about it. Apparently her mother had.

"Ma, if you knew why didn't you tell me? Why did you continue to encourage me stay with Keith?"

Sarah Owens took a deep breath, "Well, I thought it was best that you figure things out on your own. If I would have told you, you were making a mistake in marrying Keith, would you have listened?"

"Probably not," Jaidyn admitted softly.

"One of the hardest things to do as parents is to allow your children to make their own mistakes."

Jaidyn took a minute trying to understand her mother's point of view. She finally spoke up, "I want to enjoy my life, to be happy, and I couldn't do that with Keith…I want you guys to understand that I'm not leaving Keith because of the way I feel about Jared. He's always going to be a part of me but what we had was over the day that I married Keith. I was committed to my marriage. I would have stayed with Keith forever if…"

When Jaidyn's father interrupted her she expected a long drawn out speech about the sanctity of marriage but instead her father's eyes softened and he said, "Baby you don't have to explain this to us. We just want you to be happy." In truth her parents couldn't be happier to hear that Jaidyn had finally made the decision to leave Keith. Although they'd supported her they never liked him.

Jaidyn loved her family. Everything she was flowed from the foundation they had given her. Now here she was a grown woman learning lessons that no one could have taught her. No one could have conveyed to her that in the battle between your heart and your mind your heart always wins. You can change your mind but you can't change what your heart feels. Jeremiah was right when he wrote, "The heart is deceitful above all things and is beyond cure." She'd learned that the hard way.

The Christian foundation her parents had given her had proven to be her saving grace. After Chevon exposed Keith for the liar he was it was as if a light had come on. Jaidyn was forced to look at all the problems of her marriage and she turned to the only help she knew, God.

She'd once heard her pastor, Reverend James, preach a sermon called, "Surviving the Prefect Storm." She remembered the sermon so well because he'd gotten her undivided attention when he quoted Grand Master Flash, "Don't push me cause I'm close to the edge, I'm trying not to lose my head. It's like a jungle sometime it makes me wonder how I keep from going under. Ha ha ha ha." The church had erupted into laughter. His analogy made his message stick with her. He'd told the congregation that nothing made people seek God and His wisdom like trouble. He said that, "We should approach every storm with faith and trust in our Lord and Savior Jesus Christ." He'd reminded them that God would strengthen them and protect them while in the midst of their storms. He had used the words of the Psalmist David to drive his point home, "God is our refuge and strength an ever present help in time of trouble." It wasn't until Jaidyn herself was in the midst of the storms of a loveless marriage that his message became clear to her.

Through all of it she'd learned despite life's troubles she really could endure.

Jaidyn heard the doorbell ring and thought she was dreaming. When she heard voices and it rang again she turned over and looked at the clock, 3:32 a.m. She climbed out of bed to see what all the ruckus was about. She found her mother standing in the front doorway. "Russell, please come back inside."

"Mama, what's going on?" Jaidyn asked as she looked over her shoulder. Jaidyn couldn't believe what she saw. Keith had his trunk open and was throwing her clothes onto the driveway.

Mr. Owens had to remind himself that he'd promised his wife that he wouldn't lay a hand on Keith but this fool was pushing his patience. "Son, if you want your wife back this is no way to go about it." Jaidyn heard her father say.

This muthafucka has lost his damn mind, Jaidyn thought. Before Jaidyn could react her mother had repositioned herself between Jaidyn and the door. Jaidyn tried to push her way past her, "No baby, let your father handle this!"

Jaidyn acted as if she didn't hear her and moved her aside, "What do you think you're doing?"

"You want out of this marriage, I'm helping you!" Keith yelled at Jaidyn as she walked quickly down the driveway towards Keith.

"Jaidyn!" Her father yelled in a stern voice. "You get back in that house!" Jaidyn kept moving, ignoring him. "Jaidyn Nicolette did you hear what I said," her father franticly repeated. Jaidyn's pace quickened. Her father tried to stop her but it was too late. Jaidyn flew into Keith. Keith grabbed both her hands and held them, then violently pushed her off of him. Mr. Owens stepped between them and Jaidyn swung at Keith over her father's shoulder. Mr. Owens grabbed Jaidyn and shook her, *"Jaidyn go back in the house, right now!"*

"The girl's got problems," Keith yelled. Mr. Owens turned back to him and ordered him to get back in his car and go home.

Jaidyn walked into the kitchen the next morning and found Keith sitting at the table having coffee with her father. Mr. Owens was being his usual strong self, fiercely advocating on Jaidyn's behalf. "Look! You're trying my patience and I'm getting' tired. Make this your last time coming to this house. If Jaidyn wants to see you she'll call you!"

Jaidyn interrupted before Keith could respond, "What are you doing here?"

"We need to talk," Keith said. "Do you know how much I love you? I can't let you walk out on everything we have."

"You what," she asked clinching her fist. She fought to hold back the words that were on the tip of her tongue. She'd grown to love him but had never been in love with him, which only made it easier to walk away from him. "I've heard all that shit before so save it. Love is a two way street. It's about giving something to a relationship. All you seem to do is take!"

"I don't know why you can't understand that I've made a lot of mistakes. I've said a lot of things I didn't mean and I'm sorry."

"You know what? Save your breath. It's over. I want a divorce."

"Now you're talking crazy," Keith said as if she was flirting with insanity.

Jaidyn looked at Keith as if he were utterly worthless, "When I was trying to make things work, you were doggin' me."

"That's not true!"

"Hum, you can save that…"

"I just need you to understand that…"

"Understand? What am I supposed to understand? That you don't have any respect for me? That every time we're out some tramp is up in yo face or that you're always whispering in some woman's ear and as soon as I walk up the conversation ends. Am I supposed to understand the numerous times that you've come home late smelling like some woman's perfume? Or am I supposed to understand that you tripped over your own feet and your dick fell into Chevon and whoever else you've been fuckin'? It's always something with you. There's always something that I need to understand."

"I can't lose you. I'll lose my mind without you."

"There have been times that I thought I was going to lose my mind too but somehow I picked myself up and moved forward. You need to do the same thing."

"Jaidyn, I'm sorry!"

"That's for damn sure!" She said shaking her head. "But sorry can't fix this."

"Babyyy…"

"Keith if you don't stop talking to me and get out my face I'm a hurt you!" Jaidyn said looking like she was prepared to do exactly that.

Russell Owens beamed with pride. "That's my girl," he whispered to Mrs. Owen who was standing behind him. They weren't eavesdropping like she'd accused him of. They were simply standing around the corner listening to make sure that things didn't get out of hand.

Chapter 39

Keith had become more of a nuisance than Jaidyn wanted to deal with. She received so many flowers that her office staff had been instructed to start refusing all floral deliveries. He'd been showing up at her office and waiting for her to finish with her patients so that they could talk or go to dinner. The more she turned him down the more persistent he became. He had called this afternoon and asked if they could talk after work.

"We've been over this and there's nothing to talk about."

"Damn Jaidyn. You're getting on my fucking nerves with this shit. Enough is enough."

"Look I'm not with that drama today. If you want to talk to me you're going to have show me some respect. If you can't then don't call me again," she said and hung up.

She was at her wit's end with him. As she drove home she called Joanna to check on the progress of the divorce papers.

"Holloway, James and Smith Attorney's at law," the receptionist answered.

"Hello this is Jaidyn Owens is Joanna still in the office?"

"Can you please hold?"

"Yes," Jaidyn answered then listened to the music of the hold button.

"This is Joanna Holloway."

"Joanna! How much longer before the divorce papers are ready?"

"Hi Jaidyn. How are you today? Thanks for asking how my day was. I had a grueling day in court and I'm dog tired."

"I'm sorry Joanna but he's driving me crazy," Jaidyn whined in her best little sister voice.

"No problem. Your papers are ready. But I wanted to talk to you before I filed them. Have you had a chance to reconsider your stand on the property you've acquired while married?"

"The house was Keith's when we got married and I don't have an interest in his business."

"The law requires that the house be considered community property because it wasn't paid for before you were married. All community property is to be divided equally if there is no written agreement to the contrary, which entitles you to half of its total fair market value. What about spousal support and his retirement? Have you reconsidered seeking half of those?"

"Joanna, we've already gone over this. I don't want anything from him. I just want out of this marriage as quickly as possible."

"My sources tell me…"

"You're sources? What sources? Are you having him investigated?" Jaidyn asked annoyed.

"Yes! If you want to win this case we may have to play dirty."

"I don't believe you. I told you…"

"Jaidyn, I'm your lawyer. This is my job! Now listen to me. As an ex-pro football player his retirement from the NFL alone is substantial and my sources tell me that his business is doing extremely well. Since he started it he has gotten several multi-million dollar contracts and…"

"Joanna, I don't care what your *sources* find. I just want out!"

"As your lawyer I have to tell you that I think that's a mistake and I wish you would reconsider."

Jaidyn took a deep breath and tried to hide her frustration, "I know you mean well but I don't want anything from him."

"Ok. I'll sign off on the papers today and get them over to the courthouse first thing in the morning. It can take a couple of days before the constable gets the papers and serves him."

"How long before we go to court?"

"Well, I can't imagine that Keith will contest the divorce since you aren't asking for anything. So if all goes as planned we have to wait ninety days from the day the papers are filed."

"Three months! I don't know if I can wait that long!"

Joanna continued as if she hadn't heard a word Jaidyn had said, "If he contests the divorce we will have to go to mediation and that could delay the divorce even longer."

"Delay? For how long?"

"That depends on how difficult he wants to be. If he is really bothering you that much we can get a restraining order against him."

"No! That won't be necessary. Thanks Joanna."

"Try to relax Jai, this is almost over. And don't thank me until you get my bill." Joanna said with a hint of humor in her voice.

Jaidyn hung up as she pulled into her driveway. She put the car in park and made her way to her back door. As she unlocked her back door Keith stepped out of the shadows of the back yard and scared the hell out of her. "I didn't mean to scare you."

"Well what exactly did you mean to do?" Jaidyn asked angrily. "And what in the hell are you doing here?"

"I had to see you."

"For what? Did I not make myself clear, earlier?" She asked, her voice antagonistic.

Jaidyn had decided that she was going to kill which ever of her friends told him where she lived. She had intentionally not given him any of her new information. After he had harassed the hell out of her by calling her cell phone all times of the night she had the number changed. He'd set up camp at the office and she didn't want him doing the same thing at her house. Things were getting out of control. She hoped it would only last for a couple more days. As soon as he got the divorce papers she was sure it would put an end to his continuous hounding.

"Can I come in for a couple of minutes?"

Jaidyn breathed out heavily and looked him up and down in discuss, "Only for a minute. I have plans."

Just as Keith did most evenings, he'd parked his car one street over and walked to Jaidyn's house. After speaking with her he'd waited on the bench tucked between the two old oak trees in her backyard. Just as he had a hundred times before, he'd been sure to wear dark pants and a dark shirt, to help conceal his presence in the yard.

He'd never wanted to scare her, he just wanted to watch her and imagine that he was inside with her, but this night was different. As he sat waiting on her to get home thoughts of her flowed through his mind and sitting and watching her from a distance wasn't going to do on this night. He needed to talk to her, to touch her, to be with her.

"This is ridiculous Jaidyn, let me take you to dinner so we can talk."

"I said I have plans," Jaidyn said rolling her eyes.

"Jaidyn please give us a chance. Let me explain why I acted like I did."

"I've done that. All I ever wanted was for you to love me. I wanted to look at you and see the love in your eyes. I wanted you to pass me in the kitchen and hit me on my butt. I wanted to sit on the couch together and hold hands while we watched TV, instead of watching TV in two different rooms. I wanted to flirt with you while we were in a room full of people. The only time you touched me was when you wanted sex but I wanted you to touch me some other time. Just because. I wanted us to be friends and lovers. I tried to convey that to you…Let's not hurt each other anymore. It's time to end this."

"I worked hard and gave you everything I could."

"Keith you gave me material things but you never gave me you. And that's all I ever wanted."

"Baby I promise things are going to be different. I won't act crazy any more. I won't go off on you. I promise. Just give me another chance."

"I'm so tired of you pacifying me with promises you and I both know you can't keep."

"We're not the only people in the world to go through ups and downs. I wake up lonely. I miss sleeping next to you. We can work things out. I miss you. I know you've got your pride but it's time we put this shit behind us." Keith begged.

"I don't want to work things out. Nothing can take us back to where we once were. I'm moving on with my life. I suggest you do the same." Jaidyn tried to be as clear as possible without being insensitive. Keith needed to let go and she had been trying to convey that to him. He had taken their life together for granted and he still wanted more from her. She had given all she could to this marriage and didn't have anything left to give. He'd made a mockery of their marriage and no matter what he promised there was no going back.

His voice cracked as the realization of her words hit him, "I never realized your leaving would hurt so much. Can you please just give me the benefit of the doubt?"

"No, I've given all I can. How long are we supposed to maintain this illusion we call a marriage? It's time for us to stop frontin'. I don't want to hurt you but it's over."

"Can't we start over? Maybe we can date…we need to find a way to stay together. We can work this out! I love you."

"I don't doubt that you love me but love isn't supposed to hurt, and if it does that's not how I want to be loved."

"I never meant to hurt you."

"I know that but it doesn't change the facts. There's nothing you can say or do to change what happened between us. Everything I felt is gone…

the man I thought I cared for is gone. We aren't the same people we used to be."

Tears flowed down Keith's face and he struggled to get words out, "I won't stop trying until you take your last breath."

The longer he talked the more she wished he would shut the hell up and get out of her damn house. There was nothing he could say or do to persuade her to change her mind. She'd been his fool for too long. It wasn't that she was heartless but his tears meant nothing to her. After all those nights she'd cried and pleaded with him to treat her with some kind of respect. After all the nights she had to bite her tongue just so he wouldn't act a damn fool with her. He deserved to miss her. He deserved to feel the same desperation she'd felt for the past year.

She smiled to herself aware of how stupid she'd been. Once upon a time the things he said sounded so sweet. Now her eyes were opened and she realized it was all an utter crock of shit. He still thought she was boo-boo the fool and believed every word that came out of his mouth.

She remembered a time when she'd call him to the carpet on one of his lies he always found a way to justify his actions. In his own mind his excuse would justify his conduct. If she challenged him further he'd say, "I spoke to my mother and she agreed with me," which also made it right. She never thought it possible that she would get to a point that she loathed the sound of his voice but she had. She had never imagined that she would one day detest his mere presence but when he walked in her door her attitude changed. She didn't wish him harm. She just didn't want him breathing in her space and her space happened to be earth.

The conversation had already taken thirty-five minutes of Jaidyn's time. She needed to get him out of there so she could take a shower and get to the airport to pick up her friend, Anna. "Keith I don't mean to interrupt you but I'm going to have to ask you to leave. I have plans."

"Please Jaidyn." He begged. She's being bull headed and going to have to get over it, he thought. He knew things were falling apart but he hadn't known how to stop them. He was getting sick of begging her ass and wasn't going to beg too much longer. He had three or four ho's that were riding his jock for his attention. "Let me just say one more thing..." Oh here it comes she thought. "I know I can be a good man if you stay with me. I can be the man you need me to be. I can't be happy without you. I realize I need you. Please give us another chance." He said leaning towards her to kiss her on the cheek.

Jaidyn crossed her arms and backed away from him. The thought of him kissing her gave her the heebie-jeebies and she shivered, "Keith please call before you just pop up over here again."

Chapter 40

Anna had flown in for an exhibit opening at The Museum of Fine Arts. Some of her work would be premiered in the exhibit. The semi-formal private premier party was in an hour and Jaidyn and Yasmine were going to accompany her.

Dressed in a stunning black cross-back dress with a slit up the side and a pair of leg wrap black heels, Jaidyn looked like a stunning diva ready to take on the world. She had purchased the ensemble during a shopping spree she and Anna had gone on two days prior.

They'd planned an all out girl's weekend and Jaidyn was looking forward to it. The museum arranged for a limousine to pick Anna up at 6:30 p.m. Despite Jaidyn insistence on Yasmine arriving early she was late as usual. When the limousine arrived, Jaidyn had to decline Anna's invitation to ride with her so that she could wait on Yasmine.

Although Anna and Jaidyn had been close friends for years she and Yasmine hadn't had a chance to meet. It seemed that every time Anna was in town, Yasmine was busy or away on business. Jaidyn was sure that they would like each other and couldn't wait to introduce them.

Yasmine walked through the door apologizing for her tardiness. She stopped mid-sentence and looked at Jaidyn. "What?" Jaidyn asked defensively.

Although Jaidyn had always worn a smile there had been a cast of sadness in her eyes and she had begun to look haggard. Since she'd left Keith her eyes had seemed to come alive. They seemed to dance when she smiled. Her mood was upbeat and her outlook optimistic. She was finally getting back to her old self. Yasmine had missed her and was glad she was getting her life back on track. She'd always been a strong willed, strong minded, confident person. While she was with Keith she had allowed him to control her. She'd always seemed depressed and unsure of herself. Since she'd left him Yasmine had noticed that Jaidyn seemed to have been working her way back to the dignity and self-respect she'd had before she married Keith. "Nothing…You look great." Yasmine said unable to resist hugging her.

Although Yasmine didn't admit it Jaidyn knew what she was thinking. She hadn't had a peace of mind since she'd married Keith. She'd been distant and hadn't wanted to have anything to do with anyone, including Yasmine. She'd been bogged down with so much stress all she'd wanted to do after work was go home and go to bed. "Thanks. You're looking pretty fabulous yourself." Jaidyn said pulling away from her to get a second look at her outfit, "That dress is wearing the hell out of you." She was the sexiest dreadlock-wearing sister Jaidyn knew. It wasn't something she tried to be. It was just a part of who she was. She was confident but didn't flaunt it. Her dark striking beauty combined with her flirty personality and sex appeal made her a force to reckon with.

When they arrived at the exhibit they were immediately greeted by a waiter who handed them each a champagne flute. "I like the way Anna does business," Yasmine said. The place was packed. It was a haze of crystal wineglasses clinging and hushed conversations. Jaidyn surveyed the room to see if she could spot Anna.

When Jaidyn spotted Jared she seemed to hold her breath as he held her gaze almost motionless. She had gone over the guest list earlier that day with Anna and was sure she hadn't overlooked his name. He must be here with someone, she thought. He was dressed in a black suit with a black and gray tie. He smiled warmly and her knees seemed to go a little weak.

It had been three months since she'd seen him. He'd called her several times after that rainy morning she'd shown up at his apartment but she avoided his calls. Running to him when things at home were bad only clouded her issues. She needed to get her life in order without pulling anyone into the middle of her mess. Now that she'd done that, there he was, looking good enough to eat.

"Damn," Jared said to himself as his eyes traveled down Jaidyn. As usual she was wearing the sexiest damn shoes and as usual his dick came alive just looking at her. He was unable to stop the fantasy of her in nothing but those shoes standing at the foot of his bed from running through his mind.

Anna followed Jaidyn's eyes as she approached them. "Who is that," Anna asked breaking the spell.

Jaidyn pretended as if she didn't hear her, "Hey girl. This is an awesome turn out." Jaidyn said as she reached to hug her. "This is Yasmine. Yasmine this is Anna."

"It's nice to finally meet you. I feel like I already know you. Jaidyn talks about you all the time," Anna said hugging Yasmine.

"Girl, I feel like we're old friends. I'm really looking forward to getting to know you this weekend," Yasmine replied.

"So, who is the guy you're molesting with your eyes?" Anna asked Jaidyn.

"That's Jared!" Yasmine said answering for Jaidyn.

Anna's mouth fell open, "*That's Jared! Damn Jaidyn! How did you ever let something like that get away?*"

"Hm!" Yasmine said.

Just as Jaidyn was about to tell both of them to go to hell a gentleman asking Anna about the piece in the exhibit interrupted them. "Don't think you're going to get off that easy Jai. I'll be right back."

Yasmine laughed, "I like her already."

Yasmine excused herself and went to the ladies room. Jaidyn moved through the crowd and admired the pieces in the exhibit. Anna was unbelievably talented. She had seen some of her early work but she'd stepped things up and her new stuff was simply incredible.

She was caught off guard when the deep smooth cultivating voice from behind her said, "This artist is masterful and this piece...well it's extraordinary." Jaidyn's entire body smiled. He was standing so close that she could feel his body heat. His breath was warm on her shoulder. The sound of his voice sent chills up her spine. "...Are you enjoying yourself?"

"Yes and how about you?" She said as she turned around to see Jared standing there. For a moment the world stood still and they were the only to on earth. Jared was looking at her in that way that made her insides warm and tingly. It was as if she could see herself through his eyes and it made her feel sexy.

She flashed back on how wonderful sex had been with him. It was passionate. Intense. Dangerously intense. It was that kind of intensity that either scared the hell out of you or made you lose your mind. Suddenly, standing there talking to him wasn't good enough. She wanted to feel his warmth against her skin. Drawn to him like a magnet she reached out and casually touched him. Her heart still held him. It felt so good when she was near him. She had a genuine physical passion for him that tugged at the moisture between her legs.

"I love those shoes." He said smoothly.

"Thank you." Jaidyn said blushing.

"You've been avoiding me…" Jared paused but she gave him no indication that she knew what he was referring to. "I've called you several times."

Jaidyn shook her head, "I know…I'm sorry. I had some issues that I needed to take care of." She said truthfully. "I didn't want to drag you into the middle of them."

"I see." Jared said looking at her inquisitively.

Jaidyn quickly changed the subject, "Where's your date?"

"She went to the ladies room. Where's your other half?" He countered. "I can't believe he let you out looking so," he paused letting his eyes traveled down her, "Exquisite."

It was hard not to notice the lust that filled his eyes. She smiled knowing what she was doing to him. The way he was looking at her let her know she still had the same effect on him that she'd had in the past. Seeing that look made her blush like a schoolgirl who'd just been kissed for the first time.

Jaidyn was taken aback and quickly thought about what he had said to her. She wanted to say that her other half was standing in front of her but she resisted. "If you mean Keith, he and I are no longer together. I've filed for divorce." The look of astonishment on his face was unexpected. She'd assumed that Neal had told him but it was obvious he hadn't.

Jared was knocked for a loop and wasn't quite sure how to respond. The news seemed to instantaneously throw his life into turmoil.

"I thought Neal or Naomi would have told you." Jaidyn said without thinking. She wasn't sure if Naomi would say anything. She'd sworn her to secrecy, but Naomi's fierce loyalty to Jared made Jaidyn question if she would actually keep the secret. She had been in Jaidyn's office for an appointment when Keith decided to surprise her by showing up and taking her to dinner. Naomi had over heard them arguing. Jaidyn had said some very harsh things and told him he was going to have to stop coming to her office, their marriage was over. Afterward she confided in Naomi and told her of her pending divorce.

"I'm…I'm sorry to hear that." He said straight up lying. Neal had called him as soon as Yasmine told him they were separated but they hadn't mentioned that she'd filed for divorce. And Naomi had not come right out and told him but she'd hinted around it. When he had pretended not to catch the hint she'd suggested that he give Jaidyn a call to see how she was doing. "How are you doing?"

"I'm fine. Thanks for asking." She said smiling brightly.

Jared and Jaidyn were standing so close and were so enthralled in their conversation neither of them noticed Anna when she approached. "Hi, I'm Anna Monroe." Anna said poking her head around Jaidyn's shoulder.

Jared stepped to the side of Jaidyn and slid his hand down to the small of her back. Jaidyn's body stiffened at his touch. Jared extended his hand, "It's a pleasure to meet you. I'm Jared Mitchell. Your work is exquisite. I particularly like this piece." He said nodding at the painting Jaidyn was standing beside.

"Well I can't take credit for this one," Anna said ignoring the painting and giving Jaidyn the eye. "You'll have to express your appreciation to Mr. and Mrs. Owens for their work. She did turn out to be *exquisite*."

Jared erupted into laughter, "Touché."

A small look of pleasure crossed Jaidyn's face but when she saw Faith approaching them it disappeared as quickly as it had come.

Faith spotted Jared talking to Jaidyn and Anna when she emerged from the ladies room and made her way in their direction. When she approached them she slid her arm under Jared's and kissed him making it known that he was her property. "Sorry I took so long," she said. Jared appeared to be a little uncomfortable with her taking possession of him.

"Hello Jaidyn." She said trying to mask her annoyance.

"Faith, it's nice to see you again." Jaidyn said.

There was something about Jared and Jaidyn that said they were connected. It was that unmistakable look that couples had when they were intimate. Anna could see it so she knew that Faith had to see it. She could feel the tension between the three of them and tried to defuse the situation, "Hi," she said extending her hand, "I'm Anna Monroe."

Faith shook her hand, "It's nice to meet you. I've been a fan for quite some time. I bought one of your early paintings at a starving artist show on Fisherman's Wharf in San Francisco."

"Which painting do you own?"

"My First Love."

"That's one of my favorites," Anna said.

Once Faith and Jared were alone she made her annoyance obvious. "What's wrong?" Jared asked as if he were clueless.

"Why is it every time I turn around she's up in your face?" Faith snarled.

"Who?" Jared asked as if he didn't know she was referring to Jaidyn. Faith rolled her eyes. "Girl you're trippin'!" Jared said.

"Trippin' hmmm…is that why you molest her with your eyes every time she's around?"

He stared at her as if he was in complete disbelief but he knew she was absolutely right. He couldn't explain it to her because he couldn't explain it to himself. He couldn't deny he was completely enamored with Jaidyn. He just had to have her. She was a bad habit he couldn't kick. Loving her was instinctive. It wasn't something he wanted to do. It was something he did unconsciously.

Chapter 41

Keith sat in his car waiting on Jaidyn to come home. He'd rented a car and parked a couple of houses down from hers. He wanted to see what the hell she was doing and who she was doing it with. He'd done this before but had yet to catch her with anyone, but he knew there had to be someone else. The reason she left him had to be because of another man. He was sure that some brotha had whispered some bullshit in her ear and her dumb ass had fallen for it.

He'd sat under the elm tree in her back yard and watched her move through her house several times. He'd not chanced the elm tree on this night because that bitch, Anna, had been staying with her for a couple of days. He'd told her on more then one occasion that he didn't like her hanging out with that bitch. Married women shouldn't hang out with single ho's. Single bitches are jealous and fill married women's head with all types of bull shit.

360 was a club that sat atop a Downtown Houston skyscraper. When Anna, Yasmine and Jaidyn stepped off the elevator Anna was impressed. She was skeptical about where her friends were taking her when they'd entered the building and was greeted by a security guard that directed them to an elevator. They'd ridden the elevator to the thirty-third floor and were greeted by a gruff gentleman that asked to see their ID's. They'd each paid him $20 and were directed to another set of elevators that brought them to the sixty-ninth floor.

When the elevator door opened, Whitney's voice flowed over them like a smooth summer's breeze and they stepped into a room that looked like it was atop of the world. A circular dance floor lay in the center of the club. A bar sat on two sides of it. There were chaise lounges, couches and chairs set up in cozy conversational pits running along the floor to ceiling windows that were 360 degrees around the entire club. The panoramic view of downtown Houston was spectacular.

Before the ladies could find someplace to sit Yasmine noticed Jared sitting at one of the bars. "Don't look now but your boy is here." She said to Jaidyn.

"Who," Jaidyn asked looking around the club.

"Damn, how many men do you have," Anna asked sarcastically?

"He's sitting at the bar talking to some guy," Yasmine said as she waved to him.

After they found a cozy corner Jaidyn searched the bar and found Jared. They hadn't been sitting but a couple of minutes when the waitress approached them with three Apple Martini's, "Compliments of the gentleman at the bar."

Apple Martini's had long been Jaidyn's favorite. "Girl, he's knows you like a book," Anna said. Jaidyn was a little surprised that he hadn't forgotten. She quickly scribed a note on a napkin and asked the waitress to deliver it to him. Jaidyn watched him as he opened it, *'Thank you. I'm curious what else is etched in your memory.'* He smiled brightly then slipped the note in his pocket.

Someone asked Yasmine to dance before she was able to enjoy her drink. Jaidyn and Anna talked as they watched her. Yasmine was looking sexy as usual and every man in the place seemed to notice. She was wearing an open back cream colored shirt that tied at the nape of her neck with an itsy-bitsy, teeny-weeny chocolate skirt and a pair of chocolate go-go boots. It wasn't just the outfit that was attracting men to her, there was something about her smooth chocolate skin, shapely body, slightly bowed legs, and high butt that men found irresistible.

The girls spent the next hour laughing and catching up. Several men approached them and asked them to dance but they turned them down. Jaidyn occasionally eyed Jared. He hadn't moved from his spot. Julian had come in, captured his attention and he hadn't looked in their direction since.

"Why don't you go and talk to him," Anna asked?

"It's not like you're paying attention to us!" Yasmine said.

"You better tell him how you feel before somebody else grabs him," Anna added. Jaidyn pretended to ignore their comments but she'd heard everything they said and knew they were right.

As Mary J. Blige's sassy strong voice begin blowing through the club Jaidyn popped up out of her seat and made her way to the bar. She took a seat on the barstool next to him. Her palms were moist with nervousness.

"Are you ready to tell me what else is etched in that memory of yours?" She asked seductively over his shoulder. He smiled then turned and looked at her. She was wearing a pair of cream color pants that he'd love to watch her take off. Her legs were crossed and the mules she had on lightly hung on her foot. The look on her face was luring. Seductive. Sexy. It turned him on. He had to slow himself and be sure that they were on the same page.

"Springer, how you been?" Julian chimed in as he came off the dance floor. Jaidyn laughed she hadn't been called that in a long time. When they were dating he'd poked fun at them and given them the nicknames Springer and Sprung. He'd called her 'Springer' every since. At the time Jared had not found nearly as much humor in Julian's nicknames as she had, but tonight he'd laughed as it brought back memories.

"Hey Julian," she said leaning over to give a friendly hug.

"What you and your girls up to tonight," he asked?

"Just hanging out."

"Oh yeah," he said shaking his head. "You want something to drink?"

"Nah, thanks. I came over to see if I could pursue your brother to dance with me." Julian got the message and turned his attention back to Darius. When Jaidyn turned her attention back to Jared he was undressing her with his dreamy eyes. "So, Mr. Mitchell how about that dance?"

"That may not be a good idea. Your husband's friend is here."

"Markel?...I saw him." She said in a cadence way glancing in Markel's direction. "Are you going to dance with me?"

Her flippant attitude took Jared by surprise, "...Sure!" He said, taking her hand and leading her onto the dance floor.

Jared admired Jaidyn's fine ass body. She had a figure that only a black woman could. He couldn't take his eyes off her as her hips swayed to the music in an erotic seductive manner. When she turned her back to him and rubbed up against him Jared momentarily got lost in the moment and placed his groin against her nice, round, firm asset. Forty-five minutes later the two of them were still on the dance floor. R. Kelly was singing "Step step, side to side, round and round, dip it down, separate, bring it back, and let me see you do the love slide…" Jared was very light on his feet, which made him a good dancer. He always enjoyed dancing with Jaidyn because she matched his every step. They'd both relaxed into an easy groove and other couples on the dance floor watched them and tried to imitate their moves. By the end of the song they were laughing at the guy next to them who was obviously not familiar with the dance.

"Girl you've worn me out. Let's get something to drink." Jared was saying when Gerald Levert began singing. He took her hand in his and started walking toward the bar. The words of the song echoed inside her and she tugged on his hand pulling him back onto the dance floor. He quickly pulled her into his arms and held her close.

She leaned back gazing at his face. She noticed the scar on his right temple. "How did you get that scar?" She said lightly rubbing her figure across it.

"Oh, an old friend left her mark." One corner of his mouth went up into a half smile, "Something to remember her by." He said flirting with her.

Jaidyn immediately remembered their fight and the thrown glass. She gave him a sweet singsong laugh as she softly rubbed her fingers across the scar. "A lovers quarrel?" She asked in a sarcastic flirty tone.

"Something like that."

Although she knew she loved Jared, rekindling a relationship with him had been the last thing on her mind until now. Her plans were to divorce Keith and take some time to work out her own issues. A relationship at this point was the last thing on her list of things she wanted to do; but being near Jared changed that pretty quickly. To think that Jared would want to be with her was presumptuous to say the least. Lord knows she had sent him through enough changes for him to no longer view her in the same light, she thought.

"I've been wanting to ask you something since you walked in that door," he said smiling.

"What?" She asked curious at his joking matter.

"What color panties do you have on?"

Jaidyn blushed, "I'm not wearing any." She admitted with a flirtatious smile.

Her bluntness turned him on and he pulled her closer into him. The longer he held her close the more she wanted him. Gerald was singing a sexy love ballet about being made to love someone when she took a leap of faith and whispered in his ear, "You know I asked Gerald to write this song just for you." Jared looked down at her and found her looking into his dreamy eyes. He let out a soft, sexy, deep laugh, pulled her closer to him and listened intently to the words of the song.

As they held each other close the music surrounded them and flowed through them. They were holding each other so close Jaidyn could feel his heart beating. As if she could read his mind she stopped dancing and looked at him, "I was made to love you Jared. You and only you. I made a mistake. Can you give me another chance?"

His eyes locked on hers. He was completely discombobulated. "What did she say," he asked himself. He quickly ran it through his mind once, twice, and then again. He tried to blink away the surprised look on his face. What was she expecting him to say to that?

Jaidyn fingers lightly traced his check as he peered into her soul. Her lips parted a bit and she let her lips touch his. His hands slid seductively down the center of her back as he pulled her into him. He still has the gentlest touch, she thought, and these lips are still soft and warm, inviting. She loved how gentle and sensual his touch was.

"You feel so good," he whispered in her ear.

"Look at the two of them," Yasmine was saying as Markel approached them.

"Hey Yasmine."

"Markel!" Yasmine said with a cold stare.

"Who's this beautiful young lady?"

Yasmine sucked her teeth and rolled her eyes, "What do you want?"

"Come on now. I just came over to say hello and to meet your friend."

Yasmine had been vexed and down right nasty since Markel had approached them. Anna took that as unspoken advice and avoided eye contact with him. "I'm not going to entertain that bull with you so you can move on." They both looked at Jaidyn dancing with Jared then back at each other.

"What's that suppose to mean?" Markel asked.

"I ain't the one!"

"You and I both know Jai's been going through a lot. I'm not trying to start any trouble. She deserves to have some fun. Keith's my boy but he's a damn fool. Ole' boy accused me of trying to holla at Jaidyn. Then he stepped to Jai with that same nonsense. She barely talks to me because if she does she's got to hear his shit. I'm not one to get in people's business but I had to set him straight. Jaidyn don't deserve to be treated like that." Markel had told her the short version of the story. They had almost gone to war over Keith's unfounded jealousy. Keith had told Jaidyn that every time he turned around Markel was up in her face. He'd said he was pimpin' his game and knew what he was up to. When Markel came to the house and asked about Jaidyn he went off on him about his wife and put him out. Then Markel bumped into Jaidyn at lunch one day. She told him she was meeting Keith. When Keith arrived they were having a causal conversation. Keith acted a damn fool. He made crazy accusations about the two of them. He had spoken to Jaidyn so badly that Markel had to get in his face for him to stop.

Yasmine looked at him suspiciously, she wasn't sure how to take him. Although Jaidyn had told her all about the run in, he and Keith had been boys since...forever. Now all of a sudden he's Jaidyn's friend. She didn't trust his ass as far as she would throw him. "That's yo boy why don't you tell him that he's fucking up."

"I've talked to him till I'm blue in the face. Keith's a damn fool. You can't tell him nothing. After the shit his ass has put her through he shouldn't let her out of his sight. She shouldn't be in here with you on a Friday night. She should be with him. Some people don't learn until it's too late." Yasmine was surprised. Markel didn't sound like he knew they weren't together but she wasn't about to tell him. "Well, she seems to be having a nice time. So chill and introduce me to your friend."

"Anna Markel, Markel Anna." Anna gave him a dry hello and he instantly got the message.

"Look the two of them are already going through enough without us adding our two cent. So as far as I'm concerned I didn't see you guys. It was nice to meet you Anna."

Keith had a hard time processing what he was looking at. His fucking wife was dancing with that fool. His chest tightened and he could feel sweat beading up on his forehead. I've got to play it cool, he said to himself, but the stinging pain of seeing her like this washed over him like a back draft from a raging fire. If he went off it would only make things between him and Jaidyn worse. It had already been one of those days and he didn't need to add any more drama to it.

He took a seat at the bar and ordered a shot of Tequila and a Hennessey, straight up. He needed the drink to calm his nerves. Lately he'd been drinking like a alcoholic in training. The women in his life were driving him out of his mind. Chevon hadn't let him see his son since he kicked her ass after she told Jaidyn. She had filed for child support and he'd gone over to her house he found out she'd moved. The bitch had lost her mind but as soon as he caught up with her he was going to beat her ass again.

Alexia had started tripping too. She had been tormenting Shelbi by calling her house threatening to tell her husband and she had been harassing the hell out of Keith too. After he and Shelbi decided to stop letting her in on their thing she had simply lost her mind. She had cut all four of Keith's tires, thrown a cinder block through his car window, and had taken a razor to his car interior. Then she'd taken her keys and gone down the side of Shelbi's car. He was looking for her ass too. "Nothing will straighten a ho out like a little ass kicking," he thought.

Zaria was tripping as usual about not getting enough of his time. If that ho had it her way he'd damn near live with her. The one silver lining to all the bullshit was Darcy. She was down for whatever. Jaidyn had fired her but it hadn't affected her in the least. She'd found another job and was still sucking his shit like no other. Now Jaidyn has the nerve to be in here disrespecting me…uh…"She better be careful or she's next," he said to himself.

To top all this shit off, today a constable had shown up at his office and served him with divorce papers. He felt like he was loosing control and he was willing to do just about anything to get it back. His anger combined with the humiliation he felt after seeing his wife with another man's tongue down her throat was a deadly combination.

"Jaidyn," Jared said loosening his hold on her, "Keith is at the bar."

"I saw him." He was stunned as she pulled him closer to her. Being close to him made her feel alive and she wasn't about to let anyone interfere with that. She lightly kissed him on his neck and desire ran through him like a shot of tequila, warming him, stabbing at his insides.

By the time they'd finished their dance Jared had a full blown erection that Jaidyn felt poking her. "Why do you keep doing this to me," he asked seductively.

"Oh shit!" Markel said when he spotted Keith watching Jared and Jaidyn.

Yasmine spotted Keith at the same moment, "Markel do something!" She yelled.

Keith was standing in their path as they begin to exit the dance floor. Jaidyn held Jared's hand a little tighter. Shit, Jared thought, this ain't my business and I'm not going to get involved. He freed his hand from Jaidyn's, "Thanks for the dance."

Keith ignored Jared standing behind Jaidyn, "I called you last night."

"Did you?" Jaidyn said.

"You want to tell me where the fuck you were?" He asked.

"Not particularly!" Jaidyn replied annoyed.

Jared wanted no part of this conversation and began walking away from them. As he passed Keith he heard him call her a bitch and his blood ran cold. He stopped in his tracks. He never doubted Keith's love for Jaidyn but what kind of man would treat his wife like this. Jared put his hands in his pockets and looked at the floor. The profanity Keith was throwing at her made his stomach turn. He looked down at his feet and wondered why they wouldn't move. If he could take three or four steps the music would surely drown out Keith's voice.

He looked up in the direction of were he'd left Julian and Darius sitting. They must have sensed something was wrong because they were already making their way towards him. He was surveying the crowd for Markel when he heard the palm of Keith's hand hit the flat surface of Jaidyn's face. It was as if the place went quiet and the slap was the only thing he could hear. It echoed like thunder in his ears. When he turned around he spotted Markel approaching them from the right with Yasmine and Anna in tow. Jaidyn looked at Keith with wild eyes. "You ain't nothing but a fuckin' ho!" Keith yelled.

She flew at him. Julian was suddenly there, out of nowhere catching her in mid flight. Her arms and legs were swinging widely, "You son of a bi..." Tears of hot anger streamed down her face as she yelled at him, "Julian let me go! I'm going to kill this muthaf..."

When Keith raised his hand again Jared caught it. "I'm only going to tell you this once, don't you ever raise your hand to her again." Jared's voice had an eerie controlled tone to it. When he let Keith's arm go everything seem to happen in the blink of an eye. Keith mumbled something that no one heard but Jared. When the punch came it surprised everyone. Keith was knocked off his feet. Jared put his hands around his throat and pulled him to his feet.

Darius was standing in front of Markel with his hand on Markel's chest, "This ain't your fight pa'tna."

Keith was about to retaliate when Julian let Jaidyn go and showed Keith and Jared the gun he had strapped to his waistband. Julian paused, threatening Keith with his eyes. "It's your call man. Whatcha wanna do?" He asked Jared.

"I'm going to send this muthafucka home in a body bag!" Jared retorted, enraged but still holding on to an ounce of control.

"No!" Jaidyn said interrupting.

"What? You've lost yo mind!" Jared said as his blind rage boiled over.

Jaidyn shook her head, "Please don't hurt him." She said almost in a whisper. "He's not worth it." A flicker of understanding ran through Jared's mind and he let Keith go.

Yasmine frowned, "Don't hurt him?"

"Kick that fools ass!" Anna said.

Keith laughed taunting Jared. "Yo punk ass goin' to let my wife and yo boy with the gun fight your battles for you? I'm not drunk tonight muthafucka. If you wanna go head to head we can settle this shit right now."

Jared straightened his back and squared his shoulders, "I've got zero tolerance for bullshit!" Jared replied. "There ain't nothing between us but air and opportunity."

Julian pulled the gun out his waistband and slid the barrow back, loading one round into the chamber. Jared stepped so close to Keith he could feel his breath as he spoke. "I've told yo ass before, don't fuck with me! You raise your hand to her again your going to meet yo maker." Jared said through clinched teeth.

Jaidyn had been saying something but Jared's rage had drowned her out. Now she was pulling his arm and he finally heard her, "Jared please." Without looking at her he grabbed her hand. She was shaking. He took a quick glance at her and her eyes pulled him in. He'd heard that your eyes are a window to your soul and for Jaidyn nothing could be truer. Every emotion she experienced he saw in her eyes. Now he saw panic and it made him want to protect her.

Chapter 42

Jared didn't know how they made their way from the club to her bed but there they were. They had a fair amount to drink, maybe that was it, he thought. What ever it was he hoped that she didn't regret it when she woke.

It was unbelievable how good her body felt next to his. Her body was flawless and more shapely then he'd remember. It was the well-toned body of a goddess. Slender but not skinny. Firm but soft. She was shaped like an old fashion Coca-Cola bottle, curves in all the right places.

Jared lifted his head and looked at the circus of clothing tossed around the room. He smiled to himself and reminisced on the details of their evening. Normally he was the aggressor but not last night. She'd slid her tongue into his ear, caressed the anaconda and there was no turning back. The moment was more powerful than he thought possible. Their hunger for each other had taken over and everything he had been thinking seemed to disappear.

Jared closed his eyes and relived the night in his mind as if it was a movie and he was merely a spectator. Jaidyn had pulled his shirt off and thrown it on the floor. He'd removed that shirt she called a dress and it joined his shirt. Her g-string was the next thing to go. He'd picked her up and put her on the dresser. Their urgency hadn't let them make it to the bed. She wrapped her legs around him and their bodies merged, igniting an explosion emotion inside of both of them. Their kisses were deep and meaningful. It was as if their hearts were doing a dance rather then their tongues. Their souls seemed to liquefy into each other and become one.

He touched her in places she didn't know would get her hot and the heat between them seemed to take her beyond her limits. Once they were inside the inferno, sweat covered them both. Her hands were on his stomach, his on her hips. He was hovering somewhere between heaven and earth, completely under her control. His toe's curled and he'd felt a sudden burst of urgency and had tried to rush, but she'd slowed their pace and took time to play on his body like she was on a playground. She made sure she toyed with every aspect of his jungle gym. She played on the playground until her heart was content, then she climbed onto him like she was on a seesaw, up-and-down, up-and down allowing the anaconda to tease her g-spot.

Jared had fought a good fight. He'd tried to think about the NBA basketball playoffs but it didn't work. He needed to get her off of him and level the playing field before she drained him of most his bodily fluids. She swayed one last time and he exploded. Seconds later she felt the earth move through her body and an avalanche of her essence spilled onto him. With no strength left for words moans of pleasure filled the room.

They'd made love all through the night. Trying every position known to man before they'd finally fallen asleep in each other's arms. They'd been completely uninhibited. Their phenomenal craving for each other surprising them both.

When Jared opened his eye's Jaidyn was still lying in his arms softly breathing on his chest hairs. He smiled to himself, it hadn't been just another one of those erotic dreams where he could feel her thighs wrapped around his waist. It really was true. He found it hard to believe. He climbed out of bed, found his boxers, tiptoed over to the bay window, and looked into Jaidyn's picturesque back yard. He loved this time of morning. The sun was coming up but the moon hadn't gone to bed. The sunrays were just beginning to peak through the limbs on the two hundred-year-old elm trees that covered the entire yard. The cool of the night still loomed in the air. The morning dew blanketed the grass. Flowers were opening their petals to the warm radiant light of the sun. Two blue jays played in the fountain in the middle of the yard and three little squirrels searched the base of the trees for acorns.

Jaidyn woke with a feeling of satisfaction and adoration she hadn't had in what seemed like forever. Jared had given her everything she'd been missing. She stretched, smiled, hugged the pillow next to her, and thought how their bodies had twisted and turned into every position imaginable. She stretched again and noticed her back was a little sore. He'd pushed her body to the limit. She buried her face into the pillow and sniffed, his scent still lingered there. It hadn't been a fantasy he really had been in her bed the night before.

Before she opened her eyes she reached for him but he wasn't there. She popped her head up, squinted against the sunlight, and searched the room for him. There he was, all six foot-five inches of him, standing with his back to her looking out the window.

She admired his powerfully built body. He looked like a powerful stallion, tall, strong, and handsome yet rugged. He had just enough scars to let you know that he hadn't been brought up in a glass bottle, but not too many that they made his body ugly and undesirable. There was a hard edge to him that provided him with quiet self-confidence. The entire mix gave him a strong sex appeal. For an added bonus he had a dick that damn near touched her tonsils and a big ass juicy tongue. The entire combination made him irresistible.

She got out of bed and wrapped her arms around him, resting her hands on his chest and her head on his back. The smell of their night still lingered in the air. She stood on her tiptoes to look over his shoulder, "Good morning." She said in her soft waking up voice. She'd never paid much attention to this time of the morning but she remembered how he'd loved it and this morning she could see why. The morning was unbelievably beautiful. The sky was a prefect blue. The sunrays danced through the tree limbs giving the backyard a surreal glow. The flowers were just starting to bloom. The trees whispered a beautiful song as a light spring breeze blew their leaves.

The entire moment seemed so unreal but there she stood with her arms wrapped around him. It was too good to be true, she thought. She didn't want to take her eyes off of him in fear that she'd wake up from this dream.

She loved the way her skin felt against his. Loved the way he touched her. The way her heart sped up when he was around. The way her mood changed the second he was in the room. She loved loving him.

For his own pleasure, during the night someone had painted a picture of her on the inside of his eye lids so every time he closed his eyes he saw her hauntingly beautiful face. The painting was so detailed he could even see the small white birthmark under her right arm. "Good morning beautiful," he said turning to face her. "I smell coffee, Anna must be awake."

"You can't imagine how much I've missed you," she said ignoring his observation. He'd been her night school teacher, educating her in the endless possibilities of erotic passion. It occurred to her that she no longer felt that void inside. It was him she'd been missing and in one night he'd filled it. She'd wanted him since the first time she'd laid eyes on him. This had been a long time coming and nothing had ever felt so right.

He openly admired her naked body like he was a seventeen-year-old boy who'd never seen a naked woman lying in his bed before. When his hand begin to tenderly caress her back she remembered that he had always been a toucher. She wasn't sure if it was subliminal but if they were within arms distance he'd make some type of physical contact with her. It was just one more thing to add to the list of things she loved about him.

She slid her hands over his chest, embellished it with soft kisses, and pulled him towards the bed. When she turned to walk to the bed he ran his cool wet tongue down the center of her back, her blood flowed quickly. She was wet and awaiting his next move. When he pressed against her she felt his hardness and they started the morning off the same way they had ended their night.

As they lay entangled in each other's arms Jared remembered seeing her for the very first time. It was her beauty that had first attracted him to her but once he'd spoken to her his attraction was so much more than physical. They had a strange almost mystical connection. Was it possible that they could finally be happy together, he wondered.

Jaidyn lay on top of him toying with the anaconda. When she begin traveling down his chest with her tongue, he sighed as he pulled her back into his arms. "You're killing me. I've got to go home just to recuperate." She laughed light heartedly and nestled against him.

They were wrapped in each other's arms when Keith popped into Jared's mind. His brow wrinkled and his eyes narrowed, "Has he ever hit you before?" In asking the question Jared seemed to automatically put a wall up between them again. It was as if he was trying to back pedal to get some control of his emotions.

"Once, but he only did it to get me off of him. I was acting like a crazy woman." Jaidyn laughed remembering how she'd behaved. "He pushed me to the edge and I lost it. I tried my best to kick his ass…He's not a violent person. I guess he feels like he was pushed in a corner. It has to be hard for him to see me with you. I mean, it's hard when you finally realize someone you love doesn't love you the way you want them to."

Jared was quiet for a few minutes before he asked, "What am I doing here?"

She regarded his statement carefully before she replied. Realizing the seriousness of his question she hesitated making sure she said the right thing. "I'm tired of running from what I feel for you." She looked into his face trying to read his reaction. "My life is empty without you," she said sincerely.

There was a boyish uncertainty in his face, "Let's get something straight...I'm not some lovesick kid living in fantasyland. You had your reasons for marrying Keith..."

Brick by brick the wall seemed to be getting taller. She knew what he was feeling and wanted to put his mind at ease, "Can I say something?" They both sat up in bed. Jared crossed his arms across his chest and waited on her to speak. Her voice became a bit strong and she looked directly at him, "Sometimes life's lessons are so harsh that they tear away at the fabric of who we are. Keith was that lesson for me. I should have been smarter and walked away from him a long time ago. I needed to experience the things I did with him so that I would appreciate the good things that I've seemed to take for granted. I went into the marriage under false pretenses... If you walk out the door right now and never look back I'm still going to divorce Keith. I'm doing this for my own peace of mind." Jaidyn paused gathering her thoughts.

When she spoke again her tone was soft and tender, "After I finished medical school I had everything I thought I ever wanted but there was still something missing. I took some advice from my mother and looked within myself to figure out what that was." Her expression was soft as she lifted her head to look into his eyes. "All I saw was you. I tried to tell myself that we could be friends but inside I knew differently. You're the love of my life. You are the best thing that's ever happened to me. You're my meant to be. I'm tired of lying to myself. I'm tired of trying to justify loving you. I adore you and that is never going to change. I made a mistake."

Jared's heart fluttered and skipped a beat as fear momentarily gripped it. His attention was fixed on her. Her comments had taken him by surprise and somehow his heart had become lodged in his throat. This was the first time he was seeing this side of her. The Jaidyn he knew kept her feelings locked behind an iron door. It was like pulling teeth to get her to talk about how she felt. She'd always been insecure about opening up to him. She felt it gave him the ability to hurt her, but something had changed and she was straightforward and very candid about her feelings. This must have been the unabridged version of her, he thought. Her emotions were raw and fragile and it pulled at him. As if she'd taken a stick of dynamite and blown up the wall between them, it seem to disintegrate in a matter of seconds.

There was an uncomfortable silence as she waited on him to say something. When he didn't she continued, "I had to let go of my relationship with Keith because we were living a lie. I knew who Keith was long before I married him. I guess I thought I could change him, but the more I became entangled in his insanity the more I began to loathe him. Marriage is supposed to be a pleasurable experience but being away from the person I truly loved was tormenting me." Jaidyn got teary eyed as the inescapable truth came pouring out. She looked off into space for a long minute then back at him, "I'm sorry I hurt you and I'm sorry for what I did to us. I was scared. I've never loved anyone like I love you. I didn't want to get hurt."

She'd just told the man she loved more than life itself the truth she had been concealing. She'd always thought she would feel vulnerable if he knew how she felt, but she stood there with her soul wide open and marveled at the overwhelming freedom that now slammed inside her like a tidal wave. He touched her in places that no one else could reach and it had been easier than she could have imagined to confide in him.

He couldn't believe that she thought that he'd ever hurt her. "Sweetheart, I'd never hurt you…" Jared pulled her into his arms and placed his finger under her chin, lifting her head so that he could look into her eyes. "You are the other half of my soul and I love you."

It was unbelievable that someone can love me like this, she thought. "Thank you for loving me through all this. I never meant to hurt you. I'm sorry." They talked and cuddled for another ten minutes before they retreated into the bathroom to shower.

Jaidyn and Jared walked into the kitchen feeling fresh and rejuvenated. "Speak of the devil! Here comes Laila and Roy now," Yasmine said chuckling. They both fell out laughing at her reference to Laila Ali and Roy Jones, Jr.

"Good morning!" Anna said sucking her teeth.

"Morning!" Jared said.

Silence!

Jaidyn looked around the kitchen at her two best friends. They'd been her girls for so long she didn't need to ask what they had been talking about. She instinctively knew and still had enough grace to be embarrassed by it.

Jared had gotten himself a cup of coffee and was popping donut holes in his mouth when Anna said, "Ummmm," and looked Jaidyn up and down. Before she could continue Yasmine cleared throat reminding them that Jared was still in the room.

Jared knew trouble when he saw it and sat his cup of coffee down on the counter top, then kissed Jaidyn like he hadn't seen her in a week. He leaned his forehead against hers and looked into her eyes, "I love you."

Jaidyn smiled and pressed her lips against his, "I love you too." She whispered.

Yasmine cleared her throat again, *"Grrrrrrr!"* Jaidyn looked back at her and giggled. Jared reluctantly let her go and headed for the door. He looked at her over his shoulder and gave her an apologetic smirk for leaving her to face the wolves alone.

Jared hadn't closed the door completely before the girls turned on Jaidyn. Anna was the first to speak, "I see we're beaming this morning," she said with one eyebrow cocked in the air.

"Yes we are!" Yasmine was agreeing sarcastically when Jared poked his head back in the door. The room fell silent as they all looked in his direction.

"By the way," he said looking like the cat that ate the mouse, "Before Jai tells you her side of the story just let me say that she wore my ass out." The girls all doubled over in crying laughter. He kissed Jaidyn a final time and closed the door behind him. Jaidyn blushed and giggled like a mischievous schoolgirl.

"Dammmnnn!" Yasmine squeaked out.

"Do I hear a hint of jealousy?" Jaidyn asked hiding her blushing face behind a cup of coffee.

"What you hear is exhaustion! I'm tired as hell," Anna said smacking her lips. "I heard your ass all the way upstairs. What the hell was he doing to you in there?"

Jaidyn got goose bumps just thinking about their night. A sly smirk crossed her face, "Serving me some Grade A Angus beef!" She replied giving Yasmine a high five. The room erupted into laughter once more.

"Oh, come on with the details Ms. Thang!" Yasmine urged looking like a excited child waiting to hear a big secret.

Chapter 43

Joanna, Jaidyn, a court reporter, and a court mediator sat in the conference room of Joanna's office waiting on Keith and his lawyer to arrive. Keith was hell-bent on making this divorce as difficult as possible. He had counter sued Jaidyn for divorce on the grounds of adultery. Although they were legally separated he was using her relationship with Jared to support his case. He was requesting spousal support, half of her retirement investments, his house, and his business. Jaidyn was in practice with three other surgical oncologists. He was also requesting that half of her portion of the practice's net worth be paid to him. He wanted to be reimbursed for all expenses that he paid while she was in medical school. He asked for the return of the BMW SUV that he purchased for her.

Jaidyn was beginning to second-guess her decision in hiring Joanna as her lawyer. Although she completely trusted her, Joanna was still her big sister trying to protect her. She was bitter toward Keith and wanted him to pay for what he'd done to her sister, but Jaidyn refused to sink to his level. She was hoping during mediation that they would be able to settle their differences and come to an amicable settlement.

Things quickly deteriorated after Keith and his lawyer arrived. Joanna was the first to deliver a gut wrenching blow, "We have in our possession a signed affidavit from Chevon Hartman stating that Mr. Tyler engaged in an extra martial affair. Keith Justice Tyler, Jr., is a product of this affair."

"We will dispute any statements or testimony Ms. Hartman has due to her pending suit against my client."

"Mr. Joseph," Joanna began. "I also have a signed affidavit from Anna Monroe detailing a brutal attack she withstood from your client after she refused sexual advances from him." Joanna handed a copy of the affidavit along with several pictures Anna had taken after her encounter with Keith to Mr. Joseph.

Anna had been battered and bruised but not too badly, at least that's what she thought at the time. Once she was home a friend tried to convince her to go to the police. When she wouldn't call the police he convinced her to allow him to take a few pictures of the bruises in case Keith decided to lie to Jaidyn, she'd have evidence of the attack.

It wasn't until Jaidyn confided in her about Keith's child and her plans to leave him that Anna decided it was time to tell her about her encounter with him. Upon receiving Keith's counter suit Jaidyn asked Anna if she would allow her to use the pictures and sign an affidavit as to what happened. Anna was all too happy to comply with Jaidyn's wishes.

After the attack Anna had not worried very much about the bruises. She'd been more concerned about how her friend would feel. Jaidyn's original reaction to what had happened had not shocked Anna but her reaction to the pictures had. Jaidyn's eyes had filled with tears. She'd tried to wipe them away but there had been too many of them. She told Anna how sorry she was. It was the first time Anna had allowed herself to feel anything but outrage. Before their conversation was over both ladies were in tears. Somehow Jaidyn felt responsible for putting her in a compromising position.

Keith's attorney looked at the affidavit and the photos, then handed them to Keith. "The bitch is lying!" He said throwing the pictures back onto the table. "She approached me. I had to fight her off."

"Mr. Tyler please don't say anything else." Mr. Joseph ordered.

"Fuck that ho. Her ass got what was coming to her..." Keith said smiling at Jaidyn. Jaidyn looked at him like she wanted to go upside his head.

"Mr. Tyler!"

Keith's comments and demeanor infuriated Jaidyn. He was a man without care, integrity, and honor. She wondered how she could have missed that. His comments seemed to desecrate Anna even further. In her mind's eye she saw herself taking a dagger and stabbing him over and over again. She wanted to jump on him until he'd taken his last breath and been put out of his misery. It was all she could do to just sit in the same room with him. What had possessed her to marry this idiot she wondered?

She couldn't stand to listen to anymore of this. How had they gotten to the place were they had to have lawyers talk for them. She couldn't understand why they couldn't settle this in a friendly manner and not have to drag their friends into their battle. She never understood how two people who promised to love and cherish each other forever could turn around and destroy each other. Marriage required a level of intimacy unmatched by any other closely acquainted relationship. When you live with someone as your husband or wife you get to know their habits, their likes and dislikes. The way they feel, the way they think. After you've experienced the highest level of intimacy possible between two people what possesses people to go to this extreme she wondered.

Jaidyn got up from the table, looked out the window, and disappeared into her own mind. Her thoughts drowned out the arguing lawyers. She could see people leisurely strolling as they entered the Galleria Mall. They looked as though they were having casual conversations like they didn't have a care in the world. There was a line at the gas station on the corner and the traffic light was flashing. Cars were backed up in all directions. Life goes on despite what happens in this room, she thought.

She watched people come and go for a long while before she tuned back into what was happening in the room. She heard the mediator say, "Everybody calm down! This is only mediation. Maybe we should take a break." She walked over to the coffeepot and poured herself a cup of coffee. It seemed to her that this entire mess could easily be solved. Maybe she should just give him what he was asking for so that she could move on with her life. She wondered if they put a dollar figure on it how much it would cost her.

She interrupted the lawyers, "How much spousal support would I be required to pay?"

"You won't have to pay a dime! This is ridiculous; no judge in their right mind would..." Joanna recoiled.

Jaidyn interrupted her again, "What does the law say? How much and for how long?"

"The law states forty percent of your net monthly income for up to ten years," Mr. Joseph volunteered.

"How much of my retirement investments?"

"Half! But again..."

"He can have the house, the car, and his business. I don't want them. He cannot have half of my practice and I will not reimburse him for any educational expense..."

"Jaidyn we need to talk about this..." Joanna said trying to get her to think about what she was doing.

"No, Joanna we don't." She said cutting her off and returning to the list of things she would concede to. "My family worked hard to make sure that I didn't have any debt when I graduated from medical school under no circumstance will I pay him for any part of my education. Now, if we can settle on a reasonable dollar amount instead of spousal support and my retirement investments we can end this." Jaidyn had taken control of the meeting and she could plainly see that Joanna was perplexed by her intrusion.

Keith sat smirking. His attorney jotted down notes and seemed to be salivating at her foolish generosity. Joanna pretended to be absorbed in her own notes but Jaidyn knew she was boiling right under the surface. Jaidyn walked back to the window and waited on a response.

"Considering the potential amount of income you will make and due to your willingness to cooperate and not draw this out...I guess a half a million dollars would be an adequate settlement." Mr. Joseph finally said after whispering with his client.

"Hell no! That's ludicrous!" Joanna yelped.

Jaidyn ignored Joanna and considered the offer. Someone had to loose and she didn't care if it was her. "$200,000 plus attorney's fees is all I'm willing to do. My attorney can draw up the papers if Keith agrees. I want out of this as soon as possible." She had saved and invested well but she didn't have that kind of money but she'd sell her first-born and her soul to the devil to get it.

Keith had set the tone for the marriage early on. His rule was if she opened a bill she had to pay it but if she didn't open it he would pay it; therefore, he paid all the bills. Every now and then she'd feel bad and open every bill that she got out of the mailbox but Keith would complain. When she started to make it a habit he'd gotten a post office box. Since then the only thing that came to the house was her cell phone bill and her credit card bills. So, thanks to Keith she could get her hands on about $125,000 with a little finagling, but she would have to take out a loan for the other.

"No deal," Keith said to Jaidyn.

"Mr. Tyler your wife is being very generous."

"No deal," Keith said unfalteringly to his attorney. Although he was wearing a smile his mood was hovering around the edge of anger, just as it had been since Jaidyn left him. He'd been trying to keep his composure but the pain of losing her was eating him alive.

"Can I please speak to my client alone." Keith's attorney asked.

Before Jaidyn, Joanna, the mediator, and the court reporter excused themselves Joanna said, "Mr. Joseph please inform your client if he doesn't take this deal it will not be on the table at the close of this meeting." Once in the hallway Joanna begin ranting and raving. "Have you lost your mind? You hired me as your attorney, let me do my job!"

Jaidyn tried to keep her voice as pleasant as possible, "I'm sorry Joanna but this is my life and it's time that I take control of it. I want out of this marriage as soon as possible. I don't care what it costs."

"Mr. Tyler this is a sweetheart of a deal. It is my recommendation that we take it. It will allow you to put this situation behind you so you can move forward with your life."

Keith sat back in his chair and smiled, "John, I don't care what she offers me. I am not going to settle. I do not intend on letting her out of this marriage. This isn't about money. A woman like Jaidyn doesn't put much value on money. She wants her freedom, your job is to fight her every step of the way until I can figure out how to get her to change her mind. Drag this out as long as possible. Do I make myself clear?"

John Joseph had been a divorce attorney for many years. He perfectly understood what Keith was trying to do, but in his experience it never worked. When a woman has made up her mind that she wants out of a marriage at any cost, she doesn't normally change her mind. "Yes sir."

"Jaidyn's sensible; she's going to snap out of this." Keith said egotistically.

"She's only sensible because you haven't pissed her off yet. In my experience once you've done that she'll lose all sense of reasoning." Keith ignored his attorney's analysis and remained steadfast on his view of the situation.

Once everyone returned to their seats Keith's attorney informed them that they would not be taking any type of settlement.

"This is a more than a generous offer. If we go to court and win, which we will, my client will not have to pay a dime. It could cost your client dearly," Joanna said.

"I realize that but my client has decided he'd rather take his chances in court. He has expressed the desire to work things out with his wife and would like to request that they pursue counseling."

Joanna looked at Jaidyn. Jaidyn shook her head. "My client does not wish to pursue any form of reconciliation with Mr. Tyler. It would behoove us all if we could settle the terms of this divorce now."

Keith piped up, "We made the commitment for better or worse. You're being bullheaded and need to reconsider."

Jaidyn leaned forward and knead her temples. Keith was really working her nerves.

Will this fool stop at nothing? I can't believe he said that. Please keep me from reaching across this damn table and knocking his ass out.

She had been trying to play fair but he wasn't going to let it go down like that. Maybe a little show and tell would change his mind. She didn't want to have to go to that extreme but they'd reached the bottom of the barrel. They were on the brink of war and he'd left her no choice. She leaned over and whispered in Joanna's ear. Joanna asked the mediator and court reporter to give them a few minutes alone.

They were barely out of the room when Jaidyn went after Keith with a cold determination, "When I stood before God and the world and said for better or worse I felt blessed to be loved by you. I thought I'd learn to love you like a wife should, but I never did. What I felt was a blessing, turned into regret because of all the things you put me through. I've had to swallow my pride too many times. And I've had enough."

Keith pointed a finger at her like he was disciplining a child, "If you would have made me your first priority then you wouldn't have had to worry about swallowing your pride. If your ass would have been taking care of your man like you were supposed to instead of always working I wouldn't have had to turn to Chevon."

Jaidyn stared at him befuddled, "You know what, I should have left yo ass a long time ago."

"Sshhh, don't fool yourself! You ain't nothing but a stank ass bitch and don't nobody want yo ass!"

Jaidyn's blood ran cold. He'd told her that one time too many. He'd just crossed the imaginary line in the sand. This was war.

"Mr. Joseph your clients behavior is extremely inappropriate..." Joanna said.

"This isn't solving anything. Is there a point to this Mrs. Holloway," Keith's attorney asked?

Jaidyn and Keith ignored the attorneys and continued their war of words. She stabbed Keith with eye draggers as she dropped the first bomb, "What should have happened is you should have cared more about my feelings when you were laying up with Shelbi, Alexia, and Zaria. We had a good thing and you've just thrown that away because you can't keep your dick in your pants."

Keith was bewildered. He wondered how in the hell she knew their names. She must have heard something he thought. "Who the hell are they? I don't know where you're getting your information from but somebody's been lying to you. I think I was damn good to you. Any other woman would be happy if she was in your shoes."

"Yo ass was devious, trifling, shady, and you couldn't be trusted! Did you think I was crazy? Did you think you were fooling me with your little trips to the car wash at eleven o'clock at night? Do you realize the only bill

I paid in that house the entire time we were married was my cell phone and credit card bills? You didn't think you were fooling me when you made the rule that if I opened the bill I had to pay it did you? I know you had Chevon's bills mailed to our house so that you could pay them. There is no telling what else your triflin' ass was hiding."

"Baby..." Keith said trying to cool things down.

She held up her hand, "Let me finish!" Jaidyn wanted to get this off her chest. She'd been trying to be nice to his triflin', no good ass but he'd pissed her off. "I made you wear condoms because I didn't trust yo ass, not because I refused to take the damn pill. If you wouldn't have been sleeping all over town then things would have been different, maybe I wouldn't have worked so much. Do you know how many times I found Zaria's house key in the washing machine and returned the key to your jacket pocket or put it in your car."

Keith tried to maintain his appearance of control but everyone in the room knew Jaidyn had hit a nerve. He was feeling cauldron. He did the only thing he could, denied any knowledge of the women she was talking about. His father had taught him if she didn't catch you in the act or physically touch you while you were in it then it never happened. The strategy was plain and simple, it wasn't you. "Baby, what are you talking about? Who have you been talking to? With the exception of Chevon I don't know any of those other women. You need to get your facts straight. Somebody's been lying to you."

Keith had dodged the first bomb but Jaidyn was relentless and ready to deliver the second one. Jaidyn turned to Joanna and asked, "Do you have a cassette player I can use?" Joanna looked at her puzzled, but Jaidyn's facial expression told her not to ask any questions. Joanna shook her head then retrieved a small cassette player from a credenza and handed it to her. Jaidyn retrieved a manila envelope from her purse, placed it on the table and removed four cassette tapes. She put the first cassette into the player and pushed play. The first voice they heard was Keith's, "Come to me and let me take you where you want to go."

"That sounds wonderful but Cliff and the kids will be home in about an hour. By the time I make it to the spot it will be time to turn around and come home."

"Girl, you know you want this hot beef injection. We don't need to meet at the usual place. You can come over here."

"Where's your wife?"

"She just went to the hospital to see some patients. She won't be home for another couple of hours."

"Your house, your bed! You feel like living dangerously today!"

"Absolutely!"

"I'm on my way." The explicit conversation had shocked everyone. The recorder and the room were quiet.

"Does Shelbi know that you're messing around on her with Alexia? I'm sure it isn't what she had in mind when you had your three some!" Jaidyn said antagonizing him.

Keith was livid, "What the hell are you trying to pull Jaidyn. Where did you get that tape?" Jaidyn quietly loaded the next tape and pushed play. This time it was a different woman's voice but a similar conversation, "Big Daddy I'm wet just thinking about our night. When can I see you again?"

"Girl you can't handle this. I had your ass running last night."

The female voice giggled. "Yes you did," she said seductively. "But I've recuperated and I need to redeem myself. Is your wife home? Can you get away?"

"Let me worry about my wife. I've told you I run my house," Keith said authoritatively. "And while you're talking that stuff don't write no checks your ass can't cash. At some point you've got to pay the piper. You thought I got into your shit last night, today I'm going to act like a caveman and fuck the shit out of you!"

"How about the dollar cinema on the freeway in forty five minutes?"

"See you there."

The voice on the tape laughed and before they could hear Keith's response Jaidyn hit the stop button. The room was utterly silent. Jaidyn had caught Keith whispering on the phone a few too many times. When these telephone conversations would end he'd always try to pick a fight with her. When she wouldn't indulge in his insanity he'd make some excuse to leave the house, but he wouldn't return until late. The final straw happened when he came home smelling like the scent of a woman's perfume and raspberry colored lipstick was smeared on his collar. Jaidyn had gone to Radio Shack the very next day and purchased a $30 device that would record all incoming and outgoing phone calls made at their house. In her mind she'd justified the purchase by telling herself, "This man has no respect for me. He continues to sit in my face and lie so why should I have any respect for his privacy!"

She'd attached the recorder to the cordless phone next to their bed. If any phone in the house were taken off the receiver the recorder would turn on and begin to record. It didn't take her but two days to begin to intercept Keith's conversation with various women. Recording and listening to the tapes had been easy. The difficulty set in when she was faced with what to do about the things she'd heard.

After she'd heard more then she'd bargained for she disconnected the recorder. Then moved all knowledge of Keith's philandering to the back of her mind. It wasn't until Anna discovered them during her most recent visit that she remembered them. She hadn't seen or thought about the box of tapes in months.

She revealed the contents of the tapes to Yasmine and Anna. Anna seemed to be as stunned and angered as Jaidyn had been when she'd first heard them. Yasmine had reacted completely different. To Jaidyn's surprise she was not shocked or incensed by the things she'd heard. Anna and Jaidyn had mulled over the tapes hanging on every word, while Yasmine had sat by nonchalantly listening. She seemed to take it all in stride. "I'm not surprised. He's a piece of shit. And you're a damn fool for putting up with that," she'd told Jaidyn. When she'd grown tired of listening to the tapes she said, "Listen Jaidyn! You need to stop acting like Keith's doormat and stand up for yourself. As soon as he figures out you're serious about not going back to him he's going to do everything he can to fuck you. You need to use these tapes to take the upper hand. This fool has come home with a baby, messed over you I don't know how many times, and almost raped one of your best friends and you're still trying to be nice! He's lucky because I'da cut his ass a long lose a time and then I'd take him for everything he's worth. He's got you thinking he's barely making ends meet, I bet his cheap ass has investments out the wazoo. Keith may be a lot of things but he's not stupid."

Jaidyn hated to admit it but Yasmine had been right from the very beginning. She'd told her Keith would drag her through the mud and he'd done just that.

The room was saturated with silence as both lawyers and Keith tried to digest what they'd just heard. Joanna and Mr. Joseph were blown away by the potential impact the conversations on the tapes could cause.

Jaidyn had not told Joanna anything about the tapes. Joanna had Keith's business, retirement, and investments investigated but Jaidyn had continued to insist that she not look into his extra marital affairs. She didn't realize how much Jaidyn had endured during her marriage. Her heart ached for her and she wanted to beat the hell out of Keith but as Jaidyn's attorney she had to quickly put her anger in check.

"These tapes are inadmissible in any court of law." Mr. Joseph finally belted out.

"We will have to let a judge decide that. But by the time the judge makes that decision he would have already heard the tapes and the damage will be done. So it seems that your client needs to make a decision about his position on this matter."

Keith was starring a hole in Jaidyn. She picked up the key that had fallen out of the manila envelope and placed it in front of him. In case Keith had any doubts about taking her seriously Jaidyn decided to deliver the next bombshell. "You use the hotel two to three days a week. Her name is Shelbi Dennis McFadden. She's married with children. When she pages you she uses the number 1021 to let you know that she will be waiting at the hotel for you at the usual time."

She was almost right about everything except the hotel and that being the room number. That was the condo's address and the hotel passkey was from one of his weekend get away trips with Zaria. He chuckled to himself at her slip up, "Save that shit for somebody who cares! If you had been taking care of your business you wouldn't have had to worry about another woman! Shelbi is more of a woman then you ever thought about being!" He said patronizing her.

"Mr. Tyler please don't say anything else. Let me handle this." His attorney pleaded.

There he was again, throwing his egotistical, pompous, arrogant, self-righteous attitude at her, but this time she was ready for him. "Is that why you're messing around on Shelbi with Alexia and Zaria?"

"None of this information can be used in court," his attorney said.

Jaidyn stood up, placed her hands on the table and leaned into Keith's personal space, "I want to make sure you hear me." She was straight-faced but not threatening. Her demeanor demanding his attention. "These tapes may not be able to be used in court, but if I have to I will have them delivered to Clifford McFadden at his Clear Lake office. The decision is yours. If you want to ruin Shelbi's marriage along with your own I can arrange it."

Joanna decided to take a back seat and let Jaidyn handle this. She was surprised but Jaidyn was holding her own. She wasn't sure if she was bluffing or serious but Keith seemed to be regarding her thoughtfully. His attorney begin gathering his things, "Ladies this meeting is over! Mrs. Holloway my client and I will be in touch!"

"Let me ask you something," Jaidyn said not letting up. "Evidently you have a problem. Did you cover up when you were with these women?"

Keith hadn't moved. Anger shadowed his eyes. "What do you want Jaidyn," he asked sitting back in his chair.

"Out of this marriage and there will be no exchange of property or money." Since he had backed her in a corner and made her expose his dirty little secrets she might as well have things her way she thought. Shit, he'd started this roller coaster now he'd have to ride it until she decided to stop it. "I'll give you a week to consider your options."

As Keith stood up to leave Jaidyn added one final blow, "Oh and by the way, you can have these tapes. They're copies. I made them for you."

Joanna walked Jaidyn to the parking garage and blasted her for not telling her about the tapes and her intentions to use them. "Jaidyn this is not a game! Your financial future is on the line. I will not tolerate..." Joanna stopped mid-sentence as Jaidyn's face went from serious to deliriously happy. She followed her eyes, "Oh my goodness!" Joanna exclaimed. Someone had blanketed the windshield of Jaidyn's car with yellow roses. They both hurried over to the BMW. Jaidyn saw the card, pulled it from under the windshield wiper and rushed to open it. "Yellow signifies the promise of a new beginning; today you made another step towards that. Congratulations! I'm sorry I couldn't be there with you. I love you. Jared."

"What's it say," Joanna asked excitedly. Jaidyn handed the card to her and let her read it for herself. "Jared! I didn't realize he was a hopeless romantic," Joanna said.

Tears had welled up in Jaidyn's eyes. This is just one more thing to add to the list of things I love about him she said to herself. Why didn't I figure out how wonderful he was before I married Keith?

She gathered the roses, put them in her car then turned to Joanna and said, "I've been thinking...I want you to do everything you can to get me out of this marriage. I don't care what it takes. I don't want to have to give that bastard one red cent. I want alimony, retirement, everything!"

Chapter 44

Keith couldn't wait to talk to Jaidyn alone. He had a hard time believing that she would go to this extreme. As soon as he'd left the lawyers office he headed straight to her office. Once he arrived at her office he was told that she was not expected in the office. He then went to her house, but she wasn't there. He decided to pass through the hospital parking garage and found her car in her assigned parking space.

When he got to the information desk inside the hospital he told the woman behind the counter that he was Jaidyn's husband and wanted to surprise her. When the hospital operator finally found her, she was on the tenth floor with a patient's family. He was directed to the elevators and told how to find the nurse's station. After arriving there, he was told she wasn't available to speak to him. He lied to the nurse and said that it was a family emergency. She told him she was sorry but Jaidyn was in surgery. He refused to give up and struck out on his own. When he finally found her she was standing at a sink with green soap up to her elbows, scrubbing for surgery. "We need to talk."

She looked up at him and hesitated. She glanced around at the other sinks. There were several nurses also scrubbing for surgery. "What are you doing in here," she asked exasperated. "You need to leave, I am getting ready for surgery!"

"How could you invade my privacy like that?" He demanded.

"How could I...you can't be serious!" She looked at him blankly before turning the water off with her elbow. "Did you really think that you could keep getting away with all the shit you had been doing?"

"Look I'm a man and as long as I'm taking care of my business at home it shouldn't matter what I'm doing in the streets. You can't expect for me to be faithful for the next forty years. That's a ridiculous expectation! You went looking for problems and you found them. That's your damn fault. What you don't know won't hurt you."

"Unfortunately that's not true. What you don't know can destroy you."

"I love you."

"You don't know the meaning of love."

"Look Jaidyn, there is no use crying over spilled milk. It's time we put this behind us and move forward with our lives. You've made your point."

"My point? What exactly is my point?" She hollered forgetting that they had an audience. "I'm sick of putting up with your bull shit is my point."

"We both know this entire situation is just tit-for-tat. I fucked around so you went out and fucked around. I'm willing to forgive you. I know you only did it to get back at me. And you know as well as I do that you're not going to find a man better then me. You need to realize how lucky you are to have me." He said in a sexy, sweet voice.

She stared at him, his eyes were hollow, frightening she thought. "You can't be serious you arrogant, pompous, self-centered, son of a...." She stopped herself and shook her head. "Get this through that pea brain of yours. I don't want you! I don't need you! Marrying you is the stupidest thing I've ever done. You stole what I felt for you and turned it into something I loathe and hate. I refuse to be miserable for the rest of my life." She paused trying to keep her composure. Jared had warned her against being emotional with him. He'd told her when she went off on Keith he realized that he had her and that's what he wanted. But she was bitter and couldn't keep herself from saying it. "Jared is more of a man then you ever thought about being." Still holding her hands in the air like a praying Muslim she walked past him through the double doors into the operating room.

"Don't walk away from me Jaidyn," he yelled after her then kicked the linen can.

She turned and looked right through him as if he wasn't there, "Will someone please call security!"

After seeing all her patients and signing a few charts Jaidyn headed home. Jared would be there. He'd planned to cook dinner at her place. As soon as she walked through the door he knew what kind of day she'd had. She was wearing a smile but her body language was tense. The smile couldn't mask the frustrated look behind it. "Thank you for the flowers and the note," she said smoothing her wind blown hair back into place. The tone of her voice made him stop what he was doing and looked at her attentively. He turned the fire off on the blackened salmon and gave her his undivided attention. She loved the way he always did that. It made her feel like she was the most important thing in the world.

Jaidyn began washing the dishes trying not to talk about her morning. Jared pulled her away from the sink and gave her a big bear hug and kiss. When he touched her the ice crystals in her heart dissipated. He looked at her like an experienced seducer and the stress of her day instantaneously evaporated.

He felt her relaxing in his arms before he said, "It didn't go well?" Jaidyn shook her head. He had seen the hurt in her eyes as soon as she'd walked in the front door. So he wanted to approach the subject cautiously. He looked down at her questioningly. As he sent his next question to her telepathically she bobbed her head then answered, "I offered him a deal but he refused...he didn't leave me any other choice." She said about the tapes she and Jared had listened to and discussed a few days before.

Jared held her tighter and nibbled on her ear. She completely lost her train of thought. "What was I saying," she wondered. Something about Keith! Jared was embarking on a mission to help her unwind and it was working. He was caressing her body, taking his time, doing it just right, just as he always did. His fingers did a mysterious dance with the little man in the boat and she shivered. She put her hands under his shirt, lifted it and softly traced his nipples with the tip of her tongue. When he pulled her into him the anaconda was rock hard against her stomach. He softly nibbled on her neck stirring the heat inside her. The moistness between her legs called for him and inch by inch he gently answered its call.

Jaidyn was so warm and wet Jared wanted to bask inside of her but before long their groans were too deep for words and the heat consumed them both. They lay on the side as trimmers of pleasure flowed through their bodies. He held on to her tightly, still deep inside her as dreamland beckoned him.

Jaidyn woke to the crisp clean morning sunlight filtering through the wood blinds. The smell of sex still lingered in the air. Jaidyn looked at the pillow lying beside her and found a small blue velvet box. She smiled, sat up and opened the box. The box held a bracelet of interlocking diamond hearts. Jaidyn smiled and put the bracelet on. "Jesus, what did I do to deserve him?"

There was something cooking in the kitchen that seemed to be surrounding her and overpowering the smell of her and Jared's night. Maybe it was sausage, no, it had to be ham she thought to herself. She climbed out of bed, went to the dresser and put on a fresh pair of underwear. She then retrieved Jared's light gray polo suit shirt off the chair. Before she put it on she pulled it to her nose, closed her eyes, and inhaled his scent. "Ummm, damn I love this man."

After brushing her teeth she went to find out what smelled so good. She found Jared standing with his head in the refrigerator completely naked. He was humming a bar of an old Isley Brothers' song. She listened, for a second, trying to name that tune. She caught it and sung it in her head, *'hey girl ain't no mystery at least as far as I can see I wanna keep you here lying next to me sharing our love between the sheets. Bom bom bom.'* She smiled to herself remembering the good old days when music was music, rather than words set to good beats. The days when singers could sang and not just carry a tune. Her father was a music fanatic and the Isley Brothers were still one of his all time favorite groups. As long as she could remember, her parent's home was filled with sounds of music.

"Thank you for the bracelet. I love it." Jaidyn said smiling down at the bracelet.

"Your welcome." He said looking back at her face.

"Something smells good." Jared heard Jaidyn saying from behind him as he grabbed a package of grated cheese out of the refrigerator.

"I thought I'd make some Omelets. You hungry?" He asked as he turned around and saw her sexy ass standing there in his shirt.

"I'd much rather have you for breakfast," she said seductively.

A sly smile that said your wish is my command crossed Jared's face. "She's got to be reading my mind," he said to himself. Jaidyn walked over to him and began kissing him hard. Without braking their lip lock he put the cheese down on the cabinet, helped her onto the counter top, then removed the tiny thong she called underwear. He slipped inside her without a Trojan between them. The desire was too intense for him to stop and get one. This was happening more and more lately. They both knew they were playing with fire but neither cared.

Jaidyn loved having her legs wrapped around his waist but even more she loved having him inside her. If she could she would spend every waking moment with him.

When Evelyn, Jaidyn's cleaning lady, unlocked the back door and stepped into Jaidyn's kitchen Jared's hips were swaying to a melody that only he and Jaidyn could hear. Evelyn astonished and embarrassed to find them in such a compromising position, made a faintly gasp. Everyone froze as awkwardness and humiliation washed over the entire room.

Jared spontaneously took a step back allowing his dick to dangle in the air. Jaidyn hopped off the cabinet and picked up her underwear off the floor. "I'm sorry! This...ah is my...my ah...day to," Evelyn said in her heavy Jamaican accent. Evelyn's eyes instinctively slid down Jared to his muscle and she quickly tried to avert her gaze. Jared caught her eyes and realized he was wearing his birthday suit. He unsuccessfully attempted to cup the anaconda in his hands and made a quick exit.

Evelyn had come to work for Jaidyn shortly after she'd moved into the new house. She cleaned Jaidyn's house out of pure boredom rather then necessity. For the past five years she'd taken care of her granddaughter while her daughter and son-in-law worked. Now that little Chloe' was in school all day she found it hard to just sit home.

Evelyn didn't normally come until after she'd dropped Chloe' off at school so she and Jaidyn hardly ever bumped into each other. Her days rotated depending on her granddaughter's school activity schedule. The two primarily communicated through notes and phone calls. Jaidyn left a check on the refrigerator at the first of every month to cover her weekly visits.

Now here they both stood unsure of what to say to each other. "Ms. Evelyn, I'm sorry."

Evelyn seemed to have collected herself and interrupted Jaidyn, "Child don't apologize. I was young once too. I'll come back another day." She sung in her heavily accented voice.

"Wait a minute," Jaidyn said going to retrieve her checkbook. While Jaidyn was in the study she put on her thong and shirt that she was still holding. When she returned to the kitchen with the first of the month check Evelyn was gone. Jaidyn hung the check on the refrigerator and took a deep breath.

She found Jared dressed in everything but his shirt. His face was still flush from embarrassment. "She's gone," Jaidyn said relieved.

Jared's embarrassment and humiliation turned to irritation. "Why didn't you..." he started to snap.

Jaidyn cut him off, "She's not on a set schedule. I never know what day she's going to come." Jaidyn playfully pulled the T-shirt he was holding away from him. He forcefully pulled it back, trying to keep up the strong pissed off appearance. She burst into laughter. He couldn't resist her and pulled her down onto the bed. They play wrestled and laughed like children until they both collapsed.

Chapter 45

Jaidyn was sitting in the typical bumper to bumper traffic on Friday, just after 4 p.m., listening to Yolanda Adams singing, "*When I think about what You brought me through, I'm remind to praise You for all that You had to do…When I think about where You brought me from I've got to praise You like the victory's already won and I lift my hands, I take advantage of this chance to say thank you. When I think about why you loved me so…*" By the time the song was over Yolanda had ministered to her soul and grateful tears streamed down her face.

She'd put Jared through so many changes. When things had gotten hard she'd dismissed him and aborted their child. When he'd walked in and told her he loved her and wanted to fight for what they once had she'd thought her life would be better with another man and married him. During her marriage she'd ran to him for an emotional shoulder to lean on despite how she knew he felt about her. He loved her despite all the mistakes she'd made.

> *If it had not been for Your grace and mercy Father, where would I be? If it had not been for Your loving-kindness, what shape would I be in? I am so grateful for the strength You've given me. Thank you for setting me free and giving my life new meaning. With all my mistakes and my faults You've never forsaken me, mislead me or forgotten me. I've been on an emotional roller coaster for so long I've forgotten what it's like to live in peace and happiness. Praise Your name.*
>
> *Lord, I know I don't always say it but I recognize how blessed I am and I am so thankful. Thank you for blessing*

> *my life with the love and support of my family and friends. I feel so blessed to be love by Jared. Thank you Father. I know he isn't a prefect man but he is a good man. I never imagined loving someone so purely or feeling so complete. I owe it all to You. I give you the glory Heavenly Father.*

When she tuned back in the radio, the DJ was talking about how badly the city's blood bank was in need of donations. "There are multiple neighborhood donor centers around the city. You can find the center closet to you when you visit www.giveblood.com."

Jaidyn was exhausted. It had been a long grueling week and she'd been working crazy hours. She'd been called during the night several times and had gotten out of bed with Jared to return to the hospital. Jared was completely supportive of her crazy work schedule. She'd often return home to shower and change before she went into the office. Jared would often leave her a sweet note or a small continental breakfast.

Jaidyn had a distressing week. On top of all the long hours there had been complications with one of her favorite patients and she'd passed away earlier during the week. Although Jaidyn was always a professional she was still human and unable to detach herself emotionally from her favorite patients. She'd share in their triumphs as well as their defeats. She cherished the happiness they experienced when they were finally winning the battle and she held their hands and prayed with them when it was clear that they would lose the war. Cancer is a disease that wages war on every person it chooses to invade. As well as everyone around them, she thought. Its warfare is so gruesome that it drains people physically, emotionally and financially.

Losing a patient was the only time that Jaidyn truly hated her job. She'd been dragging herself through the week feeling like she was fighting a losing battle; but in the end she knew that she was winning more battles then she was losing.

After Jaidyn finished seeing patients at the office and made her rounds at the hospital she'd planned to have a few hours to herself to unwind. Jared had called her at the office earlier and said that he was going to have to work late and wouldn't be home until around 8:30 or so.

A few minutes after she had arrived home the doorbell rang. When Jaidyn opened the door a gentleman in a black suit was standing there, "Dr. Tyler?"

"Yes," Jaidyn answered with a puzzled look on her face.

"I'm Douglas. Mr. Mitchell asked that I pick you up."

"Pick me up," she questioned, "And take me where?"

"I'm sorry ma'am. I was instructed not to answer any questions but he did send this note." The gentleman handed Jaidyn a hand written note from Jared. 'This evening belongs to us. This gentleman is to deliver you to me as quickly as possible. Jared.'

Jaidyn unclipped her cell phone from her side and dialed Jared's cell number. When he answered he said, "Just do as Douglas is asking."

Jaidyn laughed, "What's going on? Where are you?"

"Passion, don't make me wait too long," Jared said in a seductive whining tone.

Jaidyn smiled at Douglas. "Let me get my purse."

"I was instructed to not let you get anything. I am to lock your door and bring you just as you are." Douglas said in a friendly tone. "But I will let you put your shoes on," he said looking down at her bare feet.

Jaidyn laughed. "I'll just be a minute."

Once inside the car, the driver drove her to a quaint little bed and breakfast that sat on a private beach on the far west end of Galveston. As she stepped out of the limousine the salt air tickled her nose and the sound of sea gulls and crashing waves welcomed her. A gentleman wearing a pleasant smile greeted her. He escorted her to the backside of the house and down a long pier where Jared was standing on the deck of a thirty-nine foot catamaran, named Reality Check.

"Welcome aboard." He said with a smile. By the look on her face he knew she was not only surprised but she also recognized the trouble he'd gone through and was appreciative. He loved making her happy.

"What's going on? Whose boat," she asked.

"Would you stop with all the questions and try to enjoy yourself!" He said taking her by the hand as she stepped on board. Jaidyn batted her eyes, pretended to pinch her lips closed, gathered the questions in her hand and pitched them overboard.

Jared took her by the hand and lead her through a small galley and saloon into an equally small but warm cabin. He instructed her to change into something more comfortable. "I didn't bring anything with me." She told him. He pointed to the overnight bag he'd pack for her.

Once she'd changed she returned to the top deck of the boat. She was surprised to find him sitting at a table set for two. Jared stood up and welcomed her with a big bear hug. She buried her head into him and inhaled. He was wearing her favorite cologne. This mysterious get away had ignited a fire inside her that she hoped he was planning to extinguish later. "What is all this?" She questioned as a gentleman delivered their dinner to the table.

"I thought it would be nice to have a relaxing evening away from everything you have going on."

"You're spoiling me."

"That's the plan Passion." It had been a long time since he'd called her that. It no longer made her angry but instead made her smile and appreciated who he was.

After dinner they sat on the deck enjoying the warmth of the sun on their skin. They talked over their day as they watched the sailboats head back to their ports. As if on cue, the sun began to descend towards the water's edge. It sprinkled the Gulf of Mexico with red, orange, and yellow streaks. The moment was awe-inspiring.

Somewhere down the road something between them had changed. The obstacles that used to prevent them from divulging everything to each other had long vanished. She'd never felt so free with anyone. In all of her past relationships she'd always held a little of herself back out of the fear of being hurt. It wasn't that way with Jared. She talked to him like he was her best girlfriend. Her trust in him had gone a step further and she talked to him about things she wouldn't dare talk about with any of her friends.

Jaidyn had lived without Jared's love and now she was living with it. The difference in the two lives was simply indescribable. Her work-a-holic tendencies had begun to change and take a back seat to her relationship with him. It was the strangest feeling to get butterflies just before she walked into a room she knew she'd find him in. Just thinking of him made her feel lightheaded and dizzy, scatterbrained and giddy. He was the man she'd dreamt of. He was her fairytale, her happily every after, and she couldn't believe that she had a second chance to make things right with him.

Once back on the dock Jaidyn thanked Jared for a magical evening. "It's not over yet," he told her. The moon was full, the sky was clear and a million little stars winked at them as they walked barefoot in the sand along the water's edge. Someone had left a picnic basket and a blanket on the sand outside the bed and breakfast. Jared picked it up, spread the blanket over the sand, opened the picnic blanket, and took out a bottle of wine and two wineglasses.

"You've thought of everything."

"I hope so," he said.

Jaidyn sat between Jared's legs, leaning back on his chest quietly watching the constant lapping of waves. A breeze washed over them and they huddled closer together. She felt completely and totally at peace. She said a silent thank you to God, closed her eyes, and drifted in the moment.

Jared had been introspective and pensive. He finally revealed what he'd been thinking since the morning they'd woke up in each others arms, "When this mess with Keith is over…I'd like you to be my wife. I don't want to prolong it."

Jaidyn couldn't believe what he was saying. She had no intention on making him wait. She wanted to be his wife as quickly as possible. She half joked with him, "You know rules were meant to be broken and if that was a proposal…I'll commit bigamy tonight!"

Jared laughed at her dry humor, "Oh yeah."

"Yeah," she said smiling but trying to sound serious.

Before returning to the bed and breakfast cottage they made love in the sand under a full moon. Back at the cottage Jared led her to a bedroom with wraparound windows, which provided a panoramic view of the gulf. He couldn't have picked a better time of year to visit this hide away refuge. Everything was in bloom. It was that time between seasons that some people like to call Spring, but in Texas they were called little slices of heaven because the only seasons they knew were winter and summer. It was eighty degrees during the day but not that sizzling humid Texas eighty. It was a warm slightly breezy eighty degrees and the evenings were a wonderful cool sixty-five. It was that time of the year that everything seemed prefect and Jaidyn's life was no exception. Keith was trying to reek havoc on her world but she was somehow unfazed by his antics.

Jared led her into the bathroom with a big old-fashioned porcelain bathtub. Candles illuminated the entire room. The bath water looked as if it was one solid sheet of lilac colored Calla Lilly petals. Just as they climbed into the warm water together and began to relax, Jaidyn's pager began beeping. Jared grabbed a towel, got out of the tub and handed it to her. "It's the hospital," she said exasperated.

"I thought you were discharging everyone today."

"I did," she said exhaling heavily.

"I'll get the phone," Jared said as he disappeared into the bedroom to retrieve his cell phone. While she was on the phone Jared toweled off and put on a robe. The entire evening felt like a dream until this point. Jaidyn hung up the phone and sunk back into the tub.

"So what's the verdict," Jared hesitantly asked.

"I had a patient come in through the ER. I'll have to go in first thing in the morning," she said in a disappointing tone.

Fearing that the interruption had put a damper on their evening she climbed out of the tub, wrapped a towel around her and then wrapped her arms around him. He cupped her hands to his chest knowing this was her way of apologizing for the disruption. He uncurled her arms from around him and handed her a small gift bag. She looked at him astonished at the elaborate planning that he'd gone through to make this night possible. Once she opened the bag she found a beautiful lilac negligée and a small bottle of her favorite perfume. She looked at him shaking her head, "I can't believe all this. Mmm-hhh...you're wonderful. Thank you."

Jared watched her get dressed then escorted her back into the bedroom. While they were in the bathroom someone had transformed the room into a love palace. A bottle of wine along with two glasses had been placed on the bed table and the soft smooth voice of Angie Stone along with the sound of crashing waves set the mood for a romantic evening.

Jared handed her a small ring box and her throat went dry. She knew he had been serious when they were on the beach but she hadn't been expecting a ring tonight. When she opened the box a small gold ring with two interlocking hearts sparkled at her. "What's this?"

"A promise ring," he said smiling. Jaidyn begin to giggle like a schoolgirl as he continued. "Every time you look at it I want you to know that I promise to love you no matter what. You are the other half of my soul."

His sincerity made her heart flutter and she threw her arms around him. Jared slipped his hands down the middle of her back to the base of her spine and once again he was an arsonist igniting a fire deep inside her, but it wasn't only between her legs. Her entire body seemed to be consumed by a heat so intense it over took her entire body.

No matter how many times they made love Jared's thirst for her was overwhelming and like any dehydrated person he woke in the middle of the night to quench his thirst with small sips from her fountain. Before the sun rose the next morning they'd made love in every position known to man.

If Jaidyn could close her eyes and wish on a shooting star she'd wish that their prefect night would not have ended so quickly. After breakfast Jared had driven Jaidyn home so that she could make her hospital rounds early. Her heart wasn't in her work, all she wanted to do was run right back home to him.

After she'd examined her patient and written a protocol for care she headed to the parking garage to retrieve her car. When the parking garage elevator stopped on the second floor Jaidyn stepped off and aimlessly walked in the direction of her car. Thoughts of her evening with Jared moved her along in a carefree manner. As she rounded the corner where her car was parked she spotted Keith leaning against the back of her SUV. She exhaled deeply thinking, "What does this ass hole want now?"

Keith spotted her coming his way and began walking towards her. "Hey you," he said showing off his incredible Colgate smile.

"What do you want," Jaidyn asked in an exasperated voice.

"I tried calling you several times last night, when you didn't answer I got worried." He waited on her to explain why she hadn't answered her phone. When she didn't, he continued, "I even came by but you weren't home." A few seconds of uncomfortable silence passed between them before he asked what he really wanted to know, "Where were you?"

Jaidyn glared at him and wondered if he knew how pathetic he was acting. She hit the unlock button on her car alarm remote then repeated her question, "What do you want?"

Her tone pissed him off, "You must have been laying up with that pretty muthafucka!"

"Do us both a favor and stay away from me," she said in a strong and demanding voice.

"*A favor!* I'm still your muthafuckin' husband," Keith shouted just as a man walked past them. They both eyed the man as he walked past them. Keith lowered his voice and got in her face. He grabbed her by the elbow and said, "You're starting to piss me off with this bullshit. You better start showing me some damn respect."

Jaidyn looked at him, wishing him dead on the spot, then pulled her arm away from his grasp and walked around him to get into her car. Keith took hold of a hand full of her hair and pulled her into him. "Don't you fuckin' walk away from me!"

She instinctively placed both hands over his and struggled to pull her head away from his grip. The more she pulled the tighter he gripped the back of her hair. He yanked her head back and forcefully kissed her. "Keith please let me go," she tried to say calmly.

"You keep acting like this I'm going to start believing you don't want me around."

Jaidyn couldn't stop herself from being a smart-ass, "Then there's hope you'll finally get the point."

Keith shot her a warning look and kissed her again. Jaidyn bit down on his lip until she tasted blood. Then she raised her leg, firmly plating her knee in his groin.

Keith let her go and cupped his balls with both hands, *"You BITCH!"*

Jaidyn took four quick steps, hopped into her car and locked her doors. She was rattled and she struggled to get the key into the ignition, but by the time he recovered she was backing out of the parking space.

On her drive home Keith called her cell. She pushed the ignore button five times before she decided to answer his calls. "What?"

"I'm sorry. I just wanted to talk. I miss you. I feel like I'm losing my mind. I can't eat. I'm not sleeping. I need you."

"Stop calling me!" Jaidyn said and hung up incensed. Keith really was losing his damn mind she thought. She couldn't believe at one point she thought everything they had would last.

She just wanted to get home to take a shower. She wanted to wash his filth off of her. It seemed that every light in town turned red when she approached it, making her ten-minute drive home feel as if it would take forever.

Chapter 46

Jaidyn pulled a single white red tipped rose and note off the windshield. Smiling, she unfolded the note, "Every time you smile an angel touches my heart, puts my value system in check and reminds me what's most important in my life." Jaidyn folded the note and put it in her purse. Jared had made leaving a single rose and a note on the windshield of her car a habit. She'd found that signature trade mark on her windshield in the most unexpected places; at the office, the hospital, her parents, the beauty shop, he'd even slipped a young sacker at the grocery store a $20 to place a note and rose on her windshield. He'd also had the lawn man place one on her car when he was out of town.

Jared had his own note pads made with a man on the bottom of them that looked like he was dizzy. The pads read, 'to: The Springier and the salutation read Love Sprung.' The first day Jaidyn received one of his notes on that paper she'd doubled over with laughter. Although the note pad never changed, the messages on them were always different and she treasured each one.

As she pulled out of the driveway an unfamiliar car passed her. She swung her head around to take a second look at the driver. She could have sworn it was Keith but dismissed the thought when the car turned into a driveway at the end of her block. "You're losing your mind Jaidyn." She said out loud to herself.

Looking down at the clock, it was almost 11:00 a.m. She'd promised Jared she'd be at his place before noon. One of the local radio stations was hosting Family Day in the Park. They were supposed to meet Neal, Yasmine, and the kids there for a picnic and an afternoon concert. The concert headliners were Morris Day and the Time and a hip-hop gospel crossover artist named Tragedy.

Jaidyn looked up at the sky as she waited for the light to change. The gray and white tinted clouds in the blue sky worried her. The weather seemed as if it might not cooperate. A few seconds later a handful of raindrops did a musical tap danced on her windshield and the sunroof of her car. When her cell phone began chirping she was reciting an old nursery rhyme, "Rain, rain, go away..."

"This is Dr. Owens," she said in a friendly tone.

"Hey Jaidyn."

"Hi Tye. I'm running a little late but I'm on my way," she said cutting him off.

"Ok but my mom wants to know if it's ok if I spend the night. My aunt called and wants to take her out some place."

"Absolutely, that sounds like a wonderful idea. I'll talk to your mom when I get there. See you in a few minutes."

Jaidyn had called Tye, the boy Jared mentored, earlier that morning to ask if he wanted to tag along with them. Tye had practically leaped through the phone. Jared had told her that Tye had been complaining about not spending anytime with him lately. Jared laughed when he told her. He'd said that Tye wasn't really trying to see him as much as he was trying to see Nicole. When she'd spoken to Yasmine the day before she'd told her that the friend that was supposed to go with Nicole had backed out of spending the day with them at the last minute. So Jaidyn thought she would please Jared, Tye, and Nicole with one simple gesture.

Jaidyn saw Tye peeping out of the window when she pulled into his driveway. Before she could get out of the car he was outside with his overnight bag in hand. "Hi Tye. Where are you going so fast? I've got to talk to your mom before we leave."

"She's in the kitchen." He said as he walked towards the car. "I'll wait for you in the car."

Before Jaidyn could knock on the door Tye's mother was opening it. After the two of them reviewed the details of Tye's overnight stay Jaidyn climbed back into the SUV where Tye was waiting.

As Jaidyn pulled away from Tye's house, she spotted the same toyota she'd seen when she was backing out of her driveway. She wouldn't have noticed it except it was fire red, dropped low like a street racer, and had some type of design on the side. When the car turned left at the corner she dismissed the thought again and continued on her way to Jared's.

Tye's excitement was evident but he tried to blame it on being able to see Tragedy in concert but Jaidyn had been young once and hadn't forgotten the signs of young love.

The rain was a steady drizzle by the time Jaidyn pulled into the parking place next to Jared's Mercedes. She and Tye were discussing alternative options for the day if the sky decided to open up and ruined their plans. "Maybe Nicole can go with us to a movie." Tye suggested as they got out of the car.

"How about we grab some lunch and go to Dave & Busters to play some virtual reality games." Jaidyn countered.

"Doesn't matter to me." Tye said trying to sound indifferent. Jaidyn smiled at his boyish nature. She knew the only thing that really mattered was that Nicole was included in whatever they decided.

"Maybe Jared will have some suggestions." Jaidyn was saying as she slipped her key into the lock of Jared's front door. His loft had become as intimate to her as her own house since they exchanged keys. As she stepped inside, Tye threw another suggestion her way, "Maybe we can go bowling." They both stopped cold in their tracks when they saw Jared and Faith in a tight body to body embrace.

Tye's eyes widened and he gasped. Jared looked up with wide eyes. "Sorry to interrupt." Jaidyn said feeling her face getting hot.

Faith felt trapped but she wouldn't run away from this. She was going to stay and fight for the man she loved. She'd been calling Jared and even stopped by but he'd been avoiding her. Now she knew why. She knew it had to be another woman but she would have preferred it to be anybody but Jaidyn. "This bitch has a key!" Her hurt feelings made her say.

Jared shot her an annoyed glance then looked back at Jaidyn and Tye. "Can you give us a minute?" Jared requested. Jaidyn complied and ushered Tye toward the stairs. "Thanks," Jared said to their backs as he watched them walk up the stairs.

He'd been completely unfair to Faith. She'd called him repeatedly but he had ignored her calls. He and Jaidyn had been back together a month before he decided to return her calls. When he did she was out of town on vacation. He left a message saying he was returning her calls but he hadn't said anything else. Faith had called repeatedly since receiving the message but he hadn't thought twice about calling her back. There had also been a time or two that she'd called and Jaidyn was laying in his arms. He'd let her talk to his answering machine.

"Now I see what the problem is." Faith said, her hurt feelings turning to fury.

"Faith I'm sorry. I should have handled this differently."

"This is why you won't return my calls or answer the door when I come over?" Jared hung his head knowing this was not going to be as easy as he'd hoped. "How long has this shit been going on?"

"Look!" Jared said agitated. "I apologize. I wasn't trying to hurt your feelings."

"I want to talk to her!"

"For what?" Jared waited on an answer but all he got from her was attitude.

"What about us?" She whined.

"Look Faith, when you got involved with me you knew that it was what it was. I don't know what you were expecting. We don't need to go through all this drama." Jared stood firm and Faith understood that she'd lost him. With as much dignity as she could muster she walked out of his apartment.

Chapter 47

Jaidyn, Yasmine, and Nicolette came out of the mall laughing happily. Jaidyn loved all of Yasmine's children but Nicolette's bubbly, out-going personality made her Jaidyn's favorite.

Keith was sitting at the end of the parking lot in his car watching the mall entrance. When the three of them came out he jumped out of his car and quickly walked towards them. He was still two car links away when he called to Jaidyn, "Can I talk to you for a minute?" Jaidyn was surprised but her annoyance seemed to mask it. She dismissively walked past him like he wasn't there with Yasmine and Nicolette in tow. Just as she reached for the car door handle he pulled her by the arm and slammed her petite frame against the car parked next to them. The force of her hitting the car shattered its window but he didn't seem to notice. Jaidyn looked at him bewildered and frightened.

Jaidyn could smell the liquor on his breath. He was unpredictable when he was drinking and she was afraid of what he might do. She tried to stand her ground and not allow his rampage to visibly shake her but she could feel her strong stance beginning to weaken. He was holding her arms so tight shock waves of pain were running up and down them. Tears were hiding behind her eyes but her defiant spirit held them at bay.

Yasmine jumped in his face after she put Nicolette in the car, "Get you're damn hands off of her or I'm calling the police."

"I'm trying to have a conversation with my wife," Keith said harshly.

Jaidyn looked from Keith to Yasmine. Yasmine shouted for her to get in the car as she dialed 911. Jaidyn looked down at Nicolette sitting inside the car. She was glued to the window. Her wide frightened eyes stabbed Jaidyn in the heart and Jaidyn struggled to hold back tears. She mouthed "I'm ok," to the little girl and a tear streamed down Nicolette's face.

"Keith let her go!" Yasmine demanded.

"Fuck you. This is between me and my wife!"

"What did you say?" Yasmine asked.

"You heard me."

Before Yasmine could respond mall security followed by police had pulled up. After everyone gave their statements. The police asked Jaidyn if she wanted to press charges, she said no and they were permitted to leave. Keith was detained for more questions.

On the way home Yasmine was extraordinarily quiet. She nervously toyed with the end of one of her dreadlocks while she drove. Jaidyn sat in the back seat with Nicolette, trying to reassure her that that the window had been broken on accident and the Keith hadn't meant to push her into it. Although Jaidyn and Yasmine were still traumatized Nicolette seemed to have bounced back and asked if they could stop for lunch.

"Can we go to that train by your house?"

"You mean Goodies?"

The little girl shook her head in excitement, "Can we sit at the bar?"

"If it's ok with your mom," Jaidyn said smiling at her.

Yasmine shook her head, realizing Nicolette was still upset but was recovering quickly. It's amazing how quickly kids seemed to move pass things, she thought to herself. After lunch Yasmine took Jaidyn home. When they were getting out of the car Keith was pulling up behind them. They all hurried inside and locked the door behind them. Yasmine went over to the kitchen phone and called 911. Jaidyn hugged Nicolette and tried to act calm although she was terrified.

Keith banged on the door and began screaming at Jaidyn to let him in. Nicolette jumped out of Jaidyn's arms and ran to her mother. Jaidyn went to the front door and asked him to leave. She told him they had already called the police but he wouldn't go away. His banging was relentless and it seemed to ring throughout the entire house.

Nicolette was frightened and huddled close to her mother. Yasmine was trying to stay calm but her temper was boiling at the edges. "You've got to do something about this before that damn fool hurts you or somebody else," Yasmine said angrily.

Jaidyn felt horrible, "Yasmine maybe I should go out there and talk to him. The longer he's out there the madder he's going to get.

"Let the police handle this."

Keith started trying to kick the door in. "Jaidyn open this fucking door."

"Keith I don't want to have anything to do with you. I've called the police. You need to leave." She yelled through the door. It seemed to be taking the police forever to arrive.

"I'll kill you before I let you divorce me!" He screamed. Just as the door gave way a policeman tackled him and handcuffed him.

While Keith sat in the back of the police car a policeman leaned in an open door getting his story. He pretended to be a prefect gentleman as he explained that he only wanted to talk to his wife. The other officer asked Jaidyn if she wanted him arrested and she said no. She just wanted him removed from her property. The officer relayed her wishes to him and told him if he came back they would be forced to arrest him. He said he would leave if they just let him talk to Jaidyn. They refused and he left.

He went back to his car and thought about what the hell he was doing. He had sat at home all day thinking about her. When she first left he thought she was angry and she'd be back. He thought she was playing games trying to get him to do what she wanted him to. But now he was drowning in his own misery. He desperately needed her. He'd almost turned his business over to his employee's because he hadn't been able to go to work and concentrate. Come hell or high water he'd made up his mind that they were going to get through this.

Keith was going overboard, Jaidyn thought. She second-guessed herself as she thought she made the wrong decision in not having him arrested. "Maybe if he'd gone to jail he would come to his senses," she thought.

Jaidyn was absorbed in thought when Yasmine told her Jared was on the phone. "Did you call him," Jaidyn asked exasperated.

"Yes." Yasmine said with an attitude.

Jaidyn snatched the phone from her and shot her a dirty stern look. Jaidyn was trying to sound calm but Jared could hear the nervous trimmer in her voice. "Why don't you come over and stay at my place for the night."

"Jared I'm fine. I don't think he's coming back." She said trying to sound confident. Forty-five minutes later Jared was walking in Jaidyn's door with an overnight bag in tow.

Jared walked in raising hell, "Jaidyn something has got to be done about him! I'm not going to continue to allow him to get in your face." Jaidyn remained silent allowing him to rant and rave. Normally, he was the worse kind of angry person. His anger was a silent, steady, withdrawn. It was the kind of anger that you never knew when its fury would be unleashed. So when he acted this way Jaidyn remained silent allowing him to get it out of his system.

"Baby..." she tried to interject.

"This is not up for discussion! I'm not going to allow him to keep runnin' up in yo face whenever he feels like it!"

Jaidyn looked at him in incredulity, "What exactly are you going to do?" Jared looked intently at her while the answer to her question passed between them. "That's not going to solve anything." Jaidyn's tone was incensed but in a concerned, loving way. His silence let her know that this conversation was over. Jaidyn let out a heavy frustrated breath. Knowing it was useless to continue to pursue this issue. There was nothing she was going to be able to say that would change his mind.

As Jaidyn lay in Jared arms, her head on his chest, his chest hair lightly brushed against the side of her face, she could hear every beat of his heart. Laying there in the dark, he held her tightly and she felt protected from the world.

Jared fit into that empty space in her life perfectly. When she was away from him she longed for the feeling of tranquility she found in his arms. It was as if nothing else mattered when he walked into the room. They were genuine kindred spirits connected by a force more dynamic than either of them could control. In him, she had finally found that magic that her grandparents had in their relationship. She'd found the man she'd spend the next eighty years with, the man that completed her.

Lord, I know You've been right here listening to my heart all along. I know that You knew what was best for me when I didn't know. Thank you for being faithful and never turning away from me when I was unfaithful and stepped ahead of Your will. Your mercy and loving kindness are forever present and I am so grateful.

Father Keith is on the edge. I see it in his eye. I'm worry that he is losing grip with reality. I'm becoming increasingly leery of him. Speak to him. Allow him to give his life to You so that he may find peace...

I need You to intercede in the festering hostility between him and Jared. On one hand I am so pleased that Jared is willing to defend me but on the other I'm scared for Keith. I can see a thunderstorm brewing inside Jared. There's an angry stillness to him that scares me. There's nothing I can do to control Jared, nothing I can do to deter him once he makes up his mind. Please speak to his heart and send him peace and forgiveness.

Lord, I love you and I need you. Reside within the walls of this house and live within our hearts. Bless us abundantly Father. In my Lord and Savior Jesus Christ Name.

Amen

Keith sat on a bench between the two old elm trees in Jaidyn's backyard, hidden by the darkness, watching her and Jared through the bay window in her bedroom. As the house drew dark so did his mood. He missed Jaidyn like crazy. Seeing her with another man was driving him insane. He had to do something to get her back, he thought.

He watched them as long as he could stand it. As he rose to walk back to his car he said, "I love you. Sweet dreams," as if Jaidyn could hear him.

Chapter 48

Jared had gotten up early to go to the airport for a business trip. He'd only be gone overnight but before Jaidyn's feet hit the floor she was already missing him. They hadn't spent a night apart since they'd gone home together after meeting at Club 360.

Jaidyn walked into the kitchen and found a brown paper sack lunch on the cabinet Jared had left for her. He had attached a note to the side of it that read, "You're so amazing. I already miss you. Have a wonderful day. Love you, Jared." Once again something so small had gotten her day off to the prefect start.

Jaidyn had seen thirty-two patients and it was time to go home before she remembered the lunch Jared had made for her. She peered into the bag and pulled a turkey sandwich, chips and a small white box with a pink ribbon tied around it out. She pushed the sandwich and chips to the side and rushed to open the box. The box contained a note and a small wishbone. The note read, "If I had one wish it would be for you to be here with me." Jaidyn picked up the phone and dialed Jared's cell phone number. To her disappointment Jared did not answer and she had to leave a message.

Jaidyn pulled the box to her chest and hugged it. She smiled as the thought of Jared trickled through her mind. The two of them had been behaving like two teenagers in love for the very first time. They talked to each other five to six times a day, popped in and out of each others offices periodically and met at home when ever possible for mid day nasty naps. When they were together their need to touch each other was completely overwhelming. Jaidyn found the greatest comfort in having his hand in the small of her back or having him stand behind her allowing the warmth of his skin to illuminate her body.

She'd begun to wonder how people in love got anything accomplished because all she wanted to do was eat, sleep, and breathe Jared Mitchell. They made love every chance they got and any place they could; on the floor, the couch, the bed, the car, their office desk, the doctors lounge, or even in the ladies bathroom at the hospital.

Jaidyn laughed as she thought about Yasmine's complaints after she and Neal had spent an evening with them. Dinner had gone fine, but afterwards they'd gone to a small jazz club where her and Jared had been completely consumed with each other. After only being there thirty minutes Jared had put on his game face and Jaidyn quickly made an excuse about having to see a patient so that they could leave. They'd gone straight home and left a trail of clothes on their way to the bedroom.

Jaidyn's excuse hadn't fooled Yasmine. She called the next morning and said, "You two are acting worse than two crack heads on a binge! No one sees you or talks to y'all. It's as if you have simply disappeared off the face of the earth. I finally convenience y'all to come up for air and y'all act like you don't want to be bothered." Jaidyn hadn't thought about it in those terms until Yasmine mentioned it, but she had to admit that Yasmine was right.

Jaidyn hadn't spoken to Jared since he left that morning and was feeling withdrawals at that very minute. I've become a junkie she mused to herself. "If I could put him in a syringe I'd inject him into my veins several times a day," she said laughing. Being with him was like being on a natural high. They didn't have to do anything special. They found enjoyment in the simple things. Watching a movie together or lying on the couch laughing and talking, cooking a meal together, or taking an afternoon drive. Anytime they spent together was special.

Jaidyn was gathering her things to head home when her receptionist buzzed her office, "Dr. Owens you have a call on line three."

She looked at the clock, 6:02 p.m. There was no way it was Jared. He told her he was taking a client to dinner at six o'clock. "Hunh," she heaved at the thought of talking to one more patient. She put the arm full of charts back onto her desk and hit speakerphone. "Hello, this is Dr. Owens." There was a momentary silence from the other end of the phone. Jaidyn repeated herself. "This is Dr. Owens."

"Dr. Owens? Dr. Tyler don't you think that's a little presumptuous?"

The blood in her veins turned ice cold when she heard Keith's voice. "What do you want?"

"I wanted to talk to my wife and tell her I loved her."

"I don't have time for games. What do you want?"

Her flat irritated tone was beginning to piss him off, "There you go! Why do you always have to play hard to get? You know I love you."

"Look, get to the point!"

"I've been calling you. There must be something wrong with your home phone. It always rings then it goes dead...I get a dial tone." He waited as if he was looking for a response but he didn't get one. He called her so much she had gotten tired of listening to him on her answering machine. She'd started looking at her caller ID before she answered the phone. When his number popped up she'd picked up the phone and hung it up.

"When's the last time you hung out with Yasmine?"

"What," Jaidyn asked. "Where in the hell did that question come from?"

"Well, I've come by the house a few times. Your car has been there, but you didn't answer the door. I figured you must be with Yasmine." Again Jaidyn remained silent. Keith was beginning to make her a prisoner in her own home. She had been home every time he'd come by but hadn't answered the door. She began using as little light as possible so that he wouldn't think that she was home. She'd also started parking her car in the garage hoping to deter him. When she could convince Jared to stay at his place they did. He always disapproved, arguing that if she had to go to the hospital during the night it required her to drive further to get to the medical center. He had only been at her house once when Keith came by and had been extremely agitated by Keith's continuous pounding on the door.

"Keith I've got to go. Please stop calling me!"

His voice now cold, "Stop calling you. Girl you're tripping. It's time to stop playing these games before someone gets hurt."

"If you're trying to make me regret the day I first laid eyes on you, you've done that. What else do you want?" Jaidyn paused regretting what she'd just said. She'd only stated the truth but she felt bad about being so blunt with him.

"I'm tired of this bull shit. When are you going to bring yo ass home?"

"What?"

"You heard me. You either move your shit back in here this weekend or else!"

"Or else what?"

"It's over!"

"Good-bye Keith." Jaidyn said then hung up. Thirty seconds later the phone rang again. "Hello." She answered incensed.

"I'm sorry. I am sick of this. I didn't mean to go off on you like that…"

"Good-bye Keith."

"Wait a minute. When can I see you? I know I haven't been the best husband but I promise I'm going to change. I promise I won't…"

"Good-bye Keith." She said hanging up.

Keith pulled the phone away from his ear and looked angrily, "You ungrateful bitch!"

Jaidyn hadn't wanted to go home to the empty house so she'd gone to her parents and then to Yasmine's. On her way home she decided to stop by the grocery store to pick up a few things. She was standing in front of nectarines, touching them, squeezing them, smelling them when Keith reached across her and took the nectarine out of her hand.

"I forgot how much you love these things." He said as he bit into the nectarine.

His presence angered her. Jaidyn's eyes were cool and dismissive, "What are you doing here?"

"This is a grocery store. Why do people come to the grocery store?" He said in an agitating voice.

"This is a little out of your way don't you think?" She snapped.

"Well my wife lives in this neighborhood. I was hoping to bump into her, and look…" He said smiling. "…Here you are."

Keith looming over her made her uneasy and had her stomach in knots. Jaidyn walked around him, put her hand held basket down, and walked out of the store.

On the drive home Jaidyn kept checking her mirrors, making sure Keith wasn't behind her. When she turned onto her street it was a little after 9 p.m., her house was a welcomed sight. The first thing Jaidyn did when she got into the house was make sure all the windows and doors were locked.

After taking a showering she went into the kitchen to get a snack. She opened the refrigerator and peered inside. Hum…tea, soda, wine, and bottled water, she said half to herself. The cold draft from the refrigerator blanketed her bare feet while she made up her mind.

Pensive, she poured herself a glass of White Zinfandel. When the phone rang it startled her. She looked up at the phone hanging on the wall and thought, that must be Keith. She let the phone ring several times before she considered answering it.

Jared thought about his evening with Jaidyn. He'd worked late and arrived home to find Jaidyn's car parked in the guest parking space. He pulled into the space next to his Hummer and put his car in park. He picked up his briefcase and the Joy dishwashing liquid a messenger had delivered to his office earlier that day. The package had been accompanied with a note that read, "You are the joy of my life. Love Jaidyn." He'd tried to call her several times but she wasn't answering her cell phone nor was she in her office. It had been a long time since they'd gone all day without talking to each other and he'd yearned to hear her voice.

When he got inside, the loft was dimly lit, and the strong aroma of food had tickled his nostrils. He'd sat his keys and briefcase down on the entryway table then walked into his living room. The warm inviting glow of candlelight vibrated through the room. The smooth sounds of Kirk Whalum were coming at him through his surround sound system. He'd stopped in his tracks at the sight of his big screen TV. There was an array of pictures of him and Jaidyn flashing across the screen. He stood mesmerized by the pictures that ranged from their first date until now. She'd even included some old video they'd taken on a ski trip with Yasmine and Neal.

Jared laughed at the sight of Jaidyn falling and him trying to catch her. They both ended up face down in the snow. Yasmine was standing beside them, dying laughing. Jaidyn reached up and pulled her down along side of them and they'd all ended up having a snowball fight.

During dinner she'd surprised him with courtside season tickets to the upcoming Houston Rockets basketball season. After dinner they'd made love late into the night.

He smiled at the memory then replayed their morning in his mind as he dialed her number and listened to the phone ring. Jaidyn had been lying in bed, her hair fanning the pillow, the soft smooth skin of her back exposed. The sheet covered her round firm ass. He'd sat on the side of the bed and pulled the sheet up around her shoulders and told her, "Please cover up before I miss my flight."

She laughed and turned over, exposing her breast. "Don't you have time for a quickie?"

He'd resisted the urge to fondle her breast and kissed her instead. "I'd be pushing my luck."

Jared tuned back in as Jaidyn answered the phone. "What?" She answered impatiently.

"What," Jared repeated, "Is something wrong?"

Jaidyn smiled when she heard his voice, just as she always did. "Hi baby."

"Are you alright?"

"I am now. How was your day?" She asked changing the subject.

"Tell me something…what are you wearing?"

Jaidyn sat down at the kitchen table. "Ah, a wife beater and a pair of boxers."

"A wife beater?" He questioned.

"Yeah. You know what a wife beater is." She said in a matter of fact tone as she leaned against the cabinet. "The white sleeveless T-shirts that the guys always wear in the movies when they beat their wives."

Jared found amusement in her analogy and a deep delightful laugh bellowed through the phone. Jaidyn was a southern girl in every since of the analogy. Even in boxers and a T-shirt he knew she was looking sexy. Her femininity surprised him. It was different than the northern girls he'd grown up around. Although they too were feminine, the difference in women from the north and south was as clear to him as night and day.

He heard her swallow something. "What are you drinking?"

"A glass of wine."

"Do you have enough for me?"

"Sure." She said taking another small sip.

"Then come open the door!"

"What? Don't play with me!"

"Open the door." He said in a seductive voice.

She sat the glass on the table and headed for the front door in hopes of finding him there. She peered out of the peephole and there he stood. He seemingly looked right at her and smiled, she shivered. "What are you doing here?" She said into the phone. She hurried to unlock the door and jumped into his arms and wrapped her legs around his waist. "I thought you weren't coming back until tomorrow!"

Jared was a delightful sight. "Mmm." He moaned as he kissed her. "Surprise." He stepped inside and kicked the door closed. She still had her slender legs wrapped around his waist when he started up the stairs.

His hands ran up and down her back massaging the tension of her day away. As his fingers tickled her spine, desire rolled through her like a thunderstorm. Jared nibbled on her neck and her earlobes as he patiently undressed her. Once undressed his tongue ran down the center of her body, traced the ridge around her belly button and then continued its exploration down her body.

When he slipped her toe into his mouth tingles ran up her back. He patiently massaged her feet, legs and thighs. Then he lightly bit her inner thigh and allowed his tongue to explore the center of her heat. Pleasurable moans bellowed from Jaidyn. Jared slipped his finger inside "The Palace" walls and his tongue slowly did an erotic dance with her clitoris bringing her to the edge of ecstasy.

The urge to have him inside her was overwhelming. She diverted his attention and pulled him into her arms, kissing him, caressing him, and loving him. She was sexually free with him and wanted to fulfill every fantasy she ever thought of with him.

He flipped her onto her stomach and inserted the anaconda into "The Palace." Jaidyn lay flat on the bed with her feet crossed at her ankles making the warm, moist spot he was accessing extra tight. He was lying on top of her swaying when a wave of unconceivable pleasure washed over him. His toes curled, goose bumps covered his body, and the universe moved. Jared's groans were incomprehensible to anyone but Jaidyn. His eyes rolled back into his head, he thrust once, twice, then he pulled out of her. It was Jaidyn's turn to lay on top of him. She inserted his love snake back inside her and before long they exploded together. Jaidyn watched his face as he released. His cum face was the most beautiful she'd ever seen.

They had given it to each other until neither could take anymore. A tear rolled down her face and he gently licked it. He too was experiencing a feeling so intense that he had to choke back tears.

They lay spooning, enjoying the warmth that they found in each other as the morning sun blanketed them. Jared's soft breath was on the back of Jaidyn's neck. His arm draped across her slender waste and her back against his warm chest. The anaconda gave it's morning ceremonial salute and she smiled as Jared pushed it into her back. "Ummmmm, good morning." She said turning to him.

Somehow Jared had become her lifeline. There wasn't anything she wouldn't do for him. He was her key to a world she had never known. There was a freedom in loving him that she cherished. Just being in the same room with him made her giddy and happy. Everyday she saw something new in him that made her love him a little more. Everyday her love surpassed the day before. She couldn't imagine not spending her life with him.

Chapter 49

The stress headaches were back. They'd become a part of her daily life. He'd pulled so many crazy stunts they had begun to instill fear in her. Keith was filled with desperation and it was beginning to scare her. Keith was becoming more and more violent. After he'd come to her house, broken a few things, and threatened her with a knife, Joanna convinced her to get a restraining order against him.

When Keith received the restraining order he was at work. He had been completely humiliated. Instead of putting distance between them it seemed to make things worse. The afternoon he received it Jaidyn went to the courthouse to meet Joanna for lunch. Joanna's court case had taken a little longer than she'd expected so Jaidyn went inside to wait on her. After the judge recessed for lunch the two women agreed on a café a few blocks away from the courthouse.

When they got into Jaidyn's car Keith was lying on the back floor. When he emerged he claimed he just wanted to talk to Jaidyn. Joanna's quick thinking helped them out of a serious situation. She told him that they could all talk while she went back into the courthouse to use the bathroom. Jaidyn slipped her the keys as she got out of the car. When Joanna returned she brought a policeman with her. He was arrested on the spot, but before the day was out he had posted bond and was back at home. That was the first time Jaidyn had truly believed that he may be capable of something truly horrendous.

Two weeks prior to that Jaidyn had come out of her office and found him waiting on her in the parking lot. He grabbed her and told her how lucky she was to have him. He'd told her if he could turn back the hands of time he would do things differently. She'd broken his grip and ran to her car. Once inside she locked the door. She nervously fumbled with the keys while he stood outside her window screaming at her. After she'd driven off he'd followed her. She had called her parents, her father had told her to drive to the police station. When she got there Keith was on her tail. She'd jumped out of the car and ran towards the door. Before she'd gotten to the door he'd caught her, slapped her several times before several policeman came running out to help her and her father pulled up. The next morning he was out of jail and harassing her again.

Then the inevitable had happened. Jared, Jaidyn, and Yasmine, were in Jaidyn's BMW, on their way to meet Neal for dinner when Jared spotted Keith's car trailing them.

Jaidyn had said, "Baby, that's not Keith's car. You're imagining things." She and Yasmine exchanged glances, giving each other that expression meaning I can't believe his ass is following us.

Either Yasmine didn't pick up on the expression or her ass was looking for trouble. The next thing out of her mouth was, "That's him. Who else do you know with a black Mercedes who's vanity plates read 'You Wish'?"

Jaidyn's head snapped back as she glared at Yasmine. Yasmine rolled her eyes and diverted them out the window. She knew as soon as they were alone that she was going to get a serious tongue-lashing.

Jared watched his rear view mirror. Keith was careful to stay two to three car lengths behind them. Then he made the tragic mistake of following them off the freeway. Jared methodically moved up and down the streets of third ward looking for the right opportunity. As Jared brought the SUV to a complete stop at a red light Keith became bolder, closing the gap between them.

When the light turned green Jared pulled the car to the side of the road and Keith followed. He parked two car lengths behind them. Jared slammed the SUV in park and hopped out. "What are you doing," Jaidyn yelled to his back. Jared ignored her and quickly walked back to Keith's Mercedes.

Yasmine and Jaidyn both turned around in their seats to see what Jared was going to do. "I'm going to kick your ass Yasmine," Jaidyn said as she watched Keith roll his window down. He seemed to be taunting Jared as he flashed his amazing smile. To Yasmine and Jaidyn's surprise Jared flashed his own award winning smiled back at Keith. From inside the car the two of them appeared to be having a friendly chat.

As Jared turned to walk back to the car, where the ladies were anxiously waiting, Keith got out of his car and said something that neither girl could hear. Jared abruptly turned around. Their body language told the girls that their words had turned angry. Jared got in Keith's face but Keith's expression never changed.

When Jared started walking back to the car Jaidyn was relieved. She breathed out a sigh of relief thinking, 'they'd had a pissing match'. Then all hell broke loose. Keith grabbed Jared's shoulder. In one swift move Jared turned around and hit Keith. Keith seemed to have been expecting the punch and answered it with his own series of punches.

Keith had done exactly what Jared was hoping he'd do, put his hands on him. Jared turned around with such quickness and force Keith never saw it coming. Jared could hear the cracking of bone as his fist met with Keith's nose.

Keith had instinctively reached for his nose. There was a plethora of bright red blood oozing from it. He'd quickly swung back landing three quick blows to Jared's body. Jared countered with a one, two, three combination in his ribs, like he'd learned in the countless hours of boxing lessons he'd had as a kid. Although Keith was wounded and bleeding he came back stronger and quicker than Jared had thought possible. He was proving he was a worthy adversary.

Jared ducked under his swing and delivered a jab to his ribs. Keith answered the punch with a right hook below the belt. Jared leaned forward, grabbing the anaconda and Keith firmly placed his knee into Jared's head. Jared stumbled away from Keith seemingly trying to recover. Keith came after him smiling wickedly. Jared pretended to still be trying to recover as Keith approached him. When Keith got close enough, Jared hit him so hard everything went black for a second. His legs were buckling when Jared hit him again and blackened his eye with a left hook. Keith lay on the ground in a fetal position as Jared stood over the top of him kicking him repeatedly with his new Ferragamo shoes. Although he could faintly hear Jaidyn screaming he didn't let up as Keith spit splatters of blood onto the sidewalk. "He's been begging for this ass whoopin," something inside Jared's head said as he tried to tell himself to back off. Jared allowed Keith to get to his knees before he punished him with another kick to his head. Keith collapsed once more like a sack of potatoes.

The fight momentarily stunned Jaidyn. She'd nervously struggled as she tried to get the seatbelt off. By the time she and Yasmine got out of the car a small crowd was gathering. The two of them had to push their way through the crowd. Jaidyn couldn't believe what she saw. Jared was brutalizing Keith and no one was trying to stop it. She yelled for him to stop but had to pull on his arm before he looked up at her, but even then he'd kicked Keith one final time.

Once back in the car Yasmine sat in the back seat waiting on Jaidyn to thank Jared for beating the shit out of Keith. Lord knows it was long over due. But as usual Jaidyn, little Miss Goodie-Two-Shoe's ass didn't think it was the right way to handle the situation.

Yasmine couldn't help but snicker when Jared looked at her in the rear view mirror. He smiled back at her and she couldn't hold her amusement to herself any longer. "Damn, you knockin' fools out behind your woman and thangs," she said with a satisfied smile across her face. "Oh you got jokes," he said laughing. Jaidyn couldn't help laugh along with them.

Chapter 50

Debra, Jaidyn's new receptionist, stopped her as she put a patient's chart down on the counter and started to move to the next room. "Dr. Owens, you have a phone call on line one."

Jaidyn let out a tiresome sigh and went to the lab area to pick up the phone, "This is Dr. Owens."

"Good morning," Jared said.

"Hey Baby. What's up," she asked wryly.

Jared picked up on her mood, "Is something wrong?"

"No, I'm just busy. I'm doubled booked, the waiting room is full, and I've got a hospital department meeting at noon. Can I call you later?"

"Sure," he said understandingly.

Debra had warned Jaidyn the day before that her schedule would be hectic so she'd gotten out of bed early and rushed right into her day, seeing her hospital patients before she'd come into the office. Her morning had been filled with problems and things just kept getting worse. She was sitting in her office leaning back in her chair with her eyes closed, waiting for her first afternoon appointment, when she remembered Jared's morning phone call.

She'd just picked up the phone and started to dial his office number when Debra buzzed her, "Dr. Owens your first patient is in room one."

"Hmph," Jaidyn sighed letting out a heavy breath. "Thank you Debra." She said as she hung up the phone and slipped her feet back into her shoes. She looked at her desk clock, 1:21, she didn't think her first afternoon appointment was until two o'clock.

"Debra I thought my first appointment wasn't until two o'clock." She said approaching the reception desk.

"Oh, aaahhh, this one walked in without an appointment," she replied, trying not to lie to her boss.

Jaidyn made her way down the hall to the first exam room and pulled the chart out of the wall chart holder. Her head was buried in the chart as she opened the exam room door. As she walked into the room she gave her normal apology without looking up from the chart, "Hello Mr. Pliske, I hope you haven't been waiting long." She turned her back to the man sitting the corner, sat it down on the counter top and began washing her hands. She aimlessly pulled two paper towels from the wall towel holder and turned to face Mr. Pliske. To her surprise Jared was sitting in a chair in the corner of the room. "What are you doing here?" She asked, her irritation instantly disappearing.

Jared smiled back at her and stood up. He had several large poster board signs in his arms, without speaking he started flashing them at her. She read the first one out loud, "Since you didn't have time to talk to me." He moved to the next one, "I wondered if you'd have time for a note?" Jaidyn was grinning from ear to ear. Jared still hadn't said a word. He moved to the next card, "How about lunch?"

"Oh honey I can't, I'm sorry. My first patient is in 30 minutes." She said disappointed.

Jared looked down at his watch and motioned for her to have a seat. He flashed the last card. It read, "No is not an option." He stepped outside the exam room door and came back with a picnic basket. Jared opened the basket, pulled out a blanket, and covered the exam table with it. Next, he pulled out two deli sandwiches along with soup, fruit, cherry cheesecake, and iced tea.

Jaidyn shook her head and laughed. "You are too much," she said taking him into her arms and planting a big wet kiss on his lips. She stayed wrapped in his arms for several minutes and let the stress of her day evaporate. She then picked up one of the sandwiches, smiled at him wickedly, and gave him the seductive eye.

Jared smiled back as if he'd read her mind, "We don't have time but I'll take a rain check."

Chapter 51

Jaidyn turned onto her street and was relieved to see her house after a long exhausting day. The floodlights were on a timer and illuminated the house giving it a warm homey feeling. She loved her new house. Maybe when the divorce was final she would check with the owner to see if they were interested in selling it.

When she pulled into the driveway the first thing she noticed was that the living room lamp was not on. It was also on a timer and would normally be on by eight o'clock. She looked at the clock on her dash broad. "9:15, humh." She said, making a mental note to change the light bulb.

Jaidyn pushed the button on the garage door opener Jared had installed over the weekend. The door came up slowly and she eased the SUV into the garage. After she turned the car off and gathered her things she climbed out of the car with an arm full of patient charts. On her way out of the garage she stopped and got a light bulb for the lamp off the shelf, she pushed the button on the wall to close the door and walked towards the back door of the house.

Before coming to Jaidyn's he tried to watch TV but couldn't. Things had gotten so bad that he didn't know where to turn. If he could just talk to her he was sure that he could get her to understand. She needed to realize that he'd never love anyone this way again. That she was all he needed. He wouldn't accept that it was over. "Does she know that I've dreamt about her every night since she left," he wondered? "Does she have any idea what it feels like when your entire world seems to be falling apart?"

I know I've been wrong on a few occasions, he thought to himself, but I've always handled my business. When she comes home I'm keeping everybody out of our business including that damn Markel and Yasmine.

Markel's been trying to push up on my wife since I met her. And Yasmine! She's a straight up bitch. I can't stand her ass. Jaidyn's just going to have to find another friend. He blew out heavily. And Mama, I'm so sick of hearing her shit too.

Keith did not have to turn any lights in Jaidyn's house on. He prowled through her house so many times when she wasn't home he now moved through the darkness with ease. He sat on the couch, thoughtful, awaiting her arrival.

His mother and Jaidyn still talked a couple of times a week. He thought about the advice she'd given him after one of their phone conversations. She'd said, he needed to give Jaidyn some time. The best thing he could do was let her figure things out on her own and if it was meant to be she'd come home. But if he kept pushing she would pull away even further. He knew his mother was right but he missed Jaidyn and couldn't stay away from her. He'd been living in a no mans land, unable to eat, sleep, or work. His nights were long and his days were filled with meaningless worthlessness. He didn't have a clue what he was doing. He just needed to see her. Talk to her. Be with her.

Jealousy had washed over him like a tidal wave and he was having a difficult time getting his mind wrapped around the idea of her sharing her nights with another man. The thought was nearly driving him out of his mind. It was making him insane.

He tensed at the thought of her divorcing him. It infuriated him. "This wasn't that fatal attraction type shit," he told himself, "I just want her to come to her senses, realize that she loves me and that we belong together. I need her to understand that everybody makes mistakes but all that's behind me. I just want to grow old with her. Before we leave this house she's going to understand that," he thought to himself.

In the back of his mind he wondered why he cared so much about this woman. Why he couldn't just tell her to go to hell like he'd done with so many other women. He wondered what made him love her so much. When he told her that she'd take her last breath before he gave up on them it wasn't trivial chatter, he'd meant every word and it was time that he proved that to her.

When Jaidyn entered the house it was dark and silent. There was no movement but it felt occupied. A nervous trimmer tickled her insides as it had on several occasions when the house had felt inhabited. She had a sixth sense about the whole thing but had moved that thought to the back of her mind and tried to leave it there. Jared had also felt it once and had joked about the house having ghosts.

She flipped on the light in the kitchen and looked around the room. Nothing had been disturbed. She pitched her keys onto the table and walked down the hall to her bedroom. She put the charts she had been carrying on the nightstand, took her shoes off, turned on the shower, undressed, and put her white silk robe on. Then she walked towards the kitchen for a bottled water, thinking about the new bath and body shower gel Jared had given her. The thought of it had reminded her that she'd forgotten it in the car.

She went over to the table to get her car keys. They weren't there. What did I do with my keys she asked herself? Jaidyn was a creature of habit. I could have sworn that I put them on the table. She surveyed the kitchen corner tops to see if she had placed them on one of the cabinets. She decided she must have put them on the nightstand with the charts, she thought. Lately, she'd been misplacing a lot of things, and things in her house seemed ill placed or somehow disturbed.

She got side tracked by thirst and opened the refrigerator door and reached in for a bottled water. She sat the bottled water on the table before heading towards her bedroom for her keys. She got side tracked again when she saw the light bulb, picked it up off the table and went in to see if Jared had mistakenly turned it off or if the bulb was actually out. When she passed the couch the sound of dangling keys chimed and in an antagonistic tone Keith asked, "Looking for these?"

The light bulb in her hand crashed into pieces at her feet. Every muscle in her body stiffened as she turned to find him sitting on the couch behind her. A bitter cold chill came over her as a dagger of fear pierced her heart. A scream got trapped in her throat. She blinked wildly and her hands dampened with fear.

She hadn't seen him since Jared had broken his nose. It hadn't healed well. There was a small bump in the middle of it and it slightly leaned to the left. She clinched the rope at her throat and quickly averted her eyes as he got up and stepped towards her. She backed away apprehensive, terrified, "What the hell are you doing in my house...how'd you get in?" Her words came out shaky, panicked, rushed. She'd never seen him sitting there in the dark. Had her eyes skipped right over him, she questioned herself.

Jaidyn was bare footed. Her hair hung onto her shoulders. The kitchen light shined through the white silk robe creating a sexy silhouette of her tantalizing body. "I'm your husband, why would you be surprised to see me?"

A spasm of fear gripped her chest. "Jesus," she thought, "He's really lost his mind." She took two steps back and felt the glass from the light bulb crush beneath her feet. Her heart was beating like an African drum, fast and hard. It was nearly deafening her. She wondered if he could hear it too. She struggled to mask her fear, "What? You're a fucking lunatic!"

Keith hadn't thought about what he was going to say. He was beginning to regret it. His eyes were shifty. It was the first time she'd seen him unsure of himself. "You know despite all the other women, I was a good husband to you."

"A good what? You can't be serious!" She said narrowing her gaze on him. "What about all the lies? Or how about all the times you made me cry? Or all the times you yelled at me? How about all the bitches and ho's you called me. Were you being a good husband then?"

"Ok, I made a few mistakes. I'm man enough to admit that."

"A few!" She countered. "I can't count how many nights you didn't come in until five or six o'clock in the morning or just didn't come home at all. And do you know how many times you told me how lucky I was to have your sorry ass because nobody else wanted me? But you were a good husband? That's a joke! I don't have time for this bull shit!"

"Why are you so bitter baby girl? I know we can figure this out if you give us half a chance. I love you. I can't breath without you."

"Love? Please, the only person you love is yourself!" She said allowing her anger to take over and make her appear unfazed by his presence.

Keith dropped his head. Realizing she was pulling him into an redundant argument that he couldn't win, and not giving him a chance to explain how sorry he was for all that had transpired between them. "We were good together," he mumbled.

Jaidyn shook her head, "Don't fool yourself. We were never good together."

That comment hurt and Keith became defensive. "It was until you started fucking around. You shattered everything we had. Do you remember how we use to hold each other all night long? Do you remember telling me that we were going to be together forever? That nothing would ever come between us, but you let another man come between us. I believed all your lies. I couldn't see what you were doing to me. You shattered our lives. Our dreams." He stopped himself, realizing how he was sounding. "We can get it all back if you'll meet me half way." Keith said looking at the floor.

"It's too late. I don't love you anymore."

"Why are you acting like this? You've changed. You're so…hateful."

"Changed! Mean? You drove me to this."

"I love you." Keith begged.

Jaidyn took a breath, trying to calm herself and hold back the hateful words she didn't want to exit her mouth.

"I want our life back."

Jaidyn's anger flared. "Do you realize what you're saying? What you're asking me?" Keith looked at her as if she was speaking Spanish and he only spoke Swahili. "You're asking me to go back to a life of misery. You're nothing but poison! Can't you get that through your damn head?"

"We just need to talk about this." Keith said pathetically. Then added, "Maybe we should go to counseling," which he had absolutely no intentions of doing.

Jaidyn's look said do you know how many fucking times we've talked about this? Do you realize how many fucking times I've heard this shit? "I want you out of my damn house." Jaidyn said walking toward the kitchen.

Keith followed behind her like a lost puppy, "Did you hear what I said? I'm willing to go to counseling. I love you dammit! I want to work this out."

Jaidyn stopped and turned to look at him, rage in her expression. She was taken aback by what she saw in him. For the first time the strong, arrogant, egotistical, self righteous jerk she'd once thought she'd loved seemed to have been reduced to a pitiful, pathetic, weak man.

The hurt was evident in his eyes. Jaidyn's rage dissolved and her disposition softened. In that split second she felt remorseful for anything she may have done to contribute to his pain. She didn't hate Keith but loathed the things he done to her, the things she'd allowed him to do to her. She hated how helpless and weak he'd made her feel when she was with him. But none of those things added together made her hate him.

In the silence of the kitchen she looked deep into his eyes and not only forgave him but forgave herself for the part she'd played in the destruction of the man standing in front of her. "Thank you Lord." She said silently as she released it all.

She hesitated then reached out and cupped his face in her hands. She looked into his eyes, not wanting to hurt him anymore but needing him to understand that this part of their lives was over.

"Keith, I never meant to hurt you and I'm sorry. But I love him, like I've never loved anyone. Please just be happy for me." She said with as much tenderness and sincerity she could.

Something inside him snapped and sent him into a cold rage, "You fucking slut." Jaidyn shrank back as he corned her in the kitchen. When he looked at her she looked straight into his eyes, studying them. They were empty. It was as if a soul didn't live there. Evil seemed to lurk within him. The thick vein in the middle of his forehead saluted her. He stepped towards her, grabbing her attempting to frighten her but she absolutely refused to show any signs of fear, and that alone enraged him. In his deranged mind he saw it as a lack of respect.

He threw her across the room. She bounced off the wall and slid to the floor cupping the back of her head in her hand. "We're going to put an end to this bullshit. I'm the best thing that ever happened to you. You're lucky to have me!" He yelled at her. He pulled her to her feet and with an opened hand hit her across the face, knocking her back to the floor.

She pulled her bottom lip into her mouth tasting the blood. The taste of it infuriated her. The anger seemed to take control of her good senses making her think she could kick his ass. Adrenaline pumped through her and she flew at him like a woman unhinged from reality.

Keith didn't want to hit her again but she wasn't leaving him any other choice. He tried pushing her off of him but she'd only come back swinging harder. This time when he hit her he slapped her over and over repeatedly hitting his target and leaving her slumped on the floor covering her head with both arms. He knew he'd beat her unconscious if he didn't tunnel his anger away from her. He picked up a few things around the kitchen and threw them against the wall in an attempt to control the anger. "Do you know what it feels like to feel you're losing your mind," he yelled.

When he finally stopped Jaidyn peeked through her arms and looked around for anything close that she could use to defend herself. Everything was in shambles. He had broken glasses and plates. The Waterford Crystal vase Jared had given her lay in pieces. If she could get a piece of the glass and stab him with it, she thought, she may have enough time to get out the door. When he turned his back she reached for a sliver of a broken plate, jumped to her feet and ran at him. As she reached him he rotated around to face at her. She drove the glass into his left arm.

"What the fuck!" He yelped, stunned, hurt. She pulled the sharp fragment out of his arm and sliced at him again. This time only nicking his cheek.

"Have you lost your got damn mind?" He shouted stumbling away from her.

She bolted for the door. He took two steps and tackled her. Standing over her he closed his fist and swung at her. He hit her so hard everything momentarily went black. An involuntary scream bellowed out of her. When she was able to see again she kicked at him but he was too close for her to get any real power behind it. She tried to hit him but he ducked and she missed. Her arms and legs felt like lead. They were heavy and hard to move. There was no real power behind the attempts to defend herself.

He came down on top of her and she took her fingernails, dug them into his face and pulled down, exposing the raw flesh underneath his skin.

Keith squealed, crawled off of her and put his hand to his face touching the spot she'd scratched, "Ah!" He pulled his fingers away from his face and looked at them. When he saw the blood he began kicking her. She tried to crawl away but there was nowhere to go. He had her backed into a corner.

Jaidyn folded into herself and concentrated on the tears that were hiding behind her eyes. She fought to contain them refusing to let him see her cry one more time. She was relieved when he stopped kicking her and began screaming profanity at her. She was unable to hear what he was saying. Still deep inside herself, her mind like a speedometer was going two hundred miles an hour. She wondered what the hell was happening. What had made him turn into this monster? What did I do to him?

When he began pulling her across the kitchen floor she didn't resist. The pain coming from her side pulled her out of her trance. "You son of a bitch, let me go!" She squealed. She tried to stand up but her foot slipped from under her. She noticed the bloody footprints across the kitchen floor. She must have cut her foot on a piece of glass when she crushed a piece of the light bulb with her foot, she thought.

Keith dragged her up the stairs to the spare bedroom and opened the window. She fought him when he tried to push her out of it. But he was too strong. He treated her like a rag doll. His movements were cold and calculating. He held her by her legs and dangled out the window. It was as if he got high off of her fear.

Now controlled by fear more then anger and adrenaline she was too frightened to move. Her first impulse was to kick but her fear paralyzed her. She opened her mouth but nothing came out. The screams were caught in her throat.

He pulled her back inside and loomed over her as she slumped on the floor trying to catch her breath. "You fuckin' bitch." He said as he picked her up off the floor by her hair and threw her onto the bed. Jaidyn scooted to the back corner of the bed in fear. As he duct taped her hands to the wrought iron pole of the headboard. He pulled the phone out of the wall and told her, "I'll kill you if you try to run!"

Jaidyn sank into the bed, horrified by his psychopathic behavior. Her fear was still pumping her adrenaline way too fast for her to realize how battered and bruised she was. She heard him shuffling across the wood floor in the hallway. She heard him stop at the top of the stairs and held her breath. When she heard the steps creaking beneath his feet she blew out a heavy sigh of relief. Sitting in complete darkness she strained to hear any movement from the other room and wondered what he'd do when he came back.

Jaidyn wondered what had pushed him over the edge? She asked herself if it was something she'd done? She thought about when he first began to scare her, it was after they'd gone to court for the legal separation orders. Joanna's investigator had dug up much more then Jaidyn could have imagined.

Once the judge heard a small portion of Joanna's argument he had scolded Keith and his attorney for attempting to withhold evidence. He appointed an outside accounting firm to access Keith's net worth. Keith was in danger of losing everything. He'd been ordered to pay $3000.00 a month in temporary spousal support. The judge had also ordered that both lawyers provide the accountants office with all financial records of Keith's business, any and all investment real estate, and his pension plans.

Keith's attorney, Mr. Joseph, had tried to argue that the house should not be considered in his client's list of assets because he purchased it before they were married but the judge saw it differently. "Do you have a written agreement stating this?" The judge asked looking over the top of his reading glasses.

"No sir, but..." Mr. Joseph said.

The judge interrupted him, "Mr. Joseph do not waste this court's time with your frivolous objections. I'm sure you know that without a written agreement the home of Mr. Tyler is considered a community estate. The total fair market value of the home is to be assessed and each party should yield half of the community estate unless your client can produce a written agreement showing otherwise."

"Your honor, I'd like to sight Johnson vs. Johnson."

"Mr. Joseph I'm aware of the case. Mrs. Holloway is your client presently living in the home?"

"No sir. She has rented a house in..."

Cutting her off, "How much is her rent?"

"$1800.00 a month your honor."

"I am ordering that Mr. Tyler pay an additional $1800.00 a month to Ms. Tyler for the residence she has had to temporarily rent."

Had that been the final draw? Had he always been neurotic? She tried not to hurt him. She wondered what had happened to make things deteriorate to this point. What could she have done differently?

Chapter 52

Sometime during the night Jaidyn had fallen into an uneasy asleep. Keith's heavy footsteps on the stairs woke her. She popped up and pulled her knees into her chest. Oh my God, why is he coming? What's he going to? She desperately tried not to complete the thought.

Keith walked into the room, smiled at her as if nothing was wrong. He cut the duct tape off her hands and a flicker of hope ran through her. He wrapped her in his arms and held her like he missed her then led her downstairs through her room and into her bathroom. He had drawn her a bath, put on a jazz CD and lit several candles. "I thought you would enjoy a bath," he said sweetly.

The way the words rolled off his tongue chilled her. She stood in the doorway and surveyed the room. She couldn't believe this whole seductive scene he had conjured up. He had damn near beat her to death now he was inviting her to enjoy herself. Keith had truly lost his mind, she thought. But she was afraid to say anything in fear of provoking him

He smiled a wicked smile at her and began apologizing for his actions. He seemed remorseful but there was a darkness to it. He told her he never meant to scare her, never meant to hurt her. He'd blamed his actions on not being able to sleep since she'd been gone. He told her how he'd basically turned his business over to his employees because he'd been unable to concentrate on anything since she'd left. He told her how Chevon hadn't allowed him to see K.J. since she'd left. He babbled on and on for the next ten minutes. His babbling was irrational and demented but Jaidyn dare not mention it. She stood quietly listening, pretending to be sympathetic and understanding. He kissed her on the forehead then left her to her bath.

Once he was out of the bathroom she began searching for anything that would help her get out of there. Maybe she could spray hair spray in his eyes or alcohol. She quietly opened the cabinet. Empty. How about fingernail polish remover? She tip toed over to the sink and opened the cabinet under it. She sighed, he had emptied all the cabinets. He'd stripped the bathroom of everything but shampoo and soap.

Jaidyn leaned against the sink and let her mind run wild with possible ways to escape. Unable to come up with any ideas she decided to climb into the tub to try to relax and think. She locked the door, took her clothes off and slid into the warm water. Every inch of her body ached. She turned the jets on the Jacuzzi tub, lay her head back and sunk down into the hot pulsating water.

She hadn't been in the tub but a couple of minutes when Jared popped into her mind. "That's it," she thought. No, no. He had flown out last night for three days of meetings with a client in Chicago. He was scheduled to take the 6 p.m. flight home day after tomorrow. She is supposed to pick him up at the airport. When she didn't show up he'd know something was wrong. He'd call and then come by to check on her, she thought. She questioned her own thinking as her imagination began to run wild. Would she make it that long? What were Keith's plans? Maybe he was just trying to scare her. Maybe he plans to do something to Jared, she thought.

She didn't know how much time had passed when she opened her eyes and found Keith standing over her. The hair on the back of her neck stood up. "Shit!" She yelled.

He loomed over her, masturbating. His movements cold and calculating. It occurred to him that he might be about to commit a crime but he moved the thought to the back of his mind because Jaidyn was his wife. "Who were you expecting?" His words were laced with ice. His eyes filled with pure unadulterated evil. He smelled of marijuana and alcohol. She knew he used to smoke a little herb back in the day but she didn't know he had started again.

"You just scared me." Her words had tumbled out of her mouth in a panicked rush. She coward away from him and shook violently.

He looked down at her with a wicked smile. Then he reached down and dragged her out of the bathtub by her hair. When he threw her onto the floor she hit her head on the side of the cabinet and a plethora of blood begin flooding the floor and trickling down the sides of her face. Tears spilled from her eyes as he loomed over her. Her bottom lip trembled and her face showed the hysteria she'd been trying to hide. She'd never seen so much rage in his eyes.

There was something about the submission he saw in her eyes that made him feel respected. Made him feel like a man and it turned him on. As he began to unbuckle his pants she slid away from him. He pulled her by her ankle and she violently kicked at him. "Don't make me hurt you." He warned. Jaidyn continued to kick at him and he made her pay for it by brutally beating her. When he dropped his pants she knew what was next, every thing went gray. She had never been so horrified. Keith was on top of her manhandling her. "Had to get him off of her," she thought. Had to fight him. No, no, please no. She tried to resist but it only made him angry, more forceful. A cocktail of terror and panic had washed over her. Her breaths were short and shallow. Salty tears rolled down her face. Somehow she was able to escape, go outside of her body. She stood looking down at herself while Keith had his way with her.

Once he was finished with her he stood in front of the sink, ran warm water on a wash cloth and cleaned himself up. When he'd finished he throw the wash cloth at her and said, "*You look like shit. Clean yourself up!*"

When he was out of the bathroom Jaidyn tried to stand up but she was dizzy, disoriented. All the blood looked as if it had been drained from her colorless face. Her stomach did flip-flops as a wave of nausea hit her. She crawled to the toilet and began vomiting. Her heart felt like it was going to explode. She scooted over to the corner, gathered her legs to her chest, buried her head between her knees and cried.

She had to pull herself together and find a way to get out of there. She couldn't let him touch her again. She had to find the courage even if it meant killing him. She looked around the bathroom again, hoping that he'd left something behind that she'd overlooked. She saw the red almost black pool of blood on the floor and reached for the cut on her head. When she touched the cut it stung. "Mmmph," she moaned as pain shot through her head.

Jaidyn was shell-shocked. The sight of the blood on her finger tips made her heart race all over again. Her mind seemed to automatically shift to a technical mode and her medical training took over. She'd spent part of her residency in the ER at the county hospital and had seen her share of this type of trauma. Her chest was tight but her breathing pattern was normal as she silently began to think from a doctor's point of view. "Ok," she said to herself. My scalp has a laceration. It probably isn't bad but because of its location there is a lot of blood.

The pain dulled as she silently went over the statistics of this kind of abuse. Domestic violence claims more lives in a year than cancer and traffic accidents combined. Seventy-eight people are raped in the Unites States every hour. She wrote the math problem in the air with her figure, that's 1871 rapes a day and 683,280 a year. Only thirty-seven percent of those are reported to the police.

She hesitated and her mind shifted again. Blackness tried to consume her. Was it really rape? Had she said no? She remembered saying it but had she said it out loud or only to herself? Her heart was thumping so loudly she could barely hear her own thoughts. Her head was splitting. Can husbands rape their wives? This was her fault. She'd pushed him over the edge. She should have known better, she thought to herself.

"No, no, no," she cried as she worked out the details in her own mind. "Keith is my husband in name only. Even if we still lived together it's wrong. Lots of women are victims of rape at the hands of their husbands. Statistics…" Her mind wondered off track. Then she pulled it back to the statistics, "Statistics…statistics show approximately twenty-eight percent of victims are raped by their husbands… Rape is a violent crime…that is more about power than it is about sex. That's it!" She said to herself bridging the distance between her technical mind and her emotional mind. "Keith is trying to regain his control over me…Violence escalates when people feel out of control…" Jaidyn fought to keep her thoughts focused. "I will not blame myself. I fought him. I said no! This is not your fault!" She yelled to herself.

Her thoughts shifted again. "I need to think about getting the hell out of here…The longer I'm his captive the more likely he is to do something… more stupid…more violent…" Her words trailed off. She had to be strong she told herself. "There is no going back. There is no talking him out of whatever he has planned."

Her mind shifted again as the walls started to close in on her. She was at the breaking point and tears rolled down her face. The rape had done something to her beyond the obvious and she was panicked, somehow injured inside.

Keith had hoped that she would beg him to take her back. He was hoping that she would plead with him to stop hitting her but she'd been stubborn and he had to beat her until his own knuckles bled before he stopped. She'd silently cried and tried to fight him back but she never said the words that he longed to hear. She never told him she loved him and that she'd made a mistake. She never said she wanted him back. If she wouldn't have looked at him so cold and dismissively then he may not have had to do what he did to her. If she'd just shown him some respect then things would be different right now, he thought to himself. He picked up his keys and headed for Jaidyn's front door.

Chapter 53

Jaidyn kept a meticulously clean house and there is nothing worse then trying to clean a house that's already clean. Evelyn had tried to talk Jaidyn into letting her clean once a month because she didn't need someone more then that. Jaidyn had agreed but insisted on continuing to pay her as if she came weekly. Evelyn felt uncomfortable taking money she hadn't worked for so she continued to come once a week although her days varied.

Evelyn mechanically unlocked Jaidyn's back door and stepped into the kitchen. She aimlessly walked through the kitchen to the hall closet were her cleaning supplies were located. As she opened the closet door recognition trickled across her mind and confusion drew her face into a frown. She closed the closet door and walked back towards the kitchen. Although the kitchen was picked up, things weren't quite right. The first thing she noticed was the wall phone was off the hook so she walked over and put the receiver back onto its base. She then turned back to survey the kitchen again. Several cabinets were ajar. The trashcan was normally in the pantry but was sitting beside the breakfast table. But what really caught her attention was the set of keys on the cabinet.

Not wanting to walk in on the same scene she had previously, Evelyn opened the back door and walked to the garage to peek inside. Sure enough the BMW was sitting in its normal slot. Evelyn went back into the kitchen and began to clean it. Hoping to make her presence known she made as much noise as possible.

After the upstairs bedrooms and bathrooms were cleaned Jaidyn still did not emerge from her room so Evelyn decided to venture into Jaidyn's private area. She knocked on the door.

After not hearing any movement or signs of life she called for Jaidyn, "Dr. Tyler." Nothing. "Jaidyn," she hollered with a heavy accent. Still nothing.

"Jaidyn...Dr. Tyler," she said as she moved through her room.

Jaidyn heard her and began screaming and crying, *"Evelyn, Evelyn, help me, please help me!"*

Evelyn walked hurriedly towards the sound of her voice. Evelyn opened the closet door and looked in. "Where are you? Dr. Tyler...Jaidyn."

"Please help me, please." Jaidyn screamed in desperation.

When Evelyn opened the bathroom door, she found Jaidyn huddled in a corner naked, with her hands duct taped to the towel rack. Jaidyn looked up at her. Her light gray eyes were terrified, she was uncontrollable trembling and her soft golden highlighted hair was matted with blood. Jaidyn's lips quivered and tears rolled down her swollen and bruised face. Evelyn screamed when she saw her then burst into tears.

When Jaidyn arrived at the hospital the only bruising that was visible was on her face and shoulders. The doctors couldn't see all the bruising on her body until she was undressed. Dr. Joyce Williams was not only Jaidyn's colleague but also someone she considered a dear friend. When Dr. Williams said, "Tell me what happened," Jaidyn's voice trembled and she broke down as she recounted every gory detail of the last twenty-four hours. The fearful look in her eyes was unmistakable. Dr. Williams had seen it many times in the eyes of other domestic violence victims.

Dr. Williams stayed with Jaidyn through her entire process. While her arm, which was broken in three places, was being cast, Dr. Williams went to speak to her family who was waiting on pins and needles. She went over a list of things people who've experienced a traumatic event such as this can suffer from. She warned them that Jaidyn's emotional state may seem out of proportion with her injuries but that was normal. She also talked to them about how emotionally difficult rebuilding her life after such a violent attack might be. She suggested that Jaidyn undergo counseling and enter a victim's group for women in similar situations for the vital support she would need.

"Joyce, we understand what you're saying but is our daughter going to be ok?" Mr. Owens asked.

She understood his question and hesitated, studying all of their concerned faces for a minute. She didn't want to say the wrong thing but the truth was that sometimes this type of trauma could change a person forever. It takes away its victims innocence and sense of control.

"Some victims are left numbed and in shock by their experience." She stated. "They are reserved and have difficulties expressing themselves. Others respond differently, they appear distraught or anxious. They may even express rage or hostility against the doctors and nurses that are trying to help them." She took a deep breath and let it out. "But Jaidyn appears to have maintained some type of control. She is jumpy and fearful but that's normal. When I spoke to her she seemed to have pulled herself together enough to know exactly what she has to do, to move pass this. I was with her during the entire process. She's very emotional but she still has her wits about her. She's very strong. One of the things that makes her such a successful doctor is her ability to deal with people during a crisis."

"This isn't someone else's life!" Russell Owens said abrasively.

Dr. Williams took a seat opposite them. Then continued to answer their questions. "That's true but I believe she has the natural ability to stay controlled and focused when everything around her is falling apart. I am hoping that she is able to do that in this situation."

"What if she can't?" Joanna frowned. "What if she can't handle this? What do we do?"

"Well, if she experiences PTSD she'll need to see a rape counselor and she'll need a good support system. If you can help her deal with one small segment of the trauma at a time she should do just fine."

"What is PTS...?" Yasmine frowned unable to remember all of the letters.

"PTSD, Post-Traumatic Stress Disorder, it's a normal emotional reaction to this type of trauma. She'll need all of you to remain close to her no matter how much she may try to push you away. She will need to feel secure and in control. When she wants to talk about things let her but don't rush her. Let her decide when she's ready to be affectionate. She may not want to be touched or hugged for a while. It's important for her to feel safe and stable. She'll need to get back to the normalcy of her life as quick as possible."

Mrs. Owens cried softly. Dr. Williams slid to the edge of her seat and cupped her hands in hers. She had been speaking as Jaidyn's doctor but now she wanted to speak to them as her old college roommate. As the girl that had eaten at their house a thousand times. As the girl who had adopted them as her second family. She took a deep breath, "Mama Owens, listen to me. Jaidyn's a fighter. When EMS brought her in here she was coherent and knew exactly what she wanted. She even insisted on seeing me. When I examined her she was emotional but in control. Her state of mind is volatile but that's not unusual considering what she's been through. The Jaidyn I know is pragmatic, stubborn and very determined. She's going to try to figure out how to get herself back on track and do that as quickly as possible. She won't be beaten by this." She said then hugged Mrs. Owens.

"Thank you Joyce." Mr. Owens said putting his hand on her shoulder.

"We've listed her under a different name for precaution. This is typical in these types of situations. I'm going to keep her here for a couple of days, just to watch her. The unit her room will be in is locked at all times for security reasons. You'll need your ID's to get in. I'll need a list of all the people that will be allowed to visit. Anyone not on the list will be turned away. You guys can see her in about ten minutes. She'll probably be able to go home tomorrow or the next day."

Dr. Williams intentionally left out how difficult it had been for Jaidyn during the examination and the police questioning. When the police took the photographs of her injuries Jaidyn had completely fallen apart. The police had allowed Joyce to stay with her and hold her hand during the heart wrenching process.

Jared was just walking into his hotel room when his cell phone began to chirp. He looked at the caller ID and pushed talk, "What up fool?"

"Hey man." Julian said in a dry dusty tone.

"I just turned my phone on. I was getting ready to call Jai. You know I'm still in..."

"Yeah I know." He said cutting him off. "Hey, ah...Neal called...your girls in trouble. I think you may need..."

"What happened?" Jared asked with an edge of impatience in his voice. He'd been feeling like something was wrong since he arrived in Chicago. He'd called Jaidyn several times and left numerous messages but she hadn't returned his calls. Before he'd left Jaidyn had told him that her surgery schedule was packed during the time he was gone so he assumed that she was buried knee deep in a case at the hospital.

"Neal says she's ok but she's in the hospital. Can you cut your trip short and get back here."

"Julian! What happened?"

Julian ignored his question and continued, "Call me back and let me know what time your flight comes in and I'll pick you up."

"Julian!"

"See if you can get a flight into Hobby Airport. It's closer. Call me right back."

"Dammit Julian, what the fuck is going on?"

"...He beat her up pretty badly and then he..."

The phone was quiet for four to five seconds. "What?" Jared's voice came by panicked.

"He broke into the house and..." Julian's voice trailed off.

Jared was silent. The news left him unsteady. His voice broke with emotion, "I'm a kill that muthafucka, Julian." He hung up enraged, hurt, confused, and feeling guilty. "Please God, please let her be ok." He begged silently as he hurried to gather his things.

Chapter 54

Five hours later Jared was walking down an airport corridor to meet Julian. His face was pale, his eyes puffy. Julian took the bag that he had slung over his shoulder from him. "Is this all you have?" He asked. Jared shook his head. They walked through the airport to Julian's car in silence. As Julian threw Jared's luggage in the trunk of his car Jared leaned against a pole and lost his lunch. Julian climbed in the car and waited on Jared.

"Man, you alright?"

Jared looked at Julian with a look that was unmistakable. The look he saw in his brothers eyes was an unfamiliar one but it was one that Julian knew all too well. He'd known what Jared was thinking since the minute he'd stepped off the airplane. Julian stared at him looking for something that told him that he was mistaken but the thought passed between them once more and he knew what Jared was about to do. "If you're thinking what I think you're thinking, you need to take a step back. See your girl. Then make a decision about what's next."

Jared didn't say anything. He just looked at Julian. Julian shook his head as if he couldn't believe what his brother was thinking but the truth was he knew exactly what Jared was thinking. He too had already dissected possible ways to get the job done.

"This shit's got me fucked up! If I just wouldn't have…" Jared's voice trailed off.

Julian looked at his brother slumped in the seat next to him with his head hanging and his heart ached. "Don't blame yourself. The brotha got something wrong with him upstairs." He said tapping the side of his forehead.

They sat quietly for a few minutes, both of them seeming thoughtful. "I need you to run me by the house to get my piece. I need to handle this before I see Jai."

"Why don't you let me and my boys handle this for you. You need to be with Jaidyn."

Jared shook is head, "I've got to do this my self!" His voice was strong and full of anger.

"You sure?"

"Yeah."

"Alright…" Julian said starting the car and slowly backing out of his parking space. "I'm down for whatever, but lets see Jaidyn first."

When Jared and Julian got off the elevator they could see Mr. Owens, Remington, and Neal standing outside her room door. When they approached them Mr. Owens shook his hand and thanked him for coming. He was glad to have Jared there. Over the past few months it was evident that he truly loved his daughter. He knew he made Jaidyn happy. At the mere mention of Jared's name she became girlish and giddy.

"The nurse just gave her something to sleep but she may still be awake." Russell Owens reported.

"I'll wait out here for you," Julian told Jared.

Jared bobbed his head and turn towards the door. He put his hand on the door and paused. His heart was beating fast and fear had a death hold on his chest. Her mother was the first person he saw when he opened the door. She was sitting in a chair with her head hung forward. Joanna was sitting on the arm of the chair with her arm draped across her mother's back. Yasmine was sitting on the side of Jaidyn's bed holding her hand and Lance was standing behind her.

As he approached the bed Yasmine tried to blink away the worry in her eyes. She got up, half hugged him, and kissed him on the cheek. Out the corner of his eye he could see Jaidyn lying in the bed, but he had avoided looking directly into her face. He was still frightened of what he might see. Yasmine stepped to the side and there she was, her eyes looked like a raccoon. Her lips were swollen, dried blood at the corner of her mouth. He stepped closer, ran his eye across her examining every bruise. Her hair was draped across the left side of her face obscuring his view. Her right arm was in a cast.

When her frightened eyes opened and stared back at him his knees gave way and he sat down beside her to keep from falling. She was ghostly pale. Her eyes were like two black holes with a gray beacon of light in the center of them. They were panic-stricken and terrified. He reached for her hand in an attempt to soothe her but she instinctively drew back and her head rolled away from him. He pulled his hand back, stood up and pushed both hands down into the pockets of his blue jeans. "I'm sorry," he whispered.

He stood next to her silently watching her while the sedative Dr. Williams had given her took affect. Jaidyn closed her eyes as she drifted into a quiet slumber.

"The doctor said she'll be able to go home in a couple of days." Yasmine muttered. Jared looked through her as if she were invisible. It was as if he could see what Keith had done to Jaidyn.

Yasmine thought she knew Jared well and had seen every side of him. She'd seen him happy, sad, disappointed, frustrated, and hurt. She'd also seen then quiet infuriated side but through it all he'd always been a pillar of strength. So when tears begin silently trickling down his face it was more than anyone in the room could take. Mrs. Owens put her hands to her face and howled as she ran from the room. Joanna put her head down and her shoulders started to shake. Yasmine turned and Lance wrapped her in his arms and she too began to weep.

Jared backed away from Jaidyn's bed and leaned against the wall. His knees buckled and he slid to the floor. He dropped his head and openly cried like her never had before. He desperately wanted to save her, to take back all that had transpired in the last forty-eight hours. He was feeling a gamut of emotions from sorrow to rage to guilt.

After Yasmine had collected herself she reached out putting a hand on Jared's shoulder then squatted in front of him and placed her hands on his. "Are you alright?" Jared wiped his face with his hand and his head bobbed. She wrapped her arms around his trembling shoulders. "She's going to be fine." His head bobbed again. Yasmine kept her arms around him for the next five minutes.

Jared pulled himself together, stood up and walked over to Jaidyn's bed. He looked like he'd aged five years in five minutes. He stood beside her with his hands crammed into his pockets and whispered a prayer;

> *In Your infinite grace and mercy renew her spirit and return her joy. Bless her with an abundance of Your love and heal her broken heart. She's been wounded and hurt beyond words, speak to her heart O' Lord. Draw her closer to You, breath hope and joy into her spirit. Help her to have faith that nothing can separate her from Your love. Grant her empowerment so that she may not be a passive victim*

of violence and hatred. Fill her with the promises You have made. Allow Your peace, happiness, and contentment to rule her heart and protect her soul.

Please forgive me Father for what I'm about to do. I just can't let him get away with this. In Jesus name.

Amen.

Jared sat beside her bed holding her hand for a long time before he got up to leave. Yasmine followed behind him. "Jared wait." He kept walking. Julian, Neal, Remington, and Lance were standing outside the door talking when he opened it.

Jared looked at Julian, "Let's roll."

Yasmine was still on his heels, "Where are you going?" She demanded. Jared didn't answer. She could feel the rage inside him. He had a determination that was unmistakable. She knew he was going to confront the beast by becoming something more horrifying then the beast himself. She stepped in front of him, "Jared don't do something stupid! Let the police handle this!" The look in his eyes was that of a lunatic, someone out of control and it scared her. There was a heinous storm brewing in his eyes that was so relentless that its fury would destroy everything in its wake.

She looked at Julian whose disposition was equally hard and cold, it was as if he was feeding off of Jared. "Don't let him do anything stupid." She pleaded. Just as Jared started to past her she grabbed his arm, he looked down at her. She softened her tone, "She's going to need you, please think about what you're doing."

"The last thing she needs right now is to have to worry about you." Neal said trying to help Yasmine.

Their efforts to calm him only pissed him off more. He did an about face and headed for Neal. Jared grabbed Neal in the collar and slammed him against the wall. "Don't you fucking tell me what she needs!" He yelled. "What if this was Yasmine?"

Chapter 55

Jared returned to the hospital to find Mrs. Owens sleeping on a roll away bed next to Jaidyn. Every light in the room was on and he wondered how either of them was able to rest. He quietly pulled a chair next to Jaidyn's bed and sat beside her. Jared looked around the room. Although he'd been in the room before he hadn't notice how nice it was. It had a very homey, welcoming feel to it. Instead of those sliding curtains most hospital rooms had it had floor to ceiling drapes. The soft brown walls were almost a tan color and looked as if they may have been sponge painted. The TV sat inside an armoire, instead of hanging from the ceiling on one of those white stands. A DVD player was attached to it. The floor had nice dark brown carpet. The headboard, food tray, nightstand, and armoire were all cherry wood. A lamp and CD clock radio sat on the nightstand. The two chairs and couch were a camel colored soft leather. This must the executive suite, he thought.

Jaidyn seemed to be having a fitful sleep. She tossed and turned, the attack now haunting her in her dreams. She screamed and sat straight up in the bed. Jared didn't hesitate when he wrapped her in his arms. She was trembling and he held her tighter. His voice broke with emotion, "It's ok baby," he whispered over her wailing.

She cried uncontrollably, drawing in deep gasping breaths letting him console her for only a few minutes before reaching for her mother. Her flinching and jerking away from him earlier flashed back in his mind and he backed away from her. Her earlier reaction had cut him like a knife but this time it was different. She was different. She hadn't pulled away from him out of fear but she was like a wounded child calling out for her mommy. Mrs. Owens sat next to her and cradled her in her arms. She rubbed her head, spoke softly to her, and rocked her as if she were a small child that had just fallen. Jaidyn responded to her mother's warmth with the innocence of a child who thought that her mommy could kiss away the pain.

The nurse finally came in and gave her something to calm her down. She fought to stay awake, afraid to close her eyes again. Her mother was looking at her wearily, she thought. She was saying something to her but she couldn't make it out. Jaidyn tried to respond to her but she couldn't get her lips to move. Everything was fuzzy. She didn't want to go back to sleep. She didn't want have that dream again but moments after her head hit the pillow the darkness took over.

Once she was sleeping Mrs. Owens suggested that Jared go home and get some rest. He politely smiled and thanked her for her concern but there was no way he was leaving Jaidyn's side. He blamed himself for not being around to protect her. If he had not been away on a business trip Jaidyn wouldn't be going through this, he thought. He knew he could have protected her.

Mrs. Owen seemed to sense his thoughts. "Jared, that man is touched. No sense in blaming yourself. There is nothing any of us could have done."

He quietly regarded her. She had very wise eyes, he thought. They were Jaidyn's eyes. He saw the same warmth in them. The same loving care that he found in Jaidyn's. His eye's clouded, he averted her gaze, and took a seat beside Jaidyn's bed.

Sarah Owens wondered when Jared left the hospital if he'd found Keith. If Jared had hurt him or even worse. He still had a hard edge about him, still dangerously poised. Her fears were worsened when he bent to sit down and she caught a glimpse of the handle of the nine-millimeter in the small of his back. "The Lord says that vengeance is His, He will repay. You need to turn all this over to the Lord...I know how much this child loves you and she's going to need your strength to get through this." She said in that loving and concerned tone that mother use. They talked for another five minutes before Mrs. Owens settled back onto her bed. Jared understood and respected what she was trying to convey to him but he couldn't let Keith get away with this.

Jared felt like he'd been awake for days. He'd tried to close his eyes but he couldn't stop his mind. He kept reliving what he imagined Keith had put Jaidyn through. His mind was clogged with worry and regret. Congested with what he should have done, what he could have done or if he just would have...

An intense pain was tugging at Jaidyn, pulling her out of dreamland but the darkness still had her and wouldn't allow her to open her eyes. She could hear the buzz in the room. She couldn't distinguish between the voices or what they were saying but she could hear them. She struggled to get her eyes to open.

When the darkness finally relinquished its control over her she opened her eyes and found her father, mother, Joanna and Yasmine quietly talking. Jared was sitting in an opposite corner with his shoulders hunched forward and his hands folded together. She watched him as he intently studied his hand. He felt her watching him and returned her gaze. His eyes softened and he flashed a sympathetic smile.

She closed her eyes trying to pull it all together. She hurt everywhere. She remembered the dream and waking up with Jared being there. She remembered him quietly telling her he wasn't going to let anything happen to her again. When she began to drift back to sleep he had been watching over her. She opened her eyes and looked for the clock, 9:41 a.m. He must have been there all night, she thought.

She looked at him again. He was her quiet, gentle savior. Her fortress. Standing guard over her. Protecting her. She wondered if he knew how much she loved him.

She flashed back to when Jared had reached for her. It felt like it was just minutes before. She remembered pulling away from him and she cringed. In her clinical mind she knew it was because of the things Keith had did to her. Professionally she was able to rationalize the mental reflex, the phobia, but it didn't ease her mind or her heart that ached for Jared. She felt ashamed, guilty. She wondered if Jared would want her after all of this. Medically she had treated patients in this situation many times during her residential rotation but nothing could have prepared her for the depth of guilt she was now feeling. It was deeper and more difficult then she could have ever imagined. Her medical mind knew she had to get control of it but her emotional mind was distort and couldn't get wrapped around the thought.

She opened her eyes and looked at Jared again. He looked like he hadn't slept in days. Inwardly she tried to battle all the anxiety she was having about him. She wanted to hug him and wanted him to hold her, but something held her back. She wanted to tell him that she loved him, wanted to tell him she was sorry for letting Keith do this to her, but she swallowed the words.

What was wrong with her, she wondered. Was it fear, she questioned. "I can't let Keith win," she said to herself. She looked at Jared with pleading eyes and reluctantly reached to touch his hand. Jared stepped towards her with an out reached hand and she involuntarily recoiled away from him still uneasy. His eyes caught her and made her aware of her actions.

Jaidyn's father was watching them from across the room. Seeing the tension he said, "Baby Girl, we never thought you were going to wake up." He sat on the bed beside her and rubbed the only part of her that didn't look bruised, the top of her head. "How are you feeling?"

She was a daddy's girl and the sound of his voice alone made her weak. She couldn't hold it together, "Daddy I tried to stop him but he wouldn't. I fought…"

Mr. Owens always appeared strong but he was visibly weakened by her confession. A sob rose in his throat, "I know you did baby. I know you did." He said pulling his little girl into his arms and cradling her.

Chapter 56

Houston Tribune
Sunday, August 24, 2004

Domestic Violence Turns Deadly

Man Killed after Beating His Ex-Girlfriend

By Christopher McCartney

Harris County Sheriff's Department deputies were called to the Dream Lakes Condominiums in the 3000 block of Sailor Crest in Clear Lake Saturday night after a resident called in a domestic violence assault in progress.

When deputies arrived shortly after 10 p.m., Virginia James reported hearing a couple arguing, a woman screaming, and then two gunshots. After knocking on the door and not receiving a response a detective peered through a window and saw what appeared to be a body on the living room floor.

When deputies entered the residence they found one gunshot victim on the floor. The victim was identified as 37 year old, Keith J. Tyler. Tyler was out on bail on separate charges of kidnapping, false imprisonment, sexual assault, battery, and domestic violence.

Investigator, John Daniels said, "It was premature to speculate about all the details surrounding the shooting but it appeared that the victim showed up drunk and had an argument with his child's mother over their child. During the argument Mr. Tyler severely beat Ms. Roberts. In fear for her life she shot Mr. Tyler in the chest twice."

Paramedics transported the victim to Clear Lake Medical Center where he was pronounced dead. Chevon Roberts was also transported to Clear Lake Medical Center where she is in guarded but stable condition. The child who's name is being withheld, was not harmed and is in the care of relatives.

A smile crossed Jared's face, "*Shhhiiiittt!*" He looked up from the newspaper, Jaidyn was sitting on the couch reviewing patient charts. Before he could gather his thoughts the phone began to ring. He was momentarily frozen in place, as a flash of anxiousness hit him when he looked at Jaidyn. The fourth time the phone rang simultaneously with the doorbell. Jaidyn sat the chart down and looked at the door. The phone rang again. She turned and looked at Jared who was sitting next to the phone. "Baby are you going to get the phone?" She asked.

"Yeah." He said dazed.

Jaidyn looked at the clock on her way to the door, 8:12 a.m. She wondered who it could be this time of the morning.

Jared snatched the telephone receiver out of its cradle. "Hello."

"Mornin' Jared. Is Jaidyn close by?" Mr. Owens asked. After Jaidyn's ordeal with Keith, Jared had refused to allow her to go back to her house, so she'd moved in with her parents. After only being there a week she'd relocated to Jared's. Her parents had objected but respected her decision.

"Yes sir, hold on a minute." Jared said still stunned.

"No, no son." Mr. Owens said in an urgent voice. "I'd rather talk to you…ah…Natalie Tyler called us this morning and it seems that Keith was killed last night." Mr. Owens listened to dead silence from the other end of the phone for four to five seconds.

"Yeah, I know. I read it in the paper a few minutes ago." Jared said. Out of the corner of his eye he could see Yasmine talking to Jaidyn.

"Does Jaidyn," Mr. Owens words became back round noise as Jared's attention turned to Yasmine as she handed Jaidyn the newspaper.

Jaidyn took the paper from Yasmine and walked towards the couch. She sat staring at the paper for a few minutes after she'd finished reading the article. The expression was unchanged. It was as if she were frozen in place.

Jaidyn could feel Yasmine staring at her. She continued staring at the paper, biding her time until she could find the appropriate response.

"I'm sorry, we'll have to call you back." Jared said cutting Mr. Owens off. The next thing Russell Owens heard was a dial tone. Jared was still holding the cordless phone when it rang again. He ignored it, dropped it on the sofa table and walked around the couch.

Jaidyn wasn't sure how she was supposed to react or how she was supposed to feel. She felt numb. A part of her was infinitely sad but another part of her was relieved. She wasn't sure if she was supposed to cry or smile. How does one react when their husband, lover, rapist, and abuser is killed, murdered?

She could feel Jared and Yasmine watching her, waiting on a response. The phone rang a third time. Jaidyn wanted to escape their questioning eyes so she snatched it off the table, "Hello."

"Jaidyn." The familiar voice said.

Jaidyn took a deep breath, "Are you ok?"

"Yes Baby." Natalie Tyler said sounding as if she was struggling to get the words out.

Jaidyn caught Yasmine's eyes asking her who was on the phone. Jaidyn averted her gaze and listened to Mama Nat. She was drawn back in time. She heard Keith saying, "I'll love you until you take your last breath." The knot in her belly twisted as the image of his face lingered in her mind. Silent tears were rolling down her face. "I'm so sorry." She said almost in a whisper. "I'll come over and see you in a little bit." She said into the phone before she hung up.

Jaidyn sat the phone back on the table and Yasmine hugged her. "Is she ok?" Yasmine was asking as a blast of nausea hit and rushed to Jaidyn's throat. Jaidyn quickly pulled away from her and rushed to the bathroom.

Yasmine and Jared remained frozen in place for several seconds trying to read each other's thoughts. Yasmine heard Jaidyn vomiting and was the first to move. Jared remained seated several seconds before deciding to see what was going on.

He could hear Yasmine's hushed voice as he knocked on the bathroom door. "You guys alright?" He called in to them. The sounds of Jaidyn's stomach contents being emptied was the only sound that came back to him.

Yasmine opened the door and he could see Jaidyn on her knees, with her forearms holding onto the toilet seat, her neck was drooping forward and her head was in the toilet.

Yasmine turned on the cold water, reached into the linen closet and pulled out two wash clothes. After she wet the wash clothes, she handed one to Jaidyn, pulled her hair up and placed the other on the back of her neck.

"Baby are you alright?" Jared repeated.

Jaidyn shook her head and started vomiting again. Yasmine looked at Jared who was leaned against the doorframe with his arms folded across his crest. She knew he was worried by the way his eyebrows were drawn together and his eyes were narrowed on Jaidyn.

Jaidyn's stomach stopped churning and she got up off the floor. "I think I need to lay down for a few minutes." She said wiping her face. At some point Jared had gone into the bathroom in his bedroom and came back with a toothbrush and handed it to her as she exited the hall bathroom.

"Are you sure you're alright?" He asked again as she passed him.

"Yes. I just need to lye down for a few minutes." Jaidyn said as she looked back at him. She had no idea what had just happened. One minute she was hugging Yasmine and the next she was feeling sweaty, dizzy, and nauseated. She got an empty feeling in the pit of her stomach and the next thing she knew she was making a mad dash for the bathroom. Now the nausea was gone but she still felt weak.

Jaidyn lay in bed for a couple of minutes before the feeling past and she was feeling better. But there was still a sense of heaviness gripping her heart. She got out of bed and walked towards the living room. As she approached she could hear Yasmine and Jared talking, "For Christ sake Jared, she was married to the man!" Yasmine was saying.

"And your point is what?" Jared said in a dry tone.

"We can't tell her how to feel."

"Don't you think I know that? But after all the shit he did to her she ought to be glad somebody killed his ass."

"I couldn't agree more. It's no secret that I couldn't stand Keith's ass but..." Yasmine was blurting out as she saw Jaidyn coming into the room.

Jaidyn pretended as if she'd not heard what they were discussing, "I'm sorry I don't mean to interrupt but its 9:30, are we still going to church?" Jaidyn asked Jared as if she hadn't heard their conversation.

Jared looked at her as if he were inspecting her and it made her uneasy. "If you're up to it." He finally said.

"Hey, are you feeling better?" Yasmine asked in an upbeat voice as she tried to ease the tension.

"Yeah." Jaidyn said as if vomiting after hearing your husband was murdered was an everyday occurrence. Silence filled the room once more. Jared and Yasmine both peered at her as if they knew she was teetering on the edge of a break down.

"Well..." Yasmine begin, "I guess I better get out of you guys way. I've got to get home so I can get my crew to service on time."

"Thanks for coming over." Jared said as Yasmine picked up her keys and purse.

"I'll call you later." Yasmine said hugging Jaidyn.

"Thank you Yasmine." Jaidyn said holding onto her a little longer then she needed to.

"Call me if you need me to go over to Ms. Nat's with you." Yasmine said flashing her a worried look.

"Ok."

"See you later." Yasmine yelled back to Jared.

"Holla at you later." Jared yelled back as he walked toward the bedroom.

Jared wasn't angry with Jaidyn. He just couldn't understand how she was feeling. Although most of her bruising was gone the cast on her arm was a consent visual reminder of what Keith had done to her. He couldn't fathom having any remorse for his death. As far as he was concerned Keith got what was coming to him. When he read the news of Keith's death all he could feel was an unbelievable sense of relief.

After he'd seen Jaidyn in that hospital bed he and Julian had left the hospital with every intention on killing him. They had broken his front door down and gone to his office but Keith was no where to be found. It wasn't until he returned to the hospital that Mrs. Owens informed him that Keith was in police custody.

When Keith was released on bond Jaidyn had begged Jared not to do anything to him. She insisted that they allow the police to deal with him. When she'd moved in with him rather than continue to live with her parents he suspected that the move wasn't just about her feeling safe. It was also about keeping him away from Keith.

By the time they'd gotten to church Jared's disappointment in Jaidyn's reaction had dissipated. She'd been through a lot and he didn't want to add to the stress she was already under. Jaidyn was sitting in the pew next to him. He was holding her hand when she laid her head on his shoulder. He kissed her on the forehead, put his arm around her and said a silent pray;

> *Comfort Natalie Tyler during her time of grief. Shower her with a peace that only You can provide. She is a wonderful woman full of goodness and love. Walk with her during this time.*
>
> *Thank you Father God for helping me to escape the temptation of killing Keith. Thank you, for holding my hand and walking me through it. If it wasn't for Your sovereign power my desire to kill him would have consumed me.*
>
> *Despite all that Keith has put Jaidyn through she still has empathy and compassion for him. I won't pretend to understand her ability to forgive him. Help me to find that same forgiveness in my heart. Please don't allow Keith's death or my attitude of relief be a source of division between us. Bond us, hold us together through this. Soften my heart and give me the gift of understanding and compassion.*
>
> *It is in times like these that I'm able to see You through Jaidyn. Her uncompromising, faith and trust in You is inspiring. I surrender to You. Where ever You lead I will follow.*
>
> *Oh, and Lord allow Your comfort and peace to blanket Ms. Tyler and her family. In Jesus name.*
>
> *Amen*

Jaidyn was preoccupied with thoughts of Keith and hadn't paid much attention to anything the pastor had been saying. She felt a profound sadness but also an overabundance of relief. It's finally over she said to herself. I can't believe it. He was my husband. I had a life with him. Why do I feel so much relief? She asked herself. I wonder what's going to happen to Chevon and K.J.

Her eyes filled with tears as Mama Nat crept into her thoughts. She was an amazing woman. After all her son had put Jaidyn through Natalie Tyler had remained Jaidyn's trusted friend. The violence Jaidyn had endured had given them similar battle scares and drawn them closer together. Natalie Tyler had vowed to stand by her only child but was remorseful and deeply hurt by his actions. She had made it her business to help Jaidyn rebuild her life. Jaidyn thought about Mama Nat's chilling confession, "Baby, I love my child and in a way I feel some responsibility for his actions. If I wouldn't have allowed him to see what his daddy put me through maybe things would be different." Jaidyn pulled her hand to her mouth to stop the sobs that were gathering there. She couldn't imagine what Mama Nat was going through right now. "I'm so sorry Mama Nat. I'm so sorry," she said silently.

Jaidyn begin to make peace with Keith's death just as the choir started to sing, "*I love you. I love you. I love you Lord today because You care for me in such a special way...My heart. My mind. My soul belongs to You...*"

Thank you for Your strength and Your divine presence in my life. Bless Keith's soul. In the name of Jesus." Jaidyn said as she lifted her hands in reverence and praise to God.

With hands still raised and her voice lifted unto God, silent tears were still rolling down Jaidyn's face as nausea crept back in on her.

Chapter 57

Jaidyn had gotten out of bed and made herself a hot cup of herbal tea hoping it would relax her so that she could get some sleep. She'd taken a long hot shower and finally she'd reviewed several patients' charts hoping the reading would help. She did everything humanely possible but her efforts were unsuccessful. Nothing had silenced her mind. When she slipped back into bed with Jared her mind was still racing frantically.

When Jared felt her slip into the bed next to him he turned and lay over her like a quilt. Silent tears begin spilling from the corners of her eyes. "Lord, what am I supposed to do?" She asked silently.

When she heard Jared begin to sore she slipped from beneath his arms and made her way through the darkness of the loft. Her mind still clogged and she needed time to consider her options, time to think, time to figure out what direction she wanted her life to go.

Things were finally changing. She could finally see the light at the end of the tunnel. It hadn't always been that way. There was a time that if she closed her eyes an image of Keith was there luring behind her eyelids tormenting her. There had been a period before Keith was killed when she was afraid to step out of her front door. Frightened to go around a corner in fear that he may be waiting for her. Now that he was dead there were still times that fear took her breath away. She may be in a corridor alone or with someone fifteen paces behind her. She would be in a parking lot and see a man approaching. There were still nights that she woke shaken, fearful, sure she'd heard Keith's voice or felt his touch. There was no rhyme or reason, no specific time or place when panic would consume her or fear would paralyze her; but these moments were happening less and less.

Jaidyn had proven to herself that she was strong and resilient. When she finally opened up to rape counselor she was seeing, it was as if she was talking about a patient rather then herself. She expressed shame and embarrassment about the things she felt she allowed Keith to do to her. The rape itself was hard to deal with but the brutality leading up to it was what haunted her. The hatred he had in his eyes had stuck with her. She had finally stopped blaming herself and was refusing to allow the heartache to take on its own life and set up camp inside her. She had been fighting hard but it wasn't until Keith death that she seemed to snap out of it. She finally seemed to put it all in perspective and was moving forward.

Jared had been wonderful throughout all she had been through. When she woke in the middle of the night in a cold sweat he was right there reassuring her that everything was all right. They had what seemed like endless nights of him having to ask if he could touch her. Hold her. After all that, why this? Why now, she questioned? Keith is reaching out from the grave trying to destroy my life, she thought. Weren't the memories he left her with enough?

After Keith was killed Jared changed back into the loving gentle man she loved. He stopped carrying a gun and stopped insisting on going with her every place she went. His eyes were no longer angry and hard. He was no longer serious all the time. Laughter once again fell between them like causal conversation.

He had been an enormous help to her and Mama Nat after Keith's death. Keith had made some very wise investments as a pro-athlete. They made him a very wealthy man. Since she and Keith's divorce wasn't finalized Jaidyn had inherited the house, his advertising business, his Clear Lake City hideaway condo, his half of a BMW dealership, as well as his multi-million dollar stock market investments. She was surprised by all the investments Keith had hidden from her but she did not want anything to do with any of it. So Jared had stepped in and helped her disburse Keith's assets.

She had consulted with Mama Nat and they agreed on how his assets should be divided. A quarter of the multi-million dollar stock market investments were liquidated and put into a trust for K.J. Keith's house was included in the trust and Chevon and K.J. now lived there. The condo was sold to an investment group. Mama Nat and Jaidyn agreed to donate the proceeds to Women Helping Women, a local refuge for woman and children trying to escape domestic violence. The organization had once helped her and Keith when she tried to leave his father.

Although nothing had visibly changed in Mama Nat's life she could now be added to the list of millionaires. Half of Keith's multi-million dollar stock market investments went to her. She resisted but Jaidyn had insisted.

Jared had overseen the buyout of the advertising business by a larger firm and Jaidyn had taken the money from the sell and purchased the lovely bed and breakfast Jared had taken her to months earlier. Jaidyn decided to keep Keith's half of the BMW dealership. She affectionately called it 'the gift that kept on giving.' The final twenty five percent of the multi-million dollar stock investment was liquidated and used to purchase a retirement home for her parents along with a cottage for herself, on a white sand, clear blue water private beach in Barbados.

Jared reached for her but she wasn't there. He felt the dampness on her pillow and knew she had been crying. Seeing her weep had always twisted his insides. It always made him ache. A few days ago this new round of tears had started and Jared had welcomed them. Since the rape Jaidyn had been changed. She seemed to hold her emotions at bay. She'd suffered in the worst way possible, in silence.

She'd been weeping for a couple a weeks. He asked her what was wrong but she'd shoved it off saying it was work and she was tired. He knew it was more than that but he hadn't pushed the issue. He lay there in the darkness looking at the ceiling, wondering what it could be. He looked at the clock, it was just before dawn. Maybe she just woke up early, he said, knowing he was lying to himself.

Once Jared's eyes adjusted to the pitch-black loft he climbed out of bed and found his way to the living room. He saw her silhouette standing in the window. She had her arms wrapped around herself like she was cold. The floor to ceiling windows overlooking downtown Houston stretched the entire length of the living and dining room. He walked heavily across the hard wood floor forecasting his approach, just as he'd learned to do this after she moved in with him. She'd been jumpy and everything seemed to scare her.

He walked around to face her and leaned against the window. Her eyes were puffy and the tip of her nose red. He touched her nose with his index finger, "Hey Rudolph." She smiled at him and he wrapped her in his arms. Jaidyn was always amazed at how much strength she found in his arms.

"Can't sleep?" He asked. She quietly shook her head as if she didn't want to disturb the soundlessness of the picturesque perfection of the downtown view. There wasn't a car in sight. The quietness of the streets was surreal. The lights of the vacant sky scrappers were peaceful. The clear night sky allowed them to pick out the constellations, which seemed to be winking at them. A tear quietly rolled down her face and dropped onto Jared's arm. "You want to talk about it?" He asked soothingly. She shook her head as tears burned the back of her eyes. He held her quietly, soothing her and hoping that she would somehow find comfort in talking to him.

When her tears dissipated the words she dreaded saying sat on the tip of her tongue torturing her. Her throat went dry and her heart sped up at the thought of allowing them to escape her lips. I was just starting to feel alive again, she thought. How could this be happening?

Jaidyn said a small prayer before she began to speak. "I'm pregnant and ...," she trailed off as tears began to flood her face. Her chest tightened making it hard for her to breathe. The words seemed to hang in the air and spread over them like a saturated blanket. She got that same sick feeling in the pit of her stomach she'd gotten when she'd waited on that stick to turn pink or blue.

She braced herself, silently panicking, waiting on him to ask the enviable question that had already passed between them. Whose child was growing inside her? It was the question she'd asked herself since the moment Dr. Turner had confirmed her suspicions. It was a question she didn't know the answer to herself. It could be Keith's. He hadn't used any protection when he raped her. But it could be Jared's. They hadn't used protection on a consistent basis since they'd been back together and they slept together the night before he left for his Chicago business trip. It was an impossible question for her to answer.

Her heart sank as Jared let go of her and quietly walked away.

When he returned to the room he turned the lamp on the sofa table on before he wrapped his arms around her once more. She wanted to turn around and look into his eyes but was afraid of what she might see there. She didn't know why she expected him to understand and be supportive. She didn't think she could have been if she was in his shoes.

They stood in silence for what seemed like an eternity. Just as the sun began slipping through the skyscrapers Jared broke the silence with four little words, "Will you marry me?" Jaidyn giggled. She wasn't sure if it was out of relief or because of the silky smooth way he'd said it. He put his hands out in front of her and opened a little black velvet box. He exposed a ring that he had purchased for her a few days before she married Keith.

When she said she was pregnant he didn't have to think about what to do. He just had to wait until the perfect moment to do it. He'd watched the sunrise over downtown Houston a million times. When the ball of fire gently showered the buildings with its soft orange and golden rays it was simply spectacular and he knew that it would be the prefect time to ask her to be his wife.

When Jaidyn looked down at the open box she gasped. Her heart nearly leaped out of her chest. Jaidyn covered her mouth with her hands astonished at the beauty of it. The ring was breathtaking. The four-carat emerald diamond was flawless in its beauty. On either side of the oddly fancy shaped diamond was a pair of tapered baguette diamonds set in platinum. *"Oh my God! Oh my God,"* she whispered to no one in particular. She swung around to face him, to peer into his beautiful face. He was intently serious. She flashed back to the day she first opened her heart to this man, but she wondered when he walked in and had taken it over. Somewhere down the road he'd become an essential part of her life. She needed him like she needed air to breathe. It was difficult for her to believe that he still loved her after all they'd been through.

Jaidyn searched his eyes for what neither of them had dared to say. She had to say it, had to tell him the truth. A tear trickled down her cheek and he wiped it away. "I don't know who's..." she whispered. Jared put his finger on her lips to silence her before she could get it all out. With tenderness on his face he said, "I don't care, he's going to be ours." He looked at her as if he wanted her to absorb what he was saying and she did. "Passion, you're the love of my life. I can't imagine life without you. Will you marry me?" Tears rolled down Jaidyn's face as her head bobbed up and down.

Epilogue

On March 6 at 4:40 a.m. with her husband at her side Jaidyn gave birth to a beautiful seven pound one ounce baby girl, Brooklyn Janell Mitchell. Both of little Brooklyn's grandmothers and her godmother, Mama Nat were also on hand for the delivery. Brooklyn was an exact replica of her mother. Her eyes were the same shade of gray and her hair a light sandy blonde.

> *Lord God, in spite of what could have happened I'm still here. It's because of Your mercy that I'm alive. I hate to think where I would be without Your loving-kindness and mercy. You've shown me Your grace despite my attempts to lead my own life. You've turned my mistakes into victories. When I was weak and didn't think I could make it, when I thought my dreams were shattered and I looked at life through a veil of tears, You were my Jehovah Jireh, my provider, my unmovable rock. Every time I lose my way You hold my hand and guide me through. You've never failed me and I am so grateful.*
>
> *Jesus, thank you for the moment of clarity when I knew there was hope. Thank you for reminding me that life is a gift. Thank you Jesus for all that You've brought me through and for refreshing my spirit in the midst of it all..*
>
> *How gracious You were when You blessed my life with Jared. He truly is the other half of my soul. His love is undoubtedly a gift from You and I will always cherish it. I am so grateful that he loved me when I didn't know how to love myself.*

> *I will never regret that we chose to give life to Brooklyn. She is an unbelievable blessing..Hummm…Bind our family with Your love Father and bless all those people in my life who supported me with the strength of their love and prayer. In Jesus name.*
>
> *Amen*

In a matter of seconds Jared's world had changed. He squeezed into the small hospital bed next to Jaidyn. He couldn't stop kissing Jaidyn's forehead. This experience had a lot more raw emotions then he could have ever thought possible.

Brooklyn was only five minutes old and he had her cradled in his arms. She was so beautiful he was nearly knocked off his feet. She stretched and looked around the room as if she was taking in this new world. She wrapped her tiny little hand around her daddy's finger and tears formed in his eyes. She looked up at him and batted her almond shaped gray eyes, and something deep inside Jared sprung a leak and tears quietly ran down his cheeks.

> *Thank you, thank you, thank you…Thank you God for seeing what I couldn't and for not allowing me to give up on Jaidyn when the Devil was whispering in my ear to walk away. You have blessed us with something that most people only dream of. Help us to remain friends and to continue to have a love that never dies. Be an unmovable force in our lives and our marriage.*
>
> *Thank you for blessing us with the precious gift of this child. You have shown me a new revelation of Your love and power. Help us to mold her, nurture her and enrich her life. Help us to be positive visual examples to her, to lead her, to encourage her, and to help her become all that You mean for her to be. Let Your grace, mercy, and loving-kindness accompany her all the days of her life.*
>
> *As I look around this room at our family I am humbled.*
>
> *I find great peace in knowing that although we are not prefect and will make many mistakes You will love us in spite of it all.*
>
> *Amen*

Printed in the United States
58664LVS00004B/247-294